VANITY FAIR. December 15, 1896

Judith Cummins after Delfico

No. 231.

THE MAÎTRE D'ARMES.

MEN OF THE DAY. No. 60.

PHINEAS AT BAY

JOHN F. WIRENIUS

New York
2014

Cover design by Judith Cummins; cover art created by Judith Cummins, after Delfico, "The Hereditary Grand Falconer," *Vanity Fair* (1873)

ISBN: 1499177321
ISBN 13: 9781499177329
Library of Congress Control Number: 2014907363
CreateSpace Independent Publishing Platform,
North Charleston, SouthCarolina

For Catherine, every word.

TABLE OF CONTENTS

VOLUME I

VOLUME II

VOLUME I

PROLOGUE

Mr. Quintus Slide, newly returned from nearly two decades in Australia, where he had been fortunate enough to earn a considerable sum of money, surveyed his newly re-acquired kingdom. Many would have thought that the making of a fortune was enough to justify a man's career, and would lead one to forget old grudges. Not Quintus Slide. He had been, until the mid-1870s, the editor of *The People's Banner*, and when he had lost his job at the broadsheet for going past the line of scandal permitted even the second tier of journalism, it had rankled. So he had written a few scurrilities about a Duchess? As if that mattered, even if she was married to the Prime Minister! The *Banner's* proprietor at the time had been weak-willed enough to give Slide the push, making him unemployable, thanks to his editorial zeal in doing the competition down.

With nowhere to go, he fled to the Antipodes, and had profited handsomely; his school of journalism seemed to take root and flourish quite naturally in Australia. And now, he had sold up, bought the *Banner* outright, and was proprietor and editor both. An unpleasant smile creased his face, and, walking into his old digs in the editor's office, he called for his secretary.

"Miss Allen!"

"Mr. Slide?" Miss Allen was a petite, handsome woman, whose severe, almost predatory, face was framed by auburn hair and the spiked tips of the winged collars on her blouses. Her rare smiles showed that she could, under different auspices, have been taken for beautiful. As it was, she remained both handsome and a little chilling. Smoothing her tailored skirts to guard against the untidiness she so hated, she seated herself in the chair opposite him on the other side of her desk.

"The file, Miss Allen. Tell me what you have found out about them."

"Very good, Mr. Slide. You have asked me to research several individuals, and their current status or involvement from a political or social point of view. These individuals were all, I believe, known to you in your previous tenure as editor."

"Yes, yes; what have you found?"

"Shall we begin at the social summit? His Grace Plantagenet Palliser, the Duke of Omnium. Liberal Member of the House of Commons for Silverbridge, until his uncle the prior Duke died, Prime Minister of the Coalition Government from 187--"

"I know all that, Miss Allen. Since the Coalition?"

"The Duke and his Duchess, Lady Glencora M'Cluskie as was, took an extended tour of the Continent when the Coalition fell. During that tour, the Duchess took sick, and died."

"Good."

"Indeed, Mr. Slide? My researches reflect that the Duchess was quite popular."

"Not with me she b----y wasn't. What next?"

"The Duke has effectively retired from politics since then—he held office in the early '80s, in Mr. Monk's last Government, as President of the Board of Trade--"

"Rather beneath a Duke, eh, Miss Allen?"

"True, Mr. Slide. My informants tell me that the Duke hungered to be Chancellor of the Exchequer or even Prime Minister again, but the former position is barred to a member of the Lords, and as to the latter, the Duke is respected, but not popular."

"No second go for Planty Pall, then. Good!"

"His children are all married: Lord Silverbridge to the daughter of the American Ambassador shortly after the fall of the Omnium Government, Lady Mary to Francis Tregear, Conservative M.P. for Polpenno--"

"Popinjay, more like! And how the Duke must hate having a Tory son-in-law! Go on, Miss Allen, go on."

"And Lord Gerald Palliser to Lady Agnes Kirkness."

"Never 'eard of 'er."

"From Scotland, Mr. Slide."

"Well, that explains that. What about"—and here Mr. Slide's voice took on an especially eager, rather unpleasant tone, "Mr. Phineas Finn?"

"Mr. Finn held office under Mr. Monk—he was Secretary for Ireland, and First Lord of the Admiralty, as under Omnium. He might have risen further, but Mr. Monk's retirement due to ill health led to a new Government, and Mr. Finn was not given office. Mr. Gresham did not approve of his independence."

"Ha! No more did he in the old days. What about now? He used to be thick with Barrington Erle."

"They remain on amicable terms, Mr. Slide, but Mr. Finn's independence does not appear to please the Prime Minister any more than it did his predecessor."

"I should have known. Erle always valued loyalty above all else."

"He still does. One of my informants tells me that he was overheard at the theatre saying that Richard III couldn't have been as bad as he is painted, since his motto was *Loyaulte me lie*."

"Eh?"

"'Loyalty binds me.' You were particularly interested, Mr. Slide, as to whether there were any connection between Mr. Finn and any ladies."

"Yes, well?"

"No hint of any impropriety. Mr. Finn appears in public quite often with his wife, the former Marie Goesler, who was in former days commonly styled Madame Max Goesler. She was very close with the late Duchess of Omnium. Mr. and Mrs. Finn appear to be well-suited. His niece, an orphan, lives with them. He spends most of his time in the House, in chambers, or at the law courts."

"Eh, Finn, practising at the bar? But his wife's as rich as Croesus!"

"Yes, Mr. Slide, and very actively engaged in her business. She has prospered these past five years, especially, although I have not been able to trace all her interests. A formidable woman."

"Takes one to know one, Miss Allen."

Bowing her head in acknowledgment of the compliment, Miss Allen resumed her report.

"Mr. Finn appears to have taken over his pupil-master's practise."

"Probably got the bug after he was acquitted."

"You mean of the murder charges, Mr. Slide? Yes, no evidence has ever been found to establish who murdered the Duke's proposed successor as Chancellor of the Exchequer, a Mr. Wilfred Bonteen. Mr. Finn's innocence having been established, suspicion rested for a time on a clergyman, the Reverend Joseph Emilius, but nothing could be proved against him."

"Nothing, d'you say? He was convicted of bigamy, at any rate."

"Yes, leading to the dissolution of his marriage to Lady Eustace."

"A rum customer herself, Miss Allen—almost certainly stole diamonds from the family she married into, and then had 'em stolen from her—what I calls poetic justice."

"Yes, Mr. Slide. The bigamy conviction was vacated when the sole witness recanted her testimony, and Mr. Emilius disappeared shortly thereafter."

"Nothing between Finn and Lady Laura Kennedy? He interfered in her marriage, I know that, though not how, or how much. Her husband went mad, you know, as a result. Aye, and then died, poor d---l."

"Lady Laura lives a quiet life, Mr. Slide. She was, it is said, her cousin Barrington Erle's principal tutor in politics, and it's also said that he owes his premiership to her, but that he sees her seldom these days."

"A falling out, Miss Allen?"

"I do not think so, Mr. Slide. She sees the Prime Minister periodically. He seems simply to feel no longer in need of her tutelage."

"And Finn?

"Normally sees her at family gatherings of the Brentford family. The current Earl of Brentford, the former Lord Chiltern, is a good friend of Mr. Finn's, and the two families spend a fair amount of time together. Indeed, Mr. Finn is godfather to the current Lord Chiltern."

"A Papist godfather to the heir presumptive of an earldom! What's the world coming to, Miss Allen? I ask you, what's the world coming to?"

"The godson has possibilities, Mr. Slide. He is often in the company of ladies of a bohemian tendency, and proclaims himself a socialist. He declines to use his title, in fact."

"Oh, yes?"

"And he is, lately, often to be seen in the company of Lady Eustace."

"Really?" Mr. Slide stretched out the word to twice its normal length, chewing it over as though it were a particularly succulent bit of toffee, and added, "And her old enough to be his mother, and a bit of a naughty one, if I remember aright. Yes, that could be quite useful, Miss Allen."

"I am glad to hear it, Mr. Slide."

"Keep yer feelers out there, Miss Allen. *The People's Banner* is back in business, and Quintus Slide has a few scores to settle, if he can."

THOUGHTS AT A FUNERAL

On a cold spring day in 189_, the Temple Church's round nave was sparsely populated for a mid-day funeral service. The bereaved family—one might question the sincerity of the long faces, as the deceased had died, in the phraseology just becoming popular, a "very warm man," but their grief seemed real enough despite the financial expectations implied—were clustered at the front of the church listening to the simple rites of the Book of Common Prayer. The mourners were, in truth, few enough; but then, the deceased had outlived his wife by many years, and the children of their union were now well into middle age. These children—three grizzled, well-upholstered daughters, and one well-fleshed son, whose bare pate caught the odd shaft of sunlight through the church's window, were dressed with a fineness that belied their somewhat coarse features.

The elegance of the Prayer Book's funeral service was only slightly marred by the murmured, slightly disjointed responses of the small crowd gathered for the obsequies. The stout frame of the grizzled man in the coffin proclaimed his kinship with the front row of mourners, and his heavily-jowled face bore an unwonted look of serenity for one who had been so turbulent in life.

Some rows behind the family, a scattering of solicitors and a handful of barristers, some of them in their gowns, had come to see off one of their own. A handful of the older congregants had known the deceased, and could tell stories his prowess in the courtroom—of his roaring defiance, face flushed, and with shabby wig askew, at the Lord Chief Justice himself. One or two had been present upon the occasion of tales that grew into later legends heard round the Temple, though now long forgotten by most even of the bar. Mr. Camperdown, perched delicately in the fourth row, could have described his own client's discomfiture at the hands of the deceased two decades before; the younger (alas, now only comparatively) Mr. Bideawhile had enjoyed vicariously the dead man's triumph in a long-ago fraud case. Mr. Bideawhile had dined out on the story for weeks—how the unparalleled Mr. Chaffanbrass (for such was the name of the deceased) had cross-examined an expert witness to the point that the witness could not accurately give his own address, let alone any opinion to which a jury could be bound to defer. Mr. Bideawhile could wax rhapsodic over the hapless witness's look of appalled fascination, for all the world like a small bird, so pinned by the glittering eyes of an advancing, hungry snake that it never even considers the option of flight.

Mr. Camperdown knew that look, having seen it precede one of hopeless resignation in the face of a peer of the realm who had been likewise rendered utterly helpless as to the colour, shape, and cut of a certain grey coat, as well as to the height of its wearer—a murderer, glimpsed in the fog by that unlucky peer. Along with the deceased, the memories of an unknown number of such courtroom tragedies and triumphs would soon be interred forever.

Very few of those whose interests had been represented by the old barrister were present to attend his farewell. This was less than surprising, as the old man's practise had been exclusively in the criminal courts, and such of his clients as were at liberty to attend the obsequies preferred to gloss over the peril in which they had once stood, rather than celebrate their rescuer. Of the small legion of those saved from the hangman or the gaol by Mr. Chaffanbrass, only two were present. Both, as if by mutual accord, were farther back even than the members of the profession. One was a lady, soberly dressed, once beautiful, and still with the lineaments of beauty in her face, and the other—

As the other will be of some note, a fuller description may be in order. The other was a gentleman in his early fifties, tall and well proportioned, with a carefully trimmed beard that hovered between brown and red in colour, except where it was streaked with white in two bands from the tips of his mustaches. His broad, expressive mouth and lively eyes denoted a man more prone to laughter than to frowns, and his brown hair was only lightly threaded through with grey. He was dressed well, but not in mourning. If truth be told, he had looked in on an impulse on his way to his own chambers in Temple Gardens. This extemporaneous mourner looked—not stricken, but rather bemused, by the death of his onetime advocate.

"I would rather be hanged, though seen to be innocent in the eyes of the world, than to be acquitted and thought to be guilty," he had declared to Mr. Chaffanbrass, again and again, in the time of his peril.

Chaffanbrass, eyebrows raised to their utmost pinnacle in scorn, had dissented from this unusual strategy, his trumpet-like voice raised in genuine outrage: "Hanged?" he had expostulated, "Never say hanged to me, me boy. You'll be acquitted, and that's final."

Mr. Chaffanbrass had not promised to secure him a similar acquittal in the court of public opinion, but had, to do him justice, been well on the way to doing so, when the accused had been suddenly cleared as if by the most romantic of contrivances—the discovery of evidence of the real culprit's guilt, by the woman who loved the unjustly accused man, who was now bidding farewell to his unlikely legal champion.

At the end of the day, thought the spontaneous mourner, Mr. Chaffanbarass had served him with great skill, and had predisposed the court to accept the evidence from abroad (which had, after all, been circumstantial in nature) against the wretch who had, in fact, committed the murder of which Phineas Finn—for such was this mourner's name—had stood accused. Phineas's own legal training had deserted him at the time of his trial, but in the more than two decades that had passed since that terrible time, he had come to recognise that his innocence, so beyond peradventure to his own mind that he had burned with resentment at acquaintances who had doubted him, if only for a moment, had needed the ferocity of a Chaffanbrass to blazon it forth.

And so he had come to say farewell to this chance acquaintance who had been of such signal use to him. In the years since, they had met but once, at a dinner at Lincoln's Inn, which Phineas had attended as a guest. The shabbily-gowned, wheezy old man had greeted him from across the room with a nod and a wink, but had not shown by any outward sign that he expected any salutation in response. Phineas, a member of the Government at the time, had crossed the floor to meet old Chaffanbrass and had taken him by the hand, greeting him as a friend. It was the only time Phineas, or anyone else, had ever seen Chaffanbrass disconcerted; the old barrister had come not to expect acknowledgement from those he had rescued.

"Why, Mr. Chaffanbrass," Phineas had greeted him, "how well you look, after all these years." And they had spoken for a few minutes, the old man seeming pleased to have been singled out by the Chancellor of the Duchy of Lancaster. Phineas felt he had behaved well on that occasion, but winced as he recalled the intolerable gossip that had been reignited by this encounter. It had done him no harm with those who were in truth his friends, but had increased the frigidity of the wind from Downing Street, then inhabited by a Prime Minister who had never loved him, and who had already banished him from the more meaningful post he had held under the prior Prime Minister.

The Government had not long outlived this encounter and the resultant flurry of rumours, and it was Mr. Gresham's last bow as Prime Minister, but still Phineas's impulsive warmth had done him no good with the party elders by associating him with, as Mr. Gresham had called old Chaffanbrass, "a dirty, ill-kempt old man who rescues wretches from the penalties of their crimes." When this assessment had been communicated to Phineas by his old friend Laurence Fitzgibbon, a junior minister at the Treasury, Finn had laughed, reminding Fitzgibbon, "'Twasn't my own crime, but somebody else's, that Chaffanbrass saved me from hanging for." Despite his assumption of a cavalier air, Finn had noticed that, while Larry had risen a little bit in each successive Liberal administration (though he was still junior enough, heaven knows), Phineas had not been asked to leave the backbenches since.

Adrift as he had been these last years in a political Sargasso Sea, Phineas knew that his friends—and especially his wife—feared he had become bitter, or resigned to his failure to carve a political career for himself. As a stray sunbeam glinted off the pillar opposite him, catching the flecks of brightness in the seemingly ebon stone, Phineas reflected that they were quite mistaken. The shattering of his trust in the Party, in the good opinion of his fellow Members of Parliament, or even in his fellow Liberals, had not begun with his arrest, but had merely culminated in that ordeal. He all too vividly remembered the closing of doors to which he had previously been a sought-after visitor when his name was—with monstrous injustice—coupled with the name of a married lady by scandalmongers. The fact that so many whom he had admired and fought beside could believe him—him, Phineas Finn!—to be guilty of murder had completed his disenchantment, not begun it.

Now, of course, the world smiled upon him. Personally popular, if not politically, Phineas had lived for nearly two decades without having to face the money worries that had bedeviled his youth. If office was not forthcoming, as had been the case—why, Phineas did not need its emoluments—thanks, admittedly, to Marie's ample income, and her extraordinary flair for business. But he never entered the portals of society these days without wry reflection, wondering who would be loyal to him should the dark times come again, and which doors would close as summarily as when he was a young man.

No, Phineas had been able to indulge his independence in a manner that had broken the heart of poor old Mr. Monk, but that had thrilled Marie when she listened from the Ladies' Gallery or read in *The Jupiter* of her firebrand's eloquence. Certainly Mr. Monk's remonstrances that Phineas needed to show loyalty to the Party to gain its loyalty in return had not moved the younger man a jot. Indeed, the younger man had not even bothered trying to explain himself to his erstwhile mentor.

Only once had Phineas tried to make that explanation to anyone, and it was not to Mr. Monk, to Larry Fitzgibbon, or to any of the friends of his earliest days, but, rather surprisingly, to the Duke of Omnium. The former Prime Minister, whose wife had been, until her death, Marie's closest intimate, had in his own shy and dry manner befriended Phineas. In the days of his own Premiership, the reserved Duke and the spontaneous Irishman had uncovered an improbable liking for one another, thrown into propinquity as they were by the friendship of their wives, and Finn imperceptibly found his respect for the Duke ripening into affection, while the Duke found in Phineas a discreet listener, who could on occasion break through the Duke's own solemnity and cadge a laugh from him.

The Duke had surprised the explanation out of him, Phineas recalled that day, as he sat in the Temple. Deputed by the new Prime Minister, the Duke had made one last effort to bring the wayward sheep back to the fold. That the Duke of Omnium would take such instructions from Barrington Erle was emblematic of the man's humility, and typical of why his own Party bore him such ambivalent love.

After his own premiership, the Duke had been viewed as a party elder, but not as one likely to seek a second helping of the cares of office. Beyond the fact that the Duke lacked the proud and dominating nature of a Prime Minister, he had been not the leading spirit of the Liberals in their full pride, but rather of a coalition that existed merely to serve the ongoing daily needs of the Nation during a hiatus when both parties needed to catch their breath, and neither was able to claim a clear mandate. As such, the Liberals conceded his necessity, but were in fact a little shamed to have served under "Planty Pall," as he was still known.

When the Duke surprised everyone by returning to a lesser office and serving in his prior self-effacing manner as President of the Council, those who were in truth already a little ashamed of him became yet a little more so—Caesar, it was said, should not rise from the cobblestones and serve under Brutus. The Duke, with his thin skin, contrived to so bear himself that none dared criticise him to his face, and spoke only of the importance of the Nation's service.

Nonetheless, the Duke had undertaken, at the request of his new leader, to speak to young Finn, with whom the Duke was known to be friendly, and of whom, the Prime Minister communicated, the Party still had hopes. The Duke had done so at Matching Priory, his country home now that he had ceded the family seat to his heir, and which was specially dear to him due to certain passages between himself and the late Duchess, whose favoured residence Matching always had been. Asking Mr. and Mrs. Finn down for a weekend, the Duke had craftily waited until the men were alone with their port.

In so doing, the Duke's poor store of craft had betrayed him; he had shut out his best natural ally, and his most influential, Marie Finn, whose admiration for her husband's growing reputation as a man of conscience was tempered by an equally natural desire to see him rise in the Party to responsibilities and—yes—power which she believed him plainly fitted to exercise.

"Mr. Finn," began the Duke as the ladies departed, "I wonder that you have declined office, despite the opportunity to contribute to our latest endeavours." (The conversation took place some five years after the final fall of Mr. Gresham, and the rise of Barrington Erle to the Premiership after a surprisingly heated contest for the leadership.)

Phineas smiled, but did not answer. The Duke cleared his throat and made a fresh attempt.

"The Nation's service, Mr. Finn, would benefit from your efforts, you know. You will forgive me, I am certain, for raising a matter of such a personal nature, but we cannot spare men who are both able and honest—as I know you to be."

By which it will be seen, by those who know the Duke of old, that he had in fact welcomed Phineas into his friendship, after what was by now a decade of close association. Phineas smiled again, but this time answered.

"Duke, you know that I have been in public life for some time, but the prospect of office holds little for me now. There was a time when I wanted it—wanted it quite badly, to be frank. But now I see the grasping and conniving for place, and the corridors of power seem—well, I won't say sullied–"

"But perhaps you think it, Mr. Finn?" the older man interrupted, adding "Yet compromise is an inherent part of any form of politics, unavoidable in small things, that one may stand firm in the great matters. Is it that you are unwilling to serve under Erle?"

"No-o," Phineas answered slowly, though indeed Barrington Erle's brand of partisanship was not, to his way of thinking, the highest form of political morality.

"Then why?" pressed the Duke.

Phineas thought for a moment. "I have views of my own, Duke," he answered at last, "views which I am re-thinking, in truth, as I see how

England is changing. I once thought that the good things of office were well-earned by our labours on behalf of the people. But now, I wonder. I doubt so much more than I did, before—my trial." The last words seemed almost forced out. Phineas never spoke of the matter, except, perhaps, to his wife. The Duke's delicacy forbade him from pressing any further.

"When I held office under you, Duke, and could directly try to ameliorate the woes of Ireland, or improve the Admiralty, *that* was work well worth doing! But then, as Chancellor of the Duchy of Lancaster—well, what work could I do in such a *fainéant* position as that?"

The Duke frowned a little, but did not try to answer the question.

"And Erle wants me, not for any meaningful post, but so that I will be under his command, and decency will require me to hold my tongue as he remakes the party in his own image. What role is it that I am offered, Duke? Ceremonial posts like Lancaster, or menial ones like Weights and Measures?"

Here, Phineas's heated blood caused him to speak unwisely, for the onetime Plantagenet Palliser, though longing to hold once more the position of Chancellor of the Exchequer, would nonetheless have stoutly maintained that there was good work to be done at Weights and Measures. But the Duke held his peace, knowing that even his closest Parliamentary friends did not share his urgent desire to bring about the happiness of a rational system of weights, measures and even—if he should ever be mighty again!—decimal coinage.

Nobly ignoring Phineas's tactlessness, the Duke reminded him, "Mr. Finn, whenever there is a change of leadership, those who have had the confidence of the previous leaders—as you had mine—are apt to find themselves pushed to one side until the need for them is felt."

Phineas spoke with his usual firm certainty. "If they are willing to be, Duke. But I find myself despising the game."

"The service of the Nation, Mr. Finn, is not a game," said the Duke, with something of reproach in his voice.

"Nor should it be," replied Phineas, "but obtaining a position in which one cannot do anything useful is, and is a dirtier game than when we were younger." And the Duke frowned again, a little more deeply than before.

"Forgive me, Duke," Phineas said at length, "I am not speaking of you, who take on whatever work you can, as long as it be useful, but of the ways in which politics are now. Or, at any rate, where my old friend Barrington would have me—my mouth silenced by his bread, but without granting me the ability to do anything to earn it."

And the Duke of Omnium sighed, knowing that on this occasion, at least, Phineas was not to be swayed.

As years passed, and ministries rose and fell—two terms for Barrington Erle, interrupted by a Conservative interregnum—the Party ceased to look to Phineas for anything but oratory. And that oratory was not always on the side of the Liberals, or at any rate in consonance with the positions the Party had taken up. Often, Phineas found himself as critical of his long-time friends as he was of the Tories. His tenure at the Admiralty had made him something of an expert on naval affairs, and so he spoke out frequently in favour of measures designed to preserve the Nation's naval supremacy. Especially Phineas warned of potential future conflict with Germany, and the Liberals laughed him to scorn. Phineas's attitude did win him some small reputation with the supporters of Empire, and he received a glowing letter from the preposterously young American Assistant Secretary of the Navy, whose *magnum opus* on sea power Phineas had referenced in a well-reported speech. The Assistant Secretary, publishing scholarly monographs while busily expanding and updating the American navy, wrote to Phineas as to a kindred spirit, which made Finn rather ashamed at his own comparatively meager achievements to date.

For that was just it; after a quarter of a century in Parliament as the member for Tankerville, Phineas still grappled with the question: What could he, a mere backbencher, do to shape the course of the Nation? Was he now merely a man with a brilliant future behind him? And how was he to justify the second chance at life procured for him by the combined efforts of his wife and the shabby, old barrister now being laid to rest? After all, Marie and he had built a life—he had a lifetime to repay her, and the payment brought such sweetness to his own life that it masked the fretting sense that he had a greater debt to pay. In a sense, it was a debt owed to Chaffanbrass—not the barrister, who had wanted nothing but his fee—but to the man. Phineas thought yet once more of overhearing the barrister, as he was leaving the cells, saying to his solicitor that he felt that he would give the blood out of his very veins to save some of his clients, and that Phineas was one such. Had he, Phineas, lived a life worthy of that strange old man's zeal?

Just as Phineas circled back to this last question, which had haunted him for so many years, the final hymn began to sound, and Phineas belatedly rose to join in. At long last, the service drew to a close, and Phineas bade farewell to old Chaffanbrass, whose brief intervention in Phineas's life had been of such moment. As the mourners began to disperse, Phineas stopped briefly to pay his respects to the bereaved family, and to take his departure. As he left, the lady who had shared his row caught his eye for a moment, and he stopped beside her.

"It's Lady Mason, is it not?" Phineas asked. He remembered the case, from his own days studying law. She had almost certainly forged a will in her own favour, but the skill of Chaffanbrass had seen her acquitted. She was old now, but he remembered how pure and lovely she had seemed in court, when all the students had flocked to see the trial.

The lady gave a wan smile and posed a question of her own: "Mr. Finn, I think?"

"Yes," answered Phineas, matching her smile with a wry one of his own. "I thought there would be more of us here," he added.

Lady Mason's delicately arched brows rose a little. "Surely not, Mr. Finn. You are here because Mr. Chaffanbrass preserved your innocence; I, to bear witness that he protected my guilt. What pleasure can there be in marking either fact? The surprise is not that we have not been joined by others, but that we are here at all."

And with that, Lady Mason swept off toward the narthex, Phineas bowing to her as she left. A moment later, he departed as well, abandoning his plan to go into chambers that day. Instead, he would return home and pass the day with his family, hoping to melt the cold uncertainty lodged in his heart by his still unanswered questions.

AT THE BEARGARDEN

Every club has its Oldest Member, who in some wise incarnates the spirit of the place. Even the Beargarden, a club in which, at its founding, youth was almost exclusively served, had seen a greying in its membership in the quarter century since its inception. Reconstituted after a brief period when its landlord and steward Herr Vossner levanted, and in the aftermath had been found to have helped himself rather too freely to its members' subscription fees, the Beargarden now survived in slightly less plush quarters. And, while not exactly an elderly man, its Oldest Member, Mr. Adolphus Longestaffe, admirably filled the role of totem of the Beargarden.

Years ago, Dolly Longestaffe had slumbered through a first class education, of whose fleece a few tufts had stuck to his mental fences. One such tuft had remained bright to him: The saying of Rene Descartes—"Old Decanted" to Dolly Longestaffe—that "In all things, extremes are vicious." And so Dolly Longestaffe had assiduously avoided extremes. He was not extremely married, nor extremely sober, nor extremely hard working. Indeed, it was in avoiding the opposite of these extremities that Dolly's difficulties lay. So he remained moderately married (in that he enjoyed his wife's jointure, and occasionally her company), moderately sober (in that he had not been rendered insensible by liquor in some years), and moderately occupied (in that he ran his eye over his steward's accountings once every six months, in order to make sure that he himself was being only moderately fleeced).

Dolly had once been tall and thin and fair, but years of moderate self-indulgence had added to his frame, without rendering him exactly gross. His hair, no longer flaxen, had grown sparse, and rather lank. He remained, however, amiable and patient, as long as gambling debts owed to him were settled promptly, for he had learned his lesson all too well in that regard. From his accustomed seat in the large bay window at the Beargarden, Dolly was able to see the street and all who came and went thereon. Dolly's amiability and patience had made him a favourite with many, and the surprising shrewdness that lurked behind those placid blue eyes was informed by an ear for gossip unmatched by any since the late Countess of Midlothian. One could justly apply to Dolly what he himself had said of the late Countess—"A veritable sibyl, who knew, my dear, everything with a precision that savoured of the prophetic, and was especially like a prophet in her ability to pinpoint who was begettin' where she oughtn't to be be-gotten."

"And therefore oughtn't to be forgotten, eh, Dolly?" interjected Savrola Vavasor, a member of recent vintage. Vavasor was a small, cherubic man in his mid-twenties who owed his exotic first name—one could scarce describe it as Christian—to his American mother; no Englishman was ever so called. She had sent him to school at Harrow, and he had served briefly in the Army in his late teens, riding with some gallantry into battle in the Sudan. After his dispatches to *The People's Banner* proved less popular with the General Staff than with that periodical's general readership, Vavasor deemed it wise to sell out, and earn a living from his pen. He had just put up for Parliament, in a well-financed campaign that owed much to his mother, a dark, queenly beauty who still turned heads (including at least one awaiting a crown, according to Dolly Longestaffe's sources—although he was prudent enough not to say so to young Vavasor). Certainly Mrs. Vavasor had cut enough of a dash at court that the Brahmins of the Conservative Party were eager to see her son elected, and Savrola was nominated for a competitive seat. Royalty did not, of course, join young Savrola on the hustings, but royalty did, it was said, speak a word in a well-placed ear, and Doting Maternity paid ready cash for election expenses, with the result that the young Savrola had taken his seat as the member for East Barchester.

Savrola Vavasor had then been put up for that considerably less exclusive club, the Beargarden, of which his father had once been a member—a member who had left England under a cloud of disgrace after a promising start in Parliament, and who had then considerately died when Savrola was a boy, before the lad's natural filial piety could be undermined by a closer acquaintance with his sire. Savrola spoke of his father infrequently, but with passion, wistfully avowing his intention to make good his father's failed political career—failed, he was certain, because of certain powerful enemies.

"Nonsense, dear boy!" Dolly had informed his young friend when he had become aware that Savrola was the son of George Vavasor, and wished to revive what he called his father's philosophy of "Tory Democracy." "Old George's philosophy stopped short after riding over anybody between him and a fox at the West Barsetshire Hunt. No, my son, your father got washed up by bad luck and worse judgment. He ran for election in a rotten borough without the readies to pay for it, and compounded his folly by alienating all his potential backers." So spake Dolly Longestaffe, Sage of the Beargarden, whose exegesis had been unchallenged for years.

"Dolly, that's not so," objected Savrola with more heat than right on his part. "My father wanted to institute reforms that the powers that be in both parties feared would break their hold on power! He wanted to introduce the secret ballot–"

"Which we have done since, my boy," Dolly interjected.

"Showing that he was ahead of his time! After the Liberal Party turned on him!"

"Turned on him? My recollection is he simply wasn't returned at the General Election. Now look here, old son, I quite liked George, but if anything drove him out of the country, it was debt and a family quarrel."

"Dolly, you don't mean to impute any scandal to my father?" Savrola asked quietly, looking like a child reluctant to quarrel with a favourite master, but preparing himself to do so at need.

"Certainly not, Vavasor," Dolly answered with a slantedicular smile that inverted the meaning of his words. "You forget that back in the old days we were all getting into debt. It's a young man's prerogative, you know. And I seem to recall he was jilted twice by a girl who eventually walked off with his inheritance—the Lord knows how she managed that. No, your father had things to provoke him, I should say."

Young Savrola sat in his club chair, unsure of his ground. Dolly Longestaffe was pretty generally right on such matters, he knew, but his father, in their one conversation of any note, had gasped out his version of the facts as he had neared death, and that utterance—a self-pitying, self-justifying recitation, comprised in equal measures of truth, half-truths, and outright lies spoken so often as to be believed by their teller as cold fact –was sacred to the son. His face reflected his perplexity, and his desire to be a loyal son and to champion his father warred with the knowledge that Dolly had never been refuted yet—and, worse luck, had known his father during the very events in question!

As Savrola struggled within himself, Dolly took in his friend's very real distress, and kindly said, as if to himself, "Of course, George was spoken of very highly before he lost that election. He had a great future before him, if he hadn't been so unlucky. I never heard of any foul play, but who knows what goes on at these rural polling places…"

The lines of Savrola's face relaxed, and he resumed his cherubic aspect at this partial withdrawal. "I don't like to be quarrelsome, Dolly, but he was my father," he murmured.

"Don't take it amiss, Vavasor, I quite understand. Shall we have a set of billiards?"

To this, Savrola readily assented, and they proceeded into the billiard room. As they went in, Dolly changed the subject:

"So how are you finding the House?"

"Peculiar, frankly," Vavasor replied. "Measures that could shape the face of the Empire for centuries are decided with as little discussion as if we were ordering dinner, and then hours are spent debating amendments to the Cod Fisheries Bill. And Barrington Erle seems to think that debate is beneath the dignity of the Liberal Party, and does rather start if we Tories raise a question! I mean, honestly, he *does* know that there's an opposition, surely? Does he expect us to join him in a lovely little bit of Liberal plainsong?"

"Ah," commented Dolly wisely, clearly more interested in his abstruse calculation of a dodgy corner shot than in Vavasor's political views.

"After all, Dolly," Vavasor continued, "Politics is supposed to be about ideas, and policies, not just whose influence you come into the House under. But not to Erle. You should see him glower whenever Finn takes an independent line."

"Phineas Finn?" inquired Dolly Longestaffe. "He ain't in any trouble, I hope?"

"Why, do you know him?"

"Not so much these days. Haven't really spoken to him in years—he's mostly a politico now, and I can't be bothered with political things. He's devilish tight with the whole Palliser clan, of course. Silverbridge was a member here back in the Seventies, and he brought Finn in a couple times. Of course, this was after the trial."

"The trial?" Savrola asked, fascinated.

"The tri-al." Dolly mimicked Savrola's tones. "Dear boy, Phineas Finn stood trial for his life, and most exciting it was, too. I think," Dolly continued with an unusual degree of thoughtfulness, "that may be why Barrington Erle ain't exactly an admirer."

"Why's that?"

"Well, Lady Laura, of course. She is his cousin, and was a tremendous sponsor of Barrington's back in the day. She married a particularly dreary Scotsman by the name of Kennedy—and one must work, my dear, to stand out for dreariness in all that Caledonian rain and honest poverty. Still, he had plenty of the readies, and all the land around Loch Linter."

"Loch Linter? Up by Linn Castle?"

"More like Loch Ness when Kennedy was still infesting the place like a Presbyterian sea monster. He went mad, you know. Well, they all do. Look at Gladstone at the end."

By now Savrola was vibrating with silent laughter. "Come now, Dolly," he managed to wheeze, "what has all this to do with Phineas Finn?"

"Well, as I say, Kennedy went mad and took a shot at Finn for being a sight too close to his wife–"

"The P.M.'s cousin?"

"That's right, Vavasor, Laura Standish as was. Lady Laura, too, if you please. Mated to the dourest of all Scots, with Phinny Finn as a second string to her bow, people used to say. So Kennedy shot Finn—or tried to, at any rate—and was taken into care until he died. Which he did pretty soon thereafter," said Dolly, then added musingly, "Probably the most consideration Kennedy ever showed anybody else, Vavasor, hey? Like the fellow in Scripture, 'Nothing in his life became him like his leaving it.'"

"Pretty sure that's from *Macbeth*, Dolly, not Holy Writ."

"Well, it's one of those dreadful, heavy suet pudding-y books, at any rate."

"And what happened to Lady Laura, Dolly—if you please?"

"Well, with her husband goin' mad, and then dyin,' and Phinny Finn on trial for murder..."

"Who did he kill?"

"I rather think you mean 'whom' there, Vavasor." Dolly was clearly enjoying himself.

"All right, then, Dolly, if we can end the grammar lesson, and get back to the matter at hand, *whom* did he kill?"

"No one, you great muff! Some politico had gotten himself clubbed to death by a parson—my, it was a boy's life back in the Seventies, eh, Vavasor?—and the parson got himself mistaken for Phinny Finn. So poor old Finn had to stand trial, and might even have been hanged, too, if the women hadn't come to the rescue."

"Lady Laura saved him, then!" Vavasor asserted.

"Lady Laura! Lady Fiddlestick! What could she have done, with the Town burning up with rumours that her infidelity with the accused had killed the Loch Ness Monster? No; not Lady Laura. Not exotic enough for Phinny, anyway. No, he gets himself rescued by a beautiful foreign adventuress, with dark hair, a contralto voice, and half the Palliser diamonds, put into her pretty hands by the old Duke himself!"

From which it may be seen, by those who know the history of our great Whig families, that Dolly's oracular quality owed more to colour and narrative verve than to strict adherence to factual nicety.

Vavasor was taken aback by a far different consideration, however. "Not Planty Pall!" he gasped, understandably.

The mere notion of the notoriously strait-laced former Prime Minister importuning a raven-haired siren by heaping the family gemstones upon her was so entertaining to Dolly that he nearly aspirated his port.

"No, Vavasor," he corrected when sobriety had been restored, "when I say the old Duke, I don't mean Planty Pall, though he is old enough these days, I suppose. I mean his uncle, the *old* Duke, who was as grand as the Queen, but a lot less sedate. He romanced this foreign woman, but after he died—leaving her the boodle—she went to the Continent, found the evidence to clear Finn, and brought it back, just at the end of the trial."

"My G-d! And they got married?"

"My dear, after all that—did he really have a choice?"

And Dolly Longestaffe, having thus spoken, bent with a well-observed grace over the billiard table, and ran up his hundred, winning the stake. He generally did, these days, and Savrola Vavsour paid up with the good grace of one who has resigned himself to habitual loss. Vavsour set up another game, and Dolly broke, thinking no more of Phineas Finn.

CLARISSA RILEY

At her well-appointed house in Park Lane, Mrs. Finn was "At Home," meaning that she was known to be ready to receive visitors, or at least their calling cards, and to offer refreshment. On this particular wet and unpleasant day, however, Mrs. Finn found herself unattended by any guests. Her husband had gone to Chambers, after several days of being unusually pensive and quiet.

Mrs. Finn was widely rumoured to have reached sixty years of age—several of those who had known her prior to her marriage swore it—and yet she had staved off all of the appurtenances of age in a truly marvelous way. Her raven-dark hair had always hung in curls, framing a face which purists had criticised as perhaps a little thin, and the curls still filled their office. Their deep hue had perhaps lightened a touch with the passage of time, and a little white had found its way discreetly through the still luxuriant hair, forming a streak that, when unbound, arrested the eye as fetchingly as if it resulted from the dyer's art, and not from nature. Mrs. Finn's deep blue eyes retained their luminescence, her mouth its mobility, and her voice its music.

Perhaps the face had grown a little thinner, or a few lines had been graven by the years into the pale, almost sallow complexion. But the most discerning observer would be hard-pressed to count her years with any certainty, such was the perfection of Mrs. Finn's art. Where her husband impressed by his frank and natural quality, her art matched that in its artlessness. Although she was several years his senior, people meeting them for the first time tended to think it the other way around. Mrs. Finn was woman enough to enjoy that fact, and Phineas was man enough to share the joke with her.

Mrs. Finn's beauty had always been that of a woman not reliant on the freshness of youth for her allure; now a little more marked by time, her spell still held good. All that money could do had long ago created a vibrant and distinctive style of dress—respectable, surely, but with a tantalizing hint of the *demimondaine*—often swathed in black, yet relieved by coloured ribbons, rubies and other rich adornments. Now, Mrs. Finn had adapted gracefully to both the changing fashions and the passage of time. She did not cling to the mode of her youth, but neither did she dress as a young woman of the present day. Instead, the basic idea that underlay the costume of earlier days—stark colours, relieved by accents in vivid hues—had been preserved, while Mrs. Finn adopted such of the simpler garments of the *fin de siècle* that showed her to advantage. The rich navy folds of her bombazine gown, relieved by an intricate pattern of jet-beaded embroidery, fell straight and true to her elegant instep from a waistline still as trim as a girl of eighteen's. A jabot of sapphire gauze set off her ivory skin and complemented her eyes.

As to her manner, Mrs. Finn remained a sympathetic listener, and a sprightly conversationalist. Although the death of the Duchess of Omnium some fifteen years before had deprived her of her only true female intimate, she still had friends who were dear to her. Of these, the closest remained her husband, who had never fallen out of his habit of coming to her with his joys and woes, whatever they might be. Another was the Countess of Brentford, once a rival for the affections of Phineas Finn, now happily ensconced in her own family, all of whom were intimate with the Finns. A third close friend was Lady Mary Tregear, the daughter of the late Duchess of Omnium. While all of the Pallisers were dear to Marie, whom they loved, and fond of Phineas, Lady Mary had come to fill, to some extent, her mother's place in Marie's heart.

If Marie had one lasting regret, it was that her marriage had been childless. Marie Finn had met her husband at a time when the hope that they might be so blessed was still possible, but the years had intervened, and by the time they married it had become improbable. When improbability had faded into impossibility, Marie felt a sense of loss, not so much for herself, but for Phineas, whose one child, a boy—born of his brief marriage to a girl from his native Killaloe—had died scant hours after his mother's life was sacrificed to bringing him into the world. Phineas had remained boyish in many ways, Marie sometimes thought, especially when watching him with the children of their friends, or with animals. He spoiled and petted their grey-and-white cat Elspeth, whom he had found crying outside the home of his old friend and onetime pupil-master Mr. Low. He would have delighted in having a son or daughter to romp with and dote upon, she believed. She was too secure in her place in Phineas's heart to feel that the lack of children had wounded their marriage, but sometimes wished she could have given him one.

Of late, the Finns had suffered another loss, that of Phineas's favourite sister Barbara, who of all the family had most resembled her brother in her ability to commend herself to those whom she liked. Barbara Riley—for she had married—had grown stout and short of breath, but had remained the same laughing, provoking companion she had been to Phineas in their shared childhood. Barbara and her husband had died four years earlier, on their way to visit the Finns for Christmas, when the boiler of their ship across the Irish Sea had exploded, killing many of the passengers and crew.

From the catastrophe of the wreck, the mother had preserved her one child, Clarissa Riley—for Barbara's romantic streak, buried beneath the folds of her good Irish common sense, had led her to name her daughter for Richardson's heroine. The mother's pertinacity in securing a place on a lifeboat for her daughter had ensured her daughter's survival, and had spared the girl the terror and anxiety the mother had felt searching the foundering ship for her husband. James Riley had perished in the sea because of the lack of lifeboats sufficient for more than the women and children; Barbara Riley had died some days after being rescued, a casualty of exposure, coupled with shock and grief. After her mother's death, Clarissa had come to live with the Finns.

Clarissa Riley emerged from the wreck a long-limbed, coltish girl of fourteen. Four years later, she was as elegant a young woman as any in London. With her mother's rich red hair, her uncle's sparkling green eyes, and a mischievous grin all her own, Clarissa missed being a beauty only to the extent that she could not take herself entirely seriously. Perhaps her face lacked repose, but it reflected her natural tendency to merriment, which had been long extinguished by the tragedy she had survived. But as the fires of her nature rekindled, Clarissa's natural vivacity returned.

Her Aunt Marie had fostered this revival, gently steering the young girl toward the innocent pleasures of life as the shock and sorrow of her losses receded slowly. In her clearest, calmest tones, Marie had urged Clarissa not to live altogether with her dead—reminding her that her parents had sought with their last breaths to preserve her own, and had saved her for more than mourning, funereal garments and grief. More than that, though, Marie had taught her how to love the living without slighting the dead, sharing more of her own history with the girl than she had with anyone in England, other than her husband. Phineas, too, played his part, merely by loving the girl both as a link to his dear sister and simply for herself.

Her uncle had, unknowingly, provided some measure of catharsis for her in revealing the fruit of many quarts of midnight oil in research and drafting in the year and half subsequent to his sister's death. On a warm May afternoon, Aunt Marie had bade Clarissa to dress and accompany her to the House of Commons. There, from the Ladies' Gallery, Clarissa had been roused from her stupor of grief by the spectacle of her Uncle Phineas denouncing the folly and indolence of the Board of Trade in allowing British vessels to sail without adequate lifeboats for all aboard.

Phineas was, of course, implicitly assailing his own party in his sharp, clear tones, concluding that: "It cannot be, and it must not be, that the lives of our sons and daughters are to be risked at sea based on a mathematical formula that assumes only a partial evacuation of the vessel, when in cases of a vessel actually foundering, there is no refuge, no safe place from which to await rescue. The rule, surely, must be simple: One soul, one seat! The amendment which I have introduced to the Navigable Waters Act, 1870, will, upon adoption in this House and in another place, rectify this grotesque, overly nice calculation, applying the common-sense formula: One soul, one seat!"

And with that, Phineas sat down, a flurry of disapprobation from those near him arising. The Tories, eager to have an issue with which to harry Barrington Erle, quickly endorsed Phineas's jeremiad. Indeed, no less a figure than the Leader of the Opposition himself rose to congratulate Phineas for placing policy before party—rubbing the Prime Minister's nose in it, rather.

"What the honourable member for Tankerville has shown us," Frank Greystock declaimed, "is that the lives of British men, women and children are not safe in the hands of the Government as presently constituted, and that independent action is needed.

At this, Barrington Erle was seen to grow red with anger.

"All good men, of whatever political stripe"—a sop to the handful of new members from poorer districts calling themselves "Labourites"—"can, and should, support this lifeboat bill that my honourable friend from Tankerville has introduced, and I pledge that the Conservative Party will provide just that support."

At this, Phineas caught the eye of the Speaker, and was given a chance to reply.

"I welcome, as all members of the House should do," he began, "my honourable friends, of whatever persuasion, to support this vitally necessary bill. But I do not condemn those among whom I have long sat for not foreseeing the necessity of this change. We have, all of us, been too reliant on standards that may have served once, when voyages across the oceans were less frequent, and ships smaller. We have been complacent, and the loss of those we love should shake us from our slumber. And so I hope that the Government will also support this measure, to reduce, if not altogether avoid, these needless deaths at sea."

Barrington Erle seldom addressed the House (other than on purely ceremonial matters) prior to a caucus, and without being sure of a majority. But if Greystock's speech had angered him, Phineas's had, in reminding him of Phineas's motives, and of the warmth of heart that provoked the unanticipated bill, touched him. The Prime Minister rose, and, to the surprise of all, especially Phineas, pardoned the breach of decorum, and the attack on the Board of Trade.

"We know," said the Prime Minister, "that with sorrow can come clarity of vision and passion, two virtues which do not," he added in a slightly arch tone, "always inspire diplomacy. Still, we take the lesson when it is given when it is based on truth, and ignore any irregularity of form. The honourable member will forgive me, I trust, if I say that the Board of Trade was following and enforcing its mandate, and that I am unaware of any negligence on the part of any man. Still, clearly, the needs of the present are no longer served by the regulations passed"—a wild start as the Prime Minister realised he had no idea how old the regulations under discussions in fact were, for he had not, in fact, an encyclopedic command of the subject—"'m'yes, passed, as I say, some years ago. In any event," Barrington Erle continued, "the thing to do when people's lives are in jeopardy is not to insist on fidelity to the dead hand of—some years ago, but—to save lives. And so," the Prime Minister concluded, "the Government will not only join those supporting the honourable member for Tankerville's initiative, but intends to see it passed this very session!"

At this, there was much tumult in the House.

"Aunt Marie, what's happening?" asked Clarissa Riley.

"Well, my dear," her aunt explained, "your uncle's proposal is being adopted by the Government and by the Opposition."

"Then it's sure to pass?"

"That might, perhaps, be a trifle over-optimistic, my dear. It's almost certain to pass is as far as I feel safe in going. Politics is a strange world, Clarissa, one in which a measure universally agreed to can nonetheless fail for reasons no one can explain."

"Why is that, Aunt Marie?"

"Men, my dear, are never entirely to be trusted—not even the best of them …"

"Aunt Marie!" The spurt of laughter shocked from the girl was the most animation Marie had seen in her since she had come among the Finns newly orphaned.

"Do I seem so very radical?" Marie Finn asked, with the quizzical smile her husband could never resist.

"No, but I think I know where my copy of *Lippincott's Monthly* got to, Madame Marie Finn," her niece replied with an assumption of severity.

"Oh?"

"When you eliminate the impossible, whatever remains…"

"However improbable," interjected the aunt.

"Must be true!" The ladies concluded together.

As they sat in companionable silence, the Ladies' Gallery began to empty. After a few minutes, Clarissa asked, in a quiet voice.

"You do trust my uncle, though, don't you, Aunt Marie?"

"The exception who proves the rule," Marie answered in her bantering tone. Then, more seriously, she said, "Yes, my dear. With all my heart. Your uncle is kind, and brave, and tried always to do what was right even when he couldn't afford the world's hostility. Like all men, he is sometimes proud, and headstrong, but unlike so many he can be made to laugh at himself. And that, my dear, is half the trick."

"What trick, Aunt Marie?"

"To finding a man worthy of your love. One who does not take himself so very seriously is more likely than most to be able to accept love, and to give it. And one who can look beyond his own nose! Yes, that is important! Look at your uncle; he was unable to do anything to save the lives of your poor parents, but he didn't just hug his grief; he found a way to try to try to prevent anyone else from feeling the grief you and he share."

"Is that why he did it?"

"But of course, my dear; why else? He did it so that his favourite sister and his brother-in-law did not die for nothing; some good had to come out of it, or he could not rest with it on his chest."

Clarissa's eyes shone, and she viewed her uncle as a very Charlemagne that day.

As the House broke up, Phineas stopped at the gangway to speak a word to the Prime Minister, so moved by his unexpected success that he forgot the title his old friend and onetime sponsor bore.

"Barrington," he began hoarsely, resting his hand on the other's arm, "Thank you. I knew your agenda was set for the Session, but I had to try–"

The Prime Minister smiled at Phineas, remarking, "Just watch out in committee, old fellow. Greystock won't like it so well if he can't get any capital out of it, and some of our chaps may help him, behind closed doors. Now, are you going to the Club, or seeing the lovely Marie home?"

"Home, Barrington. Marie has my niece with her."

"Clarissa? You must present me." And the Prime Minister of Great Britain and Ireland strode over to shake hands with Clarissa Riley, and was gracious, condoling with the girl upon her loss. And Marie Finn knew how to be gracious, in her turn; with a spontaneity she seldom showed, she pressed Barrington Erle to join their late supper.

Now, it is a fact, well known to all the world, that the Prime Minister of England does not often encounter impulsive invitations to join old friends for a meal on the spur of the moment. Such innocent, careless pleasures are denied the holder of great power, either by custom or by fear of rejection on the part of his would-be hosts, and the man who might like nothing better than a scrap lunch with a friend who knew him when his hair was dark and his face was unlined endures instead a wearying succession of State dinners, each of which might be, separately, a treat, but which become stifling when taken ten in a fortnight. Marie Finn knew this, and rewarded Barrington Erle handsomely; she made him feel like a young, rising M.P. again, with all the world before him, by the easy and matter-of-fact way in which she invited the Prime Minister to accompany them.

Barrington Erle, for all his political craft, was a warm-hearted man. If once a man or woman ever captured his affection, he was never quite able to dislodge the intruder from his heart. Although he failed to understand—and often resented—Phineas's stubborn independence, he still liked the man, and admired his wife, the sphinx who had once had a coronet laid at her feet—and had scrupled to take it. Clarissa's delight in her uncle's unanticipated success had brought colour to a face still bearing some traces of grief. Barrington Erle impulsively decided to join the Finns, and the party proceeded to Park Lane.

The servants had been somewhat startled to see their mistress entering on the arm of the Prime Minister, but had rallied, and produced a pleasant scratch supper of pheasant, pate, and some delicacies always prudently held in reserve by Marie Finn against the unexpected supper party. Marie reflected comfortably that, though their cellar was small, its contents were expertly selected, and so she led the way with the serenity of a woman secure in the knowledgc that her guests will presently be luxuriating in fine port and excellent cigars as they loosen the buttons of their only moderately snugger waistcoats. The Prime Minister found himself ensconced between the ladies—but, no; it was Barrington Erle who found himself thus placed, a freer, younger-seeming man, seated opposite his friend Phineas, not the Member for Tankerville. And the quartet feasted comfortably, Barrington Erle chatting as unaffectedly as when they met at the *soirées* of Lady Glen, herself not yet cloaked in the mantle of Duchess. For that night, had she breezed in with a puckish smile and the latest scandal, such a miracle would have been received as wholly natural, a thought that pricked Marie's heart a little as she mounted the stairs some hours later.

Since that evening, much of Clarissa's buoyancy had been restored. Now, two Seasons later, Marie felt that Clarissa was ready to take a place in Society, and to begin to circulate more. No doubt she could have introduced the girl to Society earlier, but she was *in loco parentis*, and Marie Finn had never allowed convention to dictate to her when the welfare of those she loved was involved. Marie had put off the time of Clarissa's debut until she felt her niece was strong enough, and, if questioned, had frozen her interlocutor with a glance, unless her questioner was a member of the Palliser family or another close intimate.

As to Phineas, Marie also had her concerns. As she sat in her drawing room on another wet April afternoon, reading a detective story in the *Strand* magazine, leafing through the pages of this month's installments, she sighed, trying to push her concerns out of mind. As the Prime Minister had foreseen, the bill was constantly being revised in Committee, as the operators of commercial vessels looked for a way to reduce the costs of compliance and staved off its enactment under the guise of having White Papers and studies drafted to determine if no less costly means could be found to address the concerns of the Honourable Member for Tankerville. Barrington Erle remained friendly—a little more so than he had been prior to his impromptu dinner at the Finns, indeed—but had not yet intervened.

Marie was somewhat—not too much, to be frank—concerned by Phineas's gloom in the wake of the funeral of his onetime barrister nearly a week before. Only seldom did these melancholic moods that had afflicted him occasionally in the years after his trial recur, and even then he had turned to her for solace, as he had lately. She knew of his feeling that he was under-employed, that his time to make a great contribution would soon pass away, and that his powers were not afforded their full scope. Indeed, she agreed with him that such was the case, and had foreseen the ironic position in which he stood—having stood aloof from his party for fifteen years, he now hankered after the influence that only a party leader could exercise. The bill had come for his independence, and Phineas found the cost dear indeed. That Barrington Erle, Mr. Monk, and even the Duke of Omnium had warned him of it only added to his frustration. Marie had herself been turning matters over in her mind—she was quite as good a strategist as Phineas, and if anything a better tactician—looking for an answer. So engrossed in her reflections was she that she did not hear Clarissa come in.

"Aunt Marie, can you really read that magazine upside-down?"

Marie smiled, peering over the magazine's pages. "Hardly, my dear. It's a cover."

"For what?"

"Plotting. Planning. Conspiring, if you'd care to join me."

"Certainly. Are we working for Irish independence, or conquering the Transvaal?"

"Both can wait for now, dear. No, I want to cheer up your uncle by having the Brentfords to stay."

"Is Uncle unhappy? Why?"

"Not unhappy, Clarissa, but remembering times best forgotten. And of late he has so much work in chambers.

"I don't understand why he goes so often, Aunt Marie. He doesn't like it much, I think."

"I think he likes having something specific to do. He's been out of office quite a while now. And, whether he likes it or not, the Lows depend on him."

Some years ago, Phineas's old friend Mr. Low had been stricken with a heart ailment. He lived, and had all his faculties, but was unable to attend court, or even work at Chambers with his old pertinacity. Low was reluctant—no, unable—to completely recede from legal life, and had asked Phineas Finn to step in, "just for a term or so," to ensure that Mr. Low's legal practise did not completely wither. For seven years now, Phineas had taken Mr. Low's seat at Chambers meetings, dispatched junior barristers "just until Low's return," and had himself to appear in cases where a name and eloquence would weigh more than deep knowledge of the rules of evidence.

Phineas's lack of trial experience conceded, he had kept Mr. Low's practise alive by focusing on appeals and arguments, though of late he had begun to embrace jury trials. To his own mild surprise, he discovered that he was rather good at them; his years in the House had stripped public speaking of any terrors, and with a practise ready-made for him to step into, Phineas found himself in middle age to be a well-respected, solidly established barrister.

Although it was now clear that Mr. Low would never return to work, Phineas kept up the practise, and continued to consult his old friend, who drew hope from his continued involvement, if only vicariously, with the Bar. Certainly the Lows, husband and wife, benefitted from Phineas's earnings, most of which went to the nominal Head of Chambers. But, in fact, Marie Finn was right—her husband gained as much from the arrangement as did the Lows. Phineas had work, and some money of his own, although nothing compared to his wife's ample fortune and extensive business interests. That consideration aside, however, Marie sensed a staleness within him that bespoke a frustration of his fondest hopes and dreams, and she was wise enough to know that merely inviting their dear friends the Brentfords for a stay would not work a cure, just a temporary alleviation. But that alleviation, she reasoned, would give her time for the real planning, the search for a true cure.

All this had flashed through Marie Finn's intuitive, labyrinthine mind as she bantered with her niece, and before she proposed the Brentfords' stay. Now she answered her niece's unspoken question.

"My dear," she explained, "your uncle is a political man, and one who held high office when young. Now he sees other men in office while he is on the outside–"

"But surely, Aunt Marie, the Prime Minister likes him! Why, he was quite jolly here not so very long ago! Can't Uncle go into office if he likes?"

"Ah, Clarissa, your uncle could have gone into office if he would have eaten humble pie, and served his party's leaders without question. That is what Barrington Erle expects of those who want office, and if he had done so, Phineas would be a rising man now. But instead, he chose independence."

Clarissa sat silent, unsure of how to reconcile this stark political reality with the conviviality of the supper party of which she had formed a part.

"It really is extraordinary," Marie mused after a spell, "how the English all praise independence and yet how they shun anyone who shows a spark of it. Rather like the French and modesty," she added with a sly smile.

"Aunt Marie! You'll scandalise me!" laughed Clarissa.

"Well, that will never do, so let us go instead to our respective tasks. I shall write to the Brentfords—and perhaps you will write to Lady Brentford, too, to encourage her to tear her husband away from the chase for a few days. She will scarcely do so without some reason to bring pressure to bear on him."

Mrs. Finn here showed her tactical cunning; she and Lady Brentford had always been friendly, without ever becoming truly friends, but, as Mrs. Finn well knew, the former Violet Effingham had a special tenderness for the motherless young Clarissa. And then, too, Clarissa was a special favourite with the Earl of Brentford, who had insisted that she anoint him an honorary uncle. Showing that she, too, had a firm grip of tactics, Clarissa went her aunt one better, and addressed her letter to Lord Brentford directly:

London,
April 17, 189_
A Grey, Wet Day
Dear Uncle Oswald,

My Aunt Marie and I are writing to both you and Aunt Violet—actually, she thinks that we are both writing to Aunt Violet, but Uncle Phineas says that one should always address all requests to principals, and it is really you whom we need to secure. While you are out riding, and hunting, and generally enjoying life, my poor uncle-by-blood is worrying himself pale with politics and law, and soon will go into a decline like the unhappy man in that novel you sent me for my birthday—the one whose life was being drained by three "raven-tressed women—or, rather, Fiends from the Pit!" (Really, Uncle Oswald, does Aunt Violet know that you send such lurid reading matter to young ladies? Uncle Phineas laughed uproariously when you sent it me, and said you were about as competent a duenna as a duelist.)

But this is why we need you and Aunt Violet—Aunt Marie and I, that is—to come and stay with us for a little. You make Uncle Phineas laugh like nobody else, and we think he could use a good dose of you right about now. Do say that you and Aunt Violet will come. Honestly, I can think of nothing so likely to cheer him as a nice visit from you both.

Love to you and to Aunt Violet, and remember me to Jack—whom I suppose I must start styling Lord Chiltern, as he has come of age. How nice it must be to come of age! I look forward to doing it soon, you know.

Your affectionate niece by decree,
Clarissa Riley

That her supplication would not be in vain Clarissa never really doubted. Still, she was pleased to receive a short note by return of post:

Brentford,
*April 18, 189_*
No Weather to Hunt in,
At Any Road
Dear Little Mischief,

Your Aunt Violet is writing to accept the formal invitation, and I enclose this line to inform you that your Uncle Phineas's opinions on the subject of duennas are far more to be relied upon than upon duelists. More than this, I cannot say.

Your affectionate uncle, by your grace,
BRENTFORD

Post-scriptum: Jack sends his respectful duty, by which I suspect he means his affectionate regards. Or so at least I interpret him.

And so Clarissa Riley did her part in the little conspiracy most effectively.

4

THE DOCK BRIEF

On the day the Brentfords were to arrive, unbeknownst to Phineas Finn, their host was himself in court on a minor matter for a Parliamentary friend. That friend, Larry Fitzgibbon, had been blessed with issue, but said issue had proven himself to be a blessing of a very mixed nature. The young man had been lucky enough to have matriculated into Oxford University despite having abjectly failed his Responsions, the result of the gentle bewilderment that fell upon him whenever mathematics was even hinted at, let alone approached him with bold declaration of intent. Lochinvar Fitzgibbon was reasonably proficient at Greek, muddled through in Latin, but could not even keep track of his tab at the Beargarden.

His mathematical imbecility was, he assured Phineas, who had agreed to represent him at his anxious father's request, the sole reason why he had not realised, on the night of the Boat Race, that he was "one over the eight."

"That's all very well," said Phineas, interviewing his client before their initial appearance before the magistrate, a bare three weeks after the junior Fitzgibbon had been "pinched," as he put it, "but that doesn't explain how you came to be in possession of the policeman's helmet."

"Ah," said Fitzgibbon *fils*, with his most helpless look "well, when one goes one over the eight, Mr. Finn, some of the harder-won lessons of one's education can slip away, you see. Like the distinction between *meum* and *teum*, don't you know?"

Phineas's bark of laughter surprised the younger man.

"That line was old when I was up at Trinity College, son," Phineas snorted, "and didn't work before the proctors there, let alone the London magistrates. Why don't we try youthful exuberance, general fecklessness, and a contrite spirit? Less amusing, I've no doubt, but certainly more likely to get you out of court with a fine, rather than a month on bread and skilly."

"I say, a month? Bread and skilly?" Lochinvar blanched, belying his name. "But the Pater is in Parliament!"

"And, surprisingly, that's not a defence in law, Lochy. You don't want to encourage the magistrate to make an example of you, and demonstrate the fine impartiality of English law, do you?"

"Er, no. Thanks awfully, Mr. Finn. I'll be guided by you, absolutely."

The magistrate, a red-faced countryman exiled temporarily to London, having been suitably impressed by the young Lochinvar's profound repentance, as evidenced by his pallor, stammering, and a general air of terror, and being also an adherent of the Government, with hopes of obtaining the Liberal nomination for a country borough one day, justice was tempered with mercy, a moderate fine imposed, and the miscreant sent forth to mend his ways, which in this case amounted to promptly returning to the Beargarden, and firmly instructing the waiter that from now on, his whiskey was to be lightened with a small jet of soda, though "not quite that much, mind you."

While Lochinvar made his way thus on the *via penitentia*, Phineas Finn made what many would deem a cardinal error, that of speaking with an acquaintance as the next case was called. As a young man was led to the dock, a clerk began to read to the Court the charges: Criminal mischief, trespass, riot, malicious damage to property, assault, and theft. A private prosecution, too, Phineas noted; not so common as they were, he reflected.

The defendant, a young, slim Celt, looked around him nervously, but kept his composure.

"Ifor Powlett-Jones, you have heard the charges against you -" The magistrate pronounced it "Eye-for."

"Uh, that's pronounced 'Ih-vor', my Lord," the young man shyly corrected.

"I beg your pardon?" spake the magistrate.

"My Lord?"

"What is it you are trying to tell me?" asked the magistrate, adding "And it is Your Worship, not 'my Lord.'"

"Thank you, Your Worship. Sorry about the error. But my name—it's pronounced 'Ih-vor," not Eye-for, d'you see, sir?"

"Ah, you're a Welshman, Powlett-Jones?"

"Yes, Your Worship."

"Very good. Now, as I said, Ifor Powlett-Jones,"—pronouncing it just the same as he previously had—"how do you plead to the charges—guilty, or not guilty?"

"Not guilty, Your Worship," the defendant answered, his voice inflecting a little bit at the end of the sentence.

"Are you asking me or telling me, Powlett-Jones?"

"Telling you, my L—Your Worship."

"Very good. The clerk will enter a not guilty plea. Now then, Powlett-Jones, do you have counsel?"

"No, Your Worship."

At this, the more experienced barristers began to shuffle away from the sight-lines of the dock.

"Well, Powlett-Jones, in view of the seriousness of the offenses with which you are charged, I shall authorise a 'dock brief" for you. That means, young man, that the Court will appoint counsel for you. You may select any member of the bar in court at the moment who strikes your fancy, and that barrister will be appointed counsel for you."

"But, Your Worship, I have no money to pay for counsel, and–"

"Well, of course, not, lad! That's why I'm authorising a 'dock brief' in this case! Don't worry about the money, just pick out a lawyer fer yerself."

With the exception of one elderly, patently briefless barrister pluming himself like an unlikely vulture hoping the wildebeest will fall to him, the other barristers were all studiously avoiding the defendant's eyes, patently hoping not to be selected. Phineas Finn, however, had been diverted by the exchange, and when the young Welshman's eyes met his own, Phineas returned the inquiry with a reassuring look, and a barely perceptible nod of consent to the inquiry in the young man's eyes. Visibly relieved, the prisoner exclaimed, "Your Worship—I'd like to have the gentleman on the left—him with the beard, in the second row!"

"Oh, would you then," said the magistrate. "Very well. Mr.—Finn, isn't it?"

Phineas rose from his seat. "Phineas Finn, Your Worship."

"Mr. Finn, will you accept appointment as counsel to Mr. Powlett-Jones?"

"Yes, Your Worship."

"Very good. Mr. Finn, the case will be set down for trial in due course. You'll want to speak with your client, of course. D'you wish to do so today?"

"Yes, Your Worship."

Upon which the magistrate instructed the bailiff to escort the young Welshman to an interview room. Phineas, on his way to meet his new client, stopped briefly at the clerk's table in the small dusty office outside the courtroom to the rear, and asked for a copy of whatever documents they had. As the clerk rustled about looking for a file, saying in a papery voice, "Just one moment, sir, if you please. *If* you please," Phineas heard a murmur of voices and the sound of movement from the courtroom; the sounds of a session breaking up, he judged. Sure enough, a slight scent of bay rum and a country-bred voice alerted Phineas to the magistrate's presence.

"Good of you to take on the matter, Mr.—Finn, isn't it?"

"Yes, Your Worship. I'm happy to be able to assist," Phineas answered, with somewhat more politesse that truth.

"Well, don't know that you should be, sir. Poor lad doesn't seem to have any friends or money. Not that it matters, as regards your fee, eh, Finn—'Taffy was a Welshman, Taffy was a thief,' hmm? No, you're doing this one for love, not money, me dear fella."

Phineas had practised at the Bar long enough that judicial impertinence was old hat to him, but he repressed his desire to contradict the magistrate, who had, after all, used his discretion to get Powlett-Jones a brief—more than some would have done.

"Well," he replied, "my old pupil-master would say, 'don't love them, don't hate them, just litigate them.' I'll do my best for the boy, Your Worship."

The magistrate chuckled at the aphorism, "No doubt you will, Finn. Who was your pupil-master, anyway? Sounds like he had his head screwed on."

"Low, sir."

"Abner Low? Married little Georgie Turntwhistle? Whatever became of him?"

And Phineas explained the circumstances—how Mr. Low's physical health was impaired, but not his mind, and how he, Phineas Finn, was keeping the practise going, but was not certain that it was for a good cause, because Mr. Low had been hoping to come back, but clearly now never would, and yet the Lows had, man and wife, stuck by him when he was in terrible jeopardy—

The clownish, ruddy face of the magistrate assumed a more serious mien than Phineas would have thought it capable of bearing.

"So you are that Phineas Finn," the magistrate said, "I thought you might be. Abner and Georgiana are lucky, lad. They've enough saved up, I'm sure, but Abner and I read for the Bar together, and I can tell you that, unless he's changed mightily, being completely out of the swim would kill him stone dead. No, it's a burden to you, I'm sure, but a blessing to them. You're not helping him lie to himself—old Abner's too sharp for that; you're keeping his mind at work, I'll wager. He wants to know about all the cases, does he?"

"Yes."

"And you two chew them over, think them through?"

"Yes—and he often comes out with ideas I'd miss."

"Aye, that's Abner. It's mother's milk to him, puzzling out law cases. You go on, if you can. It's a kindness, you can be sure. And tell 'em John Toogood was asking for 'em."

Phineas smiled more warmly at the man than he would have thought possible bare moments before. "You could stop by, you know. Low receives visitors every now and again. He's up to meeting with friends for an hour or two."

"Could I, d'you think? I'd like to see them again. Yes, I will. Thankee, me boy," the magistrate replied, and shambled back toward his chamber.

Out of the public eye, the young man sagged in relief into the plain wooden chair on the far end of the small table. Phineas, entering with the slender buff file, took the other chair. After the two men had shaken hands, Phineas suggested that he take a moment to look at the file.

"Hmm," Phineas commented reading the documents, "that you did, against the Queen's peace, by force of arms, ...riot, criminal mischief, breach of the peace, theft—hold on, in Pontnewydd? Surely that's in Wales, Mr. Powlett-Jones, isn't it?"

"Yes, Mr. Finn; Wales. It's my home, a mining town."

"What on earth are they sending a Welsh miner charged with a crime in Wales to the Old Bailey for?"

"For to see the Queen?" The young man's joke could not mask the disconsolate note in his voice. Phineas took another look at his client, and realised just how frightened the young man was.

"Ifor," he said kindly, "I know you are afraid, and you would be a fool not to be, frankly. But I do not assume your guilt, I am not simply here to preside over your conviction, and if I can help you, I will. Tell me about it."

There are many experienced criminal barristers who would blanch at the invitation Phineas had just extended his young client. They would point out that the barrister may not willingly call evidence that he knows to be false, and that, should Ifor Powlett-Jones had confessed to the crime right then and there, Phineas Finn would have burned his boats, and could not call his client, or indeed any witness who would affirm his client's factual innocence. It was, in short, an almost criminally reckless invitation for a criminal advocate to put to a client, and one of which the late Mr. Chaffanbrass, of great memory, would never have been guilty. Indeed, that great man would have as soon thought of setting up shop as a soothsayer as asking a client a question about the facts underlying a case, and if a junior of his had put it in his presence, a sharp buffet to the back of the head would have been deemed by him a temperate response.

Phineas recollected all this, just before his client could speak, and, for a second, contemplated reading his client a lecture about the effect of what he might say to his barrister even here and now.

But Phineas Finn was no Chaffanbrass. He did not deliver the lecture, and Powlett-Jones had made his decision.

"Pontnewydd is a mining town, sir, and I'm a miner. In my family, we all are, and that's true for most everyone in the village. 'Tis dangerous work, as you can imagine sir, and the works aren't kept up like they should be. Even still, there's always a risk of flood, or collapse. This was worse, though. It was firedamp—mine gas, sir—exploded, sir, and tore through a whole level of the mine. Well, my brother Aneurin was down in the works, at the start of his shift, and he and some of the other men were trapped in a cave-in. We went down to try to get them out, and couldn't shift the rubble. We tried, sir, you can't believe how we tried. Finally the foreman came to tell us to get out—they were afraid of another explosion. We couldn't give up, sir!"

"What happened, Ifor?"

"The engine had been turned off—all the firedamp had them worried. We took the little engine apart, and used the beam for leverage. We forced an opening and two or three of the lads got clear. The foreman was practically dancing in panic –" and here, Powlett-Jones flashed a surprisingly boyish grin. "He and some of his bullyboys ordered us up again. We were pulling more of the lads out, including my brother. His leg was broken, but he tried to help us get him out."

Phineas looked at the young man, puzzlement writ large across his brow. "I don't understand…"

"Well, the lads wouldn't stop, and the foreman and the rest were yelling that it could all cave in, or another explosion, or just the gas itself, could kill us all, and we had to stop. Some of the lads backed the foreman, some were trying to fight them off. It became a right scuffle."

"And the foreman?"

"Mr. Tudor? He tried to force us out, and the rest of the lads were afraid of him. So I –well, I hit him."

"You hit him?"

"I did, sir. He went down hard, and the boys laughed…"

"How many of the lads were lost in that gallery?"

"Only two. We got all but two out—Jim Evans and Ianto Jones."

"And that's all that happened?" Phineas asked. "Nothing else?"

"Nothing, sir."

"Are you sure, Ifor? Because if you are—wait a moment. Who owns the mine in Pontnewydd?

"'Tis a McScuttle mine, sir."

"McScuttle?" Phineas asked, "William McScuttle? Actually, come to think of it, Sir William McScuttle. He's a big figure in the party...." Phineas thought, his mind making connections.

"The party, sir?"

"The Liberal Party, Ifor. Of which I am a member myself, though not the best-beloved member. How is McScuttle as a boss?"

"He's a hard man, sir. Takes no back-talk. Refers everything to the foreman."

"And the foreman—Mr. Tudor, is it?"

"Jasper Tudor, sir."

"How did Mr. Jasper Tudor feel after you'd knocked him down?"

The boy smiled broadly. "Mad as a wet cat, he was! All the lads mocking him—well, I'm told the lads are still having a good snigger at his expense."

Phineas Finn was not a vastly experienced criminal lawyer, but he was quite well versed in the workings of politics. A big donor to the governing party who relied almost exclusively on his foreman for information. A foreman who had lost status by displaying fear in a crisis, and then was struck down by a young miner leading others ready to risk their lives to free their trapped fellows. A case, Phineas realised, in which no local jury would convict, and which the foreman needed a conviction to reassert his dominance over the workforce that had seen him afraid and then bested. Sir William may not have been Phineas's favourite member of the party, but the man might quite possibly believe in good faith that this was a riot and not a rescue under harrowing conditions.

He would need to go there. See if young Powlett-Jones was telling him the truth, as Phineas believed, but also if Phineas could produce evidence. He would need to find a theory of the case, too. Technically, you could convict Powlett-Jones on his own testimony—it would be madness, of course, but seizing and destruction of company property, striking down the owner's representative—yes, it could all go quite badly for the boy.

"Ifor, I want to do something a little risky. I want to get time to gather evidence for you, and talk to a few people about your case. It would mean that your case would not be tried until after the Long Vacation—that's not until the end of October. I don't know that I could get you released until that time. But it would give me a chance to build a case for you, to find a way of justifying or excusing what you did."

"Justifying? Excusing?" For the first time, the young Welshman looked angry. "What should we have done, let the lads die? We saved lives, Mr. Finn!"

"Yes, Ifor, you did. But you risked them too, and in defiance of the property owner. By your own account, another explosion was likely, or a cave in, and you refused to leave when the agent told you to. You used force to break machinery—all in a good cause, son, the very best!—but under the law, if you were tried today, you would be convicted."

The boy went ashen.

"Then there's no hope, Mr. Finn?"

"No; I won't say that. But I need time to work this out, to get some witnesses and some way to convince a London jury that you did what you had to do."

Phineas saw his young client's assent in his eyes before the young man spoke, and was relieved. He could have added, but refrained: "And find a reason why that fact gives the jury grounds to acquit you."

EPISCOPI VAGANTES

The Collegiate Church of St. Peter, more commonly known as Westminster Abbey, has much to commend it—magnificence of architecture, beautiful services, as well as innumerable nooks and, in the nicest possible sense, crannies, in which one might find a still place to commune with oneself, or, if one is of a mind, one's Creator.

His Lordship the Bishop of Barchester, the Right Rev. Samuel Grantly, was of such a mind on this afternoon in early May. One of the amenities of being a bishop in the Church of England, particularly one with a seat in the Lords, and with a personal reputation for fierce devotion to his faith, was that he was pretty freely able to wander through the Abbey to his heart's content. Exercising this privilege, in the episcopal uniform of apron and gaiters, the Bishop was able to meditate in the Little Cloister, meander through the quire, and pray in the Lady's Chapel. What his reflections were, what prayers he addressed to his Lord, we cannot know, for to invade that most sacred activity would be an impertinence in such a chronicle as this.

Dr. Grantly, on his knees, presented the image of a man in late middle age, were one inclined to be charitable, or at the verge of hale old age, if not. From his grandfather, who had been the Bishop of Barchester some half a century ago, he had inherited a thick mop of hair, now rendered snowy white by time, and from his father a rather unfortunately hawklike nose, as well as eyebrows that put his chaplain in mind of a falcon's plumage. That father, a noted controversialist, had been the

Archdeacon of Barchester for many years, retiring only weeks before his death. Happily, the son lacked his father's asperity, and when the son was of ripe enough years for the preferment, those who had held his father in high regard thought of the son, whose gentler mien had swept aside any obstacles. Moreover, the son had pursued a very different career from that of his father. He had shown both a firm commitment to the Catholic party within the Church of England, in an era when vestments and candles could give rise to a prison sentence, and a willingness to bear the costs of its unpopularity with the ecclesiastical powers and principalities. What distinguished Dr. Grantly from some of his compeers was his willingness to reconcile with those who sought to impose those costs. With the storm having blown itself to a pause, if not a cessation, Dr. Grantly was a natural choice to begin an effort to ameliorate future strife.

As the bishop finished his prayers, fingering a string of wooden beads in his hands to remind him of just whom he had resolved that day to pray for—a custom of his that might have, if publicly known, touched off the unpleasantness that had shadowed the earlier part of his career all over again—a footfall on the marble recalled him to the mundane.

A stranger had entered the Lady Chapel, a man also garbed in apron and gaiters, and with greying hair, a neatly trimmed short beard and dark, piercing eyes.

"Shall I withdraw, my brother, and allow you solitude for your prayers?" the newcomer solicitously asked, in a musical, almost purring voice.

Quite unreasonably, Samuel Grantly took an instant dislike to the man—an emotion he swiftly resolved to conquer—and, rising a little stiffly, answered "Not at all. I had just finished." He extended his hand. "Samuel Grantly," he introduced himself.

"Joseph Emilius," the newcomer replied, grasping the bishop's hand, and shaking it warmly. The gentlemen exited the Lady's Chapel and began to stroll the north aisle.

"Have you been newly appointed?" Dr. Grantly enquired. "I do not recall meeting you before, sir, nor do I know your name."

"Forgive me," the newcomer replied, "I was not consecrated a bishop in the Church of England, but in the United States of America."

"Ah, that would explain it. And yet, I should have thought you an Englishman by your speech."

Bishop Emilius smiled. "Indeed, I was ordained in the Church of England, but, oh, a long time ago, I was presented with an opportunity to pastor in the United States. I realised it was a call to, quite literally, a New World."

The two men promenaded a little further together, finding themselves between the tombs of the two queens. The American bishop drifted over to Mary's, while the English bishop found himself gazing in fascination once again at the effigy of Elizabeth.

"So close in death, yet so inimical in life," mused the American bishop. "One can admire each in her own way. The Scottish martyr, or a murderess? What do you think, Dr. Grantly?"

"Surely the Casket Letters settled the matter, Dr. Emilius? A murderess, I'm afraid, whatever romantic colour our Scottish friends might like to paint her with."

"And yet, can we judge her by ordinary standards, Dr. Grantly?" The American bishop crossed over to his English counterpart. "You admire Queen Elizabeth, do you not, Dr. Grantly?"

"Surely; do not you?"

"Indeed I do. But just as she could not be confined by the laws applicable to ordinary women, was not her cousin, also a queen, not to be judged by such standards?"

"In matters of state, perhaps. But the murder of her own husband? Surely you do not condone that, sir!"

"Certainly not," Emilius replied. "But the question of what actions a ruler may take to preserve the ability to rule are consistent with morality is one which I find fascinating. Was not the assassination of Darnley a matter of state, or can it merely be regarded as a matter of personal spite? Was Bothwell an adulterous murderer, or a Scots Walsingham—an instrument of state? Ah, however one looks at it, uneasy lies the head that wears the crown, eh, my lord bishop?"

"Indeed, the Bard put it well. But unlike princes, surely we as churchman follow a higher law than the teachings of Signor Machiavelli. The eternal truths of the Gospel tell us that such extremities are never permissible."

"Then you agree with me that capital punishment should never be imposed?" Emilius inquired smoothly.

"Well—actually, I do. It is, I admit, a minority position, but I have never been able to square such treatment of even the most heinous criminal with Our Lord's teaching."

Emilius's face bore a seriousness that it hitherto had lacked, as his eyes looked into those of the Bishop as though he would peel away all the layers of his personality in an effort to see the truth. Dr. Grantly met his gaze steadily.

The moment passed.

"I admire your fidelity to that teaching, Dr. Grantly," Bishop Emilius said softly. "It is a reminder to me that time has not stood still in England whilst I was away."

"And now you have returned home?"

"Only for a visit," the American bishop answered. "I have—family here, whom I have not seen these many years, and I hope to reconcile with those whom I was forced to leave behind, and not on the best of terms."

Dr. Grantly nodded sympathetically. "Yes, it can be difficult," he agreed, "when those whom we love do not understand the nature of a call. I do hope that the work of reconciliation goes well with you."

"Thank you, sir. It is surprisingly difficult. London has changed so in the decades I have been out of it, that the first obstacle is not hardness of heart, or lack of mutual charity, but mere difficulty in locating those whom I seek. I seem," he acknowledged, "to have underestimated the crass fact of change at the most simple level."

Dr. Grantly again felt unease at his unprovoked dislike of the distinguished, indeed rather elegant, clergyman before him. As they stood between the tombs of Mary and Elizabeth, the English bishop felt a need to atone for these feelings.

"I am in London for the Lords," Dr. Grantly confided, "staying with my sister, the Marchioness of Hartletop. She is giving a reception and ball in a week's time. Why not be my guest? I assure you, if anyone knows your people, it will be Griselda. She is a veritable Debrett's and Social Register in one." And in Dr. Grantly's smile, one could see the boy he had once been.

"My dear Doctor," the American answered, "you are too kind. I shall be delighted." He removed a card, and passed it to Dr. Grantly.

The Bishop of Barchester repeated the gesture, and reiterated his invitation to the American. "Friday week," he reminded his new friend, "Half seven, if I recollect."

The gentlemen (for surely a bishop, even an American one, is entitled to the designation) said farewell at the portal from the narthex to the profane world and went their separate ways. Dr. Grantly proceeded to his sister's residence, a large townhouse at Stanhope Gate, tended by the Marchioness with meticulous care that it be perfect in every detail, if a little sterile.

Not unlike, the Bishop mused, his sister herself. Oh, she had always been stoical enough to remind him of the Spartan boy who had made no complaint while the fox chewed his vitals (and what on earth had drawn Father to that tale? the Bishop thought, quite irrelevantly). But the coolness that had grown upon her from her youth onward, the strange self-sufficiency and rather curdling hauteur, mystified Samuel Grantly. Neither mother nor father had such chilling indifference—if anything, Father's defects had lain in the other direction—and his grandparents—well, Samuel did not recall his paternal grandfather, the first Bishop Grantly, terribly well, but all agreed that he had been as mild a saint as would give the Devil his shawl out of pity.

Not a bad description of his other grandfather, the longtime Precentor at the Cathedral, and the onetime Warden of the now derelict Hiram's Hospital. In Samuel Grantly's childhood, the Rev. Septimus Harding had been an unexpectedly controversial figure, resigning his great preferment on a point of principle, said some, while others, including Samuel's own father, denounced the old man's cowardice in resigning under pressure. Curiously, the Warden himself had borne it all lightly, once he felt satisfied as to his own behaviour.

Griselda was nothing like them, Dr. Grantly reflected, no more than she was like Mother or Father—she lacked the compassion that lightened Mother's pragmatism, and wholly lacked the old Archdeacon's spontaneity of feeling. Where Father could bluster and rage, but underneath longed to embrace, Griselda was—

Samuel Grantly checked himself with a shudder, almost at his sister's door. He had been about to describe his sister, his beautiful, long-cherished sister, in the secret ruminations of his heart, as dead. He did not want to believe that—could not believe that.

With a troubled heart, for he repented the thought, while worrying at how apt it seemed, Dr. Grantly entered into his sister's lovely, cold, correct household. In his perturbation, he forgot to mention his new acquaintance to his sister, and his spontaneous invitation of that other clergyman to the upcoming ball.

That other clergyman, Joseph Emilius, had walked through the streets with a nimble, rather feline tread. Years before, when he had lived in this Island, he had known want, residing at cheap, shabby lodgings when his once-numerous flock had melted away at the blast of scandal. That he, the Reverend Joseph Emilius (as he was then) had had to beg for bread from his own estranged (alas!) wife, and had been dragged perforce to a prison cell, was a memory that even all these years later could prick him with shame. Even now, enjoying a bath in his luxurious suite at Claridge's (for the Lord had requited His Servant, whose faith in his own destiny had never faltered, and his American disciples had provided bounteously for their spiritual leader at home, and now for this visit abroad), Emilius remembered the incipient panic that had fluttered in his breast at the step-by-step descent into ignominy that had shattered his English ministry. He had first lost his wife, his beautiful, vexing Lizzie, who had recoiled at his natural assertion of a husband's right to control his wife's income, and who then had gone to law with him, pretending to believe he was not in truth her husband!

As Emilius reclined in the long, porcelain-glazed tub, steam gently rising as the water lapped his midsection (regrettably, he thought, a touch more ample than once it had been, in the days when he had wooed and won Lady Eustace), he thought upon his lost wife, and rued his rashness in trying to take control of her finances.

"Fool!" he reflected, toying with the soap and thereby nearly losing it. If he had understood her better, then, and had left well enough alone, that dark beauty would still be his. So she had wanted the power of the purse! If he had seen her aright—as he could have done, for the affair of the diamonds should have educated him—he would have seen that she was not merely a beautiful, if willful, girl, but a woman who was his own mirror image—as sharp, as clever, as quick as he, and as desirous of exercising sway over others. He would do better this time, if his plans fell out as he desired.

And they might! He had, after all, been far more resilient than those barristers and the judge who tried him for bigamy all those years ago had anticipated. Convicted amidst the hue and cry of a high society that would have martyred him for a murder for which another man had first stood trial—a murder that Emilius refused to accept as any such thing, for the wretch Bonteen had, after all, been striving to destroy him by foul means—he had nonetheless confounded expectations.

Yes, at the very bar of justice, as the judge sentenced him to five years of hard labour, his eyes had met those of his accuser, the trull who claimed to have been his wife on the basis of a Papist ceremony, and her eyes had quailed. But she was unable to look away as he pressed his will onto hers, searing into her the desire, the need, to deny her own prior testimony before the man she claimed as her lord and master was taken down into vile durance. The woman—what was her name? Edith, Emilius rather thought it had been, cheekily styling herself "Edith Emilius" as if her pagan marriage had any bearing on such a Christian as he!—had confessed then and there.

He, Emilius, had spent a few uncomfortable months in prison, but had been released without a stain on his character. Or, at any rate, free from the toils and snares of the law. Naturally, remaining in England did not commend itself to him. So, with the last of his funds, Joseph

Emilius had shaken the dust of the Old World from off his feet, and had sojourned a while in New York. After a few months, the allure of travel had again called to him, and he had ventured west, until he had found a people in Utah, ready for his guidance, in need of a firm hand. They had prospered together, and only one thing was missing ere his joy could be complete. And so now the Bishop of the Saints reversed his progress once more, to reclaim the treasure that was rightfully his.

For since his precipitate departure from England all those years ago, Joseph Emilius had built up his own fortunes, but had also cherished in his heart (or perhaps we defame that organ) a craving for the woman who had once been his wife, a hunger that could not be satiated elsewhere, although it could be dulled. His rather large establishment, the community over which he ruled, needed a queen, as he needed Elizabeth, Lady Eustace. He would offer her what he now had to spare, wealth, an equal share in the joys of shaping a truly religious community, with themselves at its center, leading its denizens toward salvation. Elizabeth would enjoy the chance to shape the young almost as much as did he, Emilius thought, rising from the now tepid bath, and enfolding himself in a voluminous, heavy black robe. Yes, he reflected, she would be admirably fit to reign in Utah, in the hearts and minds of his followers.

To reign, that is, second after him.

JACK STANDISH

The Right Honourable John Oswald Theobald Phineas Standish—Lord Chiltern, in Society—was in a position that would have excited the disapprobation of his relatives and friends, knew it, and, flushed with emotion, did not care.

While the position was unaccustomed—for the young Lord Chiltern did not habitually spend his time on his knees at the feet of a beautiful woman, and indeed, if asked, would have asserted that a gentleman should do so precisely once, when asking said woman to become his wife—the knowledge that his family would disapprove was all too familiar a feeling to the young peer. That his family would have, in this case, good grounds for the expression of disapproval—for the woman in question, though *certes* beautiful, was almost his mother's age, a notorious *demimondaine*, and a woman whose entree into society endured, but only barely—well, this would not have weighed much with Lord Chiltern, either.

Because Lord Chiltern was a socialist, a scholar and an aesthete a well as an athlete, he would have rejected the notion that the age of his beloved should enter into his calculations, for he believed in complete equality between the sexes, and, though he would inherit a title (and, indeed, bore one now), he viewed that privilege as nothing to perpetuate, and thus, should a marriage of true minds not bear fruit in the form of children—why, Jack Standish would rather marry for love, than marry merely to breed. Assuredly he would not allow himself to pass love by merely to perpetuate a title that he despised, and indeed, did not use. Among his friends, and whenever he was not absolutely forced by his parents to employ it, he was known simply as Jack Standish.

One might have thought that his father, the notoriously choleric Earl of Brentford, might have taken firm action with regard to his heir's attitude towards the title. And, indeed, the Earl was entirely capable of, and predisposed to, such action. The fires that had so blazed in his youth had been banked, not extinguished. But with respect to his son, the Earl was handicapped by his fondness for this elegant, intelligent heir, who was so unlike himself, and yet withal a man to respect. "Yes, yes," he had answered the boy's Aunt Laura when she had upbraided her brother for tolerating Jack's political tendencies. "No doubt he thinks and reads a lot of nonsense, Laura, but whoever heard of a Standish—other than you—thinking and reading at all, hey?" And the lad's prowess with a sabre reassured him that his son wasn't like some of his overly bookish friends; one had only to watch Jack lunge with swift, predatory grace to realise that he was no milquetoast.

Such swift, predatory lunges had not availed Jack Standish with the lady to whom he now knelt, burying his face in the flowing folds of her gown. Semi-recumbent before her, he drew his breath in sharply, as he felt his beloved's fingers sweep through his hair. A gesture at once intimate and humiliating, he thought, unsure whether he was receiving a lover's caress, or one more fit to be given a dog by its mistress. Torn between extremes of feeling, he groaned, loudly enough to provoke a silvery laugh from her.

"Poor darling," she teased, "do I hurt you?"

"You do, Lizzie, you do," Jack answered. "I love you, and you fend me off like—like a child."

Lizzie Eustace—or, more formally, Elizabeth, Lady Eustace—stroked Jack's hair again. "I am old enough to be your mother," she said, before adding a trifle complacently, "Though I believe your mother is some years older than me. Isn't better if I treat your....enthusiasms as harmless?"

"You are not so much older than me that I cannot love you. Not so much older than me that I can't join your heart to mine. Marry me,

Lizzie," Jack implored—a request he had never foreseen himself making, and yet one which he could not, at that moment, forbear from making.

Lizzie's fingers lost their playful languor; her hand formed a fist, and pulled Jack's head from the folds of her dress, tilting his head back so that she could look into his eyes. To his astonishment, her face was severe, her eyes blazing, her beautiful lips set in a firm line. Jack Standish, who rode fiercely to hounds, and had fenced bare-bladed among the *schlager*-men of Heidelberg, and had not felt fear, met the gaze of his lady-love with a thrill of terror that only added to his desire for her.

"Never, Jack, never," she said, in clipped, emphatic tones, "never offer marriage to a lady as a means to seduce her. It's cruel, and it is beneath you. There is better stuff in you than that, and you disappoint me." Releasing her grip on his hair, Lizzie Eustace thrust him off and strode away from him, seating herself on the settee at the far end of the room. Red-faced, still kneeling where she had left him, flushed with adoration and need, Jack almost crawled to her in his anxiety to rebut her charge. Something in the way her eyes flashed recalled him to himself, and led him instead to rise.

"Lizzie, I meant no such thing," he said hoarsely.

"And that is what makes it so iniquitous, Lord Chiltern," she snapped. "A desire to marry a woman of my age may be foolhardy, but it at least does no dishonour to either gentleman or lady. But a younger woman, one who had not already experienced life's hardships and betrayals as have I, might be deceived by your soft words and false promises."

"I intended no falsehood," Jack Chiltern replied, "made no promises, but only said that your age should not prevent us from joining hearts."

"Yes," the lady answered, with a sardonic smile that suited her dark beauty admirably. "You promised nothing, but imply all, Lord Chiltern."

"That is not my name!" the young man roared.

"No, of course not," she answered. "Lord Chiltern must be sober, responsible. Jack the Young Socialist may believe in free love with Mr. Wells, and throw himself at the feet of women of a certain age, purely in the spirit of an experiment, to learn how it is done."

"No!"

"No?" she asked, rising to face him. "Well, if you so want me, you have only to ask, after all." And she smiled, at once mocking and daring him. A thousand contradictory thoughts crashing through his mind; his desire for this woman, matched only by his eagerness to prove himself not the boy she thought him, outweighed all the qualms her notoriety and occasional cruelties had fostered, and brought him once more to his knees before her.

"Lizzie," he entreated, "please don't refuse me. Please, say that you can love me."

She cupped his chin with her hand, and with a Delphic smile, asked, "Ah, but in what capacity, my dear?"

"As my—my wife," the young man stammered. "As the woman to whom I will pledge myself in marriage, to love till death parts us."

And Lizzie Eustace's thumb and forefinger drew his chin upwards, bringing him to a standing position, like an angler drawing his prey from the depths to the surface, and then into the open air. Jack found himself standing, with Lizzie gazing at him almost hungrily.

"Oh, Jack," she said, in a little, gentle voice, "I accept. I will marry you."

And she sealed his lips with a kiss, his first from a lady not a relative, unless one were to count his courtesy-aunt Marie, and different from any he had previously imagined, more passionate, more thrilling, and yet more earthy, than he ever thought a kiss could be. The scent of her, the warmth of her body—none of these had entered into Jack's reveries of love. Jack Standish's head swam and, as he pressed into Lizzie, found not the shy yielding he expected but rather a matching pressure. She subtly, inexorably, took control of the kiss, and he found himself to be the one yielding to her.

Never one to surrender, Jack rallied his forces, and met his beautiful antagonist head on, only to find her outflanking him, cutting off his retreat, and, ultimately, leaving him no option but capitulation. He struck his colours.

That evening, Jack Standish, haunted by a strange feeling of disappointment, strolled toward the Finn's residence in Park Lane to meet his parents and godparents, as well as his "cousin" Clarissa, whom he remembered as a schoolgirl, still and quiet after the death of her own parents. As he entered the Finn's residence, he could hear the familiar sounds of chatter in the drawing room—his own father's sharp staccato laugh, Phineas Finn's more musical one, the slightly arch, dry tones of his Aunt Marie scoring a point in one of her Congrevian marital tilts at her husband, and another feminine laugh he could not place, one which sounded like glasses cunningly played by an expert hand. Certainly not Mother, he reasoned, and advanced toward the drawing room as Meier announced him.

"Lord Chiltern, Madame," the butler intoned, raising a slightly ironic eyebrow in response to Jack's reproachful glance.

Jack entered the room, and, spying his mother in the near corner, advanced to her first, greeting her with a kiss. She returned the salutation, gently. Violet, Countess of Brentford, had been a pretty girl, and was a striking woman even still; she had not lost that air of sympathy that had made her so admirable a listener for the young Phineas Finn. After greeting his mother, Jack turned toward his hostess, who was draped elegantly on a seemingly precarious divan.

"I know, I know, Jack," Marie Finn greeted him with a shrug expressive of mock-despair. "I have told Meier again and again that you are to be announced in the manner you have requested, but he ignores me. Meier?"

"Yes, Madame?"

"You are a snob, my friend. You are aware of that, I hope."

"Indeed, Madame. It is what fits me for my position." The butler bowed and exited.

Jack's father, Oswald, Earl of Brentford, guffawed—no other word will do, although it has long been well established that a peer constitutionally cannot guffaw.

"You see, my boy," the Earl japed, "not even the middle classes you set such a store on want you to join them. They like having an aristocracy to look up to."

Before Jack could interpose any words, Phineas Finn countered his old friend's argument for him. "I hardly think Meier is representative of the British working class, do you, Brentford? The real question Jack should think through is whether the title might give his arguments added weight or whether it detracts from them."

"I have thought about that, Uncle Phineas," the young man replied, coming forward to shake hands with his host, and then veering to kiss his hostess' cheek and murmur a quick "Hallo, Aunt Marie." He continued, "But surely the use of an illegitimate title–"

"Ho!" interspersed the Earl, but with no real heat behind it.

"Surely the use of an illegitimate title," his son continued, perhaps a little louder than before, "even in a good cause, is to legitimate it. It seems to me –"

But the party was not to discover what seemed and how it seemed to Jack at that moment, because he turned to the window seat, to greet the room's last occupant. But instead of the schoolgirl "cousin" he expected to behold, he met instead a willowy young woman, garbed in white, with a crown of glorious red hair, and lively green eyes.

"Hello, Jack," said Clarissa Riley.

Jack Standish stood mute, stricken by the beauty of the woman addressing him. Where he had habitually favoured Clarissa with the condescending regard befitting a big brother, this woman had gained a maturity, a poise, that the girl had lacked. And she had become a beauty, too, a lady—one to whom one could devote oneself—if one were free.

At last he began to understand the feeling that had accompanied him as he left Lady Eustace's home. He felt—cheated, somehow. Manipulated, even. More, he felt a little foolish. Oh, Lizzie was beautiful—yet how would she fit in his life? The notion of inviting her as his wife to dinner with the Finns had not perturbed him, until he realised that Clarissa Riley was no longer a girl, but a woman grown.

"Jack?" Clarissa asked. "Have I changed so? Is something wrong?"

Jack had received a gentleman's education, and thus had learned the art of using many words to say nothing when placed under pressure.

"Wrong? No, of course not, Clarissa!" he said. "I was just declaiming against my own class—poor Father is quite tired of that by now–"

"Mother could do with rather less of it, my dear," quoth the Countess of Brentford, the former Violet Effingham.

"—but what I should be doing," the young man continued, "is praising the virtues of those who bring such freshness and light into the world as you represent."

Marie Finn raised an eyebrow at this; the young man was clearly unaware that his smitten response to Clarissa's beauty (which she had spotted instantly, despite the boy's persiflage) had led him to steer inexorably toward a grotesque insult to his hosts. She besought a way to seize the conversation, and move it elsewhere, and, as she readied herself to pounce…

She found her sally forestalled by a warm chuckle from her husband, clapping his hands in applause.

"Well said, Jack," Phineas said, the laughter still in his voice, "for the English to pay tribute to the Irish shows that you are every bit the radical you say you are, and an artist, too."

"Artist, Uncle Phineas?" Jack's realisation of his blunder showed in his nervous response. The boy was fond of them at heart, Marie thought, and had meant no offense. "No wonder he wanted to eschew his title—it divides him from those he loves," she thought.

"Artist." Phineas reiterated. "After all, how do you properly praise Ireland and the Irish? Why, as leavening the English stodge."

Marie Finn smiled, and added, "The sugar that makes the porridge palatable?"

Violet, Countess of Brentford, made a noise that in Violet Effingham would have been a snicker.

"I hear you laugh, Countess," Phineas mock-admonished his old friend, "but you will confess, surely, that without the Irish sweetening, the English would lack a certain lightness of touch that we bring."

"Oh, indeed," the Countess readily conceded, while looking fondly at her own lord. "We would miss you painfully. But we would muddle through in our own solemn, stolid way, surely, Oswald?"

"Undoubtedly. One can have too many raffishly charming duelists, Finn. Especially the kind of duelists as are likely to promptly lose the duel, and go on to marry a charming, exotic lady of mystery—who herself turns out to be as great a lady as any born on our shores."

"La, you compliment me, Earl," said Marie Finn, "and, really, what better note upon which to ring for dinner. "As she suited the action to her words, she added, "Jack, will you bring Clarissa in. I think we of the older generation want to flirt among ourselves, and there is no reason, my boy, why the younger should not do the same."

"Of course, Aunt Marie," he answered, offering Clarissa his arm, and leading her in.

As he did so, she smiled, and said, "Your secret is discovered, Jack."

He flushed, with his memories of Lady Eustace's seductive voice, her scent, and her taste still vivid.

"My secret?" He held her chair for her, and she descended gracefully.

"Yes, Jack, your father has revealed all. And to think I was so impressed by your austere aesthetic taste, sir! But Uncle Oswald has disabused me, and I. Know. All." There is no orthographic way in which to convey the charm of Clarissa's pauses, nor of her quizzical smile.

"All, Clarissa? Not even a member of the Socrates Society at Oxford, such as myself, knows all," he replied, a grin tugging at his lips.

"And how would the Socrates Society view your taste in Gothic literature, sir?" she asked pertly, her own smile breaking through the assumed severity.

"My taste? Gothic?"

"Uncle Oswald sent me a sample from your collection, Jack," she explained, "When Aunt Marie scolded him, he said it was the only way to get it out of the house, and save your morals."

"By inflicting the indecent volume on you?"

"Naturally," she replied primly, "he was quite sure of my incorruptibility—even at the prospect of three scarcely-dressed–"

"It wasn't that dreadful vampire book, was it?" At her nod, he laughed even harder. All pretense of debate was dropped now. "Oh, Clarissa, whatever did you make of it?"

As he listened to her reply, he realised that this young lady was as charming as Lady Eustace, and so much more natural. More, he could be free with her, discoursing without fear. The fact that he feared Lizzie Eustace in some way he could not quite describe was both a part of her fascination, and appalling to him. As he felt himself relax in the company of his beautiful cousin—by courtesy only, the happy thought occurred to him—he wondered if he was really, truly in honour bound to Lady Eustace.

THE MARCHIONESS ENTERTAINS

Winifred Vavasor scrutinised herself carefully in the mirror. Her mouth quirked into a wry little smile as she surveyed herself. The heavy chestnut hair piled upon her head was still lustrous, her eyes clear and sparkling in their famed arctic blue, and if their setting was just slightly more hooded than in her youth, her luck had held true, because their creamy, thick-lashed lids gave her a deceptively sleepy, sultry gaze. Her features were still firm, her lips supple. As to her form, in her own practised judgment, she filled her cobalt-blue House of Worth evening gown to admiration. Shoulders and arms still firm enough to justify their exposure sloped downward to a graceful bust that well supported the rather daring *décolletage* of the dress, tapering to a bodice that demonstrated beyond peradventure that her waist remained slender. As for the skirts, they flared out gracefully, with only a little floral decoration—how clever, she thought, of Jean-Philippe to see that too much adornment could make a woman look like one of the Christmas trees her more plebian fellow Americans were wont to admire in the Fifth Avenue shop windows of a holiday season!

Winifred did not miss America. She had buried two husbands there, one a disgraceful, drunken American ruffian, the other a disgraceful, drunken British ruffian, whose surface charm had deceived her into believing that she was bettering her lot in life by uniting it with his. She had met her second husband in America, after returning from a sojourn in England, only to find that an English gentleman was often no better than an American desert rat. Well, only a little better, perhaps, she amended, recalling that the first time George Vavasor had lifted a hand to her, her riding crop had provided ample defence; against her first husband, she had needed a pistol.

Now in England again for her son's sake, Mrs. Vavasor meant to enjoy herself. Savrola had wanted an English education, and, although Winifred had felt that Groton would have done just as well, she had returned to her late husband's native land.

Savrola's career at Harrow had been rather disappointing, but his time in the Army had shown him to be both capable and courageous, and because Winifred had been much sought after, she had been able to assist him through her social connections. Now, as Savrola strove to make a name for himself in politics, Winifred wondered what to make of herself once he was married and set upon his way. She had enjoyed helping him to get started in life, almost living vicariously through her son, but now that he was on his own way at last, she needed to find her own path. She had lived through too much to be a mere appendage to her son, however dear he was, and doting grandmamma was not a role she hungered for.

In fact, Winifred had turned to her son only when he was old enough to be an interesting companion. In his early years, she had been too busy preventing his dipsomaniacal father from getting his hands on her money and from taking out his temper either on her or the boy. Fortunately George had been a coward as well as a wastrel, and it had only taken one cut at his cheekbone with the aforementioned riding crop to educate him. Emotionally, however, Savrola had suffered more than had she from his father's madness.

Winifred had done her duty by her late lord, providing him medical care, looking after his needs, and, as long as he kept a civil tongue in his head, condoling with him on his wasted life (that last-named service had not required any lies from her, at any rate!)

But it had cut her to see her son's hero worship for his father met only by a sort of puzzled contempt. Ultimately, Winifred thought, George could only despise anyone who cared about him. Winifred Vavasor had no more time for such wretchedness, and, whatever she did do from here, she would never again hitch her wagon to anyone who did not simply adore her. Better to be alone than to suffer another man's mistreatment—or worse, another memory of another Englishman rising unbidden in her mind—another man's pity.

No more of that; Winifred had learned from her experience. She would choose happiness over misery. And the Royal Personage who so desired her...Well, he had so many others, Winifred smiled to herself. Let him hunger. Unsated appetites never cloy, and, while she enjoyed the Court well enough, she had no desire for the heavyset, aging *roué* at its center, thinking himself a very Jacques de Casanova on the strength of the adulation that came his way because of the fortuitous fact that one day he would be King.

Ascertaining in the mirror once more that she was as beautiful as was needed for tonight, Winifred exited her room, and proceeded downstairs to meet her son. Her American training bade her to arrive promptly at the time designated on the invitation, but years of living in England had taught her better than that. The Marchioness would keep, while she had a glass of wine with Savrola.

Lady Laura Kennedy stood at the outer fringe of the crowd gathered in the Marchioness's drawing room. It had not been ever so, she reflected gloomily. Once upon a time, she recalled, she had been at the core of such crowds. Admittedly, not at the Hartletops'—political gatherings had been more her *forte*, whether at her late father's town house, or at weekends at Brentford. She had even been courted at Gatherum Castle, the peculiarly-named Palliser seat. The Hartletops were more—well, vapid; society creatures who toiled not, nor did they spin.

Of course, the same could have been said of the Old Duke of Omnium, who had allowed his houses and prestige to be used for the Liberal Party's benefit, but himself did nothing but carry on in a grand manner through a life of wenching and self-indulgence.

Lady Laura caught herself up sharply there. That thought sounded more like her late, mad husband Robert than like the sober but contented woman she had once been. Clearly, envy was working away at her.

But it was too, too hard for her to be relegated to a widow's life, listening to that foreign minx Madame Max Goesler's horrid trilling laugh ring out in response to a sally of Phineas's that Laura herself could not even hear, placed as she was at the outskirts of everything! It brought out all the old jealousy, the anger at herself for having rejected Phineas when he had loved *her*, not the foreigner, and foolishly tossed away the life she could have had, all for the sake of guaranteeing her brother an income that he had turned out not to need. All futile, in the end, her sacrifices.

These many years later, Laura had little enough to take pleasure in. There was her nephew Jack, of course, and her political role as Barrington's shadow adviser—as the Prime Minister's hostess, confidante, and strategist, she had been saved from rusting away altogether. Still, while all these kept her engaged, alive, yes, Lady Laura had been made for more.

She had kept her looks—in fact, her lanky frame, somewhat raw-boned and mannish in her youth, had aged into a distinctive, rather queenly mien, which suited her well. Her dresses were simple, but of the highest quality—modest, clean lines, but none of the crude carnal appeal that some ladies affected these days. She sniffed as she glanced disapprovingly at the Vavasor woman, showing off her milky shoulders and bosom in a startlingly blue gown; the very image of mutton dressed as lamb. If anyone were to ask *her* for whom the American hussy had so adorned herself -

But alas, nobody here seemed to want to do so. Nor, indeed, to ask her about anything else. Lady Laura was beginning to learn that a middle-aged, unmarried woman, however exalted her rank, could be invisible.

Oh, Barrington had thrown her a wink; Phineas himself had greeted her with a warm smile that still had the power to disturb her, and even his wife (or, as Laura persisted in thinking of her, Madame Max Goesler, the notorious adventuress) was cordial. Violet's affectionate greeting rang false to her, and Oswald seemed constrained somehow. Was it because they were staying with the Finns, instead of with her? But what an absurdity; Laura did not mind that a bit. Oswald and Phineas had been friends for decades, and—well, Laura knew her house was less cheerful than she would wish it. She seemed somehow to have lost the knack, unless politics was involved.

She turned away from the crowd, and left the drawing room, repairing to the library to try to shake the funk that was deepening her mood to indigo. As she swept through the guests, she brushed past a rather sinister, almost feline, clergyman—a bishop, she corrected herself automatically, noting the episcopal uniform—and an old soldier—a general, she recalled, though his name was eluding her at the moment; big and stalwart looking, she reflected, but something just not right about him, and a Tory, in any event; no need to apologise there. And sure enough, the big-whiskered old soldier leered at her as she passed him by, and turning to the bearded bishop said, "Doyenne of the Liberals m'lud. A Blue Book in blue stockings. Rather fine legs, for 'em, mind, but still..." Noting from the corner of her eye that the bishop, rather than reproving the old reprobate smiled amusedly and cast an appreciative eye her way, Laura walked on, only to be arrested by a sharp, angry voice.

"Disgusting!"

The General raised an inquisitive eyebrow.

"Such discourtesy to a lady in a house where she is an invited guest," Plantagenet Palliser continued, his usually pale face flushed a little, his voice holding a slightly more resonant timbre than it normally did.

"Well, so am I, old cock, come to that," the General replied indifferently. "Still," he continued, "no offence intended. I apologise, Lady Laura, for my offensive remark, and only hope that the admiration behind it can excuse my crudity." Turning away from her, the General said to his companion, "The billiard room is excellent here, and since the last member of the family who cared to play died in the Hindu Kush in '54, the table is in excellent condition. Shall we adjourn?"

The bishop bowed in Lady Laura's direction, and then in the Duke of Omnium's.

"Well played," he said, with a slight upward quirk of his mouth, and joined the departing old soldier.

The Duke reached out his hands to take Lady Laura's, and, his eyes meeting hers, asked if she wished to be alone. Laura shook her head, clearing away some of the anger and the embarrassment of having been talked about in such a way by such a man, and let him lead her to the library, and sit her down on the chaise lounge.

"A glass of wine, Lady Laura?" he asked solicitously.

"No, thank you Duke," she answered, and then burst out laughing.

The Duke of Omnium, looked at her perplexedly, worrying that she was giving way to hysteria.

"Oh, dear, oh, dear," Lady Laura gasped, "what will you think of me? It's just...it was too awful, but also too, too funny. That dreadful old humbug calling you, of all people, 'old cock.'"

"Me of all people, Lady Laura?" he asked, the lines more deeply graven in his face than they had been a bare moment before.

"Yes, you," she answered, the laughter mercifully ceasing. "You who are courtesy and kindness itself, you, who ask nothing and give much, and will not let anyone approach you...you are nobody's 'old cock', Duke, let alone that vapid soldier's." An uncharacteristic touch of mischief enlivened her grey eyes.

"We have known each other many years," the Duke carefully replied, "yet I am unaware of anything I have ever done to warrant your generous estimation of me."

Laura Kennedy rose to meet him at eye level. Tall she was, though she had not carried herself so for years, striking, though she had for too long faded into the background.

"Are you indeed?" she asked with more force than she had hitherto used. "Reflect. I saw at first hand your generosity toward a man shunned by society, when all the world turned away from him. I saw you serve as Prime Minister, and patiently bear with all of the petty treacheries men reserve for their benefactors. And I saw you accept service again, at a level beneath your worth, simply to do the Nation's business."

"I have done nothing but my duty," the embarrassed peer stammered.

"You say it as if that were routine. It is not. And to do one's duty in the face of contumely, with no reward? No, my lord, you stand convicted, I am afraid."

And the Duke was bewildered by the clever flash in those clear grey eyes, the broad smile of a woman who had not smiled freely for too many years. "Convicted of what?" he asked.

"Idealism. Be careful, Duke; it can be most harmful to one's well-being."

Now it was Plantagenet Palliser's turn to laugh—a sharp, staccato bark.

"You arraign me for idealism? You? Who have patiently laboured for the Party since you were a girl, smoothed over countless disputes, reconciled adversaries over the teacups—not to mention instructed our Prime Minister in statecraft–"

"Nonsense, Barrington's quite clever; he only needed to learn how to manage people..."

"And to master details, and read those Blue Books that cur referred to so cavalierly, and to actually do the work of a statesman. And who taught him that, pray? And why? Idealist!" The Duke pointed a finger at her.

"Guilty."

"Ah, you admit it?" he pursued.

"No, no; I was pronouncing the verdict on you, sir."

And Plantagenet Palliser, whose laugh had been only a sharp little bark since he had become again a single man, laughed loudly and long. Laura Kennedy joined him, and their pleasure in one another's quickness rang out for a good many moments.

As their laughter died away, the Duke heard the orchestra playing a waltz from a distance. Acting on the spur of an impulse, he asked, "Shall we join the others? May I have this dance?"

With a grave nod of her head, Laura consented. Taking her hand, the Duke led her from the Library. As they walked toward the ballroom, passing the billiard room, they heard the click of ivory upon ivory, and a ball tumble into a pocket. They did not hear—or was it merely that they affected not to hear—the sardonic tones of the old General, saying "Well, if nothing else, I've done that chap a bit of good," nor the smooth answering chuckle of his partner.

Clarissa Riley watched the dancers from the sidelines with awe. How confidently, how surely they moved! She had been trained by a succession of dance masters since her childhood, but always doubted her ability to move with the grace of her Aunt Marie, who was now laughing as Uncle Phineas propelled her surely, swiftly, about the floor. Or, for that matter, "Uncle" Oswald, galumphing about the dance floor while Aunt Violet patiently, unobtrusively made up for his ragged steps, and sudden lunges. Or even that distinguished older couple—the long-limbed Lady Laura, of whom she'd heard so many rumours, skillfully, sedately waltzing with a slim, lantern-jawed old man, whose greying hair merely heightened his air of distinction.

She did not recognise every guest at the ball, but many of the dancing pairs, either jointly or singly, were familiar to her: Her disturbingly handsome "cousin" Jack, dutifully whirling with a beautiful, if older, woman, whose ivory gown belied the strong impression of danger and avidity she exuded, but who smiled as pleasantly as did a gentle matron; the Prime Minister, carefully steering another striking woman in a stunning bright blue gown, her red-brown hair cascading down her neck; aging clubman Dolly Longestaffe, with his nondescript but pleasant wife, waltzing in perfect time to the music and each other, but with rather less speed and effort than the other dancers.

All these, and many others whom Clarissa did not know, swimming rhythmically amidst a sea of the ruling classes of the United Kingdom of Great Britain and Ireland, the British Empire, assembled as guests of the enigmatic Marchioness of Hartletop, whom Clarissa had never yet seen.

As the dancers moved through and around each other, as so many of them had indeed threaded in and through one another's lives, and even, at times, in and through Clarissa's own short existence, Clarissa's desire to spot the woman who had brought them all together beneath one roof became more acute. She looked around the room, trying to discover her hostess—a woman noted both for her extreme loveliness and for her equally formidable coldness—but could not see anyone answering to her notion of what a Marchioness of Hartletop must be. Nonetheless, when she at last admitted the fruitlessness of her quest, those who, like

Clarissa, were not dancing made an interesting enough show to engage her attentive gaze.

Not far from her stood a clergyman—a bishop, from his apron and gaiters—tall and spare, with a receding hairline and a beaky nose, but with kind eyes, chatting amiably with an old woman who had been querulously complaining about the Church with a quacking voice over her sherry, but now, wrinkles smoothed quite away, smiled almost charmingly.

An old man, of military mien, but with a jolly smile, leading Clarissa to assess him as a kindly, grandfatherly type, was himself scanning the room, sharp eyes picking out and recording interesting features. Farther along, another clergyman, indeed, another bishop, this one dark, bearded and saturnine, followed the beauty in ivory with his eyes, assessing, thinking—

Clarissa's reverie was broken into by the sudden appearance of a cherubic young man, only a few years her senior, whose clothes seemed a little too big for his frame, and whose steely-blue eyes contrasted pleasantly with his vivid red hair.

"Hallo," he said. "I'm Savrola Vavasor. I sit in the House, on the opposite side as your Uncle, so if this constitutes consorting with the enemy, tell me so, and away I'll fly. No? Splendid. Well, then, ah, we *could* dance if you'd fancy it, but I can't guarantee your satisfaction, though I'd try my best. What might be more of a plan," he rattled on, musingly, "might be if we were to step over to yonder balcony, and get away from the madding crowd. I could show you the stars. I'm reasonably good on stars, you see. Dancing, well—no guarantees there, I'm afraid."

Gravely, Clarissa agreed to be shown the stars.

HOW THEY CHIRPED OVER THEIR CUPS

Dolly Longestaffe quite enjoyed these things, and was in a slightly better than average mood. He steered his wife over to the Finns, and greeted them with a happy smile.

"Hasn't Her Grace done us proud, Finn?" he asked and then bowing to Marie Finn, added "How-de-do, Mrs. Finn. What's your secret, dear lady, you look just as you did in the Old Duke's time, and here's me looking like that frightful portrait Wilde promised me, instead of the gilded youth himself, eh?"

"Ah, there was your error, dear Mr. Longestaffe," Marie answered, "You take your fashion tips from Mr. Wilde, who promises everything and delivers only epigrams, while I take mine from Mr. Stoker, and merely avoid the sun."

"And here's me thinking you'd cut yourself shaving, Phineas," Dolly replied.

He then cast his eyes around the room.

"Look at them all, Finn. New enmities, new romances blossoming around us. Political coalitions forming. And Planty Pall dancing? Surely a harbinger of the End of Days, hmm?"

Phineas followed Longestaffe's gaze, and his eyes lit upon the Duke and Lady Laura slowly but gracefully revolving about the room. His quick intuition—as well as his keen awareness where Lady Laura was concerned—discerned her heightened colour, her carriage, and, most of all, her smile. *Ah, if it could be so*, he thought, and making an excuse of bringing Marie and Mrs. Longestaffe a claret cup, strode across the room to a balcony. He stepped outside, and breathed in the night air.

Lady Laura dancing! Lady Laura smiling again! Could it be that, after so many years, the blight would pass from her life, and the shadow of guilt from his own?

For all these years he had forced himself to remember that it had been she who had turned him down, that her unhappiness stemmed from her own decisions—to reject him for the gloomy Scot, and to marry for money. From that decision had flowed much unhappiness for him, too, and the fact that he had won through to freedom and a second marriage that had brought him much joy—well, that joy had a few shadows, and one of them was the sorrow he felt for Laura, whom he could no longer love as he had once done.

In his youth, Phineas had loved easily, spontaneously—there was Laura, then Violet, and before any of them, his own poor dear Mary. He had come back to Mary, as he had promised, but uneasily, bound by oath, not by spontaneous feelings. When he had proposed to Laura, he had truly felt passion for her, a passion which revealed his tenderness to Mary as facile—calf love, really, the first stirrings of a hobbledehoy's romantic urgings, attached to a "suitable" girl. Lady Laura, her sophistication, her ease in the corridors of power, and that razor-sharp intellect—something he had not been taught to look for in love—had enchanted him. Her rejection of him had left him disconsolate.

But then he had met Violet, more conventionally feminine, and thought he had found love there. Laura, having sworn to be his "sister" in rejecting him, had tried to aid Phineas in his wooing, against Oswald's interests. Perhaps she was able to do so, he thought, because she sensed, at some level, that Violet Effingham was too conventionally feminine for Phineas, that his felt passion for Violet was as much a declaration that he would not be permanently marred by Laura's own rejection of him. It would explain her inveterate hostility to Marie, another wealthy *habituée* of the corridors of power, but one whose exotic otherness made her an even better match for Phineas.

Yes, Laura had been jealous from the start of Marie, who had, for no discernible reason, chosen him, and frankly offered herself to him. Phineas had turned her down, but all along feelings for "Madame Max," as she was then known, had been growing within his breast. When he returned to London after Mary's death, his old facility—or changeableness might have been a better term—had left him, somehow. He had given up on love, and striven only to build a career. And yet, even after his great happiness came, and Madame Max became Marie Finn, Phineas's tenderness for the woman he had once loved, and who was so tragically wounded, retained its power make his heart ache.

Reading far too much into a single dance, Finn! He thought, and went off to retrieve the claret cup.

But, oh, if it could be…

Lady Mary Tregear watched the dancers indulgently. She was in what her late Mamma would have called "an interesting state," and had no desire to be on the floor, but she did love watching the dance. Her husband sat next to her, one hand gently resting in hers, the other wielding a cigar. Frank dug his elbow gently into her side and gestured with the cigar, drawing her attention to an older couple she did not at first recognise. Then she placed them with a start: Lady Laura Kennedy and—Papa! Dancing, seemingly of his own free will—a sight not seen since Mamma would chivvy him to lead her out, generally with the mock-reproachful moan, "Oh, really, Plantagenet, can't you be as dutiful a dancer as you are at standardizing coinage!" She remembered the rusty chuckle such a plaint would bring, and the feeling of safety and warmth their by-play gave her.

Lady Mary knew Laura Kennedy as an odd duck, a political pedant in petticoats, and was surprised to see this gangling, gawky woman moving so fluidly in her father's arms.

She missed her mother sorely at that moment; and just then, she hated Lady Laura.

It's just one dance, she thought miserably; and then, more tolerantly, *And even if it were more, do you really want him to be alone and ever more isolated until he dies?*

Clarissa Riley decided that she loved the stars, and even as Savrola was getting tangled in the constellations, and trying to brazen his way through—Clarissa knew quite well that there was no such constellation as the Royal Unicorn—she loved being on a balcony, on a balmy night, being shown the stars by this ginger-haired, sweet-faced, funny young man.

The Rt. Rev. Joseph Emilius had waited patiently, biding his time, as Elizabeth waltzed with her young partner. Young, and, he thought, just a touch unwilling. Emilius saw the distracted movements of the young man's eyes to a balcony where, moments before, a flame-haired lady of about an age with Elizabeth's partner had stepped out with a very different young man, also red-headed. A slight, sad smile crossed his face. As the orchestra stopped, the young man took Elizabeth's hand, and said some words that Emilius could not make out. She shook her head crossly, but he let go of her hand, and left her.

Emilius walked swiftly but unhurriedly through the crowd, passing the young man who had lately partnered Lizzie. Something about the set of the cleric's face impelled the dancers out of his path, and he soon found himself at Lizzie's side.

"My dear," he greeted her, "do not lower yourself to pursue that stripling."

"What do you take me for, Joseph, the sort of woman who chases after men?" Her hand, which had been languidly waving a fan as he approached, snapped the trifle of painted silk and ivory shut with a violence that nearly cracked its delicate spines. Her nostrils flared with a barely contained anger that threatened to break loose. She continued, in a voice almost loud enough to be heard by their neighbors, "He was on his knees to me just days ago! On his knees, begging me to marry him!"

Emilius recognised the slight trembling of her frame from their married days, and knew the crisis was near for her.

"I don't doubt it, my best-beloved," quoth the bishop, as he firmly steered his onetime wife across the floor and out of the ballroom, "but let us not forfeit your dignity for a child's inconstancy."

She went with him, but the trembling persisted, and he could hear the words under her breath, "begged me," and then, moments later, "practically crawled to my feet." He managed to pull her into a closed-off sitting room, re-sealing the doors behind them as the inevitable tempest broke out.

Lizzie fought against her rage, as she always did, but it was, as so often, a losing battle. Rocking back-and forth with the last vestiges of self-mastery, she trembled, her hands working.

Not wanting Lizzie to disgrace herself by destroying the knick-knacks dotting the room, Emilius took the only action that occurred to him; he kissed her firmly on the lips, holding her tightly, inhaling her scent, her taste, basking in her warmth, missing from his arms for so long. Lizzie opened herself to the kiss, yielding, then turning it back against her erstwhile husband, one hand seizing his hair, while she poured out her rage into the kiss, biting his lip, her body pressing him up against the wall. Emilius felt a wave of desire wash over him, and found himself yielding to her attack. She broke the kiss, and stepped back. Then she struck at him with her full strength, one of her rings striking him in the corner of his mouth.

A lesser man would have cried out; Emilius let out a long breath, and raised an inquisitive eyebrow.

"We are not married any longer, sir," she said emphatically.

"No?" he asked, "There's a remedy for that, you know."

"Why? How many wives have you now?"

"Seven at last count, Lizzie."

Her laughter was notably not hysteria, but genuine. A good sign.

"Elizabeth, I am wealthy, I am powerful, I have everything that I want—except you. Our marriage was unsuccessful–"

Her laughter this time was louder, but still genuinely amused.

"Yes, Joseph," she smiled, "any marriage that ends up with one of the happy couple jailed for bigamy could perhaps be called unsuccessful."

"I was acquitted."

"You really were not, Joseph. The conviction was annulled—like our marriage—because that Bavarian fool—"

"Bohemian," the husband corrected.

"Batavian, Bohemian—regardless, the woman was a fool, and let you somehow persuade her to recant her testimony. We remain divorced, although you remain—for now—free."

"For now, my dear?" the bishop enquired.

"Who knows what you've been up to since last we met? Besides, I'm engaged to be married, Joseph. You saw me dancing with my *fiancé*."

"I did. I also saw him leave you to pursue another woman, so I shouldn't rely on his fidelity, were I you. And you hardly kissed me like an engaged lady, did you?"

Lizzie smiled. "I hardly kissed you like a *disengaged* lady. But—have it your own way. No, I did not, Joseph. You were always awfully good when I was upset. I should thank you, I suppose, even though it was a frightful liberty."

"You're quite welcome."

"I could have you arrested for assault, of course. With your record and our history…"

"With your record and our history," the prelate replied, rubbing a meaningful forefinger across the welt already beginning to rise upon his lower lip, "you might not be believed."

Lizzie smiled again, mischievously. "Shall we put it to the test?"

"Do you want to?"

Lizzie considered a moment. "No," she answered at length, "but gratify my curiosity, Joseph: Why should I consider remarrying you?"

"Because I have grown wiser, Lizzie, and would not treat you like a heedless girl this time. I've spent nigh on twenty years berating myself for that mistake. You and I were both meant for the better things. For wealth, yes, and prestige. But as much as that, we were meant to govern. To rule."

"To rule?" she asked, incredulous.

"To rule," he repeated firmly. "I am a bishop in the American West. In our large territory, we are effectively sovereign. And as bishop, I am the first man."

"But America is a democracy, surely?"

"In the States, yes. But I hold power in a territory, a long stretch of country where I am effectively a sovereign."

"Under the Congress, and a Governor, I seem to recall."

"Oh, my dear Lizzie. You can be naïve. The Governor is my man. In my part of Utah, I am supreme."

"Surely, Joseph, there are any number of women panting at the prospect of becoming your bride, then."

"Oh, there are. But none of them are you, and so they will not suffice."

"I am engaged to marry a Lord, the heir to an earldom, Joseph. Why would I pass him up to re-marry you and be queen of a desert?"

"Better to reign in Utah than to serve in London? Besides, I know you. You don't have to playact with me. I admire you just as you are, not as you try to persuade others that you are. Are you not, at long last, tired of playacting, Lizzie Eustace?"

When she did not answer, he said, "Besides, the choice may be simplified for you. I strongly suspect that if we go back to the ballroom, we may be in time to find your *fiancé* brawling with the one red-head over the other red-head."

"I must go," Lizzie replied, her face set.

"Think on what I said," the bishop answered.

"Oh, I shall. But I will not release my young lordling. You will forgive me, Joseph, if I acknowledge frankly that, while I quite like you, I don't remotely trust you."

Savrola Vavasor realised that Clarissa had rumbled him when he tried to show her more constellations than the ones he in fact knew. But he didn't want this part, this precious part, of his evening to end. She seemed to be enjoying it too, he thought excitedly, or else why should she smile and solemnly nod as he drifted off into further and further absurdity? Finally, when he sketched out the constellation of the Golden Lion of Granpere, she could bear no more and began snuffling with laughter.

"No, no!" she cried, "I've read that novel! No, you are a fraud as an astronomer, Mr. Vavasor, and I can't believe in anything you say."

The pair laughed conspiratorially.

"I confess," Savrola admitted, "I ran out of real constellations some time ago. But it is such a beautiful night, and I simply couldn't bear to go in."

"You could have let me decide whether I wished to stay, instead of corrupting my young mind–"

Unfortunately, Clarissa never got to finish that sentence. Jack Standish, having followed them onto the balcony, came out just in time to hear it, and, as his father had so often done, flew into a rage.

"Corrupted her?" he roared, "You have corrupted my young cousin, you d—–d scoundrel!" And before Savrola could untangle himself completely from the telescope, Jack Standish punched him in the jaw, knocking him back into the telescope, over which he stumbled and fell. Jack waded in, barking "Stand up! Stand up, d—n you!"

Clarissa screamed.

As a matter of historical record, the first two people on the scene were Bishop Emilius and Lady Eustace.

"Gentlemen!" the bishop called out, "This is most unseemly. Stop it at once!"

Savrola Vavasor shook off the remnants of the telescope and assumed a boxing stance.

Lady Eustace commanded, "Jack, step back and leave off this nonsense."

Both men rather unskillfully threw a punch. Bishop Emilius, trying to part the combatants, instead managed to be on the receiving end of both blows, and collapsed, winded, into the telescope's shards. Clarissa screamed a second time.

Dolly Longestaffe, who had been watching all this, transfixed, from the doorway, was startled to see that, as Vavasor bent down to assist the fallen clergyman, Jack, still in a Chiltern rage, punched him again.

Vavasor fell on the bishop, and, before Jack could do any more mischief, Dolly Longestaffe, to everybody's surprise (but nobody's more than his own) stepped in and seized the young man.

"Don't do it, Jack!" Dolly called out, "don't strike a man when he's down! They'll cut you in every house in society!" Jack turned on Dolly, ready to strike him, jaw muscles working. Fist raised, he caught sight of Clarissa's tear-stained face, and Elizabeth Eustace's contemptuously composed visage.

He fled through the house, out into the night.

AFTER THE BALL

As Jack Standish hurtled through the ballroom on his way out of the Marchioness's home, his mother glimpsed him and tried to intercept his course. Her son was moving too quickly for her, and he was already out of range of her voice unless she was willing to make a scene. She cast about for help, looking for her husband, who had drifted off to speak with a hunting friend after their dance together. She spied Phineas returning with the claret cup.

Seizing him by both arms, Violet gasped out, "Something's happened, Phineas—Jack just charged out of here like, looking for all the world like Oswald used to at the worst times. Help him!" she beseeched her old friend and onetime suitor.

He met her gaze.

"Find Oswald," he instructed her, "You and Marie clear up whatever's happened here. I'll find Jack, and see he comes to no harm."

Without another word, Phineas strode swiftly through the crowd. At the door he asked the man, "Lord Chiltern. Which way?"

"Th-that way, sir," the doorman's shaken voice replied, in the accents of Phineas's own native County Clare. "In a divil of a hurry he was, too!"

Without bothering to retrieve stick, glove, or coat, Phineas began his pursuit.

Meanwhile, Violet sought out Marie Finn, apprised her of the situation, and told her of Phineas's mission to find and, if possible, rescue his godson.

Imperturbably, Marie nodded her head, and said to the Marchioness, "We had better see what happened." She swept toward the balcony where she found Clarissa sobbing, as Dolly Longestaffe, Savrola Vavasor, and a footman struggled to raise the injured bishop, who was now bleeding freely from the side of his mouth, and sporting the beginnings of a black eye.

Vavasor was stumbling over a series of apologies, cheeks as red as his hair, while Longestaffe waspishly barked out instructions and commentary.

"Help me get the poor old chap into a chair, Vavasor," he grated, "I'm not a porter, and don't want to carry him through the streets. And," he added as they dropped the bishop somewhat unceremoniously onto a chaise just inside the ballroom, "you can do your atoning later. Punching out the clergy just isn't done, old boy."

A small crowd gathered around the stricken man—a crowd that notably did not include Lady Eustace, who had decided with considerable aplomb to absent herself quietly from the immediate scene. Marie drifted silently to the weeping Clarissa, and enfolded her in her arms.

"What on earth?" asked Bishop Samuel Grantly, joining his clerical brother.

"Roughhousing," replied Dolly Longestaffe crisply. "These two young muffs—hi, where did Chiltern take himself off to?" he interrupted himself.

"What do you mean, where did Chiltern take himself off to?" asked that boy's father, glowering at Dolly.

"Oh, no you don't, Lord Brentford," the latter pertly replied. "'Tisn't my fault your son and young Vavasor got into some sort of scrape, and the bish here tried to separate them and got knocked down for his pains."

"Knocked down? In my sister's house?" repeated Bishop Grantly.

"Knocked down? A bishop? In my house?" asked a severe, but feminine, musical voice, with all the gentleness nevertheless leached out of it.

The Marchioness had deigned to visit her guests.

Phineas Finn paced quickly through the streets, trying to catch up with his godson. He was sure he had gone in the right direction, yet no sign of the boy was to be seen! Not wanting to call out for him, Phineas cogitated. Where would he head? Not the family home; Lady Laura would find him there. Certainly not the Finns' residence; although he would be welcomed there by the staff, the presence of his formidable father would suggest that he refrain from going there. So—where? It was late, Phineas mused. He pulled out his watch, straining through the thickening fog to see the time. No good! He rummaged in his pockets, and found a box of Swans. He pulled out a match, struck it, and viewed his watch in the short-lived blaze. Half-past eleven. Phineas knew only one place where a young gentleman could find admittance at this hour, and repaired to the Beargarden.

When he arrived, the Club was rather sparsely populated. Phineas asked the porter, a slabsided, thickset man, "Lord Chiltern?"

"Sir?"

"Is he here, man?"

"No sir. His lordship is not here."

"Do you know where I could find him?"

"I could not say, sir."

"Could not or would not, blast you?"

Another voice, clearly inebriated, called out, "Doesn't Bunny want to play, then? I'll tell, for a fiver."

Phineas walked past the porter, and confronted a middle-aged clubman seated at the otherwise empty bar, about the age of Dolly Longestaffe, but nothing like so well-preserved. Florid of face, whiskery but without the commitment to have a proper beard or even a moustache, dressed in the height of a fashion designed for younger men, Phineas's new interlocutor had come to the condition that Dolly Longestaffe had managed to avoid: Pathetic.

"You know where I can find Lord Chiltern."

"Oh, indeed, I do, indeed I will, for five quid. Otherwise, my memory is quite apt to have holes in it, d'you see." He grinned slyly.

"Sir Felix, I really cannot advise—" the Porter interrupted.

"You be blowed, Hammond!" the wreck so-addressed replied. "Well?" he asked Phineas, "do you care to—how do you lawyers put it? Refresh my rec-recollection?"

"You know me?" Phineas asked, surprised.

"You have lawyer stamped all over you. And that bog-trotter's brrrrrogue? Surely I have the honour of speaking with Mr. Phineas Finn, the Pallisers' lapdog?"

Phineas removed a five pound note and, holding it up for inspection, crinkled it. "Surely you think better of me than that?" he asked. "After all, I would be happy to give a friend a little money to tide him over—the sort of friend that would help me find a mutual friend who's gone missing. But I don't buy secrets."

The inebriate grinned more widely. "Oh, we're friends, Phinny," he said, leering. "And I'll help you. His Lordship has repaired to the Half Moon, where all the lovely Fabians practise their free love." He reached for the note.

"And where is that?" Phineas pressed.

"Praed Street. Near Craven Road."

Phineas handed over the note.

"A brandy, since we're such good friends?" the old sot wheedled.

Phineas nodded at the barman, and plunked down a coin. "Forgive me if I don't stay, Sir Felix," he said, and walked out into the night.

Griselda, Marchioness of Hartletop, had been, in her youth, widely hailed as the most beautiful woman in England. A body of opinion would still award her the palm, though she was no longer young by any definition. Her finely chiseled features, her red lips, her abundant blonde hair remained almost entirely untouched by time; what few marks maturity had carved in the perfect mask of her features added an impression of strength, not age. Her figure was trim, her waist narrow, and she moved as freely as in her girlhood.

What distinguished the Marchioness most, however, was her coolness. Normally placid enough, and with a certain brittle charm, the

Marchioness could be quite restful company in her indifference to those around her. Tragedy, comedy, sorrow and joy alike, had all literally left Griselda unmarked. She treated all around her with equal politeness, and equal lack of concern, even the young Marquis, her son. In black (because it suited her fine porcelain skin and golden hair, not out of any sorrow for her dead husband), she floated through life politely receiving the obeiesances and attentions that her beauty had accustomed her to as her due. As long as all was well, she condescended to exchange pleasantries. Now, however, all was most decidedly not well.

Her voice like the tinkling of ice breaking under the runners of a sleigh, she asked Savrola Vavasor, "Did you strike the bishop under my roof?"

Blushing, Savrola replied, "Not deliberately, Your Grace—the other man–"

What Savrola would have said about the other man will never be known, as Her Grace had heard enough.

"Go."

"Your Grace?"

"You are dismissed. Withdraw." Griselda turned from Savrola as if he had already left. A few moments later, he had.

The Marchioness cast her eye on the injured man. "You were injured, my lord, in striving to separate two of my guests who were misbehaving?" she asked.

"Yes, Your Grace," Emilius replied.

Samuel Grantly, listening intently, could not resist giving voice to the flippant thought that crossed his mind. "The Church Militant, indeed," he murmured. "How Father would have approved."

The Marchioness, not bothering to respond to her brother, added, "I greatly regret the occasion, sir, and am grateful to you for your chivalrous deed. The young lady is unharmed?" The Marchioness tossed this question to Mrs. Finn.

"My niece is unharmed," that lady replied, and indeed, at Marie Finn's words, Clarissa turned to face the Marchioness.

"Poor child," the Marchioness said, in a kinder if still clinical tone, "visitors to my home are not usually treated so. You must return, and allow me to make amends."

"Y-yes, Your Grace," stammered Clarissa, adding, "you are too kind to me."

"Hardly. My guests do not assume a risk of fisticuffs. As to you, sir," she returned to Bishop Emilius, "You are at Claridge's, I am informed?"

"Yes, Your Grace," Emilius replied, too dazed (and frankly a bit over-awed) to venture beyond that safe harbor.

"You shall come to us as our guest. We shall have your things sent."

"Your Grace is too kind," the Bishop said, "I assure you it is not necessary."

Griselda, Marchioness of Hartletop made a short chopping motion with her right arm that brought back to Samuel Grantly, more than any portrait could, the memory of their father.

"Of course it is necessary, sir. I owe you a debt, and wish to have the pleasure of your company. You will grant me this, I trust?"

A small smile tugged at the bishop's lips, still bleeding from Lizzie's ring. "Your Grace honours me," he said in his most musical voice, "I am delighted to accept."

The Half Moon, effectively a workingman's pub run by a motley consortium of Fabians, Fenians, artists, and hangers-on of the three, should really have been closed under the licensing laws. But it had, with the help of a radical solicitor, incorporated itself as a club, and therefore could remain open at the pleasure of its members. The pub sign, a wooden representation of a guillotine blade, hung over the entrance, and served to put Phineas right as to the politics of the club's habitués; he was visiting the radicals.

What surprised Phineas was just how jolly the radicals were. Oh, a strange mix; undoubted gentlemen like Paul Montague, over in the corner hobnobbing with young Tavy Robinson and a scruffy-looking Jack Tanner. Across the room, Phineas saw journalists—the music critic Corno di Bassetto, whom Phineas read regularly, enjoying his rhetorical flourishes—and poets, such as Bunthorne, holding court on the opposite side of the saloon. Phineas even spotted a client, his wife's banker, old Ezekiel Breghert, for whom he had handled a rather delicate matter some years ago, arising out of a sundered engagement. Breghert, who had been clearly relishing a debate with a dandified young man and his young lady, saw Phineas, rose, and walked over to greet him.

"Mr. Finn," he greeted the politician, "I have never seen you here. Welcome. Has your good wife persuaded you to investigate the Society?"

"No, Mr. Breghert," Phineas replied, "though we are buying seats for Bassetto's new play."

"Good, Mr. Finn. An intellectual feast awaits you—though not, I suspect, a typical night at the theatre, hmm?" The old man winked at the lawyer. But, as the light struck Phineas's face more squarely, Breghert perceived that all was not well.

"Something is amiss, my friend?" he asked, "Nothing to do with the trust?" For, upon hearing that his onetime *fiancée*, widowed young, had fallen upon hard times with the death of her father, Breghert had settled an annuity on the hapless woman, lest she become utterly dependent on her brother's charity.

"No, not the trust," the Irishman replied. "Ezekiel—my godson, Jack Standish; is he here?"

"Upstairs, I think. He rushed in here about an hour ago."

"Do you know which room?"

"Come," the old banker said, "let us find him." Breghert questioned the factotum, who in any other such establishment would have been frankly called the landlord, and was directed to the last room on the left. The two men mounted the stairs, and passed by the sleeping quarters available to members as bedrooms. None were in use that evening, until they reached the specified chamber.

"Shall I leave you?" asked Breghert.

"No," Phineas answered, "he may be unwell and I might need help." Phineas knocked gently at the door, then, upon receiving no answer, opened it. On the bed, under a blanket, lay Jack Standish, snoring deeply. His finery from the ball was scattered throughout the room, and he was evidently clad only in his shirt, minus the wing collar, and his small-clothes. A cut glass decanter stood on the bedside table, and a reservoir glass. Both appeared to contain a green liquid. Phineas sniffed it, and a bitter scent masked by an odor of licorice, filled his nostrils. He peered at Breghert inquisitively.

The old man nodded unhappily.

"The Green Fairy," he said, continuing, "Absinthe. A spirit made of wormwood; quite strong. Judging from the state of the bottle, your young friend has drunk deeply of it. Unwise. It is said to inspire poets to brilliance, but drive more prosaic men to madness. Your young friend is not, as far as I have seen him, a poet."

"Have you tried it, Ezekiel?"

Breghert guffawed. "I?" he asked. "Can you picture a more prosaic man than an elderly banker, working in the City of London? No, no, my friend. Even in my young days, I wouldn't embrace the Green Fairy."

"I don't know, Ezekiel," smiled Phineas in his relief at having found Jack. "I'll tell you who is more prosaic: the bankers who *don't* join the Fabian Society, don't debate poetry with the Duke of Dorset–"

"Oh, you recognised him, did you?" smiled the old man.

"Yes, I did. And I won't even mention your least prosaic facet of all, as it falls under the heading of a client confidence…"

"Do not, I beg you. It would pain me. I cede the point, Mr. Barrister Finn. But I will not drink the absinthe, and I urge you to refrain as well. The good Madame would never forgive me if I led you to vice."

"Agreed. Perhaps we can turn our clear heads, though, to the problem of getting this young man home, or at least letting his parents know where they can find him."

"It is easy to tell you are not a parent, Phineas," Breghert answered, with a sigh. "You will go home to the lovely Madame after stopping off to inform the worried mother and father, and I will go downstairs and continue educating the unfortunate Duke and the charming but somewhat untraveled Miss Dobson to the realities of the way we live now."

"And then?"

"I am sleeping at the Club, and will bring the young man home on my way to the office tomorrow."

"What if he wakes before you?"

"Not after embracing the Green Fairy, he won't. I drink barley water, at my age, and need little sleep. I will probably have to rouse him in the morning if I am not to have luncheon here."

"Rather out of your way, though, isn't it?" asked Phineas, reluctant to impose on his friend, yet seeing no better solution.

"It's Saturday." Breghert shrugged. "I should not be working at all. Helping a fellow mortal on my way to violate the Sabbath might stand me in good stead." He smiled, and added, "Now go home to your lovely wife, and tell her that her affairs remain in good order. Unless her husband tempts me to try a dance with the Fairy, that is."

10

FACILIS DESCENSUS AVERNO

The Earl of Brentford scowled at his morning tea. He bitterly regretted acceding to his friend Finn's suggestion that he accompany the barrister on his trip to Wales, where Phineas hoped to get evidence that would assist him in his efforts to free his young client. At the time, it had seemed a good enough suggestion; the scene the night after Jack's brawl at the Hartletop ball certainly indicated that matters had progressed beyond his ability to deal with them, and leaving the matter in the hands of the lad's mother and that wily Penelope Phineas had married might just work.

Not that the former Madame Max could make a worse hash of matters than had he! The boy had met them at the Finns' home the next morning, pale, clearly unwell from an excess of drink, and reeking abominably of rotted licorice—the report that Jack had pickled himself in this absinthe rotgut Phineas had described had rendered Marie Finn grim, indeed. She had shrugged her shapely shoulders before going to bed and murmured that she had seen many a good man become much less so from its use on the Continent, and fixing the Earl with a sympathetic eye, had comforted him by saying "Never mind, my lord, it is not the poison the boy drank we need to worry about, it is what is poisoning him from within—and that, my friend, can almost always be rooted out." Her calm certainty had eased the anxious father in the dark hours of the morning after Phineas returned from his midnight hunt for the boy and reported him safe—or, at least, safe enough.

How typical of the Finns, the Earl thought, to take his family's troubles on themselves, and how very odd that his closest friends should turn out to be an Irishman—a Roman at that!—on whom he had once drawn a pistol, and a woman once suspected of having been the mistress of an elderly debauchee. And she Jewish, too, come to think of it. Not that you'd ever know; she and Phineas had been married in the C of E, as the only religious authority that would marry 'em without one or the other converting. An unlikely pair. And yet, they had eased themselves into his heart as readily as they had made their way into Society; all these years later, the words he had offered in his friend's defence were more true than when he had spoken them, and could be extended to the man's wife.

"I have known him well," Brentford had said those many years ago, and would have said that very day of both, "and have loved him dearly. I have eaten with him, and have drank with him, have ridden with him, have lived with him, and have quarrelled with him, and I know him as I do my own right hand." Of all his friends and associates, only this improbable pair had his unshakeable trust.

The next morning—or, rather, later that same morning—a washed out, nervous Jack had presented himself to his parents and the Finns. As Phineas and Marie rose to leave the Standishes alone, he had waved them back to their chairs.

"I'm sure Jack wishes to apologise to you at once. It's a pity Clarissa isn't down yet, so that he can beg her pardon, as well."

The boy winced at the name of Phineas's niece, and Oswald acknowledged inwardly that he had taken a wrong tack.

"Apologise?" his son retorted, with something of a sneer in his voice. "For what? Punishing a Lothario in the act of corrupting my cousin?"

Phineas Finn flushed a deep red. Brentford, who had observed his friend in his rare instances of profound anger, recognised the symptoms. Fortunately, Marie intervened. "You take things too literally, Jack," she said, not unkindly, "you mistook a pleasantry for a confession."

"I suppose that's what Clarissa must say." The young lord attempted to brazen it out, though he looked quite queasy.

"Indeed she does say that, Jack," Marie Finn answered, with a preternatural calm, and a soothing voice. "And I and her uncle believe her. So, I think, should you, my friend."

"Oh, I believe in *her* innocence," Jack shot back, his voice rising to almost a cry, "but not in that b——d's; we all know what his father was—yes, and what his mother is!"

Violet had almost jumped out of her chair at that; worse, Brentford had seen Clarissa arrive just in time for that indecency. And that, he reflected gloomily, had prodded his own Chiltern temper.

He had roared something or other at the boy; couldn't remember now just what he had said, but the look on his son's face—hadn't seen him look so pale and, well–frightened—since he'd last had occasion to whip him, back when he was still a young shaver. The boy had said simply, "I apologise," to everyone in a rather general way, and had backed out of the room, and then run to his Aunt Laura's. Wouldn't see anybody, Laura said. Hadn't eaten for the rest of the day, she'd added.

Yes, he'd made a hash of it all, and Phineas was right enough in suggesting that Brentford join him on his quixotic effort to gather evidence, so they "fled the jurisdiction," as Finn had put it, leaving for Wales the next day. But it was such a sodden midden of a country—or at least, so it seemed to him! Phineas seemed to like it well enough. After the dismal trip by train, the barrister had perked up considerably, no doubt the result of being surrounded by all these bloody Celts. He kept pointing out what might have been beautiful vistas, had they not been spoiled by the rain and, more lastingly, by the filth of the mines.

Oswald had resolutely stayed in the hotel of this little mining town, the Tanfor on Richmond Road. The musical voices of the maids and landlady had some charm for him, although the food was merely serviceable—though the hotel-keeper, known as "Daffyd the Knife" for his carving prowess, would have resented that characterization. Still, the people, at least those who were not awed by his rank—a dreadful bore, that—were amusingly pert. And they'd taken mightily to Finn, of course, not just because of the man's "dubious Irish charm" as the guv'nor had once put it, but because he was there to fight for one of their own, a young roughneck who, Brentford gathered, had done some property damage in saving some lives in a cave-in. Brentford couldn't see what the fuss was all about, quite frankly, and said so in the saloon bar that first night—"After all," he'd harrumphed, "if the blasted mine was caving in, what kind of fool worries about the machinery?"

That flash of insight earned Brentford a round on the house, and a curious look from Phineas. Nonetheless, Finn spent several days compiling dossiers, drafting affidavits, and all kinds of legal folderol that Brentford shuddered to think of.

And then, on the first sunny day that this blighted little village had given them, Phineas proposed an excursion.

"I think I have to actually see it."

"See it? See what?"

"The mine, Oswald. It might help me better frame my defence of the lad, if I actually know what happened, what it was like."

"I've never heard a lawyer say that before," the Earl retorted, laughing.

Phineas grinned, a little ruefully. "Chaffanbrass would be appalled, I admit. Still—going down a Welsh coal mine. Aren't you even a bit curious?"

"Good God, Finn, of course not! Let me tell you what you'll find: a dank, dark hole. It'll be dark and dank. There: I've saved you some time, let's go on a real excursion."

"No, no," Phineas smiled even as he shook his head. "I must go. That chap in the bar—the one you liked so much–"

"The lad's uncle, you mean? Geraint, wasn't it?"

"That was his first name—Geraint Powlett-Jones. I have to go see him."

"When?"

"No time like the present."

"Right; I'll get my coat." Phineas looked confusedly at his friend. The Earl explained, "Whither thou goest, Phineas. I still think it's a tom-fool idea, but I did sign on for the tour."

They found Geraint Powlett-Jones ensconced in the bosom of his family. A burly, florid man, with greying hair and a dark, thick moustache, he was placidly sipping tea, while his nieces, nephews, and his dogs creatively made havoc in his little thatched cottage. When he saw Phineas and the Earl approach he shooed them all outside.

"Phineas, *bach*, Your Lordship," he greeted the two men.

"Bach?" the Earl inquired. "Have you been writing music, old boy?"

"*Bach*, milord," said Geraint Powlett-Jones, "is a term of endearment. And the fact that this gentleman has come all the way from London to try t'help our Ifor entitles him to it, and requires me to confer it. I've been to London, gentlemen," he continued, gesturing them to chairs, "and I don't think that lawyers generally do that sort of thing, now do they?"

Phineas sat down, a trifle embarrassed. Oswald beamed. "Don't hangers-on get credit, too?"

"Your Lordship is an Earl. Whilst every Welshman has noble blood—I am myself descended from Owen ap Owain—it would not accord with guest-right to be unduly familiar with an Earl."

The Earl smiled. "From you, Mr. Powlett-Jones, the title 'Oswald, *bach*' would confer more, not less, honour."

"So be it. Now how can I serve the cause, gentlemen?"

Phineas explained his plan, while Powlett-Jones drank his tea.

"Aye, 'tis a good idea. A sound idea. A very fine idea—if I can get you past Jasper Tudor."

"The agent?"

"Agent, foreman, whatever you call the likes of him in the English. In the Welsh, the proper term for a man like Tudor would be *siacal*. And the shame of it, him being of Royal blood."

"What does *siacal* mean?"

Geraint Powlett-Jones grinned. "Jackal, Oswald, *bach*. But one with teeth, on his own patch. So mind how ye go."

The two travelers looked at each other, and nodded, taking the information on board, as it were; Powlett-Jones rose, and said "Is it today then that you'd be wanting to do this? Because we should go straightaway, afore it gets too late."

They walked to the pithead in almost absolute silence, the ruined valley stretched out before them. When they reached the shed, Powlett-Jones accosted a boy who looked no older than twelve. "Hi, Daffyd! Is Mr. Tudor about?"

"Yes, Mr. Powlett-Jones, he's in the shed," the lad replied, jerking his thumb in the direction of a little, ramshackle building.

The Earl could not forbear. "Isn't he a bit young to be working here? He can't be thirteen!"

"He's ten, Oswald, *bach*," the Welshman replied matter-of-factly, if a little sadly. "The little ones are often at the pit, as they can get in places we grown-ups can't. Any accident is sad, but saddest of all is when the little ones are taken."

"Does it happen often?" Phineas asked.

"Not as often as ye might expect. Even yon *siacal* has his ideas of right and wrong, and tries not to put them at too much risk."

A tall, sturdy man, with a full head of dark hair and a red beard was now approaching. He greeted Geraint with a nod, and then asked. "And who may these gentlemen be?"

"Friends, Tudor, from London. Here about the law-case."

"Friends is it, then? And what is it they'll be wanting?

Phineas Finn answered, "To go down the mine, and see what a level like that which caved in is like. To understand what happened better."

"And what affair is it of yours? This mine is private property, and has its way to pay. We don't offer tours for the gentry."

"I am Ifor Powlett-Jones's defending barrister. I have a right to examine, on his behalf the *locus in quo*—the place where it happened."

"Aye, but ye can't; it's all caved in. And d'ye have a judge's order, then?" After a short pause, he said "Thought not," and turned contemptuously to Powlett-Jones.

"Are these men really who they say?"

"Aye."

"And ye'll go down with them? Make sure they come back all sound? And that they do nothing they ought not to?" Powlett-Jones, nodded his assent, and the foreman nodded.

"All right," he said, "Go, then, if you've a mind. I'll not have it said that I denied any man his right of law. You go, and see what you need—and then leave, d'ye hear?"

Tudor left them, and the visitors looked at Powlett-Jones in some perplexity.

"He's got his own standards, has Tudor. They're mean and grasping, but he has his own ideas about what's just." They followed Powlett-Jones into the changing area, and put on coveralls, boots, and a helmet with a light and a mirror to reflect that light. As a last step, a heavy, long neckerchief was presented to each of the gentlemen. "Put it on," Powlett-Jones commanded. And then they followed him into the man-engine. As they began their descent, Powlett-Jones, with the ease of long practise, lit the candles, and readied the lights.

"They'll be some lanterns down there," he assured his guests.

"Isn't that dangerous?" Oswald asked.

"That's mining, Oswald, *bach*," the Welshman replied with a shrug.

The engine took them down slowly, with fewer jerks and starts than Phineas had envisioned. The dark grew quickly impenetrable, and even their little lamps were of no use here. As if reading his mind, Geraint said, "We light them above to have less open flame below."

The feeling of walls closing in around him was one Phineas Finn remembered from childhood nightmares. Now it was, in very fact, exactly what occurred as the shaft narrowed and the lights cast peculiar shadows against the walls; Phineas glanced over at Oswald, and in the flickering, diffuse light, Oswald looked almost an old man—Phineas could see, for the first time, a resemblance between Oswald and his father, the old Earl of Brentford. Powlett-Jones, between them, looked ghostly, like a revenant of another time. The seams of the walls, rough-hewn and raw, occasionally refracted the light or glinted; otherwise, it formed a rippling black tunnel dividing them ever further from air, light, and life.

As they went further and further down, the dust began to make its presence felt.

"Raise yer neckerchiefs!" Brentford and Finn obeyed Powlett-Jones's command, muffled by his own kerchief. Breathing through the coarse fabric, Phineas could feel the dust enter his nose and mouth, despite the barrier. When the man-engine stopped, they saw that they were at a small bridgehead from which several small tunnels branched off. Unhesitatingly, Powlett-Jones bore left, crouching to avoid striking the top of his helmet—and the precious lamp—against the tunnel roof.

The three men trailed through what seemed to Phineas an interminable twisting series of tunnels, resisting several turn-offs, only to enter a wider gallery, a crudely excavated area almost the size of a ballroom. The walls were being worked on by men with tools, the exact nature of which the poor lighting prevented Phineas from making out. The chunks that were being carved from the wall fell toward, if not always into, large basket-like vehicles which reminded Phineas of nothing so much as the laundry-carts for linens he had seen at the hotel he stayed in on trips to Ireland. To his horror, he saw around each such vehicle, small figures darting about, stuffing coal into sacks worn about the neck and shoulders, and periodically emptying the sacks into the cart.

As the gallery had been expanded irregularly—the miners' pickaxes tended to explore the walls with the best yield, not to create a pleasing symmetry—wooden props had been put up to shore up the ceiling. The very ground beneath their feet shifted, as they walked through the dust, gravel, and spoil created by the mining that had gone on here before. No engine was visible, which informed Phineas that he was not yet as far into the mine's workings as he wanted to get.

Though their environs seemed as appalling as a Doré illustration of Dante, they were clearly in a well-worked out, relatively safe part of the mine; the work was more of a scraping of the sides to make sure that all the useful coal had been stripped from the walls. Phineas knew that the area Ifor and his companions had been in at the time of the accident had been at the cutting edge of McScuttle's exploration into the depths of the hillside. He began to stride toward one of the tunnels, only to be seized by the back of his overalls, and pulled forcefully back.

"Oh, no, Phineas *bach*!"

"But I need to see–"

"No further," the Welshman was implacable. "The further ye go, the easier ye can be lost, or a cave in could happen, or a bit o'ground give, and ye break yer leg. Just—just look about ye. See the men. Smell the reek, and the must, and feel the dust in yer nostrils, yer hair, yer eyes, and mouth. Isn't that enough to help you picture that day? They were tighter in, and fewer pit props. No ponies there."—Phineas had not even noted the little beast in the corner, attached to a cart. "No children, either. That much ye can give Jasper Tudor, as well. McScuttle'd have 'em throughout the mine, but Tudor? He'd feel obliged to attend the funerals."

Phineas looked about him, taking all the details, the sounds, the heaviness of the air, the clogging of his nostrils, his ears, and the taste, even through the coarse fabric barrier, of the dust under his tongue, an almost salty, ashy taste, the feeling of grit between his teeth. Phineas looked around once more. Brentford was stoic, immobile. He would follow Phineas deeper into the bowels of the workings, Phineas knew, but would as lief leave.

He nodded. "All right," he said to Powlett-Jones, "all right. I've seen enough."

They headed back to the surface, and the pithead baths. As they ascended, Phineas doubted he would ever feel clean again.

11

SIR WILLIAM MCSCUTTLE

The afternoon after their visit to the mine had been spent in scrubbing themselves clean, and in a nap. After supper, they glumly had a glass or two in the public bar. Geraint Powlett-Jones was there, answering Phineas's questions, of which there were many. The Welshman's blunt good cheer, and his patent liking for the two men he inaccurately but amusedly termed the *Sais*, lifted the dark mood each had fallen into, and, although it was an early night, it did not end as dourly as it might have done. Thoughtful, saddened by the conditions he had seen, Phineas shook his head at the thought that all he had witnessed was for the enrichment of a member of his own Party, a man Phineas had met at conferences and events over the last few years. A man, in short, on his side of the political fence.

As he drifted off to sleep, the strange role of Sir William in all this revolved about in his mind. The next morning, over breakfast, he raised the matter.

"Look, Oswald," he said, "Something's just off about all of this. I don't understand why McScuttle is pushing this case, and I can't believe it's all down to a scrappy manager wanting a bit of his own back, particularly now that I've met Tudor. I need to see McScuttle."

"Well, what's to stop you?" the Earl of Brentford asked, harpooning a sausage with his fork.

"McScuttle himself, for one," the barrister replied. "He doesn't want to see me, and we're on his patch."

"So what do you do?" The Earl had a reasonably good suspicion of what, but wanted to hear it stated.

Phineas grinned at his friend. "Now the Earl of Brentford earns his corn."

"Oh?" The Earl grinned back.

"McScuttle's ambitious; he can refuse to see a somewhat independent backbencher easily enough, but the Earl of Brentford? The head of the Prime Minister's family? And Lady Laura's brother? I don't think he'd dare, do you?"

The Earl, shaking with laughter. "Bounder. That was the word I was groping for earlier, Finn. You're a bounder."

"Not a cad, though?" Phincas askcd.

"Certainly not," his friend answered, "I've never seen you in a check suit, and hope never to do so."

They set out after breakfast, asking Daffyd the Knife for directions to McScuttle's home. "You mean Haggis Hall?" the hotelier asked, giving the residence the name the owner's employees referred to it by. "You won't find him there. He'll be at the mine office." Brentford shot him an inquiring look. Phineas shook his head; he didn't want to try to intimidate this rooster on his own dunghill, but to use Brentford's rank and position on the man where he was most vulnerable.

"Ah, but will we find Mrs. McScuttle in?" the burly peer inquired.

"Well, that you will," the hotelier answered.

"Isn't it Lady McScuttle?" Phineas asked.

"Oh, yes. Forgot that he'd been knighted. Don't know what Barrington was thinking, there."

The road to McScuttle's home led across several fields that, although lying fallow, had not been clawed up to scavenge coal from the earth's heart. They followed the stone walls pointed out to them by Daffyd the Knife, which, while marking property lines now long made obsolete by death or purchase, nonetheless formed a helpful guide to the Coal Baron's hall.

The friends enjoyed their leisurely stroll, and Oswald even broached the subject that was still plaguing him. "So, the lad—what should I be doing, Phineas?"

"For now, nothing."

"Really?"

"He was suffering the results of that ghastly green liquor. He was humiliated by having gotten into a brawl at the Marchioness' home. And then, to cap it all off, he used an obscene term to describe a rival and was crude about a lady—and in the presence of Clarissa."

"A rival?" the Earl asked gently.

"I'm rather afraid that may be the case, Oswald. Two incidents, both involving Clarissa, And his anger at young Vavasor seemed, well, a little excessive if his sole interest really is protecting my niece's honour."

"Hmmm."

"I'm not matchmaking, Brentford, and neither is Marie, if that's what you're afraid of."

"Hey?" The Earl's laugh boomed out. "Oh, Finn, I wouldn't mind if you were. My father would've had apoplexy, of course, but having you as family—well, Clarissa would be worth even that."

Phineas stared at his old friend a moment, saw the twinkle and his eye, and rolled his own eyes in mock exasperation.

"Only the nobility," he said, "still think that condescending to their inferiors is gratifying to them."

"Isn't it?" asked the Earl. "It certainly is to us."

At Sir William's home, a Tudor-era manse somewhat spoiled by the replacement of the original windows with more modern efforts, and with sundry other modern conveniences grafted onto the pleasant original structure, the friends had not long to wait for Sir William. His Lady, a sweet faced Welshwoman, had seen to that, and it was all Brentford could do to ignore the plump footman running toward the town to fetch his master. They made small talk with Lady McScuttle for a while; that lady, upon learning that Phineas had a niece who had recently come out into Society, prattled away happily of the McScuttle daughter, Leonora, at that very moment in London "being finished," as her mother put it, causing Phineas to suppress a smile as he pictured the poor girl in the hands of the cabinet makers of Wardour Street, until the drawing room door opened precipitately, and they were greeted a small, white-haired personage.

Sir William McScuttle had one of those faces that deceive; he looked as though he would be more at home in a pulpit preaching comforting truths, not hellfire. The lineaments of his features professed gentleness, kindness, and an overflowing mercy, an impression belied by the reptilian hardness of his obsidian eyes.

"Lord Brentford, Mr. Finn," he greeted the pair, "what an honour and a surprise"—leaving no doubt in the minds of his auditors which had provided which. "How may I serve you, gentlemen?"

The Earl made the running first.

"Sir William, as you know, my family has a great tradition of public spiritedness," he began rather heavily.

"Indeed, my lord—though you are not as active in such spheres as was your late father," the mine-owner replied.

"Oh, I keep informed," the Earl answered, "but my cousin Barrington Erle—but of course, you know Barrington, don't you?"

"Not to speak of."

"Oh, we must amend that state of affairs. I just wish this little political unpleasantness could be dealt with first– "

"What little political unpleasantness would that be, my lord? My protection of my property against the vagaries of vengeful employees?"

"Vengeful?" Phineas interjected. "I was given to understand that there was a cave-in and a rescue attempt at issue."

"Aye, so they say. But we know better, don't we my lord? No, my lord, what we had here was an offence against the just rights of property and property holders. I admit that they seized the occasion of the cave-in, but we all know what was really at stake…"

"Surely it was the saving of lives," the Earl said.

"That's what they'd have you believe, my lord. 'Twas nothing less than industrial violence."

"But there was a cave-in, surely?" the Earl asked, confused.

"Aye, my lord."

"And the young man who has been charged…Powlett-Jones?"

"Your friend Mr. Finn knows the name quite well, my lord. He's sought to belabour me about this case several times."

"Wasn't the young man's brother trapped under the rubble?"

"So the men say, my lord. But that was just icing on the cake for them. They were there to break and smash, whatever the excuse."

"But why on earth….?" Brentford's question dried up. He started another. "If the roof was collapsing, then…" This time, he did not so much run dry as perceive that Phineas was shooting a look in his direction that more clearly commanded silence than could any utterance. However, the knight began to answer the first, uncompleted question.

"Why? Why do men employed by a fair but stern master revolt? Because they do not keep to their rightful places. Discontented with their own lot, they look enviously at their betters, and see what decades—or even generations—of patient toil have amassed, and their one thought is to filch it. Filch it for themselves, not even understanding that in so doing they sign and seal their own death warrants. Such as they cannot use money to grow more money; they have only wasted their substance with riotous living, and then find themselves pleading to fill their bellies with the husks that the swine did eat. No, they are like children, and need a firm hand."

The Earl of Brentford cast about for help. Phineas answered, "How can you be so sure that these men were set on destruction, not rescue?"

"Because that young man you are defending, sir, that very selfsame young man? He was after organizing the hands."

"Forming a union, you mean?"

"Aye; a union. They've talked of getting the Fed in. And that man of yours," McScuttle wheeled and addressed Phineas directly for the first time, "is the leader of them trying to bring in the Fed. So don't tell me they'd not as lief smash up my machine, aye, and paste my manager, while they're at their mischief. All in the name of socialism, of course—a dangerous, nay, a deadly brew of *Liberté, égalité, fraternité.*"

Phineas, who had only just retrieved the Earl's son from the revolutionaries of the Half-Moon, but had not sampled the deadly brew served there, was hard-pressed to deny it without smiling. He contented himself with one last question.

"So, Sir William," he asked, "is it fair to say that your impressions of young Powlett-Jones were formed from his connection with this 'Fed'? I mean, was he otherwise up to the job?"

"Aye, he was up to the job," the old man growled. "Up to both jobs, if you ask me. A fine lad at digging up the coal—and of spreading sedition."

It took some little while to make their farewells, with the Earl pouring oil upon the McScuttle troubled waters by expressing an insincere, but not unconvincing, delight at the thought of re-encountering the knight and his lady in London. And, when that proved insufficient, Brentford then added that he hoped to hear more from the knight—that the Party needed to hear his views, and to profit by them. That restored the benignant aspect to McScuttle's face, and removed the crease from his Welsh wife's forehead.

As the friends began their amble back to the Trafon, the Earl carefully waited until they were out of McScuttle's grounds, and remarked, "What a dreadful little man! Not like any other Scotsman I've ever met!"

Phineas laughed out loud. "Scotsman!" he exclaimed. "He's no more a Scot than you are! *Mc*Scuttle, not *Mac*Scuttle. He's a countryman of my own, though I hate to own it."

"But he sounds nothing like you do—or did, even a quarter of a century ago," the Earl protested.

Phineas sat down on the stone wall they were following back to Pontnewydd, laughing all the more. "I'm from County Clare, he's from, oh, Donegal, maybe, possibly Sligo." Seeing the incomprehension on his friend's face, Phineas explained, "He's a Northerner, Oswald, I'm a Southerner. I'm a Catholic; he's an Orangeman. Different cultures, different accent."

"Like the Americans? I mean, without the slavery, of course."

"Not to hear Larry Fitzgibbon tell it, Oswald, but, yes, without the slavery. Just general privation and oppression."

"You're not joking, are you?"

"No; the Famine was the worst of it, but the damage is still—appalling." Phineas mused. "When I had office, I tried to do something about that. It is so hard to convince even the best Englishmen that they are capable of tyranny."

The friends were silent for a moment.

"More so than other men?" asked Brentford.

"Perhaps it only seems that way, because the English have such high ideals, and yet are so able to ignore them."

"And yet, you've thrown your lot in with us, Phineas."

"Yes. And I don't regret it, Oswald, on the whole. We're bound together, the Irish and the English, at least for my time. But only when the Irish can be heard will we know how our destinies as a people will be worked out. For now, I try to remind the English that an Irishman is not just a comic chap in the music halls."

"You wouldn't do on the stage, Finn. Now McScuttle, on the other hand–"

And the friends stood up, and resumed their stroll.

"What next?" asked the peer.

"Home. London. I've compiled a great deal of information, and need to sort it all out. And, with any luck, Marie and Violet will have moved matters forward in that other case—*In re Chiltern.* Time to find out, I think."

THE LETTERS OF LADY EUSTACE

The night of the ball, Jack Standish had fled the scene of his own impetuosity, and from his own mother. His initial thought had been the Beargarden, but, knowing he would be sought there, he turned away from the door, and hurried away to Praed Street, and the Half Moon. Once there, he had accosted the factotum, the Faithfull Follett, as Jack was wont to call him in better times, and demanded a bottle of the Green Fairy, with results that have already been seen. That morning, he awoke to find Ezekiel Breghert sitting in a chair at the side of his bed.

"So, you are awake," the old banker observed cheerfully. "All the better. I should get to my office, and I have promised to see you safely home."

Jack lurched from the bed, and into the water closet, where he was violently ill.

"My company does not normally bring about that result, Lord Chiltern," Breghert remarked as the still-queasy peer returned to the main room.

"Jack …please," the younger man managed to gasp. Seeing his reflection in the glass, he added, "I cannot present myself to my Aunt Laura like this."

"No? Surely that is what Aunt Lauras are for, no?" Seeing Jack's gloomy visage, the old man sighed. "Very well. I have had shaving things brought, and your man should be here with fresh clothes soon. Can you bear to eat something? No, perhaps not..." Jack's convulsive twitch at the mention of food convinced the old man that the idea was ill-timed.

When Jack was bathed and dressed, Breghert took him by cab toward the old Earl of Brentford's townhouse, now Lady Laura's home. Before they arrived, however, Jack changed his mind, and asked the driver to take him to the Finns' residence in Park Lane.

"Are you sure?" the old banker asked, as Jack exited the carriage. "Maybe better later—or tomorrow. Your Aunt will be easier, I suspect."

Already feeling anxious, Jack shook his head. "'If it 'twere done when 'twere done, then better it were done quickly,'" he quoted.

"Yes, my young friend," the old man answered, "But will it be? Come, listen to old Breghert; I told your godfather I would look out for you..."

But Jack Standish mumbled "'twere better 'twere done quickly," thanked the old man, knocked on the door, and was admitted, with results of which we already know.

When Jack arrived at his aunt's home, he let himself in with the key she had given him for his own use when in London, and went directly up the stairs to the comfortable apartment known in Lady Laura's establishment as "Jack's room." Instinctively, while passing the hall table, he picked up a letter addressed to him, and when he achieved his room, he closed and locked the door, kicked off his shoes, and lay down on the bed. The fact of the letter finally registered, and he opened it. In a neat feminine hand, it read:

September 15, 189_,

My own dearest love,

I write these lines, stricken by concern as I am by your sudden departure from the Marchioness's ball last night, and in the earnest hope that they will find my beloved fully restored to himself. I know not by what instinct you divined that some man was trespassing upon your little cousin's innocence, but you will be pleased to hear that Her Grace exiled the wretch at once. The poor child was dreadfully shocked by all that went on, and also—alas, poor little girl!—wholly lacked the sang-froid to hide that she liked the attention. She will, I am sure, grow up to be a fine young woman, and even now is a biddable, tractable child, though scarcely ready for a ball. She would no doubt have been far more comfortable in a pinafore, superintending the younger children at a nursery tea.

But as to our wedding, my love. I suppose we must fix a date so that our announcement can be in the Jupiter and the Times. How like a queen I felt as you knelt at my feet and pleaded for my hand, and how much more so I shall feel at the altar, when our union is solemnised before God and our friends—and, of course, your family!

Write soon, my own one! Every moment we are parted is an age, until I am assured by your own dear hand that all is well, and that you will soon be once again in the arms of

Your own loving
Lizzie

Jack groaned. He crumpled up the letter, pulled the coverlet up to his chin, and immediately resumed his prematurely broken slumber. He slept heavily.

The lingering fumes of the absinthe in his system must have birthed a dream in which he, draped in a peer's coronation robes, staggered behind a woman similarly garbed, carrying a heavy, coiled-up chain that led from her wrist to his wrists, which were bound together. The woman turned to look at him and he saw that it was none other than Lady Eustace—not the beautiful siren he had always known, but a hard-faced, predatory virago, whose hair was shot through with grey, and whose skin had altogether lost that suppleness that enchanted him. The phantom-Lizzie tugged at the chain, laughing with cruel enjoyment as he staggered in her wake, and led him through a palatial hall.

As she frog-marched him, dragging him past all the members of Society who had known him since his cradle lining the walls of the hall, he made out his own father, hanging his head at his son's ignominious fate. And there was Phineas Finn, his uncle in all but blood, consoling his father. "Never mind, Brentford," the Irish M.P. was saying, "you have other sons, *they* can restore your lost honour..." His own mother, face tear-stained, turned her back on him, while Mrs. Finn smiled enigmatically.

But worst of all was when the phantasm dragged him past a little cluster of children, among whom he spied Savrola Vavasor, in a blue sailor suit and sailor's hat, energetically riding a rocking horse, while Clarissa Riley, in a little pink pinafore, gazed up at him adoringly. He stopped to remonstrate with her, to tell her that he found her beautiful, and could be so much more to her than the boy on the horse, but the phantom-Lizzie chuckled again, and gave the chain a tremendous jerk, and he lost his balance, and was falling before her, falling, and—

Jack came to on the floor, tangled in the bedclothes, and hearing a frantic knocking at the door. "Jack!" his Aunt Laura called out, "Are you hurt! Can I help, my dear? JA-ack!"

He twisted out of the bedclothes, and found his feet. Stepping over the mass of covers, he opened the door a crack.

"I'm all right, Aunt Laura," he said, "just fell asleep again after a late night. And had a bad dream," he added.

"I heard you calling," she said.

"Calling? I wasn't calling you, Aunt." He tried to smile in his usual way.

"Indeed you were not," she replied with some asperity. "You were calling Clarissa. I'm sure the servants found it most edifying. Now straighten yourself up and dress for dinner. And meet me in my study in ten minutes. I think we had best have a few words."

"I-I don't really fancy dinner, Aunt Laura."

"Don't you? How unfortunate. Because you'll be present for it, I assure you. And I further assure you that having this conversation with me will be considerably less difficult than having a similar one with your father."

"Yes, Aunt Laura," Jack replied.

Pleased with her success, Lady Laura smiled. "Good. Full fig, mind. No lounge suits." Scrutinizing her nephew's disheveled state more closely, she amended her instructions. "You may have fifteen minutes, Jack. I suspect you will need them."

The door closed, and Jack slowly began to ready himself for dinner. A scant few minutes later, another knock at the door sounded, and his man Partridge came in. Querulously, Jack asked "What kept you? I've fewer than ten minutes to get downstairs, or Aunt Laura goes on the warpath."

"Beg pardon, sir," the valet replied, "but there was a delivery for you, and the messenger was most insistent that it be placed into your hands. It took some time to—er—persuade—him to go."

"Ah. Good scout, then. Well done."

"Thank you, sir. Do you desire the letter now, or after dinner?

"Oh, blast. I suppose I'd better have it over with."

The valet complied. Jack instantly recognised the handwriting on the envelope, tore it open and read:

*September 17, 189_*

What! He had slept the clock around? Or had he? A flash of recollection came to him, of having crept down to the larder in the night and having raided it to sate his hunger. Yes, and his thirst! There was no absinthe at Aunt Laura's, but now he spied an empty whiskey bottle on the floor beside the bed.

His Aunt's firmness made sense now. He resumed the letter:

My only one, my beloved Jack,

I am somewhat worried that you have not replied to my last letter, my dear. I do not mean as yet to chide you, for the night was late, and the day is not even—as of yet—over. Still, you know that a girl [Jack snorted as he read Lady Eustace's self-description] *treasures the many attentions she receives from her accepted lover, and that the swiftly waning days between engagement and the bliss of the wedding are sweetened so very much by the myriad attentions with which a parfait gentilhomme is wont to shower his Lady.*

I should not have written merely to say this, of course, but have news which I should communicate to you most urgently. It seems that there are those saying that you and that ginger cur Vavasor (the half-American mongrel whom you had to punish for his attempt to debauch a mere child, a veritable baby, really, years away from being eligible for matrimony!)

are in fact rivals for the little girl's hand! Yes, I know the story is as wildly fantastical as anything that clever Mr. Dodgson ever wrote, but that is what I heard Hermione Longestaffe saying at Lady Monogram's just this afternoon at tea.

Well, I scotched that absurd rumour, of course, and was only too be pleased to do so by telling them of our engagement, which naturally put paid to any gossip concerning little Miss Clarissa—poor infant!

In my joy at our betrothal, I was wearing a favourite old ring, the diamond my poor lost Florrie gave me (all those years ago) [the last four words were heavily scored out, but Jack managed to decipher them] *several years ago, and I'm afraid that when they all assembled to congratulate me, Hermione most kindly catching up my hand as she embraced me—well, she mistook that old ring for an engagement present from you! Droll, isn't it? I was so diverted by receiving the congratulations of all the assembled matrons of Society that I quite neglected to correct her mistake. I suppose it's just as well, my dear, as really you should have given me a ring when you proposed the other day - but how can I blame your sweet (impetuousity)* [also scored out, but still legible] *impetuousness for not wanting to wait to propose until you had done so? What fun we shall have remedying the error together!*

Well, the announcement of our engagement was doubly pleasant news for the assembled ladies, my dear, because, of course, nobody wanted to believe Hermione's gossip—and to give the old tattle-tale her due, she was the first to profess relief that the rumour turned out to be somebody's wicked fib. And then I realised how I could best defend your honour—and I'm sure you will be most pleased with me—I have sent in an announcement of our engagement to both the Times and the Jupiter! Isn't that delightful? Oh, you are so very, very welcome, my darling, and please know that I always will rise to defend your honour whenever needed!

Such a long letter—and two in as many days, as well! I really must close, or you will become dreadfully spoiled, and expect such effusions every day. And, of course, you may have them—as long as you are a good boy, that is.

Always your very own, as you are ever, ever, mine,

Lizzie

He read the last lines, thunderstruck, and, feeling like the proverbial condemned man expected to choke down every bite of an overly hearty last meal, Jack passively submitted to having his suit brushed, and his tie tied. His spirit groaned within him at the thought that he must now, in his still weakened condition, inform his Aunt Laura that tomorrow's papers would tell all the world of his engagement to the a woman of his aunt's own generation, and, moreover, one who had been known for decades as the most infamous adventuress in England.

Dinner was interrupted at the Finns' Park Lane home that evening. The Countess of Brentford, Marie Finn, and Clarissa Riley had sat down to a cold collation after Phineas and the Earl had left that afternoon, their wives assuring them that they should go to Wales as planned. "My dear friend," Marie Finn had assured the harassed peer, "Jack is safe for now, holed up at his aunt's, and you two probably should not meet until we have seen what is leading him to act in this unprecedented way. A woman's touch, do you not think, Violet?"

The Countess had agreed; she knew the warmth of her husband's heart, yes, but also that of his temper, and her mother's instinct was telling her that Jack needed delicate handling right now; clearly something was amiss, something that was upsetting the balance of her boy's mind, and his father's rough-and-ready handling could only lead to disaster as things presently stood. "A woman's touch is best for this, Oswald; Marie is right." And so the men had decamped, leaving their wives to grapple with this situation that escaped their skills.

Tomorrow, the Countess and Mrs. Finn had decided, they would storm Portland Square, and force a showdown with Jack. Clarissa had been left out of their deliberations, but her heart ached for the handsome young lord she had idolised since her arrival in England. He had always been so good to her, so kind! And then, just two nights ago, he had assaulted Savrola, ripping from her a pleasant, dreamy encounter with a charming young man who had wanted her company—hers!—enough to make up silly stories merely to prolong their conversation. Clarissa struggled to identify the angry, brutal young man who had wrecked her evening, leaving it shattered it along with the telescope on that fatal balcony, with the hero of her first years in England. She simply could not fathom it. She picked at her food miserably, while her two aunts—one by marriage, the other by adoption—gazed sadly at her, and conducted a desultory conversation about nothing very much.

It was rare that one could hear a knock at the door from the dining room. But the fusillade of raps bombarding the front door penetrated far into the house. When Meier swung wide the door, he found Lady Laura Kennedy on the doorstep, in the act of athletically swinging her parasol handle at the door to deliver a second round. Meier adroitly stepped sidewise, Lady Laura stayed her hand, and the butler's head was spared any direct insult.

"Madame?" the unperturbed butler inquired.

"Your mistress," Lady Laura demanded, "quickly. She's in?"

"May I inquire…" Meier got no further, as Lady Laura stepped into the townhouse, giving her name, and saying, "I must see her at once. Tell her—tell her I regret intruding, but it is imperative that she and the Countess of Brentford see me immediately."

But the two ladies so demanded were present already. Marie Finn, calmly wiping her fingers on the napkin she had neglected to put down in her haste to reach the door, said, "No apology is necessary, Lady Laura. You are most welcome in my house. What has disturbed you?"

Lady Laura turned to face her hostess, acknowledging her with a nod that was almost a little bow. But it was to her sister-in-law that she spoke.

"Oh, Violet!" she exclaimed, "He has run away! How can we find him?"

AS THE DUST SETTLES

The Countess of Brentford was, quite simply, dumbstruck by her sister-in-law's revelation.

Marie Finn, however, was not.

"Did you search his room?" she asked pragmatically.

"Search his room?" Lady Laura asked. "I tell you, he has run off! His man helped him dress for dinner—and then, he simply did not appear! His overcoat is missing, and so are his gloves, and Jack himself has simply—vanished."

Mrs. Finn remained patient; too much lay between her and Lady Laura for her to allow any frustration to show.

"For any indication as to why he left, or where he was going?" she explained.

When Lady Laura shook her head in the negative, Mrs. Finn commanded, "Meier, the carriage and my wrap. Violet, will you come with me?"

The countess found her voice. "Of course," she answered.

Back in Portland Square, the ladies searched Jack's room. Lady Laura, finding the first billet-doux from Lady Eustace crumpled up on the floor, let out a whinny of despair.

"Violet, Madame—Marie," she corrected herself, using Marie's Christian name for, as far as either could recall, the first time, "Listen to this." And she read the letter aloud.

"My son, under the spell of that abominable woman!" Violet exclaimed.

By this time, Marie had spotted a second screwed-up twist of heavy paper, and pounced on it with the avidity of Elspeth in her kittenhood.

She untwisted the discarded letter and read through it quickly. "Tcha!" she hissed.

"What is it, Marie?" asked the distracted mother.

Marie Finn read the second letter aloud. Then she asked, "Laura. Are you on the 'phone?"

"The 'phone?"

"The telephone exchange," supplied Violet.

"Yes, of course. We are," Lady Laura replied, "Jack was most insistent that we should be, and I indulged him."

"We must avert this announcement's being published," Mrs. Finn declared. "Once it is in the papers, Jack will be delivered bound and gagged into that woman's hands."

"But how can we stop it?" wailed Violet.

"Leave that to me. Laura," Marie inquired sweetly, "where is the instrument?"

Lady Laura Standish led Mrs. Finn to the instrument, and she and Violet watched in astonishment as Mrs. Finn, apparently quite well-acquainted with the mysteries of the telephone, reached her quarry in short order. Their admiration grew as she deployed a remarkable combination of threats, flattery and promises on the respective editors of the *Jupiter* and the *Times* to induce them to embargo the announcement.

With the pro-Government *Jupiter*, she cast the announcement as a practical joke, designed to hinder the Government by linking the Prime Minister's family with a fading *demimondaine*, a "dirty trick" she called it, in a phrase that would echo in the Editor's ears, and ultimately find expression in other circumstances. With the anti-Government *Times*, Mrs. Finn coyly played it as a similar strike—a stab indirectly aimed at the Leader of the Opposition, Frank Greystock, who had once, long ago, had his name linked with the same withered flower. Mrs. Finn represented the spurious announcement of the Chiltern-Eustace betrothal as having been done with the intent of resurrecting talk of long bygone youthful indiscretions on the part of Greystock, in the hope of scotching the possibility that the Leader would receive a "K" in the New Year's honours list as a gesture of respect from across the aisle.

In both cases, she urged the importance of keeping her, Mrs. Finn, sweet-tempered on behalf of the editor, as her husband was sufficiently well-placed on the fringes of his own party and yet friendly with those high in the councils of each that she could reward her friends in the Press with "'Stoops,' as I believe you gentlemen in the Press call them. No? Oh, it is 'scoops,' is it? Yes, I may be able to assist you to some 'scoops,' my friend, if you do not connive at this vulgar prank in embarrassing my friends through disseminating a false announcement."

Finally, Mrs. Finn drew from her quiver the poison-tipped, politely-used threat, both the explicit one of litigation and the implicit threat of Government displeasure, hinting that both the Government and Society would delight in Lord Jack's (Marie was careful to work her godson's title into as many sentences as possible) libel suit against the newspapers for linking so promising a young man with a raddled harridan whose own family had sued her for theft. Throughout these mirror-image conversations, her manner was pleasant, even charming, and she never once raised her voice.

Under the relentless three-pronged attack of Mrs. Finn, the Editors each succumbed, leaving the field entirely to her. She had utterly routed Lady Eustace's most potent tool at making her desires an accepted public actuality. She had done so, remarkably, without leaving the chair in the Library nearest the instrument, and in the time it took for the tea to be made and served.

Violet smiled wanly. "I do believe you've managed it, Marie. How on earth do you do it?"

"A combination of running my own business for decades, and watching dear Glencora behind the scenes. She could have been the first Prime Minister in petticoats, you know."

"Not to be ungrateful," Lady Laura interposed, clearly greatly relieved, "but now—what do we do about finding Jack?"

"That is more difficult," Mrs. Finn answered. "We must first find out where he has gone in order to address that difficulty."

Violet pondered, then rose from her chair and rang the bell. When the elderly butler wheezed into the room, she asked, "Chalmers, his lordship left some things behind. I need to have them sent on to meet him…" her voice trailed off.

"To Lochlinter m'lady?"

"Oh, is that where he's going," the Countess mused, "And I thought it might be Oxford…"

"No, m'lady, Lochlinter."

"Thank you, Chalmers. That is all for now."

As the butler withdrew, Lady Laura asked, "Should it be you or I, Violet?"

"Both," Mrs. Finn answered. The other two ladies looked to her. "We don't know Jack's state of mind. Some times in one's life call out for one's mother, others for one's aunt. Which this is, I do not know. Be prepared for either, and leave London to me. I have put out the principal blaze, but Lady Lizzie is still to be reckoned with."

On her husband's return three weeks later, Marie Finn, after dining with him, Clarissa, and the Earl of Brentford, waited until the latter two retired for the evening. When they had done so, and Phineas had lit his pipe, an old Peterson that had seen much wear, and Elspeth had taken her wonted seat in his lap, Marie passed her husband a letter which had been delivered two days after the Marchioness's ball. The envelope was sealed, leading Phineas, after noting the return address, to cast a quizzical gaze at his wife.

Casually, he remarked, "You steamed it open, of course."

Vibrating with silent laughter, Marie tried to protest her innocence.

"Quite well, too, I might add," the barrister continued. "Only a little damage on the left flap. Perhaps a bit too much spirit gum, though…" he mused, trailing off as if in thought.

"Bah!" Marie declared, through her laughter, "Before you returned to practise at the bar, you never noticed such minor –"

"Deceptions?" inquires Phineas, his fond look removing the barb from his words.

"Minor courtesies, such as allow marital life to proceed more smoothly," his wife answered, causing his laughter to burst out with such gusto that an irritated Elspeth leapt from her Papa's lap and joined Mrs. Finn on the settee.

When his laughter had subsided, Phineas remarked, "I never could tell which of you corrupted the other."

Marie smiled. "Lady Glencora and I each educated the other in her own way, my dear," was all her reply.

"And what," Phineas asked, "does Mr. Savrola Vavasor want from me, I wonder?"

Smiling serenely, his wife advised him, "I couldn't possibly say. Better open his letter and find out, do you not think so?"

With another bark of laughter, Phineas did just that, and read the enclosed letter:

*September 16, 189_*

My dear Mr. Finn,

I am writing to you because, as you are no doubt aware, I have been placed in an invidious position vis-à-vis yourself and yours by the public quarrel foisted upon me by Lord Chiltern, whom I know to be closely connected to you. I hasten to assure you that I do not write to enmesh you in this quarrel, which I hope will be resolved by Lord Chiltern's recognition of his misunderstanding of my perfectly innocent conversation with one whom I greatly respect and, if I may say, admire, but to assure you that she of whom I write, Miss Clarissa Riley, acted with complete discretion and is entirely an innocent party in this foolish misunderstanding.

Phineas reeled from the length of this sentence, but, having spent some time in Chancery, managed to persevere. The letter continued, requesting an audience with Phineas at his chambers, or at his home. Savrola professed his respect for Phineas, across party lines, and desired an opportunity to speak with him about a matter of mutual importance, "though," Savrola wrote, "I daresay of more importance to me than to you, at any rate at the present moment."

Phineas drew on his pipe, and patted his leg. Elspeth knew the signal, and returned to him, curling up in his lap, and busily began kneading his leg. All the laughter gone from his face, he asked his wife, "Have you spoken with Clarissa?"

"No," she answered. "I wanted to see how you felt about the matter first."

Phineas stood up, dislodging the justifiably outraged cat a second time. She protested with a short yowl, and went off to complain to Meier.

"How do I feel about the matter?" Phineas asked. "Some young Tory—seemingly a good enough sort, from what I know of him, but whose mother is an exotic American lady who's in with the Prince a bit too tight for any decent woman, some say–"

"I seem to have heard similar things said—and by the same cats-about-town, too—about certain other ladies you ultimately came to like very well," Marie Finn replied, with her most inscrutable expression and tone.

"Am I being tug, Marie?"

"Tug?" she asked. "Translation, please."

"Pompous. Proud. Conventional."

"For a Fenian socialist flirting with Fabianism, my dear—you are."

"Am I a socialist?" Phineas asked.

"If half of what you said over dinner about the treatment of those miners in Wales is true, who could blame you?"

"It's all true," her husband answered. "The men—and boys, too—work beneath the earth, in the dark, with the constant fear of flood or fire. Their hours are long, their pay risible—disgracefully low. They have no homes but what McScuttle provides, no stores but those he owns—and at which he overcharges them shamefully, making sure they can never save enough money to get away from the mines. Legalised slavery, in short. The work is dirty, as well as dangerous, and when the men finally do get home, their wives boil water, and then pour it into a cast iron tub in the kitchen, and the men scrub themselves as clean as they may."

"Such things are not unknown, my love," remarked Mrs. Finn, in tones more sympathetic than her words.

"I know, I know. My father was a doctor in Ireland, you know—and not in the City. Still, there's poverty and poverty, you know. My father's patients weren't being poisoned by their work."

"And the miners are? You are sure of this? I mean, more than others who work in dirty environments"

"Oh, yes. The miners know it, too. They get tumors and growths, and die of cancer at appalling rates. And the dust down the mines kills them, too. They cough it up, and it seems to tear their chests apart. They call it black lung, and make grim jokes about their life expectancies—who will see out the coming winter, or how old Rhys has been knocking on heaven's door…and all of this against that constant backdrop of dark and dread, in the bowels of the earth."

"My dear, you sound as if you have been down there yourself."

"Of course I have, Marie. I went down as close I could get to the collapsed level where it all took place—where Powlett-Jones saved his brother and the rest. It was darker than anyplace I have ever been—darker than a starless night in the middle of the country. And close—the air from the ventilating furnace—a furnace, with all that fear of fire!—was stifling, hot, and damp, and you could feel the bits of dust and rock tearing at your mouth, your nose, your throat as you breathed them in and out."

"Phineas!"

"And the men joke, and sing, and pretend it's as normal as having breakfast with Oswald at the inn."

"Because to them, it is," Marie said soberly. "Normal is what you live every day, whether for weal or for woe. Women and men adapt to life under circumstances they could never have imagined, when those circumstances make up their lives."

"Now you are speaking from experience, I rather think." He walked over to where she sat, elegant, lovely, a lady in every line of face, form and accouterment, and, crouching before her so that their eyes were at a level, placed his hands lightly on her white shoulders.

"Indeed. I have told you of my youth, my dear," she said, meeting his gaze steadily. "But perhaps I have rather spared you the more sordid aspects of life in a ghetto. When you met Madame Max Goesler, you met a rather finer creation than the little shabby Jewish girl who knew hunger, and want every day, and who most of all longed to be free, not just of these grim specters, but of a society that said to her: These are all you deserve, little Jewess. Be grateful for them, for we let you live." She slid her arms beneath his, and rose, so that they were standing, in a loose embrace, and transfixed his eyes with her own.

"So my dearest one," she said, "If you wish to throw in your lot with these dispossessed who do not even know that is what they are, I shall as well. You wish to kick over the traces? Do so; we are invulnerable to the sneers of the cats-about-town. But where your heart lies, your mind and your arm must go. And I, of course."

She leaned in slightly, and kissed her husband on the lips.

"I am going up now," she said. "Do not be too long."

And with that, she left him.

Phineas sat down again, and picked up his pipe. He drew in a breath, and the crackling of banked fire in the bowl heralded the smoke as he pulled it into his mouth. Not quite the same, he mused, as those poor devils in Pontnewydd, or worse, Brynmawr. That had been the place to shock him, really. The company stores there overcharged by as much as a third, and between the ironworks and the mines outside of the town, much of the landscape had been so badly charred and gutted as to remind him of his Dante.

Returned from whatever foray she had been on, Elspeth brushed against his trouser leg, and reared up onto her hind paws. She jumped into Phineas's lap, and resumed her long-interrupted kneading.

Maybe it was the soothing influence of the affectionate little beast's presence, but he found his thoughts drifting into more hopeful facets of what he had seen in Wales. A young miner had gotten himself elected to the Urban District Council of Brynmawr, and had been delighted—but not overwhelmed—to meet an M.P. who was taking an interest in the welfare of the miners, especially in young Powlett-Jones, whose plight alarmed and affronted many of the men. Gwyn Jennings, his name was. Yes, he had potential. Part of this new Labour Party, and more willing to question the Liberal Party's verities than Phineas was, the pair had nonetheless struck up a rapport. Jennings had argued that the Liberal

Party was too rooted in tradition—in the Eighteenth Century and in the early Reform Laws—to be an effective advocate for the working men and women of England, let alone Wales, where their eyes seldom strayed. Over a tankard, Phineas, had tried to disabuse him of that notion, but had found himself half-persuaded to Jennings' arguments instead.

After nearly a full generation in Parliament, what had Phineas seen the Liberal Party accomplish on behalf of those most in need of its intervention? What help there was for the poor came mostly from the churches—and not even, always, the Established Church, but quite often fringe characters like "General" Booth and his ragtag Army of women and enthusiasts bringing "Soup, Soap, and Salvation" to the most hungry. Admirable, yes, if quixotic.

And then Phineas Finn bethought himself of how long it had been since he had done anything that could be termed quixotic, and his easy gibe at the Salvationists seemed cheap. But what did they do for the working man or woman? How could they play a role in reforming civil society, to bring justice to those who were so brutally exploited?

Could the Liberal Party? Could he?

Perhaps this trial could answer that last question, at least, he thought.

The cat, having had her fill of affection, leapt lightly down and darted off into the darkened portion of the house. Phineas knocked the spent ashes out of the pipe, and replaced it in the rack. Meier looked in, and inquired if "that would be all." Phineas bade the man good night, and began mounting the stairs toward the refuge of their bedroom, where he would find Marie, her comfort and good sense.

A CONJUGAL SCENE

Since he was so cruelly buffeted by the combatants, and then forcefully pressed by the Marchioness of Hartletop to partake of her hospitality, the Right Reverend Joseph Emilius had been conflicted in spirit, a rare occurrence for that man of great talents. Even a man of his social ambition and overweening desire for preeminence and attention could scarcely hope for greater public acceptance then to have the Marchioness expiate the sins of her guests by lionizing him among the bluest blood in England. And yet, the canny streak that had saved him from many vicissitudes warned him now that his place was perilous. Bishop Emilius had, in his youth, been a scholarly lad, and had read the tale of Icarus. The blazing sun, wilting wax-mounted means of ascent, and the headlong fall from dizzy heights were prominent in his mind in these days.

While the bishop was in no way amenable to the claims of English law—absent evidence that would not now, could not now, ever be provided, regarding a certain blow struck on a long-ago night—he was keenly aware that his great project stood upon a precipice. His social antennae were sensitive enough to know that the woman he desired to wed anew was herself accepted but gingerly, on the implicit condition, as it were, that she give no further cause for offense. Hence, his predicament. Those old enough to remember the precise nature of the scandal that had engulfed their marriage could, if given any ground to do so, connect the charming American bishop staying at the Hartletops' with the disreputable foreigner the mob had branded him back then. Were that to befall—well, he, like Icarus, could tumble from the skies, to the jeers of those who had once persecuted him. Indeed, the fall would be so easy to precipitate! In sum, were his name to be remembered in conjunction with the very woman whom he needed desperately to find and court, the game was up.

Yet the bishop was a man of some mettle, persistent, and not easily turned from his goals. He had, *certes*, several cards in his hand that might yet see him through.

First, he was ensconced in the most respectable, indeed eminent, of homes, and this by no request of his own. He was the invited guest of the undeniable doyenne of high society, a queen only slightly less eminent than she who wore the actual crown. And then there was his own not inconsiderable title—he was a bishop, and thus by definition a paragon of virtue. Aye, a paragon injured in a vain but valiant effort to maintain the peace in his hostess' own home.

What on earth had he been thinking when he had thrust himself between those two young fools, Emilius wondered, distracted for a moment as he ticked off these assets. He was a little ashamed to own it, but he rather thought it was the tear-streaked face of that young girl as her night of enchantment was shattered about her. He had, quite simply, pitied her. How ironic that she should belong to Phineas Finn! Ah, well, he had no objection to doing the fellow a good turn; he could even, in his own conscience, acknowledge to owing Finn one, or even two, of them.

So: He was a bishop, a brave man—a gallant bishop, then—and a member of high society, residing in the home of a Marchioness. Who in the world would look for an accused bigamist, suspected of other, darker, acts, in all of these?

Second, he had the sublime docility of the British public in its submission to the press. Yes, the press, his onetime harrier and foe, which had corrupted his splendid, English cognomen to a crude sounding Bohemian parody thereof. The two need never be connected again, as the memory of the former in his time in England had been utterly eclipsed by the taunting use of the latter.

But how to find Lizzie, he asked himself. Bishop Grantly had naively suggested that he, Bishop Emilius, ought merely ask the Marchioness where he could find his onetime wife, trusting to her encyclopedic knowledge of society. Of course, that very knowledge could, under even the most delicate questioning, bring about the very fall he earnestly desired to avoid. In any event, that risky course appeared to have been mooted by the serendipitous appearance of Lizzie at the Marchioness's ball, but her swift departure in the wake of the altercation that had laid him low meant that, after a promising start, he had no obvious way of finding her.

Staying with the Marchioness did have certain advantages, however, and one of them was the ebb and flow of pilgrims who came to adore at the Marchioness's shrine. She seldom favoured devotees below the rank of baronet with her physical presence, but those who presented themselves on her "at home" days would be entertained with tea and seed cake. As one of her two guests in residence—Bishop Grantly remained for the Parliamentary session—Emilius was getting to know a wide cross-section of Society, from tuft-hunters to toadies, fading Corinthians and aspiring courtesans, all seeking the imprimatur of Griselda, Marchioness of Hartletop.

Bishop Emilius had a gift for dealing with these aspirants, he found, effectively treating them as he did members of his flock. He simply encouraged them to share their hopes and fears, reposing trust in his (now-exalted) clerical status. In the old days, of course, he would have used the knowledge he gained from these conversations to increase donations to his ministry, either by using the information himself, or by encouraging the donor to support his ministry more enthusiastically, either as a penance for some sin revealed, or, more pragmatically, as a means of salving the ministerial conscience for withholding confidential information that could assist the police with their inquiries. After all, a member of the Church who was tithing—and the good bishop had never gone beyond requesting the biblical tithe, however tempted he might be; he was far too intelligent to drive his parishioners too far—deserved the protection and silence of his spiritual director.

He had no need for tithes here, of course; for the past three weeks, he had been extravagantly fed and housed by the Marchioness, and he had, unusually, been telling Lizzie the plain truth when he told her that his flock back home had amply provided for his needs. Still, he kept his ears open, looking for an opportunity to engineer a meeting with his former wife.

It was that old soldier with whom he had been speaking at the ball—the one who had sneered at Lady Laura—who finally resolved his problem. Not that Emilius had caught the old man in an indiscretion; rather, the old man gave him the information he besought out of sheer good nature—or, more likely, mischief. The old man's sharp eyes had grown sharper as he noticed Emilius subtly bringing yet another conversation to Lady Eustace, and, after the gull had left without enlightening Emilius, the old man snorted.

"Too subtle, bishop. Much too subtle for this rabble."

"General?" The bishop stalled for time.

"You're very interested in Lizzie the Liar, aren't you? Oh, aye, no need to pretend puzzlement—I've made that face myself, not knowing if I was with friend or foe. Friend. Well, as near enough as makes no difference."

"Lizzie the Liar?" Bishop Emilius asked, mellifluously.

"Oh, don't play the purring prelate with me, Joe!" the old soldier scoffed. "I was in England for that mummery with the family diamonds she pretended to have had stolen so that she could actually steal 'em herself. And the lady's proclivity for saying what old Swift would call 'the thing that is not' is common currency in Society, tho' no one will admit it."

The bishop looked askance.

"You still don't get it, I see. I know who you are," the old man rasped, "and what you were widely believed to have done back in the Seventies. And I don't care a rap."

He chuckled a bit at the bishop's wary expression.

"You're quite good, old son. Really, you are. You give nothing away. A lesser man would be declaiming innocence, striding up and down the room, all that music-hall nonsense. But not you. You'll leave me to make the running, until you're quite sure you're safe. Well, you are. Quite safe, I mean. From one rogue to another, I'll make it a free gift to you: Lady Eustace rides in the Park on Wednesday and Friday afternoons. She lives right off the Park, these days, in a townhouse old Florrie left behind. Her son owns it, but he's off at Cambridge, poor devil, studying Aeschylus—no doubt in an effort to understand his childhood."

"And where on the Park is this townhouse?" At long last, the bishop dared a question.

The old soldier smiled, pleased to see the fox break cover.

"East side. She lives on Green Street; rides 'til just before teatime and then goes in. You'll catch her there."

The bishop gravely thanked the old soldier, bowed to him, and prepared to leave the room.

"I'm not entirely sure I'm doing you a favour, mind you," the old man said as the bishop made his way to the door. "Lizzie was the death of old Florrie. Be careful she doesn't see you off, too, Your Grace."

The bishop turned, and bowed again, a touch of irony in his smile. "I am touched to the heart by your concern. But I, too, have studied my Aeschylus."

The old soldier smiled back. What a pair those two would make, he thought —if they didn't finish each other off, that is—and he reclined in his armchair, his uneaten seed cake ignored, as he drained the brandy-and-soda he favoured.

The following Wednesday, Joseph Emilius dressed with especial care. The day was moderately cool for October, the crisp air savouring more of September, with the last vestiges of summer still asserting their presence. The bishop promenaded about the Park's west and northern side, hoping to intersect with Lady Eustace's path rather than have to await her by her door. Luck, as had so often been the case with the bishop, stayed true to him, and he soon espied his onetime wife atop a sorrel horse, riding with great style and skill. Her riding habit of black with scarlet trimmings set off her deep, rich hair, and her formal high hat gave piquancy to her proud, lovely features. Emilius felt the old unquenchable yearning arise, unbidden, and, as she brought her horse to a full stop and the groom took the reins, he stepped forward to assist her from her seat.

Lizzie smiled down on him from her perch, and accepted his hand. She dismounted gracefully—even Lizzie Eustace's most caustic critics would acknowledge that she was graceful in her movements—and met her former husband's penetrating gaze.

"My dear Lizzie," he greeted her, "how very lovely you are today." His voice was a monotone, almost hypnotic.

She responded by raising her riding crop, and stroking his cheek with the thong. Lady Eustace's groom, having been in her service some time, studiously averted his eyes.

"My dear bishop," she said, mimicking his monotone, "how very familiar you are—to a lady not your wife."

"Not by my choosing," he answered, "and a mistake that I hope to rectify."

She trailed her whip down his cheek, to his neck, caressing him with it, lingeringly, slowly, down to his chest.

"It is rare, surely" she mused, "for bishops to presume upon their cloth in courting. Is such presumption worthy of punishment, I wonder"—and here the whip flew to the other side of the bishop's face, touching his cheek with just enough force to sting, but not enough to mark—"or is true Christian devotion to the state of holy matrimony, and thus to be encouraged?" And with these words, the crop began its sinuous downward path again.

The bishop's normal cool composure had given away to a strained sincerity. "I have come halfway around the world solely to find you again, that my joy might be complete."

"Oh, my dear bishop—or shall I call you my lord?—surely so romantic an answer as that warrants at the very least an offer of—tea. And I can promise you a savoury respite from the Marchioness' endless seedcake. Come," she said, crooking a finger and favouring her suitor with a smile that promised a signal absence of nursery fare, "into my parlor we go." And the bishop obediently trailed in her wake.

Lizzie Eustace's townhouse, Portray House, was, as the old soldier had told the bishop, not her own, but rather belonged to her son. It was named for the Eustace family seat, Portray Castle, and had thus far been left largely within Lizzie's dominion by the absence of the current Sir Florian, her son, who remained at Cambridge. Lizzie had furnished the house stylishly, with stark, vivid colours, paintings by Rossetti, Millais, DeMorgan, Archer, and others of that school. The black-and-white fantasies of Aubrey Beardsley could be spotted as well at irregular intervals, less colourful, if disturbing nonetheless. But Burne-Jones' "The Beguiling of Merlin" was given pride of place in her drawing room, opposite a startlingly vivid "Omphale and Heracles" –French, by the look of it, and thus indiscreet as a matter of course - and a small bronze of Diana and Actaeon. Damask swathes abounded in the room, and a small bookshelf within the mantelpiece itself sported morocco-bound editions of Wilde, Dowson, Swinburne, Keats, Huysmans, and Rossetti, along with a shabby little brown volume that the bishop recognised as an edition of the failed play from some years ago *The Noble Jilt.* Lizzie had flaunted her familiarity with German literature, as well; the rare complete set of *Das Vermächtnis Kains* occupied a shelf beneath a small table upon which stood a newfangled stained leaded glass lamp, adjoining what was clearly her favourite chair.

Lady Eustace bestowed herself upon her welcomingly broad leather wing chair. She looked over at the bishop, who, without waiting, had taken the chair opposite her.

"I may be seated?" he enquired smoothly, with a hint of cheekiness.

"Ah, Joseph," she sighed. "What a pity that a man so admirable in so many ways proved himself so utterly unsuitable a husband."

"My dear?"

"Do you honestly think I could entrust myself to you again, after you tried to wrest control of my fortune from me? I am no simple girl, to be ruled by a husband, but you tried to do just that."

"You are a girl no longer, beautiful as you are," he replied, "and I am not the man I was then—or, rather," he amended, with a much more open smile than was his wont, "I know better than to repeat the mistakes I made then. And, quite frankly, I no longer need to."

"Explain," she invited.

"As I said at out last meeting, Lizzie, I am rich. I am established in the American West, and any desire I have for suzerainty I have is more than amply fulfilled in my role there. From you, I want…what you clearly want." And he gestured about the room.

"Oh, Joseph," she laughed, "most excellently well done! And my fortune?"

"Shall remain your own. Use any lawyers you like, tie it up in any way they and you deem fit. My own means are abundant, and it is you only that I desire."

"Me only?" She smiled. "I believed every word you said…until those, Joseph. Try again."

"I mean, of course, that I do not desire your money. If you know of the sect over which I preside, you know that there is a wide scope for each of us to employ our God-given talents for the moral edification and instruction of those entrusted to our loving tutelage."

Her smile broadened just a touch. "You paint a lovely portrait, Joseph, but I think my *fiancé* might object."

It was his turn to laugh, now, a cross between a chuckle and a purr. "He is far more likely to object to your describing him as your *fiancé*, from what I have observed. My understanding is that, after he had beaten up another stripling over his attentions to some chit of a girl barely out of the nursery, he went on a spree in some low pub, and fled to Scotland. Of course, young love may have different conventions since I was last in the country, but I would hardly call that a propitious beginning to your engagement."

Lizzie Eustace frowned. "You always did have a flair for finding out all the scandal. I am surprised at my *fiancé's* absence from Town, I confess, but think you are taking a rather dark view of the circumstances."

"Oh? I have seen no announcement. And surely so noteworthy a betrothal would not have escaped my most vigilant eye." At this unwelcome truth, her frown deepened.

"It has been—delayed," she answered curtly. "But I have not released him from his promise, and I need not. If I marry Jack, I shall be Countess of Brentford eventually - "

"If his parents die before you," the bishop smoothly interrupted, "although, being in their—shall we say 'prime'?—they are not that much older than you are."

This observation was uttered with such an air of mocking gallantry that Lizzie's hold on her temper seemed about to fray, but she checked herself, and returned the compliment, with interest.

"—and you offer me 'suzerainty' over some cow town in America. Why, I cannot even be sure that, as your wife, I could be addressed as 'Lady Elizabeth!'"

"Are you so entitled now? And even if you were, my dear Lizzie, I assure you that if a question of protocol is too abstruse for you, it will not even occur to our little flock. And 'our little flock' is not quite accurate. My bishopric covers a region the size of Shropshire, and I am the ultimate authority there. And you would be, after me, absolute queen of–"

"Of the cows? I rather think not. As for 'suzerainty,' surely you mean after you, my dear?" Lady Eustace smiled lazily, confidently.

"In the eyes of the community, if not in fact," he temporised.

She laughed prettily, a musical sound. Her amusement was short-lived, however, and her tone sharpened. "And my lordling? If he should be unfaithful, as you suspect? What shall I do with him?"

"What do you wish to do with him?" the bishop asked.

"I could make him marry me, you know. The threat of a breach-of-promise suit, with all the resultant scandal, in addition to Jack's own sense of honour? Yes, I can still have him."

"If you want him," the prelate answered. "But why marry a man so unwilling—surely not merely for the chance of a title only a little more exalted than that which you already bear?"

Lizzie's pretty smile turned quite cruel. "Perhaps—to punish him? Perhaps—because the thrill of the chase can be savoured, not only by men, but by we of the fairer sex?"

"Would you ruin your own life for so brief a satisfaction?"

"Oh, Joseph," she said, "Ruin my life? No, sir, I would not. But a young man with a conscience is far more likely to suffer under those circumstances than a woman—at least, a woman such as I."

The bishop leaned forward, and urged, "He is not worthy of you, and you should not waste yourself on such a man. I can provide you with–"

"No doubt. But do I want that which you can provide? Tell me, Joseph, will my life with you be as—rewarding—as life with my little lordling? Can you offer me the satisfactions he can?"

"All of them, and more," he replied.

"I wonder. But here I am, prattling away about such matters without giving you tea! Shall I ring for tea, or would you rather see the rest of my art collection first? I have many *objects d'art* you might find—rewarding." And Lizzie loosed the power of her gaze on her onetime husband.

Deliberately keeping his voice steady and controlled, the bishop declared, "Let us satisfy our other senses before sating our appetites. The art, I think."

"Ve-ry good, Joseph," she purred. "Let me show you the way."

And rising from her chair, Lizzie Eustace led the good bishop from the room.

LOCHLINTER

Lady Laura Kennedy, as is well known, had become the chatelaine of Lochlinter upon the death of her husband, something over a year prior to the marriage of Madame Max Goesler to Phineas Finn. Reclining on the faded maroon plush of her seat on the train to the town of Linter, the nearest railroad station to the castle, Lady Laura looked out on the scenery with a jaded eye. How she had hated Lochlinter for these many years! Even during her husband's lifetime she had hated the dreary place, made yet more dreary for her by her husband's presence.

In their early days together, he had enforced his weary Sabbaths on her, depriving her of the political books that were her only connection to the partisan fray that was so vital a part of her life, let alone the novels with which she occasionally rested her busy brain. No—Robert had required her to read "improving" volumes of sermons, dating back, most of them, to the Seventeenth Century, as anything subsequent to that era was suspiciously latitudinarian, in his eyes. Later, before their marriage ruptured irrevocably, Robert had tried to win her to a more tractable course of behaviour by presenting her with Knox's *Trumpet Blast Against the Monstrous Regiment of Women*. The gift had only brought the day forward on which she bolted from him to her father's house.

Indeed, Laura could only remember one day at Lochlinter with anything approaching fondness—one sun-filled, pleasant day, spent in the company of Phineas Finn, a day that had ended in the triumph of receiving an offer of marriage from him, and then in the tragedy of her refusing him. A day, she had long been wont to remark to herself, that had wrecked her efforts to build a life fit for a woman of talent and ambition. But now, on the wearisomely long trip to Scotland, she had viewed the matter anew.

Yes, she had loved Phineas Finn. Yes, her love had been thwarted by her own well-meaning refusal to accept him. And yet, what a burden she had—she saw now—imposed on herself and on him! She had mourned their brief love for far longer than the time they had shared together, while he had built a life that gave him much of what she had pushed away.

It was not that she loved Plantagenet Palliser, she thought to herself, as the train neared the station. She could not be so quickly moved by a brief, if charming, encounter. Admittedly, she had felt something quite like the magic that had once passed between her and Phineas with the former Prime Minister. But not love. Surely not. Still, something in Laura had been awakened by the experience that led her to regret how much of life she had shut herself off from. Dour Aunt Laura, sour Aunt Laura, the brain-box and blue-stocking! She was, she must be, more than that.

The train was pulling into Linter. The bleak confinements of her brief married life to a man she had never been able to care for reached out to enfold her again. Not comfortably, like a blanket, but restrictively, like a strait-jacket.

She looked over at her sister-in-law. Violet had been, remarkably, sleeping in her side of their compartment. Laura found Violet comforting, but often unfathomable. So calm, when her son's state of mind could only be guessed at—when his acts had been increasingly rash and self-destructive! Laura, the boy's aunt, was desperately anxious about him, but his own mother was able to sleep these past hours away.

The train slipped into its berth, slowing, then stopping altogether, after a brief jerk, sufficient to rouse the Countess of Brentford. Violet came awake with a start. She looked out into the rain-swept morning, and recognised Linter Station. She stretched herself in her seat, looking less like the Countess she had been for so many years and more like the gamine who had captivated Oswald so long ago. Her own Aunt, the dreaded Lady Baldock, had once called her a "pug-nosed puppet"; for a moment, Laura, her friend since girlhood, admitted that the old dragon had not been entirely without foundation for what she still deemed a slander. A slander, yes, but a caricature of the real woman, and for a split second, Laura smiled at the old beast's metaphor. Silently, Laura vowed once again not to age, as she had been well on the way to doing, into a yet more fearsome version of that not-so-*rara avis*, the noble *dragonne*.

The ladies were the sole passengers for Linter. They got off of the train, porters trailing them with their baggage, and the stationmaster, whom Lady Laura had telegraphed from Edinburgh, had a fly ready to receive them. The stationmaster bustled out to greet them, fawning over Lady Laura with a brusque obsequiousness that only a Scot in the presence of his laird could manage. For five centuries, the lord or lady of Lochlinter had been the mainstay of the community; Lady Laura, though seldom physically present, was generous in her support of the estate. Where Robert had been close-fisted, Laura had used her inheritance to make the land bloom and the people and beasts of Linter thrive. The loyalty once shown to Robert's dreadful mother, and then to the Mad Laird himself, had, slowly but inexorably, transferred itself to Laura.

As the rain fell gently upon them, the ladies crossed to the fly and took shelter within. Their cloaks and bonnets had kept off the worst of the rain, but Laura felt glad to be in motion again; the Scottish chill had begun already to creep into her bones. Jack had always loved the weather here; her semi-annual duty visits had been lightened by his presence, and she regretted that, upon her death, Lochlinter could not go to him, the one person whom she knew who truly loved the place. Now it was his refuge, which she and the boy's mother were to breach.

The fly took them to the great gate, which swung open at their approach. Though stealth was not possible, Laura had hoped to arrive inconspicuously enough that Jack would not take warning and renew his flight. As the fly approached the house, Laura gazed once more on the imposing gothic pile of Lochlinter. Its rough-hewn stone and timber held no charms for Laura, but had enchanted Jack from his boyhood on. Odd, how she had let her blighted romance with Phineas colour her perception of the Great House that was hers for life, and that had so entranced her nephew. This time, she felt something new as she crossed the threshold. Her heart lifted as she entered the one place on earth whereof she was undisputed mistress, and she realised that here, at any rate, she had not merely done her duty; she had brought light into a dark place.

MacTavish, who had long ago replaced Robert's loyal man-of-work, swung the door wide. "Welcome tae Lochlinter, Lady Laura," he greeted his patron. And through his high manner, adopted to mark her arrival with the decorum he had always seen as her due, Laura recognised his pleasure in welcoming her.

How had she missed it? Lochlinter was alive with possibilities, its stones warmer than she had ever noticed before. The staff, the tenants, all those for whom she had provided out of duty, but more thoughtfully and generously than ever had Robert, had seen their lot improve, and noted that their Lady had loved them more than did their Laird. Both had, in truth, been distracted, embittered. But Laura's conception of duty had been deeper, more generous than Robert's. And now she had, at long last, the reward her pains had earned: she realised that she was loved, if only by her servants.

Now as she entered the great hall, and looked at the faded trophies of centuries past, an irrepressible smile broke through her formal mien. "MacTavish," she said, "Lochlinter has never been so welcoming in my lifetime." The little Scot bobbed his head, and clucked delightedly. As the housekeeper swept into the hall, Lady Laura greeted her with a smile. "Mrs. Quirt, how nice to see you."

"Lady Laura." The unsmiling countenance of the housekeeper did not change a jot as its owner curtseyed—but the curtsey was perhaps a shade deeper than usual.

Violet came in at length, looking about the Great Hall, which she had not visited in well over a decade. The two servants bowed and curtseyed respectively, and the countess advanced toward MacTavish. "Where is his lordship?" she asked.

"In the Library, m'lady," the little butler answered. And Violet swept off in its direction. Laura intercepted her briefly, and asked if her sister-in-law wanted her company.

"No," the countess replied, "let me see my boy first, Laura." And Violet continued her progression to the library. Laura instructed MacTavish to payoff the hired fly and Mrs. Quirt to make up the bedrooms for herself and her sister-in-law, and decided to take a look around this seemingly new Lochlinter.

Seated behind the heavy mahogany desk in the library, Jack Standish wondered which of the two women he dreaded seeing most, his mother or his aunt. These past days at Lochlinter had been a much-needed escape from the trap in which Jack found himself. But it was a temporary refuge from the trap, he knew, not a true escape, and his desperate cudgeling of his brains to find a sure way out of the snare lovely Lizzie the Liar had set for him—well, these efforts of Jack's had not borne fruit. As far as he could see, he was bound to marry Lizzie the Lamia (for Jack favoured Aristophanes over Aeschylus), or else, he supposed, be haled by the lady into court, where he would be forced either to convict himself out of his own mouth, or lie, and earn the righteous contempt of the woman he had already wronged by precipitately changing his mind after having once pledged his word.

But, no doubt irresponsibly, he had cherished his refuge from his predicament, and now the arrival of his mother and aunt signaled that the bill for his reckless folly had come due. The rap on the door—recognisably Mother's—heralded, not the arrival of a much-loved parent, but of that bill.

"Come in," he called, shooting his cuffs and straightening his tie. He rose and walked out from behind the desk, and crossed the floor toward the door. His mother met him near the center of the room, where she embraced him, and kissed his cheek.

"Hello, dear," Violet greeted her son, "how nice to see you."

"Hello, Mother," Jack answered guardedly. "Won't you sit down?"

"I will," she said, suiting the action to her words. She made herself comfortable in a large, throne-like chair. Jack retaliated by sitting behind the desk, opening a volume of Spenser, and immersing himself in it. His mother observed this, and let the silence stretch for a minute or two before breaking it.

"So, darling, did you happen to read your engagement announcement in the *Times*? Or perhaps in the *Jupiter*?"

Jack gave a guilty start, and tried to stammer out that the *Times* took too long to get to Lochlinter, and he didn't take the *Jupiter*, even when in London, so, no, he hadn't seen the—engagement notice did she say?

Violet looked at him coolly. She thought for a moment, as her son ran out of steam. "Oh, Jack," she said pityingly, "Thank heavens you never wanted to go on the stage. I've seen more convincingly feigned surprise from your Father, and we all know how hopeless he is at dissimulating. No," she continued, "you didn't see anything about your engagement, because your Aunt Laura found the letters Lady Eustace wrote you, and your Aunt Marie managed to, well, let us say, *persuade* the editors to suppress the announcement. So that, as far as I know, right now, only your aunts and I are aware that you have made an offer to Lady Eustace, and that she has, it seems, accepted you."

Jack Standish blushed. There was, quite simply, nothing he could say that would help him. "Mother, I–"

She waited for him to formulate some response. When none eventuated, she continued: "No, I was very pleased to hear that you were contemplating matrimony, although I would have preferred finding out about it from my son directly rather than from the press, so I should be grateful, I suppose, you left those letters behind. Your Father's breakfast would have been quite spoiled. But at least," and here Violet's voice rose a half tone, "at least you gave real thought to whom you should marry. And what an original choice of a bride you made! A woman with a son almost exactly your own age—no doubt you'll be good friends. As for Lady Eustace's reputation, well, what would you? On the off chance she can still bear *you* a son, any child she bore you would probably sneak your Father's watch out of his pocket and sell it to a pawnbroker!"

"Mother!"

"No, no, Jack, it's all right. I'll just lock my jewel case when you come to visit and hope my daughter-in-law doesn't force it open." And at last the brittle gaiety she had assumed broke down. "Oh, Jack," she moaned,

"She's a bad woman, my dear. You've gotten engaged to a bad woman, a woman who has no love in her, and will use your youth and abuse your trust." And the countess gave way at last to the terrified mother, holding back tears by sheer force of will.

Jack came out from behind the desk, and crouched down by his mother. He raised her chin, and met her eyes.

"I know," he said. "And she knows that I have come to realise that she is—what you have said. Don't you see, Mother, those letters were written to entrap me—to bind me to her, because she had discovered that I was desperate to break it off with her?"

"Truly?" Violet gripped his hands and gazed searchingly into his face.

"Of course! I realised I had made a fool of myself as soon as I came away from her to meet you and Father at the Finns' I don't know which was worse, the notion of presenting that—that simpering Jezebel—to Father and to you, or realising that I had pledged myself to such an artificial creature—when all along, the real flower was blooming away, right in front of me." He stopped, realising that he had disclosed more than he meant to.

"Clarissa?" his mother asked.

"Clarissa," he confirmed, "I know that she hasn't birth to commend her–"

"We can overlook that," his mother assured him.

"Or much money–"

"Nonsense, Phineas and Marie would see her right on that score."

"And she's not of our class, really–"

"Jack, stop." He looked at his mother. "All that you say is true, and in any other circumstance, would pose a difficulty. But Clarissa is the niece, and ward, of your Father's best friend—a man I esteem greatly, and of a woman who, though unusual—eccentric, really—I esteem almost as much as I do her husband. They move in our circles, have been loyal friends to us, and your father loves the girl already. I think a little qualified optimism is in order, here, I really do."

"Could you love her as a daughter, though?"

The mother weighed her answer. "Yes. She is a good girl, and one who is dear to many who are dear to me. If you love her, I shall as well." She paused for a moment. "I do hope that the idea that we'd find Clarissa unsuitable is not why you became entangled with the far less suitable Lizzie Eustace, my dear boy."

"No, Mother. Lizzie—Lady Eustace was very—charming."

The Countess made a noise that in a woman of lesser rank could only be described as a snort. "I have no doubt that she was, and suspect that 'charming' only scratches the surface."

"I really cannot describe how she made me feel."

"Not, at any rate to me, I suspect. Pray, Jack—don't try." Violet sighed. After a moment, she added: "You could do worse to confide in your Uncle Phineas, you know, Jack. He was a susceptible young man once, and would be more understanding than you may think."

"What am I to do, Mother? I do not believe for a moment that Lizzie will release me. And if she brings an action for breach of promise–"

"You must speak to your Uncle Phineas, Jack. He is a lawyer, and can advise you better than can I, or your father." Violet rose from her chair. "Come," she said, "we must let your Aunt Laura know that you have not gone mad."

Mother and son began to walk toward the door, arm-in-arm.

"Does she think so?"

"I am sure she is concerned," Violet responded.

As they walked to the door together, Violet began to laugh. Her son looked her, taken aback. "Oh, my dear, it's easy to see that you've been in Scotland." Her son regarded her blankly. "Simpering Jezebel? You sound like the Elder of the Kirk!"

For the first time since the disaster at the ball, Jack Standish laughed with a real sense of mirth. Together, mother and son went in search of Lady Laura.

"BUT HE HAS WON MY HEART"

Clarissa Riley had been withdrawn since the night of the Marchioness's ball. Simply, she had gone from exultation to terror in a matter of seconds. The instantaneous transformation of Jack, for whom she had long cherished a schoolgirl passion, even after she ceased to be a schoolgirl, from paladin to brutal thug, savagely attacking Savrola, pummeling a bishop, and then fleeing the scene of his crime—for crime it was to Clarissa, make no mistake—had shattered long-held daydreams and her very real affection for him.

In the weeks between the ball and her uncle's return from Wales, Clarissa had tried to come to terms with what had happened that night, with Jack's flight to Scotland, and then, with the shocking news that Jack was engaged to Lady Eustace. Aunt Marie and Aunt Violet had let that slip in their hasty putting together of a trip to Scotland for Aunt Violet and Lady Laura Kennedy.

Clarissa was revolted. Certainly Lady Eustace was beautiful, but she was surely old enough to be Jack's mother. And even if she wasn't, well, my stars, the stories about her that Clarissa had heard! She had been married, not once, but twice before, and, as if that and her age were not sufficient to debar her as an appropriate consort to her noble cousin-by-courtesy, she had been married to the very man who, all Society knew, had committed the murder for which Clarissa's own dear uncle had very nearly been hanged! Had Lady Eustace otherwise been in herself all that a woman should be, Jack should never have considered her just for these reasons. But in fact, in addition to her age, and her more than dubious connections and past, she was a woman of notoriously bad character.

Just how bad her character was, Clarissa could not say. She knew that Lady Eustace had a reputation for untruthfulness—Uncle had referred to her in conversation as "Lizzie the Liar", thinking that Clarissa was not paying attention—and she had heard Aunt Marie refer to Lady Eustace simply as a thief. More dreadful still, Uncle Oswald had once intimated to his son, while Clarissa was in the room, that worse yet remained undisclosed. Clarissa was not sure exactly what precisely this "worse" betokened, but clearly it had a dark edge to it, because Uncle Oswald was not easily shocked, and his reference to Lady Eustace had conveyed not just disapproval, but, well, shock.

At the ball, before all the trouble, Clarissa had seen Lady Eustace. She was, admittedly, very lovely, with her dark, abundant hair, wide eyes, red lips, and a lush but not overripe figure—but she also seemed somehow frightening to Clarissa. There was a barely restrained fury about her, and a hunger in her eyes that daunted Clarissa, and whispered to her that Lady Eustace was a woman on whose mercy she would hate to be dependent. How could Jack look upon such a woman and love her? What did this say about him?

And poor Mr. Vavasor—or, as Clarissa had already begun to call him, in her most secret heart—Savrola! Clarissa had liked him terribly. She had never had an admirer before, and, in fact, had found him charming—his rumour, his sense of the ridiculous, even his bumptiousness. She liked his bright blue eyes, his thatch of red hair, his surprisingly dainty hands. She liked that he liked her, and even better, liked that he recognised her as a woman, and one worth setting himself out to charm. Since the ball, although she had glimpsed him several times, she had not heard anything from Savrola Vavasor. She kept hoping she would.

On a Wednesday morning shortly after her uncle's return, Clarissa found herself in the library, browsing the illustrations in the new *Le Morte d'Arthur*. They were interesting, Clarissa thought, but rather fantastical to her tastes. There was something of Lady Eustace in them—overripe, not physically, but spiritually. Her uncle walked in, and kissed her good morning.

"My dear," he said to her, "I don't mean to drive you from the library, but I have an appointment in a few minutes, and had rather thought to speak with my visitor in here."

"And so you need to drive me from the library," Clarissa teased with a smile. "I shall go, then. But let me first pick out a book to take with me." And Clarissa began to scan the shelves. A respectful knock on the library door preceded Meier, leading in Phineas's visitor.

"Mr. Vavasor, sir," the butler announced.

"Show him in, Meier," Phineas instructed, and to her astonishment, Savrola Vavasor entered the room. Phineas greeted his guest as Clarissa began to walk out of the room.

"Good morning, Miss Riley," Savrola said to her formally, but with a pleasant smile. She noticed that the flesh around his left eye was still a little blue—the last remnant, she suspected, of a bruise inflicted by Jack.

"Oh, Savro-Mr. Vavasor, your poor eye!" slipped from her before she could stop herself. Savrola Vavasor's quick, delighted smile removed her compunction, as did his next words.

"It's well on the way to being healed just for seeing you, Miss Riley." And, indeed, both his eyes shone upon Clarissa in a most convincing fashion.

Uncle Phineas sighed, a little too loudly, and then said, in his normal kindly manner, "Perhaps you and Mr. Vavasor can visit with each other when we've discussed the business he wished to see me about, Clarissa. Will you be at home?"

"Yes, Uncle Phineas; I'll be in the conservatory." And, taking *Le Morte d'Arthur* with her in her confusion, she left, closing the door behind her. After ascertaining that Savrola required no refreshment, Phineas sat in a comfortable brown leather club chair, gesturing Savrola to its mate opposite him.

"Well, Mr. Vavasor," asked Phineas, "how may I be of service to you?"

Savrola Vavasor stirred uneasily in his chair. At length, he found his voice.

"Mr. Finn," he said, "I wish to ask your niece to marry me, and have come to ask your permission."

"I see." Phineas thought for a moment. "You cannot have seen her very often," he ventured.

"No, sir, only a few times. But enough to see that she is unique. Enough to have come to love her."

Phineas nodded, slowly. "And how do you know this?"

Even as the words left his lips, a sense of his own hypocrisy reproached him. Was Savrola Vavasor any less likely a suitor for Clarissa Riley than Phineas Finn had been for Violet Effingham? Or for Madame Max Goesler, back in the early days, when that lady had so signally made her views known? As to Lady Laura Standish, as she had then been, he could acquit himself of hastiness, remembering the hours upon hours of political discussion and strategizing they had shared before any thought of asking her to share his life had crossed his mind. Of course, he thought, that marriage had never taken place, and who knows how well suited they would have been, while the marriage he *had* made, to Marie, had succeeded beyond his fondest hopes.

Savrola was struggling to reply to Phineas's rather difficult question. "That she is beautiful," he answered carefully, "I need not tell you. That she is kind, I can attest from my own experience—her concern for myself and for the unhappy clergyman who was involved in the, the unfortunate events at the Marchioness's—

Phineas interposed, "I should tell you that Clarissa confirmed your account of that matter in every particular when I asked her. Had she not, my answer to your letter would have been quite different."

The young man relaxed somewhat, and smiled a bit. "I knew she was truthful, sir, and so had no doubt on that score, sir, but it is good to have confirmation that she is exactly as I knew her to be—blade straight, true and brave."

"Brave?" Phineas mused, a slightly quizzical expression on his face. "Am I so terrible a guardian that she should fear to confide in me?"

Savrola was young enough to take the bait. "No, sir! Not at all," he replied anxiously. "But she was brave enough that night—she didn't flee, but held her ground. Because of her courage, it did not become a question of my word against Standish's."

"Jack Standish is the son of my closest friend, and my godson," Phineas began.

"I know it, sir. And I do not mean to pursue any hostility against him for just that reason; I would not hurt Clarissa—Miss Riley—or yourself so."

Phineas nodded gravely.

"My point was merely to explain how I have come to know Clarissa's—Miss Riley's—sterling qualities. In answer to your question, sir, I love her, quite simply. And I believe that I could make her happy, if I were to be so fortunate as to win her heart."

And there it was, Phineas thought. His generation had taught their elders the limits of parental authority, and had themselves been similarly schooled—he thought of his friend the Duke of Omnium, forced to yield, after a longish struggle to not one, but two of his children; of Lady Laura, who had broken her marriage, and forced her father to champion her cause, despite the late Earl's belief in marriage's indissolubility, and of even an overbearing husband's right to the company and care of his wife. In each case, the strong will of the children and the love and lack of ruthlessness on the part of the parent had led inevitably to capitulation. No, Phineas had learned that the heavy father was a thankless role, to be resorted to only *in extremis*.

"We are of course, divided by politics," he commented neutrally.

"True, sir," Savrola agreed. "But we are both men of honour, and I have admired your willingness to take your own line when you disagree with your party."

Phineas smiled. "It is true that I am not the most faithful of disciples. But it is no way to get on, you know. Am I right in thinking that you will need office to support a family?"

Savrola shifted uneasily. A point to me, Phineas thought.

"Ultimately, yes," the young man admitted. "My late father left no estate, and my mother's means are ample to support her and myself, especially as my writing brings in a helpful modicum, but, yes, I will need to carve out a political career to support a family."

"Is that all you have to say?" Phineas enquired, "No questions about what my wife and I would do for our niece?"

Savrola's reply was almost a growl. "It's your niece I want, sir. I am no fortune hunter. If I am lucky enough to win Clarissa, I'll expect no more of you."

Phineas laughed gently. "You'll do, Vavasor," he said. "I have to admit that I didn't know your father; he'd left England by the time I arrived, but I can't say that I admired what I heard of him. No, no, don't get restive; I understand he was your father, and I mean no insult to his memory. Just to say that you at, any rate, seem to be made of good stuff."

"I am my father's son," Savrola Vavasor answered, "and I believe that my sense of honour came from him."

"Tell me what he was like." Phineas invited, curiosity getting the better of him.

"I don't remember him ever being well," Vavasor admitted. "His health broke when I was a boy, and he wandered in his wits until his death. He lost his seat in the House due to betrayal, and it embittered him. My poor Mother had to care for him, and he was very weak from my earliest memory of him. But he told me often of his struggles in Parliament, of his efforts to challenge the Old Bulls of the Party and bring about reform, only to lose his seat and his inheritance."

This was so wildly at variance with what Marie had heard from her acquaintance Alice Grey as to suggest that they were discussing entirely different men. Alice had described her cousin only reluctantly, and with loathing—as if their onetime engagement had so sullied her that even now, on the brink of old age, and after a long and happy marriage, the memory made her feel unclean. Despite this, Phineas retained his grave, pleasant demeanour. "Does this have anything to do with why you do not share his political allegiances?"

"Yes, sir, it does. How could I be a member of the party that had treated him so shabbily? And, in his latter days, his views had shifted—he thought that the only hope for the reform of England was the Conservative Party instilling a more democratic ethos—'Tory Democracy' he called it."

Phineas, considering the man under discussion, thought that Savrola must be reflecting the ravings of an embittered man who was seeking to justify his own failures, but he could understand the son's taking a different view.

"How did he lose his inheritance?" he asked.

"My cousin, his *fiancée*, was led to believe that he was unworthy of her, and their engagement broken. Worse, the rumours became so widespread that his share of the family fortune was left from him to my cousin, the father of the very same lady who broke their engagement."

"How very difficult that must have been for him, and for you," Phineas commented.

"Yes, sir," Savrola concurred, "You see, even now, after all these years, your view of my father has been formed by his enemies, and by the rumours they spread against him."

"He must have been very grateful to your mother, and all her care for him." Phineas probed.

"His illness made him too distracted, too uncomfortable to realise all that she did for him. He was tetchy, even to her."

"I hope, at least, he was kind to you."

"I was a disappointment to him," Savrola answered glumly. "Not good enough at school—mathematics were my bane—not as handsome, or as good on horseback, or on the playing fields as he had been. I'm sorry to say that I let him down all too often, sir."

"Did you? I wonder." Phineas rejoined. Then, choosing his words carefully, he continued, "Even the best fathers can make the mistake of trying to live through their sons, and holding it against them when they realise they cannot do so. My own father was a doctor, and long hoped that I would outgrow my love of politics and law, and follow in his own way. A father who was an invalid could all too easily fall into the trap of wanting his son to retrace his paths, with happier results, and resenting any deviation on the part of the son."

Savrola could not reply; emotions that he could not express had been stirred by Phineas's words.

Phineas stood up, and walked over to the fireplace to give Savrola a moment to master himself.

"Neither the Finns nor the Rileys are highly born," he said casually, leaning against the mantle and facing the young man, who had politely stood himself, again. "In that respect, your mother might think you are making a *mésalliance*."

Savrola's cheeky grin returned at this. "Mother's an American, you know," he replied, "and from the West, not the East, where they can afford to get stuck on these things. I may be a Vavasor on my father's side, but as a westerner, I'm a bit of an alley-cat on Mother's."

"And yet your mother has all of Society at her feet." Phineas said with a smile.

Savrola returned the smile, "She could charm a duck out of the water," he answered fondly. "She's the best mother a chap could have, Mr. Finn, and has the best heart in London."

"Have you spoken to her about your intentions?"

"I have. She admires your wife greatly, and tells me that she finds your reported speeches most diverting."

Phineas chuckled. "I find her charming already," he laughed, adding more seriously, "Savrola, you have my consent to speak to Clarissa. If she can love you, we will be happy to expand our family circle wide enough to encompass a Tory."

Savrola strode to Phineas and took his hand. "Thank you, sir!" he said. "With your permission, I won't say more just now, but, well, I should so like to see if she can spare me a few moments..."

Phineas's smile broadened. "Oh, I daresay she can. She'll be in the conservatory."

Gabbling his thanks, the young man left in search of Clarissa.

He found her in the conservatory, the sunroom at the back of the house in which she and her Aunt Marie had spent many happy hours discussing and planning the orchid displays in which both ladies delighted. Neither did the actual planting; Meier, whose passion for the flowers truly was extraordinary, cultivated them, nurtured them, and did so with the usual offhand competence that masked his fanatical attention to detail. Clarissa was looking at a particularly magnificent specimen Meier had successfully grown from a cutting. The orchid, a startling ebon colour, was Meier's crowning achievement to date, and even his assumed air of indifferent competence could not be maintained.

"You see, Miss," the butler was saying, "the *cymbidiella falcigera* is rare; quite rare. To grow it from a cutting has not, as far as I know, been done yet in England, and it is, I am pleased to say, thriving."

"It is extraordinary, Meier, but perhaps a bit—sombre, isn't it?"

"Sombre?" Meier asked, clearly shocked. Clarissa's laugh rippled from her, delighted to have just this once got in under Meier's stoic guard. Perceiving he was being made sport of, the butler shook his head mournfully, and prepared to make his departure. He did not sulk, precisely; rather he cast a reproachful look at Clarissa in the manner of a basset hound before whom a rabbit had the bad taste to frisk, inviting, as it were, the tired dog to give chase.

"Oh, Meier!" the girl exclaimed, "I am sorry. I am just a little nervous, because Mr. Vavasor has been such a time with Uncle Phineas."

"Mr. Vavasor, is it, then, Miss?"

Casting about to make sure that she and her old friend were not observed, she nodded wordlessly.

"And not, then, Lord Jack?"

Again ensuring they were unobserved, Clarissa shook her head negatively.

"Ah-h!" the servant breathed, "You are wise, Miss. That other, he would not make you happy, for all his rank."

At just that moment, a knock sounded on the conservatory door, and Savrola Vavasor was admitted for a second critical interview, more critical even than that which he had just undergone with Phineas Finn. Meier showed the young man in, and closed the door behind him as he left.

Savrola Vavasor never could remember what exactly happened thereafter. He remembered saying "Good morning, Miss Vavasor," and from there, events were a blur.

The historian's duty requires affirming that Savrola did, in fact, greet her as "Miss Vavasor," to which Clarissa replied, with a rippling laugh, "But I am Miss Riley!"

Without any thought, Savrola asked, "Oh, please, can't we change that?"

Laughing harder, Clarissa threw a sidelong glance at Savrola that completed his devastation and answered "To what? I can't be Miss Vavasor, it simply can't be done."

"No, but you could be *Mrs.* Vavasor, you know. Honestly, you could get used to me, and I do love you ever so much!" And seeing nothing forbidding in the blushing, laughing face of the girl he adored, Savrola promptly dropped to one knee, looked about, snatched a nearby rose from its stem and exclaiming, "Oh, the deuce!" when a thorn pierced his thumb, extended it to Clarissa with a wistful, hopeful look that touched her to the heart.

Clarissa had often dreamed of the eloquent and elegant marriage proposal to which she would ecstatically yield her consent, she had never dreamed that she would be laughing as she accepted it.

Some time later, when Savrola, his wounded thumb nicely bound up in Clarissa's pocket handkerchief, had pulled a ring from his waistcoat—"Not Mother's," he assured her, "that one brought neither of them luck."—kissed her, and was led to the door in a state of dazed joy, Clarissa drifted gently into the Library where her uncle, pipe wafting its fragrant smoke aloft, was moodily staring into the fire.

"Well?" the nervous uncle asked.

"Mr. Vavasor has asked me to be his wife." Clarissa said, her voice suspended between laughter and tears.

"And?" demanded Phineas Finn, the suspense beginning to get under his skin.

"And—and I have accepted him."

Putting his pipe down, Phineas walked over to his niece, gently took her hand, and led her to the settee, where they sat down together.

"Are you sure?" he asked, adding, "He does not have money, his politics are not ours, and his family has a tragic history."

"But he has won my heart," Clarissa answered.

BEFORE THE TRIAL

Ifor Powlett-Jones looked smaller and younger in his prison uniform. Ill-fitting and rough, it accentuated the youth's pallor and his schoolboy air. Phineas noted the kindness the boy evoked in the warders, and drew some comfort there. Still, his interview with Ifor had not gone as well as he had hoped. The young man was falling into despair, he feared, and had listened very politely to his barrister without taking much on board.

His solicitor, the younger—or, to give him his proper place in the sequence, the youngest Mr. Camperdown, seemed to have the same concern. As they walked away from the Scrubs, he murmured to Phineas, "No fight left in the boy."

"I know," Phineas replied.

"He put a good face on it for months, but now the jury will look at that lugubrious wretch and know he's guilty," the solicitor complained.

"They may think it, but they'll know nothing of the kind. He acted with the intention of saving life, not damaging property."

"Oh, aye? You can make that argument, Mr. Finn, but when the prisoner in the dock is staring down at his shoes like a whipped cur, all the life gone out of him, what else are they to think than that he's guilty?"

"That he's been locked in a box for months, in a foreign country, with nobody to speak to but warders who presume he's guilty because they presume everybody's guilty, and with prisoners who mostly are guilty? That he's terrified and confused because he saved the lives of every man-jack who got out of that collapse, and instead of thanking him for it, society is looking to put him in prison until he's a very old man, indeed? Maybe, just maybe, they need to understand that a boy his age can't be locked away from the sun, the grass and fresh air for months at a time without being reduced to a terrified wreck."

Mr. Camperdown snorted. "Tell that to a juryman from Whitechapel—he'll have a laugh at that. Or elsewhere in the East End. Limehouse salubrious enough for you? Or our factories? Much sun and light you'll see in one of those. What about the chimney sweeps? Did you hear about the sweep's boy who got caught in some toff's chimney and died in the flue because the sweep was too drunk to realise the boy had grown and the toff's lady wife didn't understand the lad was actually going up there, and could get stuck?"

Phineas looked at the normally quiet Mr. Camperdown with a new eye.

"You're not the quiet, careful lawyer your father is, then, are you Mr. Camperdown?" he asked.

"I'm every bit as professional as he is, Mr. Finn, but I see what's happening in Britain, even if he doesn't. And even if you don't either, being in Parliament and all."

"What do you mean?" the astonished Phineas asked.

"Money is pouring in from all around the world. British trade has never done so well as it is doing now. But do we invest the money on making England—let alone Wales!—fit to live in? We do not, Mr. Finn. We treat the working men—and women—aye, and children, too!—like slaves, not caring if they drop dead, and do even worse for the really poor—we just let their part of Town rot, not even sending in the Law until some lunatic is cutting up women we neither care about nor even notice till after they've been butchered."

Phineas winced a little at the memory of the rash of killings in Whitechapel a few years ago.

"I'm no Fabian, Mr. Finn, let alone anything more extreme. But all those cranks and agitators? Heaven bless me, I sometimes think that they are closer to the truth than we good drab lawyers are."

And the two men parted, leaving Phineas troubled. Troubled, not just about the state of his political soul—those concerns had been percolating through his mind since his visit to Wales—but, far more prosaically, about the state of his case. He knew that he had a sympathetic client—if he could but rouse the lad from his despairing torpor—but knew that he needed more; a justification for the jury to acquit. He remembered what Low had always said about juries, and for a moment could see his old pupil-master not as he was now, but in the flood of health, his finger stabbing upward in a minatory gesture.

"A jury," Low had been wont to declaim, "has the right to discharge any accused for any reason—or at any rate, the power. But it is not enough for them to want to exercise that power. It is the duty of the barrister to provide them the legal grounds upon which they may lawfully and properly exercise that right."

Phineas had not yet found that legal ground. He mounted his carriage, and instructed the driver "Home."

As the carriage rattled off toward Park Lane, he changed his mind. Why had he not had the sense to run all of this by Low months ago? If anyone could see a legal justification—or excuse, even—for the boy, it was Low! He rapped the roof of the compartment with his stick, and heard a sepulchral "Sir?" from the box.

"Change of direction, Williams. The Lows, instead."

"Very good, sir," the coachman sighed resignedly.

Phineas pulled out the gold hunter Marie had given him for his last birthday, when old Doctor Finn's open-faced watch had finally given up the ghost. With any luck, Phineas would arrive in time for tea, and Mrs. Low would delight, as she always had, in spoiling Phineas.

Years ago, of course, she had felt the need to keep her husband's *protégé* on the straight and narrow—deploring his too-early pursuit of office, for example and his original decision to leave the bar and devote his full time to political life. But when his hour of trouble had come upon him, Georgiana Low had been staunch, as had her husband. And when Phineas had come through, she had not rejoiced, but simply nodded, declaring that she had always known that justice would be done.

For a few weeks after Phineas's marriage, she had been over-awed by the glamour of his wife and her dazzling resources. But Marie had soon won her love, her own continental common sense dovetailing nicely with that of the barrister's wife. Mrs. Low's affection for Phineas had only grown in the years he had kept the practise afloat, to the point that her scolding was transparently an expression of her maternal regard for the Irishman.

After he rapped on the door, and was admitted, Mrs. Low beamed at him, greeting him with words that belied her evident pleasure at his arrival.

"Phineas Finn!" she declared. "Just dropping in for tea, young man? Uninvited? Well, I suppose you must have some. Still, if you had given me some warning, I could have laid on something a bit nicer for you. As it is, you'll just have to make do."

And taking Phineas by the hand, she led him into what the Lows called, quite inaccurately, the Combination Room, which in any other home would be the parlor, but which had bookcases on all the walls, stuffed with legal *curiosae* and treatises, from Eames's *Glanville*, to the new Selden Society edition of *The Mirror of Justices*, as well as a first of *Blackstone*, prettily bound in buckram with rich red and gold titles. Low's reading had always been wide, but in his forced retirement, it had broadened even more; Phineas espied a copy of the controversial American tome, *The Common Law*, which Low had pronounced sound, if disconcerting, after meditating on it for six months.

The old lawyer was leaning back in his favourite chair, an old battered wooden basket with a high back and arms. He always had sworn it was more comfortable than any armchair he had ever sat in, and when it became clear to him he could not expect to return to chambers for an indefinite time, he had asked Phineas to bring it to his home. Phineas complied, of course, and Low was comfortably settled in it, with a little table at his right hand. The barrister was sallower than he had been when in health, and breathed a bit more stertorously than in those days, but, in a well-worn brown suit and a crimson dressing gown, looked alert enough, eyes lively, moustache drooping over his lip.

"Phineas!" he greeted the younger man enthusiastically. "What brings you here, my boy? Take a seat, give me all the news." And his eyes gleamed hungrily for a problem to distract his too-long unchallenged mind.

"A case, Mr. Low, that's due for trial in two weeks, and which I haven't quite found the right theory for."

"Oh," the old man asked, "a bit at sea, Phineas? That's not like you. Tell me all about it."

And Phineas did just that, with Mrs. Low silently directing the parlourmaid as she set up the tea things and brought in the tea and cakes—cakes that had clearly been baked that very morning, belying Mrs. Low's warnings of the meager fare to be expected. After he finished rehearsing the facts of the case, including his visit to Wales, Phineas found himself with an appetite.

"Necessity," said Mr. Low.

"Hmmmph…," replied Phineas Finn, finishing a slice of tea-cake. "I thought of it, of course, Low," he clarified, "but then I remembered the case from about ten years ago—you know the one, the wrecked sailors in the dinghy who were lost at sea for weeks, and cast lots to see which of them would be eaten…"

"What a ghastly thing to discuss over tea," Mrs. Low interjected, clearly not at all disturbed by it. "More cake, Phineas?"

"Yes, please, Mrs. Low."

"You of course are referring to *Regina versus Dudley and Stevens*, Phineas," the senior barrister said.

"That's the one, Low. They defended on the ground of necessity, and were convicted."

"So you ruled necessity out, did you?"

"Only after making sure that Lord Coleridge disallowed the defence," Phineas rejoined. "After all, the mere conviction does not say very much. But I looked up his opinion, and he rejected the very notion of a necessity defence."

"To a murder charge, indeed, he did. But what happened to the unfortunate sailors, Phineas?"

"They were pardoned. I don't want to have to rely on a pardon, Low."

"Why not? You're a member of the party in office at the moment. Still, I take your point; they may not be reliable in such matters. Oh,

Phineas, Phineas! You never did have the tenacity to be a truly first-class lawyer!"

The old barrister laughed at his onetime pupil's hurt expression.

"Not that you haven't been a good friend to Georgiana and me, and not that you haven't done a splendid job at keeping the practise up, Phineas, but you never did care to dig through the books, my boy. Help me up will you?"

Phineas helped the older man from his chair, his wife handed him his stout ebon stick, and with some support from Phineas, the sick man tottered into his study, a squarish room just off the parlor, swathed with dark green drapes and furnished largely in browns and greens. Mrs. Low swiftly turned on the gas lamps, while her husband made his way to a large bank of small drawers, each with a small label in Mr. Low's spidery hand. The light brown wooden cabinet, which ran nearly the length of the wall, had been known in chambers as Low's "ready reckoner," a summary of every case decided by the courts of England, and every treatise the old man had read, since the day he was called to the bar.

"D," the older man murmured, "D for defences, subset N for necessity." He found the right drawer within seconds, and, as it was closer to the floor, asked for a chair, which Phineas supplied. Low sat down, and pulled out a drawer expertly; he ruffled through the little cards and pulled one out, wedging a blank card perpendicularly to keep the withdrawn card's place.

"Here it is: 'In every law–'" the old man intoned with relish, pausing to interject, "–that bit's probably an overstatement—still—'there are some things which, when they happen, a man may break the words of the law, and yet not break the law itself; and such things are exempted out of the penalty of the law, and the law privileges them, although they are done against the letter of it, for breaking the words of the law is not breaking the law, so as the intent of the law is not broken. It is a common maxim, *Quod necessitas non habet legem*.'"

"Eh?" Mrs. Low asked.

"Phineas?" the elder barrister invited.

"Right, 'That which is necessary has no law.'"

"Oh, dear, worse than I would have expected. *Necessity has no law.* It is from *Reniger versus Fogossa*, 1550; Serjeant Pollard's argument." The old man looked contentedly around the room. "You can make something of that," he said.

"I don't see how," Mrs. Low stated. "The other boys—the sailors—tried just that, and failed."

"Yes, yes, Georgiana—but that was a case involving cannibalism, my love; this is the tearing off a component of a piece of machinery to save the lives of the men. The former is a little more ethically fraught, I feel sure we may agree, yes?"

"True," Phineas added, "but I am concerned about the whole political aspect of the case; the notion that Powlett-Jones was interested only in getting at the boss is madness, of course but the mine owner genuinely appears to believe in it."

"Did you not tell me that one of the trapped miners was your client's own brother? I should think a jury more likely to believe that was his motivation, shouldn't you?"

"Just so, and yet, I can't help but think that this case is likely to be presented as a case of the rights of property."

"Perhaps," the old barrister replied. "Still, at least you have something to go on—an alternative way to frame the events. At any rate, that's better than nothing."

And with that, Phineas Finn realised, he had to rest content. Not so Mrs. Low.

"So, Phineas, my dear," she said, as the party returned to the Combination Room and tea, "we read the announcement in the *Times* about your niece Clarissa's betrothal to a Mr. Savrola Vavasor. Are you and Marie pleased?"

"We are, Mrs. Low," the younger barrister replied. "He's a good lad, and I think he'll go far."

"Is not his mother—a trifle…fast?" Mrs. Low asked, concerned.

"Perhaps a little," Phineas acknowledged, "but she is an American lady, and a little less versed in our way of doing things than might be ideal. Still, when Marie had her and Savrola to dinner, she was remarkably friendly, and really quite gracious."

"Bad blood on the other side," Mr. Low commented.

"You mean George Vavasor?" Phineas asked, and, at his pupil-master's nod, agreed. "Yes; a dreadful man, from all I've heard. But his cousin Alice and the rest of his family are good people—even though they are on the other side politically, as is Savrola."

"First good thing I've heard about the boy," grumbled Low, who was beginning to tire.

"This, too—he loved his father as much as that wreck of a man let him, and has tried to redeem his errors by living a better life. I'd have preferred a good Liberal," Phineas confessed, to a snort from Low, "but he seems to me a good boy. In any event, I think Oswald—sorry, Brentford—was rather relieved; he didn't have to decide whether to approve a *mésalliance* between my niece and his son, which he was vacillating about all the time we were in Wales, and Savrola has made it clear to him that he will hold no grudge against Jack. Besides, Savrola has passed the two most important tests, Mrs. Low," he added with the cheeky grin that Mrs. Low could not withstand, even now.

"What's that?"

"Most importantly, Clarissa loves him. Almost as important, Marie likes him—and then, to cap the globe, Meier knows no bad of him."

"Meier? Your butler, Phineas?"

"Hardly just that, Mrs. Low; Marie's eyes and ears. If he'd been a bad 'un, Meier would know."

"Abner," Mrs. Low said to the older barrister, who was just beginning to doze, "Did you hear that? Marie has a kind of spymaster for a butler."

"D—d clever of her," snored the old lawyer, and surrendered to Morpheus.

Mrs. Low made a helpless little gesture, and escorted Phineas to the door. "Thank you for coming, dear boy. It means a great deal to me, and even more to him. Was it helpful?" she asked.

"Oh, yes," Phineas answered. "Very helpful indeed. I'm not sure we can get him off with necessity, but Mr. Low always taught me that even if they want to let a fellow off, you still have to show them a way to square it with their consciences. I think we may be a lot closer than we were two hours ago." And with that, Phineas kissed his hostess good-bye, leading her to make the noises commonly recorded as "pish" and "pshaw" even while she blushed with pleasure, and told him to save such nonsense for Marie. As the door closed behind him, Phineas walked off in the direction of Park Lane, his heart a little lighter.

MATCHING PRIORY

Matching Priory, the residence of the Duke of Omnium when not in town—for he had ceded Gatherum Castle to his eldest son, Lord Silverbridge and his bewitching American bride, the former Isabel Boncassen, well over a decade ago—was especially dear to the Duke. Likewise, the old M'Cluskie place on the banks of Loch Lugan had gone to Lord Gerald, his younger son, on his marriage eight years since, while the Horns and the town house in Carlton Terrace belonged to his daughter, Lady Mary Tregear. The Duke had even purchased a second house in Town and deeded it to Silverbridge, to facilitate his attendance at the House. Alone of all his properties, Matching Priory the Duke had retained for himself, and he made himself at home there when he was not staying with the Tregears.

Many of his acquaintances found this love of the Priory strange. Matching was no showpiece, unlike Gatherum (which had obtained its admittedly silly name from a royal jape during a visit from the King on a visit soon after the Restoration, and which no duke would alter). Still, prone as he was to endow his children with all good things, it had not been generosity alone that had led him to retain only Matching for his own use.

This is not to say that Matching lacked its attractions. It was a large building, very pretty, with two long fronts; but it was no more than a house. It was neither a palace, nor a castle. One could hardly call it a mansion without exaggeration. Matching's claim to prettiness came in part from its gabled roofs, four of which surmounted the side of the house from which the windows of the drawing-rooms opened out upon a lawn that served to separate the house from the old priory ruins. Indeed, the lawn not only led to, but surrounded, the ruins, and crept inside them, creating a kind of flooring within the old chapel, the old refectory, and some of the old cloisters. The walls of the cloisters had in large part survived intact, despite the iconoclasts' best efforts during the Civil War, and where they stood, the stone pavement remained. But within the square of the cloisters, ruin had prevailed, and the floor was all turfed. The old Duke, in his frivolous way, had in his youth placed a large modern stone vase in the center of the open space, and out of its broad basin depended green tendrils and flowering creepers, trailing to the turf, and resting thereon. In sum, a charming house, but a surprisingly modest residence for the Duke of Omnium, and for a former Prime Minister.

But Matching Priory was where the Duke's fondest memories had all taken place. It was at Matching that his wife had been least distracted, most affectionate; at Matching, she had found some peace in her often fretful, often sensation-seeking life; and it was at Matching, in the never-deconsecrated grounds of the ruined Priory, that her remains had been laid to rest. The local vicar had quailed at this, claiming it was irregular in the extreme, but the bishop of Barchester had overruled him—not, the Duke felt sure, because of his status as a peer of the realm, but because, as one widower to another, he had seen into the Duke's grieving heart, and was not minded to deprive him of any solace.

In the chill of a late October afternoon, the Duke was in the ruins of the old Priory, at his Duchess' grave. Over the years since her death, Plantagenet Palliser had spent much time here, at Matching, communing with her ghost, in a way, telling her all the troubles of each day, as he watched his children strike out in their own directions—Silverbridge making a bit of a name for himself as a legislator, Gerald as a Scots laird, Mary as the wife of a Conservative member of the House—which last still chafed the Duke, on occasion, although his son's return to the fold had long ago plucked the bitterness of that fact from his heart. Of late, he had taken to telling her of their grandchildren—little Planty, a small Marie, named for her closest friend by the daughter who had found in

Mrs. Finn something of a substitute for the mother too soon lost, and a Gerald, named in graceful salute by the eldest brother for the younger.

He saw Glencora's influence in each of them, children and grandchildren alike, and was glad of it—gladder of it, admittedly, in the grandchildren than in his own children. The waywardness of his children in their youth had been a burden to him, but now, in a sense, he missed it. For, he admitted, he was lonely now that they had plunged into the full stream of their own lives and cares. Oh, they were good to him, loving and affectionate, Isabel, especially, making room for him in her heart, but their own concerns predominated—as indeed they should, he reminded himself with his usual justice.

And he loved his grandchildren, in his slightly dry, rather hesitant manner. Fortunately, little Marie saw past his shyness with children and ran to him without reserve, but little Planty already had his grandmother's wiles and wit, teasing him with one breath, and wheedling treats out of him with the next. How he wished that Cora had lived to see them! She would have delighted in them, swooping down to spoil them with her familiar wry smile, knowing that the games and pleasures of the day were both means and ends to their little hearts. Cora could have romped with them, outfoxed them, and made them love it—as indeed she had so often done to him. He lacked that spontaneity, and it grieved him.

Of late, his visits to her grave—for to him, the whole ruin was now her shrine—had been rote, an effort to recapture a communion with her spirit that had faded over years. Wherever Glencora's soul was, he could no longer feel her presence, except as a memory. And, though he yearned for her with all his heart when he turned to those memories, he had realised that, quite simply, he did not wish to grow old alone.

Plantagenet Palliser had ever been one of those men who did not seem young when they were so, and now that he was nearing old age—for he had not been fifty when his wife died, and was not yet sixty, though it loomed—did not seem old. He had so dedicated himself to work that its demands had made him middle-aged in the flood of his youth, and yet his vigor was still unimpaired. When he had been invited to the Marchioness's ball, he had been, he could admit to himself now, curious to see how Griselda had aged. Long ago, he had come quite close to defying convention, and the expectations of his family, by asking her to run off with him, soon after her marriage to Lord Dumbello—she, a mere nobody, Griselda Grantly, merely the daughter of the Archdeacon of Barchester. The cool refusal of the lady herself had thwarted that plan, and the resultant swift action of his uncle, his predecessor as Duke, had led to his marriage to Glencora. After more than a decade as a widower, Plantagenet had been mildly curious to see her again.

He was astonished at her evergreen beauty, as were all men, but her iciness repelled him. Had this been all that she was when he had so desired her in the flower of her youth? Had she, even in those days, been, not a warm, living blossom, but merely a brilliant facsimile, carved in ice? If so, he had his decades with Cora to thank for no longer desiring a woman who gave nothing but an imitation, however artfully crafted, of life. Life with Cora—her quicksilver moods, her laughter and caprices, and the warmth that underlaid them all—had unfitted him for life in the Arctic regions in which the former Griselda Grantly's spirit resided.

Far from being disappointed, Plantagenet found himself relieved by the Marchioness's lack of allure. Oh, they had bowed and smiled to each other, and she had been perhaps a touch less frosty toward him than to her other guests, but so chilly a warmth he would as lief be spared. No, he had been preparing to leave the ball when he found himself roused to anger by the mistreatment of a lady, and then found himself, surprisingly, drawn by her company.

Lady Laura Kennedy! Tall, one could almost say gawky—Cora's favourite word for the lady, in truth—yet somehow nonetheless a fine figure of a woman, even now, and one whom he knew to be earnest and good. Plantagenet Palliser had always liked women, found feminine company more enjoyable than that of men, and he had always taken pleasure in Lady Laura's good sense, and in her political acumen. He was surprised to find himself thinking of her as charming, though; it was not a word he had ever applied to her previously. Charm was a word he associated with Cora, and it was a surprise to him now, nay, almost a shock, to associate it with so different a lady.

He had not danced since Glencora's death.

He had been jovial at his children's weddings. He had made toasts, welcomed Tregear, Isabel, and Agnes to the family, as well as their relations; he had carried himself so that all men said that he was a man of few cares, one who took special joy in the happiness of his children, and was thoroughly contented to see them marry after their own hearts' inclinations.

But he had not danced.

One pair of eyes there had been, sharp enough, and shrewd enough, too, to see through his gaiety. And now, confronted with two facts, the meaning of which he could not be sure of accurately deciphering on his own—that he did not want to grow old alone, and that he had, only just recently, danced—he felt he needed to call upon his old friend, and more than that, *her*, Cora's, special friend and ally, for yet another kindness after many already received by him and his from those trusted hands.

The Duke rose from his perch on a little marble bench commanding the best view of the ruin, and walked swiftly across the lawn and into the house, not stopping until he was in his study, at his desk. He wrote:

My Dear Mrs. Finn,

I find myself in need of advice respecting a matter of which I fear I am no competent judge, and can think of no person whose judgment would be of greater assistance and worth to me than would be yours.

I intend to be in Town a week hence, and beg leave to wait upon you at your earliest convenience.

Pray extend my kindest greeting to Mr. Finn, whom I look forward to seeing in Town.

Faithfully yours,

OMNIUM

Three days later, by return of post, he had her prompt answer:

My dear Duke,

Of course I am happy to provide any assistance to you of which I am capable. Your letter sounds urgent; I shall make myself available at any time you care to name.

I remain, very truly,
Dear Duke of Omnium,

M. Finn.

The Duke was tempted to send back a line disclaiming any urgency, but did not how to do so without involving himself in a lie. Worse, how could he call upon Mrs. Finn to hold herself ready to advise him in so delicate a matter, and then insult her by treating it as a triviality?

No, wisely or not, the Duke realised, he had exposed his unsettled heart to her, and, to at least obtain the benefit flowing from his confession of vulnerability, could not retract it. Besides, he thought, she knew him too well, and knew that the mere fact of his asking for advice was extremely rare. In the three days that passed since he had written his letter to her, the Duke had thought of flying to London immediately, rather than waiting the whole week he had mentioned in his letter. He had been uneasy since the mailing of his letter, and the receipt of hers this morning had not set his mind at rest. Rather, like a patient confronting a dentist for an extraction, he was growing palpably anxious about what Mrs. Finn would say to him.

Would she accuse him of infidelity to the memory of her closest friend? Or would she jeer at him as an old man who sought to join in the laughter and life of his fellows all too late? Having missed the ball, as it were, and without Cora to mediate the world for him, was he fit for nothing but the long political grind and then solitude?

As the Duke fretted over his morning coffee, Mrs. Finn's reply at the side of his plate, he fancied he heard a bit of a bustle outside, near the door. Hopefully not some messenger from London with another white paper that Barrington Erle needed his opinion on, the Duke thought to himself, and poured himself a little coffee rather than ring. As he took a sip, he sighed, hearing voices and a clattering in the hall. He stood up, to meet whatever jack-in-office the Prime Minister had chosen—really, it was intolerable to have all the cares of office with none of the ability to directly influence things, Plantagenet thought, not for the first time, as he strode out of the dining room and into the hall.

Where he beheld Marie Finn, casting off her wet hat and coat, handing them to the housekeeper and calmly ordering a fresh pot of coffee to be brewed.

"My dear Duke, you have only yourself to blame." So said Mrs. Finn, as she refreshed herself with a second cup of coffee. "You are not known for seeking counsel, my friend, and generally when you do so, it is genuinely important."

"But I had no intention, Mrs. Finn, of dragging you from your home and family…"

"*Sicherlich, tatsächlich*. But here I am, Duke, because my husband, who is preparing for a criminal trial, was almost as concerned as was I, but unable to come down with me. And, knowing you as we both do, we immediately concluded that you were wishing you had specified an earlier day, while refusing to advance your timetable by an instant."

At this, the Duke had to laugh.

"Am I so stubborn, then?"

"But of course! But 'stubborn,' no, that is not the word. 'Self-denying'? That seems closer to me, Duke. Do you not yet understand that you have friends who love you, and to whom you can repair without setting an appointment a week in advance? That to see you is not a burden, but a pleasure? And that if you need our help, we are only too ready to provide it?"

"I am justly reproved," the Duke answered.

"You are," she replied, "but only because you should know by now that too much diffidence can be a denial of friendship in its own way. So, as a friend, I demand: tell me how I can help you."

Again, the Duke laughed, this time more readily than before.

"Ah, Mrs. Finn," he said, "What have I done to deserve a friend such as you? Very well, I shall."

And the Duke unfolded his story to Mrs. Finn, holding nothing back, his normally dry voice grown softer in the telling. He told her of his lonely state, of the slow slipping away of his feeling that the Duchess was near him, of the repulsion he had felt for the Marchioness, and of the unexpected warmth he now felt for Lady Laura Kennedy. He described their exchanges at the ball with the same precision he brought to an analysis of the savings to be brought by moving to a decimal system of coinage, and only a little more evident emotion.

When he had finished his recital he looked to her, for all the world like a schoolboy who knows he has erred in his sums, and said: "No doubt I seem very foolish, asking to see you over an old man's fanciful hopes—or do I seem base in betraying the memory of my poor Cora?"

Mrs. Finn answered immediately, in her firmest voice. "Neither, my dear Duke. You loved my dear friend very much, and she loved you. No doubt it was not always easy, or restful; love never is, is it? But when Glencora died," Mrs. Finn continued, "you did not die with her, and she would not wish you to crawl into your grave whilst you are still breathing."

"You speak as if you knew," the Duke commented sadly.

"Indeed I do. My dear Duke, how can you believe you would betray her memory by marrying more than a decade after she is gone? You have been grieving her these many years, and at the first sign that you are ready to live again, you prepare to scourge yourself for the sin of doing so? Surely you are wiser than that!"

"You truly think so?" the Duke asked, his voice catching a little.

"The fact that you loved her so much is what has held you apart so long. My Phineas did not wait a decade after his poor wife died before marrying me, did he?"

"He was younger, and the young heal more quickly," the Duke defended his friend.

"True. But poor Phineas had also married a girl he had outgrown, thinking he did right in doing so. And he had some love for her. When her death freed him, he mourned for her most sincerely, but not for so long. You loved Glencora so deeply that it took many years to heal from the wound of having her torn from you. Do not regret being made well again; she would not want you wounded until the day you die!"

The Duke, unable to speak, nodded quite slowly.

"I am going to leave you for a bit," Mrs. Finn said. "I need to change after my journey, I'm afraid. May I have my usual room? I would like to stay the night—the roads are in a poor state with all of this rain, and I, too, am not as young as once I was. So we shall have time and opportunity to speak at greater leisure, should you wish to."

The Duke rose, and, still not trusting his voice, nodded. Mrs. Finn left the room, and mounted the stairs. She went up to her room, where her luggage had been brought, and a fire built. After she had washed and changed, she looked out of her window, over the old Priory. There, in the rain, as she had expected, was the Duke, swathed in a large Inverness cape and wearing a wide-brimmed hat, walking once more around the ruins.

Lady Laura Kennedy, Marie Finn thought to herself, as she watched the solitary man make his circuit in the rain. Her relations with Lady Laura had always been marred by the Englishwoman's jealousy—and her seemingly inexhaustible ability to persist in it. As the woman in possession, it had always fallen to her, on the rare occasions when a meeting could not be avoided, to be gentle and pleasant to her rebarbative would-be rival.

Since the ball, though, she had noticed a change in Lady Laura. She had been tentatively pleasant, even calling her by her given name. At the time, she had ascribed this to the circumstances—the urgent need to strike a counter-blow to Lizzie Eustace's little plan to entrap Jack into marriage by presenting their so-called betrothal as a *fait accompli*. But if this new-found amiability were to betide more, why, Marie would like nothing better than to see Lady Laura settled into a happier frame of life. She could like her former rival much better, she thought, as Duchess of Omnium than ever she had previously done as Phineas's embittered *amie d'antan*.

Most importantly, the Duke's choice might have seemed strange to many, but not to her. Like Lady Laura, he was addicted to politics, to policy, and was high-minded almost to a fault. Lady Glen had brought him down from those heights, and forced him to commingle with lesser humanity by her raillery and mischief. Could Lady Laura do as well? Perhaps not by those means - in fact, clearly not by those means, but quite possibly by dint of simply loving him—if she could at last be free of the shadow that her old infatuation with Marie's own husband had cast over her life. After some thought, Marie knew how to advise the Duke further, if indeed her advice were asked.

Marie cast one final look out the window. The Duke had, at long last, come in from the cold and wet.

PHINEAS FOR THE DEFENCE

The Central Criminal Court, or the Old Bailey as some (especially, regrettably, many who practise at the Bar, and hence should know better) insist on calling it, was a quaint little building at the time of the events which we chronicle here—small, that is, for a busy courthouse. There was already talk in high circles of tearing down the old pile, and replacing it with a new building, one large enough to accommodate the number of trials which took place there, due to the no doubt deplorable ebb in morals as the Century drew toward its end.

Marie Finn declined to attend Ifor Powlett-Jones's trial—not even to accompany Clarissa, who was afire to see her uncle defend the hapless young Welshman. The Earl of Brentford agreed to accompany Clarissa instead, and then her *fiancé* completed the party. Mrs. Finn had her own reasons for not wanting to set foot in the Old Bailey again, as the place brought all too vividly to mind the sheer terror that had gripped her throughout Phineas's trial. She contented herself in remaining home to welcome back Violet, Jack, and, perhaps, Lady Laura, due home that day or the next. She suspected that a careful reception would be required.

In her private soul, she was not sanguine as to how Jack would take the news of Clarissa's engagement, Violet's reassuring telegram about Jack's calmer state of mind notwithstanding. Neither the mother nor the aunt had remarked the burning look Jack had given Clarissa before dinner at the Finns,' but Marie had, and the fight between the young lord and Savrola seemed to her more a battle of rivals, and not a cousin's mistaken overreaction to a witticism. Jack's violence did not otherwise make sense to her, even allowing for the Chiltern temper, the stress Lizzie Eustace had placed him under, and the fact that he had been—dining.

She supposed she could have telegraphed news of the engagement to Violet, or even to Lady Laura at Lochlinter, but she was reluctant to do so. She did not want to appear to be suggesting that the news was in some wise pertinent to Jack, or to hint that he was a *partie intéressée* thereto. After all, she could quite simply be wrong. And even if she were correct in her intuition, calling it to Jack's attention could reveal to the acute perceptions of youth that his unhappy status was found out. No, Jack would be informed in London, but not, at least, by her, Marie Finn reasoned. And she would not attend the trial.

But the Earl of Brentford's party did attend, and were, by virtue of their host's rank, invited to take seats with the judge on his bench. The peer, the young Tory member, and the comely young red-haired lady arrayed behind the judge struck an oddly casual note against the formal setting. Clarissa gazed around the wide expanse of the courtroom, taking in the crowd, the heat, and, as her aunt had correctly forewarned, her nostrils tautened at the intolerable stench that grew as the room filled up, jam-packed with a motley assemblage of humanity, mostly shabbily dressed, working class people come to witness one of their own accused of a crime against the laws of property. Clarissa raised her scented handkerchief to her nostrils, pretending to dab her face against the heat, and was glad that in bringing it along she had, as in so many things, been guided by the wisdom of her Aunt Marie.

For Phineas's great fear had come to pass; a handful of articles in the *People's Banner* and in the *Jupiter* had depicted the accused as an angry radical, eager to destabilise the social order, to take from the creators of industry (and thus the generators of the wealth of the Nation) the means of production, pursuant to the vile atheistic teachings of the agitator Karl Marx. In a leader in the *Banner*, Quintus Slide had dared, after many years of treading warily, to fire a somewhat muted broadside at young Powlett-Jones, and the "conspiracy of radicals" of which he was a part. Along the way, Slide managed to cock a snook at Powlett-Jones's defender, the "formerly fire-breathing Celtic dragon, who, after years slumbering in a cavern lined by a lady's loot, has awoken, seeking to bathe today's society with the flickering fires left from long-fled youth."

"Mild, for Slide," was Phineas's only comment when Brentford pointed it out to him, adding "I rather think my old friend Quintus's fires are the ones flickering—when they aren't taking the waters, that is." Brentford remembered that remark as he beheld Phineas enter into the courtroom with Mr. Camperdown and a young, pale clerk. Catching sight of Quintus Slide as he came in, Phineas made an ironic bow to the journalist as he processed toward the bar. Startled, Slide—grown greyer and a good deal fatter than Phineas had recollected him—returned the greeting, leading Phineas to flash a real smile in his old antagonist's direction.

Phineas moved to his seat casually, spreading a few papers, placing his pen just so, and looking around the courtroom until he saw Brentford's party. As the judge had not yet entered, the barrister tipped a quick wink to his niece and smiled at Brentford and Savrola both. Phineas extended his hand to the leading barrister appearing for the prosecution, a gaunt, balding man only a little past his own age, but looking older. This barrister, Sir Simon Slope, had once been Solicitor-General, and in that capacity had been the junior barrister for the Crown against Phineas himself. It was thought that this unusual re-encounter was a stratagem on the part of Sir William McScuttle, an effort to rattle Phineas by placing him in the same courtroom in which he had stood trial for his life, against the very man who would have seen him hanged.

Brentford smiled, a trifle grimly. That little stratagem did not appear to be working, if Phineas's calm good humour in shaking the hand of his adversary, and exchanging some pleasantry with him was any indication. He mentioned the fact to Savrola Vavasor, who let out a soft whistle.

"The cheek of it!" he exclaimed softly. And Clarissa's white hand gripped his own, and her milky flesh paled even more as she gazed in horror at the man whose energies and skills had been directed at the hanging of her beloved Uncle Phineas for another's crime.

But now the usher was declaiming "Be upstanding!" and the judge was making his grand entrance: Sir Lemuel Bullfry, large and pouched, with deep-set eyes, resembled an amphibian, a fact that, combined with his name, had earned him the obvious soubriquet. Still, he bore the scarlet and ermine well, and played his part in the medieval mummery that ornaments the process by which years of a man's life—nay, his very life!—may be deemed forfeit. But to call the pageantry in which the trial is cloaked mummery is to display ignorance of its purpose, the solemnization of one of the great functions of the people acting as a community, the weighing of guilt or innocence, and the meting out of the communal judgment on the accused. For the criminal trial is many things—a search for truth, a drama, a battle in which every technique of rhetoric and wit is brought to bear in the contest for victory. But it is nothing quite so much as it is a crucible testing the characters of all involved, though none so harshly as that of the accused, which must, unless it is of true steel, crack.

Phineas Finn had not cracked. Neither, though, had that other man, Joseph Emilius. If ever they were to meet, each would have the measure of the other in a way that very few could understand, almost none who had not undergone the ordeal they each had survived. While the one man strove to use his days to do good, and the other sought to bend the precepts of good to his own uses, both had faced the extremity of fear and shame—and had come through intact.

Now the test was upon poor Ifor Powlett-Jones, young, and without the friendship, or the education, or the sheer anger that had strengthened the man now defending him in his own hour. Phineas met the lad's eyes as he was put into the dock, and tried to will some of his own confidence and buoyancy into him. The adrenaline of arriving at the day of hazard had revived poor Powlett-Jones a little, and he stood in the dock, dreadfully pale, but composed, the trembling in his hands suppressed by his grip on the rail of the dock. He looked terribly young, and terribly innocent.

In the newspapers that evening, Sir Simon's opening read rather as though it had been drawn from one of the leaders from the *Jupiter*. Though lacking the personal venom of the *People's Banner*, it was, in its own urbane way, deadly, depicting the accused as a young brigand, wholly dedicated to the overthrow of the very industrialists who made Great Britain's preeminence in trade possible, in hopes of replacing it with a worker's collective. He finished up with an invocation of the rights of property, the sole basis for a just and equitable society, the one means by which the poor would be lifted out of their sorry lot. Strangely enough, the lack of venom with which Sir Simon delivered his words, sometimes in a papery near-whisper, sometimes in a flat drone, lifted his words above the cries of a hound baying on the scent to seemingly irrefutable scientific propositions.

Phineas rose, and began his opening quite simply. "My learned friend," he began, "has suggested that this is a case about the rights of property. It is not. The property my client is charged with vandalizing—the engine—was lost in the cave-in. It has not been dug out—cannot be, the mine's engineers say, because the roof has been destabilised."

Phineas continued, warming to his theme:

"My learned friend has told you that this is a case about capital under siege by labour. No, gentlemen, it is not. Do not be gulled. This case is far, far simpler than that. It is a case of men underground, and of duty—duty performed heroically!—when that ground collapses. The paramount duty, surely in such circumstances, is to save life. All that the man I have the honour to represent is accused of stems from his performance of that first, most basic duty—to save life! Yes, the rights of property sometimes must bend to that imperative. I may take your hose without your permission to put out a fire to save life. Because, ultimately, the lives of men underground are precious in a way that the engine cannot be. It cannot think, feel, fear, love or pray. It can only remain behind, and be buried in the collapse of the cavern roof. Nobody weeps for it; a new one can be purchased. But the men saved by my client's actions—the men who owe their lives to Ifor Powlett-Jones? You will see them, and hear them. You will rejoice in their preservation. And you will, when all the evidence is placed before you, I know return the only verdict which justice and the law can support: *Not Guilty*."

Sir Simon called his first witness: "Sir William McScuttle!"

Phineas could not see to what end the mine owner would be called; he was not even in Wales at the time of the cave-in.

"Sir William," asked the prosecuting barrister, after eliciting the witness's name, titles, and ownership of the mine affected, "are you acquainted with the accused?"

"I am, m'lud," the industrialist answered.

"And what do you know of his character?"

"I object, m'lord," Phineas rose.

Bullfry grunted inquiringly.

"I object on the ground that character of the accused is not properly at issue."

Sir Simon responded, "M'lud, the character of the accused will be drawn into question when he testifies, and by having Sir William testify now, we can afford a basic courtesy to a very busy man who should not be held captive to the timetable of the defence, or its caprices."

"What have you to say to that, Mr. Finn?" croaked the Judge.

"My Lord, I have not yet determined whether to call my client, or to call character evidence on his behalf, and therefore this evidence is not proper at this time, at the very least."

"Nonsense," grated Sir Simon, "how else can the defence try to establish its claim that the accused acted solely to save life under desperate conditions? That is your contention," he added, a sneer beginning to grow visible on his face, "is it not?"

Phineas replied, "Why, any one of the trapped miners my client's action saved, or those brave men who remained behind with him can testify to that..."

"Objection!" thundered Sir Simon.

"My Lord, I merely answered counsel's question..." Phineas answered with a barely perceptible smile.

Bullfry waved them both to silence.

"The objection is overruled Mr. Finn. Should the accused not testify, I can always instruct the jury appropriately."

"My Lord," Phineas interceded, "the members of the jury cannot unhear testimony, no matter how hard they try to do so. The Court's ruling infringes my client's right to remain silent should he choose to do so and–"

"Your exception is noted, Mr. Finn. Continue, Sir Simon."

"Well, Sir William?" asked the onetime Solicitor General.

"His character was a bad one, m'lud. Aye, he was a dab hand wi' the work, I'll give him that, but he was always one for complaining, and agitating that the men should have a union. He wanted tae bring the Fed in…"

"The Fed?" asked Sir Simon smoothly.

"The Federation, a group of radicals obsessed with the idea of dictating tae employers how they are to run their shops, and–"

"Objection," said Phineas Finn, in a bored manner, only half rising from his chair. Savrola Vavasor smiled to himself, recollecting what Phineas had told him over dinner the night before. "Only the tyro pounds his fist on the table, and shouts his objections in front of the jury. The seasoned barrister yawns them, conveying to the jury that the question is silly, improper, misplaced—but ultimately unimportant." And, indeed, his manner seemed as uninterested that of as an elegant cat refusing a dog's dirty plaything.

"Mr. Finn?" the Judge inquired.

"The witness is speculating as to the state of mind of a group of men whose motives and conduct are not at issue in this case."

Bullfry heaved a mountainous sigh. "Sustained. The jury will please excuse us a moment, and retire to your room, if you would, gentlemen?"

After the wizened little clerk closed the door behind the last juryman, the Judge spoke, in a deliberately pleasant tone. "Mr. Finn, I admit that these objections of yours may have technical merit, but they are impeding the progress of this matter. Might I ask you to be a little sparing in peripheral matters?"

"Of course, my lord. I will only object when absolutely necessary."

"Thank you, Mr. Finn."

The jurymen trouped in again, and took their seats.

Sir Simon resumed: "So you knew the accused to be a man of radical convictions?"

Phineas, with a slight air of diablerie, half-rose, and pertly said, "Objection, my lord."

So it went for most of the morning; Sir Simon seeking to draw opinions from the coal magnate, Phineas harrying him at every turn. As the morning drew on, Judge Bullfry began sustaining more of Phineas's objections, and the pace of testimony slowed even more. At the luncheon break, Phineas rose to bow to the judge with a smile and an air of cheerful respect; Sir Simon bolted to his feet like a man with a grievance mightily seeking to restrain himself. After the judge and his clerk departed, Sir Simon expostulated. "I say, Finn, you don't give a fella much leeway!"

"Now, now, Slope," the Irishman answered, "Can't be helped if you're having an off day."

"Off day?"

"Well, I've never known you to frame questions so objectionably before. I know it's not deliberate–"

"Certainly not!"

"But I can't let them pass, you know, when they're as objectionable as that. Must protect the record, after all. Never mind," Phineas said, "I'm sure you'll do better in the afternoon."

Savrola watched raptly, a smile tugging at the corners of his mouth. Brentford was suppressing a sharp bark of laughter by stuffing his handkerchief in his mouth, feigning a cough. Clarissa looked at both of them, confused. When they descended from the bench and Phineas escorted them to a little room, the husband-to-be grinned broadly, and Brentford gave way to laughter. Clarissa, annoyed, asked, "What was that all about?"

Savrola answered, "The oldest billiards trick there is, modified for the law courts."

Brentford answered, "You tell your opponent that he's watching the wrong ball…"

"And he can't help but do just that!" Savrola declared, jubilant.

And Phineas Finn smiled.

"I do hope Sir William thought it was worth his pains to get Sir Simon Slope in to prosecute," he said, vibrating with silent laughter. "What a stroke of good fortune that Sir William was the first witness, so he could see for himself just how badly I was rattled to face Slope again."

THE GLADIATORS

By the end of the first hour after the luncheon break, Sir Simon, visibly weary, seemed to think he had finished with the coal magnate, having been allowed to give his witness an opportunity to explain the evils of trade unionism, and the resultant tainting of any deed done by young Powlett-Jones by the malice he bore employers and all property holders.

With that portion of his duty done, Sir Simon subsided into his seat. As the witness made preparations to leave the box, Phineas arose.

"Good afternoon, Sir William," he began, "just a few questions for you." The magnate, startled, looked at the judge, who nodded, and composed himself for Phineas's expected broadside.

"Were you in Wales at the time of the incident in question?"

"No-o," Sir William answered, probing for the trap.

"So it follows that you saw nothing of what happened on the day and time in question?"

"That's right," the truculent mine owner declared, "But I heard all about it after, and I–"

"No doubt, Sir William, but I'm only asking what you yourself saw, in your own experience."

"Why, nowt at all, man, I was in London that day."

"Very good, Sir William, then let us pass on to something else, shall we? Have you ever had a conversation, yourself, I mean, with Ifor Powlett-Jones?"

"Myself?"

"Yes, that's right."

"Well, no, I can't say that I have–"

"You cannot?"

"No, not myself..."

"Have you ever heard the accused give a speech?"

"That one?" the industrialist barked a laugh. "No, no, he's always quite the little chap-pel boy in public. Butter wouldn't melt in his mouth, would it?"

"Thank you, Sir William. Have you ever heard—with your own ears, mind—the accused give any kind of opinion about the mine, or mine owners in general, or working conditions–yourself?"

And at each question, Sir William replied, simply, "No."

"Other than what you may have been told by others, have you any knowledge of the opinions or views of Ifor Powlett-Jones?"

"No, but–"

"Thank you, Sir William," Phineas interrupted. "Have you any direct, personal knowledge of his involvement with the union?"

"Aye! I saw him talking with that Gwyn Jennings."

"That would be the same Gwyn Jennings who is a duly elected member of the Urban District Council for Brynmawr?"

"Why, yes–"

"Other than his speaking with a duly elected representative of the people of Brynmawr, any other direct knowledge of his views?"

"I know he joined the Fed!" the industrialist, red-faced by now, roared.

"Anything else?" Phineas asked.

"That's enough for me!" the angry mine owner declared.

Phineas then turned to his primary interest in cross-examining McScuttle at all.

"Sir William, this case is a private prosecution, is it not?"

"Aye, it is." The glowering man almost snarled it.

"And you have brought it, am I correct?"

"I have done—as is my right!"

"Why?" Phineas asked, in defiance of every law of cross-examination—at the back of his mind he saw Chaffanbrass wince, heard Low decry a cross-examining barrister foolish enough to ask a question to which he did not already know the answer—yes, and a non-leading one at that!

"Why? Why, because of the damage to my property, of course!"

"The damage to your property? Do you mean the engine?"

"Yes."

"Is it not buried with the rest of the machinery at that level?"

"Aye, it is—what of it?"

"Well, of what conceivable use is it to you?"

"What?" The mine-owner seemed flummoxed. "What d'ye mean?"

"Can it be dug out?"

"Nay, of course not! 'Tis too unstable, most of the level has since caved in, ye fool!"

"So Powlett-Jones's use of the shaft–"

"Beam," corrected the mine owner.

"Thank you, beam," Phineas accepted the correction, "damaged a machine that is lost beyond retrieving?"

"Aye, that's right."

"You acknowledge he saved lives?"

"'Course I do." The industrialist looked surprised that the question should be put.

"So—and I just want to make sure this is absolutely clear to the members of the jury, Sir William—even though Powlett-Jones's actions saved twelve men's lives, and only damaged a machine that was lost in any event, you believe these actions were criminal?"

"Of course I do," the little man said, calm again.

"Why?" Phineas asked.

""'Twas my machine, and my foreman said him nay. 'Twasn't his place tae decide, but my foreman's."

Phineas, astonished, was done. "No further questions," he informed the judge.

"Thank you, Sir William. You are excused," said Mr. Justice Bullfry, after Sir Simon declined the opportunity for redirect examination.

The rest of the day passed surprisingly swiftly, and established the main facts quite smoothly. The fact of the cave-in was, of course, not subject to dispute, nor was the rescue of the miners. A handful of witnesses established, without cross-examination by Phineas, the tearing of the beam from the engine, the use of it to free the captive miners, the effort on the part of the foreman, one Jasper Tudor, to prevent the dismantling of the engine, and his resultant quarrel with Powlett-Jones.

Phineas cross-examined Tudor, who, removed from his home country was merely a large, glowering Welshman, but could not shake him from his story. He stoutly insisted that he had not used force to try to recall Powlett-Jones to his duty, but had only once grabbed the boy's arm to get his attention.

"And he swung at me, then, without listening to a word I'd to say!" Tudor repeated again and again. The man was simply not to be swayed; he had either been rehearsed to perfection, or truly believed his testimony.

Worse, even a few miners who were patently sympathetic to Powlett-Jones went some way to corroborating him; Tudor had not been violent, but had been shouting, they said, advocating caution and a quick evacuation.

The next day, the defence presented its case. Miner after miner told of the panic below ground when the cave-in took place, and that Powlett-Jones had rallied the men to the rescue of their trapped brethren. Powlett-Jones's older brother, more self-assured than the defendant, passionately described what it had been like for the imprisoned men to hear the foreman ordering that they be abandoned, the fear of death by suffocation—or what might have been even worse, by slow starvation—and the sudden hope when they heard Ifor and his shift-mates coming to the rescue.

"We thought we were doomed, sure, sir," Aneurin Powlett-Jones testified, "and but for Ifor, doomed is what we'd be. I'd never have got home to wife or childer again. My little Gwyneth and Megan would be fatherless—not to mention the little one on the way!"

Ifor perked up at that, as at some welcome news, Phineas noted; he hoped his brother had not been so foolish as to think visiting was impermissible these past months.

Through it all, Sir Simon had not done much cross-examination. Now at the lunch break, Phineas was confronted with one final hurdle: whether to call his client.

The matter was far from simple. Powlett-Jones could not add anything, Phineas believed, on the riot, destruction of property and related charges. He had established all the facts he needed for his claim of necessity from the witnesses he had called, and even from the prosecution's witnesses. It seemed clear to Phineas that if the judge charged the jury that it must consider necessity as a defence, and the jury did its work, then Powlett-Jones would be acquitted. Even if the judge did not charge necessity, but allowed Phineas to argue it, he was in with a chance. But, because they had been arguing off to the side, and not all of the miners had been willing to risk their employment by coming to London to testify, Powlett-Jones was the only witness who could refute Tudor's claim that he had not offered any violence to the young unionist.

Unsure what course to take, Phineas decided to skip luncheon, and instead meet with his client. Powlett-Jones was keyed up, anxious. Phineas explained the situation to him, and asked him, "Well, Ifor?"

"I'll—I'll try, sir," was the best the young Welshman could offer.

When he was sworn in, though, Powlett-Jones seemed to take heart. He answered Phineas's questions crisply, directly. While the young man was far from relaxed, he had enough wit and force of character to say his piece, finally given the chance.

After eliciting Powlett-Jones's account of the cave-in and Tudor's command that the level be evacuated, Phineas asked him about the rescue effort.

"Mr. Powlett-Jones," he asked, "was not Mr. Tudor properly in charge?"

"He was," Ifor agreed readily enough, "but the man was dead scared. Looked like a whey cheese, right enough. And his orders weren't making sense, Mr. Finn—tellin' everyone to leave, but then sayin' that the men left behind'd be rescued later."

"And that did not make sense?"

"No! There was no later, Mr. Finn! Ye could see the rest of the roof strainin' and once it gave, why, there'd be no way back in."

"What happened next?"

"Mr. Tudor got more and more frantic as we began to take out the beam—sayin' 'it's company property, lads, if ye break it, it's our jobs—all our jobs'—as if that mattered! My brother was trapped back there, and my friends—Dai Llelwellyn, Huw Evans, poor Ianto—we were too late for Ianto." The young miner fought to regain his composure.

"And then?

"Mr. Tudor grabbed me, hard, and spun me around. Said we'd be the ruination of the whole town, that we'd get ourselves killed, too. His face was like I'd never seen, his jaws champing, and straining—and he was cursing, too—not like him, that; he's well-spoken enough–"

"Mr. Powlett-Jones, after he spun you around?"

"He jerked on my arm a couple times, wouldn't let me go. So, I—well, I hit him."

"To hurt him?"

"No, sir!" Powlett-Jones's voice carried real incredulity, and shock at the notion. "To get free! To save my brother and the rest!"

Phineas down, Sir Simon up.

"I put it to you, Mr. Powlett-Jones, that you enjoyed striking Mr. Tudor."

"Put it where ye whist, it's not true."

"Mr. Powlett-Jones," Mr. Justice Bullfry interrupted, "Sir Simon Slope is doing his duty in cross-examining you, just as Mr. Finn has done his duty in examining you. He is required to ask these questions, and pert answers to them will do your case no good, young man." The judge's words and tones were less minatory than yesterday, Phineas thought. Despite his lapse, Powlett-Jones had done himself some good, as long as he didn't wreck himself on the rocks of Sir Simon's cross-examination.

Sir Simon agreed, apparently, because his hitherto bloodless manner quickened, as he chased Powlett-Jones up and down the various ravines of the facts, trying to tangle the witness up.

"So you like Mr. Tudor, then?" the former Solicitor General asked.

"I do not."

"You disliked him?"

"Aye."

"But your testimony is that you didn't enjoy striking him? Seeing him at a disadvantage? Finally being free of his power, and in a position to tell the men what to do yourself?"

Phineas rose. "My lord," he objected "Any one of those questions on its own would be unobjectionable, but having them fired all at once—well, cross-examination by Gatling gun may be very dramatic"—and here he gave the Solicitor General, who was, truth be told, panting a little bit, a stern look—"but it hardly allows the witness to answer. And it is, surely, the witness' answers that constitute evidence, not the questions."

That earned Phineas a weary smile from the beleaguered youth. Mr. Justice Bullfry agreed.

"Sir Simon," he reprimanded the barrister, "I do not believe that you gave the witness an opportunity to answer any of your questions but the last." The barrister visibly flushed, and, plainly annoyed with himself, apologised, both to the Court, and, with a return of his normal manner, to the accused.

That did not betoken any gentler line of questions. Sir Simon began to probe Powlett-Jones's purported hatred of his employer ("I never met the man!"), of bosses, and of capitalism in general. He asked if Powlett-Jones was familiar with Marx, with Shaw, or with di Basso's scurrilous writings. Fortunately, Powlett-Jones remembered the three rules Phineas had given him: Don't try to pick the answer that puts you in the best light, don't be too quick to agree, and never, ever guess—say only what you remember. Powlett-Jones did admit to his admiration for Gwyn Jennings, the miner now rising in local politics; to his belief in unions as a good, but never wavered from his earlier testimony that the rescue was motivated by his anxiety and fear for his brother and other mates.

The blizzard of questions began to confuse the young man somewhat, and so Phineas interposed an objection here and there to allow him time to get his bearings. Sir Simon chipped away at his exchanges with Tudor, pressing him to recall the foreman's exact words. Ifor admitted that he could not do so, but remembered the sense of them. Sir Simon worried away at this, trying to catch the young man out. Although Powlett-Jones was becoming bemused by the barrage, Phineas stayed his hand. The day was now late, with shadows creeping into the room, and the glow of the autumn sun had almost faded from the courtroom's windows. Where one last ray slanted into the room, motes danced in its fading beam. Phineas surreptitiously checked his watch; nearly quarter-past five! The session had run later than he had thought.

As Sir Simon's cross-examination seemed to repeat itself, doubling back to areas already covered, Bullfry grew visibly impatient. When Sir Simon paused to check the sheaf of notes piled beside him, the Judge interposed.

"Have you very much more, Sir Simon? The hour is late, and we have kept the jury past the usual time."

"One moment, please, m'lud," the barrister replied, conning his notes once more. "Ah, just one or two more question, m'lud. Mr. Powlett-Jones: Are you a delegate of the Fed?"

"No, my lord," the witness answered.

"Are you a member of the Fed, Mr. Powlett-Jones?"

"Yes, my lord." Exhausted, overstrained, as he was, Powlett-Jones doggedly held to his brief. Heartened, Phineas recollected the words of an old clergyman he had once met, "It's dogged as does it, Mr. Finn," the old man had said to him, and here was Powlett-Jones demonstrating that very lesson.

"And do you agree with the Fed's philosophy of employing violence against unjust employers?"

"I agree with the Fed's philosophy," Powlett-Jones began, "but it–"

"Thank you, Mr. Powlett-Jones," said a beaming Sir Simon Slope, and, his silk gown rustling about him, resumed his seat.

Phineas rose, "My Lord," he began, "the witness must be allowed to complete his answer. I do not believe—"

Tired out by the long day, Bullfry snapped, "He appears to me to have answered the question. If you believe it necessary for him to elaborate, you may re-direct in the morning. We stand adjourned."

"Pray note my exception, my lord," Phineas grated. "The witness is on the stand, and the matter can resolved in bare minutes."

"Minutes which we will also have in the morning, Mr. Finn," the judge responded. "Your exception and objection are noted for the record. And this Court is now adjourned until the morning."

On their way out, Clarissa asked her uncle, "Why was it so important to you to ask poor Mr. Powlett-Jones to finish his answer tonight?"

Savrola looked grim at this, suspecting he knew the answer.

"Because, in the morning, when Ifor testifies that the Fed does not in fact advocate violence, the jury will have already spent all night thinking that it does, and that he agrees? And, as you said at the beginning of the trial, they cannot unhear what they believe they have heard?" he offered.

"Very good, Savrola," Phineas answered, his frown deepening, "but that's not all of it, my boy. Slope will argue in closing that Ifor and his lawyer had all night to cook up an innocent gloss on his testimony, and that what they thought they heard him admit is the most credible testimony he could have given."

"Will he argue that?" Brentford asked. "That would be scandalous!"

"Surely the jurymen are not so easily misled, Uncle," Clarissa offered, resting her hand on her Uncle's arm.

And with that, Phineas Finn had to strive to content himself until the morning.

"NECESSITY KNOWS NO LAW"

The next morning, Clarissa Riley, Savrola Vavasor, and the Earl of Brentford resumed their favoured seats behind that of Mr. Justice Bullfry. Savrola felt jaded, exhausted as if he had been down in the arena with his putative uncle-in-law, but without the justification of fighting the case alongside the older man. He slipped his hand beneath Clarissa's, and lounged in his uncomfortable seat, waiting for the day's proceedings to begin. Phineas had, for the third day running, pleasantly shaken hands with Sir Simon, and passed a few remarks that would, the younger man devoutly hoped, unsettle the former Solicitor General.

Brentford, seated on Clarissa's other side, resembled nothing so much by this stage of the affair as a dyspeptic eagle. Essentially a countryman, his stay in the municipality had been extended far beyond his initial intentions, but he was too engrossed in the trial to leave now. Nonetheless, the suspense of the case was taking a toll on the older man.

Clarissa, by contrast, was crisp and composed, calm, and seemingly proof against all tension from the combat she had elected to witness. Savrola strongly suspected that her sunny confidence was in part assumed to buttress her uncle's performance, but he found it awfully convincing. He thought to himself, "I wonder if she is bluffing it out? If so, she could play onstage for a living..."

"Be upstanding in court!" The stentorian call to the pre-battle formalities came, and the judge took his seat.

"Mr. Finn," Mr. Justice Bullfry inquired, "have you any further examination of the accused?"

"Indeed I do," answered Phineas, and re-called Ifor Powlett-Jones. The re-direct was mercifully brief—Ifor was looking wan and faded, if resolute—and entirely expected: Ifor denied that the Fed advocated or engaged in violence, affirmed that he did not himself advocate violence, and Phineas rested.

And then Sir Simon surprised Phineas: He did not ask Ifor a single question. Not one.

Before closing arguments, the jurymen were sent back to their room, while Phineas and Sir Simon wrangled with Mr. Justice Bullfry. Phineas began by urging the Court to charge the defence of necessity, Sir Simon countered with *Regina v. Dudley and Stevens;* Phineas replied that the defence might not, as Lord Chief Justice Coleridge had opined, apply in cases of cannibalism, but this was not such a case.

"Surely that case involved acts which were *malum in se*, my lord, while this one involves acts which are, at worst, *malum prohibitum*."

"What is Uncle saying?" a clearly frustrated Clarissa hissed in a whisper to Savrola.

"He's saying that cannibalism can never be justified—it's inherently wrong, and thus inherently unlawful—whereas breaking a piece off of a machine is not; it's only wrong because it is prohibited by law, and therefore can be justified where the reasons underlying the law do not apply."

Phineas, who was in fact saying just that, took heart from the fact that Sir Simon was slightly distracted by the whispering going on behind Mr. Justice Bullfry, who himself was equivocating on what he should do.

Phineas tried to push him over the edge with Serjeant Pollard's famous argument from *Reniger versus Fogossa*: "*Quod necessitas non habet legem.*"

"What?" hissed Clarissa Riley again.

"'Necessity knoweth no law,'" translated Mr. Justice Bullfry, with a glare at the unfortunate girl.

Sir Simon pounced, "From an argument by counsel, m'lud, not a ruling of the Court."

Mr. Justice Bullfry pondered. "True," he said weightily, "but one which the Court permitted. And one which I will permit counsel to make. But I will not so charge."

"Very good, my lord," acknowledged Phineas, accepting the half loaf offered.

"Thank you, m'lud," said Sir Simon, pleased to have staved off a judicial endorsement of the defence's main plinth.

The jurymen trouped back in to the box.

Sir Simon up, Phineas down!

Sir Simon began his closing speech by noting that he did not even bother asking the accused any questions about that morning's testimony. "After all, gentlemen," he reasoned, "After an entire night to think of an innocent-seeming way to explain away yesterday's devastating admission, of course the defence was able to come up with a story against which no evidence could be found. But you know what you heard, gentlemen! An explicit admission, from the Accused's own lips, not only that the Fed advocates the use of violence against employers, but that he himself does so as well. You heard it, gentlemen, and it is corroborated by the testimony of Sir William McScuttle, and by common knowledge of the filthy lengths to which these desperate brigands will go!"

Much more in this vein flowed from Sir Simon, along with a painstaking summary of the undisputed facts in the case—the cave in, the wresting of command from Tudor, the striking of a blow against the man who, even by Powlett-Jones's own testimony, offered him no violence, but only sought to arrest his reckless gambit and save those men who could be safely evacuated. At which point, Phineas leaned forward, and murmured into his instructing solicitor's ear, "I think I liked him better when he was trying to get me hanged."

Over an hour later, Sir Simon came to his conclusion, urging the "preservation of private property, of order, of safety by the only verdict that the evidence justified: Guilty—on all charges."

Sir Simon down, Phineas up!

"Necessity, gentlemen, knows no law. The man who stands before you accused, was in a dark, tight place, dust-covered, choking on tiny airborne pieces of coal and rock, tearing at his throat. A brother ordered to abandon his older brother, friends, and fellow workers, and leave them to be buried alive. And for what, gentlemen? To leave undamaged an insentient machine about to buried with those living, breathing men, and which was, as even its owner admits, beyond rescue, let alone repair. Those dozen men, gentlemen, would have quite simply died for nothing whatsoever.

But Ifor Powlett-Jones chose not to leave them there, but risked his own life, in a successful effort to save life. A *successful* effort! Twelve men, whom you have seen and from whom you have heard, who would be buried in the ashes, dirt, and rubble that covers the wretched machine which the gentleman I have the honour to represent is charged with having taken a piece from! Are not their lives worth recognition? Is not the saving of these living souls—fathers, husband, brothers, friends—a higher good, worthy of the approbation of the law? Must we not admit, in the words of a wise Frenchman, that it is 'true that there were exceptional cases, that authority might be put out of countenance, that the rule might be inadequate in the presence of a fact, that everything could not be framed within the text of the code, that the unforeseen compelled obedience?'"

And Phineas did his best to point out to the jurymen that the accused had sought to answer the question about the Fed's philosophy the night before, but had been cut off by counsel for the prosecution—"perhaps by an accident, perhaps by mistake, perhaps," and here his voice took on a sharpness it had hitherto lacked, "in full knowledge of the confusion that would result."

Finally, Phineas argued that the blow to Tudor had been delivered under great stress, and under dire necessity only to prevent the panicked foreman from further hindering and rendering more perilous with each second the rescue attempt that had succeeded for all but two of the men left behind. "Who knows if the delay caused by that foreman's grip and his efforts to prevent the rescue may have meant the difference of life and death for those two men." And from her privileged seat, Clarissa saw that Jasper Tudor, in the gallery, seemed to wilt a bit at these words.

"Do for this man," Phineas concluded, "what he was able to do for twelve others: rescue him from the clutch of the law, and send him home to join the brother he loved so well that he risked his life to save him, and for the friends for whom he was prepared to risk all. Give the only verdict which the facts, the law, and justice require: *Not guilty*."

And Phineas lowered himself into his seat, and, removing a handkerchief, mopped his brow.

Mr. Justice Bullfry, in his charge, was scrupulously fair in his marshaling of the evidence. He did not opine on either side, but sketched out the possible interpretations each side urged for the disputed facts. But he made no mention at all of necessity.

The jury retired to their room to deliberate, without food or drink. The increasingly pale Ifor was taken below, and Phineas and Sir Simon cast wry looks at each other. Clarissa and Savrola came down to the floor, and the girl embraced her uncle. Sir Simon approached, and asked to be presented to the lady and her intended. Phineas did so, but with less than usual of his customary cordiality. Still, both men followed the forms, knowing that the strain of the case, and of blows possibly too hard-struck, would fade over time. Brentford scowled at the entire spectacle, hungering equally for a verdict and a resolution and for his luncheon.

After what seemed an eternity later, but in hard truth was only slightly over two hours, the jury returned to deliver their verdict. When the foreman handed up the note to the bailiff, and the note was brought to Mr. Justice Bullfry, there flickered across His Lordship a barely discernible expression of surprise. He announced the verdict, count by count, from the most serious to the least, a ringing series of "Not guilty" verdicts until the very end, the count of simple assault against one Jasper Tudor, whereupon Mr. Justice Bullfry's refrain changed: "Guilty," he read. Ifor Powlett Jones supported himself by his arms; his legs went weak. A cry from the gallery was quickly suppressed.

Asked if he had anything to say in mitigation, Ifor only shook his head.

Mr. Justice Bullfry praised Ifor's courage, his manliness in saving life, and hope was again kindled in Phineas's breast. He acknowledged the cruel circumstances, and how the error of an instant could taint what was a heroic performance under many criteria.

Phineas's spirit began to soar again—only to crash back to earth, as he heard his client sentenced to five years imprisonment.

By the time Phineas Finn reached home that night, he was wan and exhausted. After four days on trial, he would have expected to be fatigued, but he had hastily bade Clarissa and Savrola farewell, and had bustled Brentford off to see the Home Secretary, with whom he had been at school.

"We must obtain a pardon for the poor boy," the anxious barrister said to his friend.

"Why not just appeal?" asked the Earl pragmatically.

"On what grounds? The indictment was sufficient, and the Court had jurisdiction."

"Oh, I'm sure that the court made some errors along the way," the Earl said airily enough, though, truth be told, he was greatly disappointed.

"That's not all that helpful in this case, Brentford," Phineas sighed. "Oh, were Powlett-Jones convicted of a misdemeanour before the King's Bench, I could move for a new trial. But assault is a felony, and, in any event, the trial was at the Bailey. I could argue that Mr. Justice Bullfry made a legal error in declining to charge necessity, and that error amounted to misdirecting the jury, but that's by no means sure—the most recent case is against us, and even if we were to sue out a writ of error, we could very well lose."

"What about that ruling at the beginning, where Sir Simon was allowed to put in evidence about Powlett-Jones's character before you'd decided whether to put him in the box? That seemed pretty rum to me," the peer suggested helpfully.

Phineas smiled wanly. "Not bad, Brentford, not bad," he replied. "It would require Bullfry to agree to reserve the case for the Twelve Judges– "

The bewildered peer looked at Phineas blankly. "The Twelve–"

"No, no," Phineas said, with a faint suggestion of a laugh, "not any theological body, but the whole body of common law judges. They meet at Serjeants' Inn, and can review a point of law. We might even get Powlett-Jones released, pending their review. But realistically, I think our first step is the Home Secretary."

"Phineas, if you are going to seek a pardon for the lad, it should surely be done in the normal course. Descending on the Home Secretary on the very day he is sentenced can only prejudice that application, surely."

"True enough, but I do not want to file a due course application," the barrister said grimly. "In a case where the accused was acquitted of all but the least serious crime charged? Where the sentence is relatively short? They'll deny, quite simply, because they'll treat the case as a mere grudge among lawyers."

"Is it not?" the Earl asked quietly.

"You know better than that, Brentford," Phineas answered his friend. "I don't care much for Sir Simon, but barring that last little trick, he was no worse than most prosecuting counsel. But I care very much about poor Powlett-Jones. Five years in prison will destroy that boy. And when he comes out—what kind of future will there be for him? No," Phineas continued, resolute, "What we need is for the Home Office to investigate the matter, and recommend a pardon, not merely yawn at a lawyer's submission."

"My dear fellow, I really don't know how much help I can be," the Earl cautioned. "Old school ties fade, rather, when it comes to politics, and we were never close..."

"You can stop temporizing, Oswald," Phineas smiled affectionately at his old friend. "I want you to make small talk with the Home Secretary while I work over his Undersecretary."

"Thank God," the Earl sighed. "I'd hate to have that boy's life in my hands—one cross word over hunting and the poor devil'd get the rope, or transportation to Australia. I take it you know the Undersecretary?"

"Yes. And by great good luck, it's somebody who owes me a thumping great favour: Larry Fitzgibbon. Indeed," Phineas grinned mirthlessly, "you could say Larry got me into this pickle, so it's time for the Party to come to the aid of all good men."

When they arrived at the Home Secretary's office, the Secretary himself descended and greeted Brentford, with all the enthusiasm of a weedy boy who has since surpassed the hero of his schooldays. He bore the peer off into his *sanctum sanctorum*, and began regaling the Earl with all his accomplishments since they had "pu'd the gowans fine." Brentford submitted to this rather barbarous treatment without complaint, as it left undefended the real target.

"Hallo, Phineas," Laurence Fitzgibbon, member of the House of Commons, Undersecretary of State, greeted the barrister. "How did it go down the Bailey?"

"Mixed result. Acquitted of just about everything else, but sent down on the assault charge," Phineas answered, watching Fitzgibbon's face fall a bit at the news.

"Oh, bad news, Phinny!" the Undersecretary condoled, using the nickname by which he had called Finn by in the days of their political youth. "How high the tariff?" he inquired.

"Five years," Phineas told him soberly.

"D—n it. Poor little devil. I'm sorry for him, Phinny, indeed I am. And for you, too, of course—that goes without saying, I should think. Any grounds for a reservation? Misdirection?"

"Some, but weak at best. The fact is that the jury got it wrong, Larry. That's why I'm here. An investigation and a recommendation for a pardon could set the whole matter to rights, and if you—and why, Mr. Fitzgibbon, are you wagging your head at me in that decidedly negative manner?"

"You can't blame me, Phinny; you know what himself is like–"

"You cannot tell me that Lord Fawn has a pronounced view on this matter. You simply cannot tell me that. I know him of old, and–"

"Indeed you do, Phinny, and that's half the problem. His Lordship don't like you, and it's as simple as that."

"And for that he'd consign an innocent man to five years imprisonment and a life of infamy?"

"No, and you know that. But convincing his Lordship that the jury got it wrong, and that the man is innocent, *that* would be next to impossible. With Mr. Phineas Finn defending, the task gets that much harder. And with Sir William McScuttle closeted with the P.M. as often as he is, that makes it even harder still."

"McScuttle has been oiling around the Prime Minister?" Phineas was astonished. There had once been a time when he would have known that well before Fitzgibbon. He had not realised how little he had been involved in the affairs of his Party in late years. Another cost of his vaunted independence, it came to him; he was no longer in the swim.

"Oh, yes. And he has gotten the P.M.'s ear, you know. McScuttle has coalmines, steel mills, and a lot more. He has money, and is willing to spread it around to make more."

"What, are you saying that Barrington–"

"Certainly not, Phinny. But a wealthy contributor can help the Party hold a dubious seat, y'know. We're past the old days, when each member could underwrite his own costs. More and more falls on the Party. And where's that money to come from, eh? The McScuttles of the world."

Phineas opened his mouth to speak, but Fitzgibbon forestalled him.

"Oh, and don't look so woundedly virtuous, Phineas. I remember a time when you came in as a member for Loughshane—the rottenest of all rotten boroughs, wasn't it? Or Tankerville, that first time—that was a clean fight, was it? You can hold the place until you die, but that's pretty much because you have a bit of fame, a bit of charm, and you married a woman as rich as she is beautiful—well, the luck of the Irish, Phinny smiled on you, and Barrington Erle, and, in its way, McScuttle. Everyone but poor old toiling Larry." And the heavy face frowned.

Phineas's sour look lightened momentarily. "You appear to be doing well enough, Mr. Undersecretary. Why leave yourself out?"

"Oh, please yourself. But d'you think Lord Fawn is the cynosure of Downing Street? He's terrified of the P.M., and terrified he'll be turfed out of office if he blots his copybook. And you can be d—d sure that he'll not run counter to Sir William, who represents industry, and is flooding the Party coffers, on a doubtful case. The P.M. would not be pleased. And Lord Fawn"—and here the Undersecretary looked around to ensure that there were no auditors, and, comforting himself that it was so, continued: "I say, and Lord Fawn may in fact not be the most illuminating light of all our peerage, but he ain't as dim as that."

Phineas nodded wearily. "Then it is to Barrington that I must go."

"I wouldn't, Phinny. He's got a lot of time for you, but there's something going on in the ranks I don't like. A leadership challenge, maybe, and Barrington's got the whip hand because he's got control of the lolly. And if he doesn't keep that control—why, Planty Pall has another former Prime Minister to join him on the sidelines. And much as Planty Pall hates to be outside looking in—well, Barrington'd hate it even more."

Phineas nodded again, then, brightening a little, asked "How's Lochy?"

"Still a fool. Came back from Court whining that you threatened him with bread and skilly for a month. Told him I wished I'd thought of it mesef, and told him I'd do it, too, if he ever did anything so idiotic again. Thanks for getting the poor chump off the hook. Sorry I can't repay you in kind."

The two friends shook hands. Phineas was making ready to go, when he heard Brentford's voice.

"Good seeing you again, Fawn. Yes, we'll have to dine soon."

He departed the *sanctum*, smiling with something less of his usual geniality, seized his hat and his stick, and began to make his exit. Frederick, Viscount Fawn, tall, and frayed and perhaps a little anxious underneath his conscientious manner, trailed after him, "Name the date, Brentford!" he called, and then stopped short. "Ah—Mr. Finn, is it not?" he said bowing a little. Phineas bowed to him as well.

"Yes, my lord. I was just seeing Mr. Fitzgibbon on a matter of Parliamentary business while you were with Lord Brentford."

"Ah, very good, Mr. Fitzgibbon," the Viscount said to his junior. His Lordship then asked, with a slightly peevish air, "I take it the matter has been resolved satisfactorily, Mr.—ah, Finn?"

"Mr. Fitzgibbon was very—illuminating, my lord."

"Then I'll wish you a good afternoon, shall I, Mr. Finn?" And Phineas saw that it was after four. He made his departure, and, with the disgruntled Earl in tow, began to make his way toward Park Lane and dinner.

The family party that had convened for a glass of wine before dinner was atypically subdued. Violet was fretting about her son, concerned about how he would react to the news of Clarissa's betrothal. Marie, having heard the tale of the day, its triumph and its tragedy both, from her husband, was fretting about him. Brentford was vexed that the excitement had come to so unpleasant an end, and cross at the notion of feeding Lord Fawn—"a waste of good woodcock," he finally burst out over the soup. With a momentary smile, Phineas, himself in a brown study, suggested feeding the Viscount beef.

"Beef!" The outraged peer repeated. "It'd be a waste to feed a sick chicken to that fluttering ninny. *Beef* shouldn't be thrown away so, either." He cheered up for a moment. "I could offer him venison. Very young venison, eh? Let Fawn eat fawn?"

When the gentlemen were withdrawing for port and cigars, Savrola, who had been most atypically silent through the meal, pulled Phineas aside for a moment.

"I don't mean to suggest anything you might feel inappropriate—us being on different sides of the aisle, I mean, and I doubt Barrington Erle would approve—but I know a way you could put pressure on the Home Secretary to pardon Powlett-Jones."

"Oh? How?" Phineas asked.

"Well, Mother is good friends with the Prince," the younger man offered shyly, "and if you spoke to her, and she spoke to him, then the Prince might speak to the Home Secretary–"

"Or even the Prime Minister, if needed–"

"Yes, if needed, and, well, the Prince doesn't interfere often, but he *will* be King, and, inevitably, that must happen–"

"I understand. You understand that this could put both of us in a position that might be—awkward."

"Not me, sir," Savrola differed. "My Party's not in power, and I'm just a novice backbencher. You—that's another story. You might think it rash. But—well, I felt I should make the suggestion. I could sound out Mother, if you like."

"Yes. Do so."

"Are you sure, sir?"

"I am," replied Phineas Finn, his face set. Then he added, grimly smiling, "*Quod necessitas non habet legem.*"

"ABSINTHE MAKES THE HEART GROW FONDER"

The very evening that Ifor Powlett-Jones's cross-examination concluded on such an unfortunate note, Savrola and his mother had been invited to dine with the Finns. Marie had warned Mrs. Vavasor that, as her host would be in court, she might find the party less carefree than she had hoped it would be when they had initially fixed the date, and offered to reschedule. Mrs. Vavasor had declined, saying in her return note that, as her son would be at the trial all day in the company of her future daughter-in-law, she would be afire to hear about what would be uppermost on their minds. So the ladies were together, awaiting the return of what Mrs. Vavasor had wittily dubbed "the Court Party," enjoying a preprandial glass of wine.

At about seven o'clock, a knock at the door was heard, shortly followed by Meier leading in the Countess of Brentford. She greeted Marie Finn with the warmth warranted by decades of intimacy, kissing her on the cheek. If she was surprised to see Mrs. Vavasor, she covered it well, shaking hands in a friendly manner.

"Mrs. Vavasor," the Countess greeted the visitor, "I know that our sons have quarrelled, but I trust we need not. Before you answer, please know that my son returned with me this afternoon from Scotland, and he is quite cognizant that he was in the wrong, and owes your son a full apology."

Winifred, who knew that the Countess had been staying with the Finns, had been prepared for a confrontation with her if necessary, and was disarmed by Violet's frankness.

"Your husband has already offered peace to me, Lady Brentford, and I would much rather be friends," Mrs. Vavasor said readily, "with those so close to one who is now to be most dear to me."

Violet shot her friend an interrogatory glance. Marie Finn answered her without excluding the newer visitor. "My niece has accepted a proposal from Mr. Vavasor," she said in her gentlest tone, "and her uncle has given his consent."

The Countess paled a little, but smiled. "I congratulate your son through you, Mrs. Vavasor. Clarissa is a girl I have known her whole life, and love most sincerely. Your son is most fortunate."

Winfred's sharp eyes told her that, despite the Countess' warm words and matching tone, something was amiss. "Forgive me, Lady Brentford, if I seem to pry, but you seem surprised to hear of the engagement. It was published in the *Times* some days ago."

"I have just returned from my sister-in-law's Scottish house, Mrs. Vavasor, where my son had been staying. We have all just returned, I should say, as Lady Laura and Jack—my son—travelled with me. And my sister-in-law does not take the *Times* up at Lochlinter, so we none of us had heard the happy news."

"Ah, that explains it all." Mrs. Vavasor passed it off with a light laugh.

The "Court Party" bustled into the room just then, with Phineas complaining aloud that "Old Bullfry shouldn't hold long sittings if he can't stay abreast of what's happening 'til the very end of them," Brentford exclaiming with pleasure at the sight of his wife, and Clarissa shyly accepting a kiss from her betrothed's mother.

Brentford greeted Mrs. Vavasor with cordiality, and remarked "Wine? Splendid. Could use some after that dusty courtroom, eh, Finn?"

With an enigmatic smile, Marie rang the bell for Meier. Barring an eruption from Jack at the news that Clarissa was affianced to Savrola Vavasor—news that he must receive within days, if not hours—she and Violet had patched up a peace in the wake of the quarrel at the

Marchioness' ball. All might yet be well, she reflected, if only Jack would have it so.

The next evening, Jack Standish headed to the Beargarden. After his travels, he had needed to sluice the dirt of the road from his person, and to sleep. He had slept through much of the day, and had lazed about the rest of it, perhaps having a little more wine than was ideal. Now, though it was a trifle late to dine, he wished to take the temperature of London Society after his unfortunate *contretemps* with Savrola Vavasor. He had been sufficiently catechised to realise that he had been thoroughly in the wrong in his actions at the Marchioness,' and he even had been brought to see that he owed that bumptious Tory an apology. He did not much relish the notion of tendering it, but, yes, since it was he who had resorted to fisticuffs, it was he who was in the wrong.

And, in truth, he was ashamed. When he had flown into his wild rage, he had lost, not merely control of his own behaviour, but some degree of perception of the situation in which he found himself. So he had not realised that the man he had punched had been a clergyman, let alone a bishop. And in the heat of the moment, he had not realised that he had nearly struck a man when he was down, or even Dolly Longestaffe, who was holding him back. He simply *was*—lashing out, striking at and hurting those who hurt him.

Afterward on such occasions, when memory returned, shame at what he had done often scalded him. But in that terrible moment when his rage boiled over, he knew nothing but that need to strike, to destroy—and he shuddered even now at the thought. He had ever relish the old stories of the *Táin* Phineas Finn had told on dark, wintry evenings, but not those featuring that most furious of Celtic heroes, Cuchulain. His own rages were too reminiscent of that beserker's for comfort. He knew that his own father had had similar lapses, but had, with passing age, mastered them.

Jack intended his return to the Beargarden as expiation. As a good Socialist, the *flâneurs* who infested the Beargarden were, at best, by turns comical or pitiable relics of the old order which even now changeth, yielding place to new. But they were also his friends, schoolmates and playfellows alike, those with whom he had gamboled as a boy and gambled as a young man. Their respect, while it should not matter to him, did. Their love mattered more. And so, squaring his shoulders, and screwing his courage to the sticking place—Jack entered the Beargarden.

He was a member in good standing, and so the porter greeted him cheerfully enough.

"Hallo, Hammond," Jack returned his greeting. "Chops still available in the dining room, then?" On being assured that was the case, Jack entered the dining room, and found it only sparsely populated. But among the few members there was one whom Jack both feared and needed to find.

The Oldest Member was finishing his sweet course, a moderately large chocolate concoction Jack could not identify, so splendid was the progress Dolly had made upon it. A cup of coffee steamed gently at his side, and he made happy gustatory noises as he made further inroads. And then he perceived the figure standing in front of him, waiting to break in on the finale of his meal, and lowered his heaping spoon in dismay.

"Oh, dear," the nonplussed Dolly murmured, "Chiltern."

Rather than issue the usual remonstrance, Jack burst out, "I say, Dolly, I was beastly to you at that d——d ball, and I beg your pardon."

Dolly's face lit up at that and he waved Jack to a chair. "My dear boy," he greeted the prodigal, "have a little fatted calf, and we can go into the card room together. Or do you fancy billiards tonight?"

Jack sank with relief into the proffered seat, ordered some grilled chops, and watched as Dolly finished communing with his sweet course, then rang for another pot of coffee, a bottle of brandy and two snifters. As Jack awaited his meal, he poured himself a large snifter, which he steadily, but unhurriedly, drained. Dolly diverted him with the news of the day—a threat to Barrington Erle's premiership being mounted by some of the younger members, as well as rumours that Planty Pall might be courting again—that he had come early to town, and, instead of staying with his daughter at Carlton Terrace, had booked a suite of rooms at Claridge's.

"And the ladies' bush telegraph is signaling that it's the Marchioness herself he's interested in. Oh, aye, Jack. When she finally deigned to put in an appearance, who did she make sure escorted her around the terraces? Planty Pall himself. Hard to believe, though, isn't it? I mean, he's never remarried, and it's ages since poor darling Lady Glen was lost—oh, there was a hostess for you! Always a sly joke, the latest scandal, and a good laugh."

As Jack recharged his glass, and set to work, Dolly twittered on.

"But come to think of it, the rumour was years ago that Planty Pall nearly went off the rails before his wedding to Lady Glen. I remember my sainted Aunt—courtesy title, I assure you, dear boy; nobody could seriously call my late, unlamented Aunt a saint, except as a courtesy—saying when I was a boy that Planty Pall had nearly run off with the Marchioness herself."

"Dolly!" expostulated Jack.

"No, no; it's true, Jack. You must remember that, forbidding and proper as the Marchioness has become, back then she was Lady Dumbello—and had only recently become so; most people knew her, if at all, as simple Griselda Grantly, the Archdeacon's daughter. It's quite possible that the old fire still burns," he mused.

"Under that permafrost?" scoffed Jack. "Fancy a dry old stick like Planty Pall kindling any woman's haystack!"

"Ah. But it's just the dry, well-seasoned sticks that burn the hottest," Dolly began.

"Congratulations, old man," said a voice from over his shoulder. Jack rose and turned, finding himself facing a newer member.

"Congratulations, Benskin? What for?"

"Why your engagement, you great muff! I don't know the lady, but I hear she's a beauty, and rich, too."

"Engaged—to a rich lady, who's a beauty?" Jack was thunderstruck. Mother and his Aunt Laura had assured him that the threatened announcements had been suppressed by Aunt Marie; what had gone wrong?

Seeing Jack's confusion, Benskin turned to Dolly Longestaffe. "Dolly, you told Sumner that your wife had the news from the lady herself, didn't you?"

A stricken Jack swiveled his head to see Dolly, who confirmed, "Why, yes; yes she did. Hermione was taking tea with Lady Monogram, and the lady herself breezed in and told everyone there. I doubt there's a lady in London who hasn't heard the news, by now, Jack."

And Jack realised that for all of Aunt Marie's cleverness, his *soi-disant fiancée* had nonetheless scored; with Jack absent from Town, she had spent the past month spreading the story of their engagement. Jack collapsed back into his chair, and Dolly waved Benskin on.

"What's the matter, old chap?" he asked Jack, concern written across his brow.

"She can't have..."

"Nobody thinks the worse of you for her being a bit older, Jack. She's got tons of the readies, and if your family ain't as solvent as it ought to be, well, that's an old story these days."

Jack drained his brandy, poured himself another snifter, to the brim this time, and gulped it down. "No, no, Dolly—I can't marry her..."

"My dear fella, of course you can. At least she's still a looker, and gad, those wild panther eyes of hers would lead plenty of chaps to forget *anno domini*."

"But I don't love her, Dolly!"

"Well good heavens, man, d'you think I was burning for my Hermione when we got married? 'Course not. Stands to reason. But we jog along very pleasantly nowadays. So, you see, old son, marrying for money can work out fine if you're just moderate about it."

But Dolly was speaking to the back of his interlocutor, who was stalking toward the billiard room in pursuit of Benskin. Dolly followed suit, hoping to prevent another Chilternian explosion. He arrived in time to find Jack denying his engagement, still calm at least on the surface, but quite firm. "No, no," he said emphatically, and with the particular precision of a young man who has had perhaps a bit more brandy than is ideal while waiting for an order of chops he has not had the opportunity to consume, "I cannot marry Lady Eustace," he said, "sensible tho' I am of the honour she would so confer upon my house, because my heart belongs to another."

"Oh?" Benskin asked. "And to whom does your heart belong?"

Jack quaffed most of the large snifter still in his hand, and slopped more into it, filling it well above the customary level. He drank deeply of its contents.

"Gentlemen," he explained owlishly, "I love—and believe that I am fortunate enough to have the love of—a lady who does not, perhaps bring birth or wealth to me, but who excels in beauty, youth, and the indefinable charm of goodness."

"That's all very well," Sumner called from across the billiard table, "but who the d—l is she?"

"The lady to whom I intend to get married is none other than that lovely waif, niece of the long-term friend of my family, Miss Clarissa Riley."

This announcement produced a sensation, but not the one Jack had anticipated. Instead of bursting into effusive back-thumpings, his interlocutors turned rather pale and seemed to be regarding him with—surely, not pity?

"You cannot be serious," Dolly asked, "can you?"

"I am indeed," the young peer, swooping his arm in a bold gesture, which, alas, sloshed some of his brandy on the table.

"Careful, there!" cried out a member, "you'll ruin the pile on the table!"

"But, Jack." Dolly Longestaffe spoke as if to a child. "Miss Riley is already engaged to be married."

"She is not, sir!" Jack thought this was an excellent leg-pull, and waggishly pointed a finger at Dolly. "Her guardian uncle is my own father's closest friend, and I'd know."

"The engagement was announced days ago," Dolly replied. "Here, where's that paper—Niven, you're in the corner with the *Jupiter*; flush the ruddy thing out, will you?"

As the youth so addressed obeyed, the less-fogged portions of Jack's brain began to doubt that this was so excellent a jape as he had previously thought it.

"It's true, Jack." Dolly tried to reach the younger man.

"Oh," challenged the drunken peer, "well, then to whom is Miss Riley engaged then, hey? Who's the lucky man to be?"

Dolly drew in a breath, and answered, just as Niven approached Jack from the side with a newspaper.

"Couldn't find it in the *Jupiter*, Dolly," the youth said, handing the broadsheet to Jack, "but here it is in the *Times*."

"It's Vavasor, Jack. She's going to marry Savrola Vavasor."

And, snatching the broadsheet, Jack scanned the page, and saw that it was true. He gulped twice, but said nothing. He mutely handed the paper back to Niven, and crossed the room, pulling the bell. When the porter arrived, Jack instructed him curtly, "A room for the night. And, Hammond—a bottle of the Infuriator."

As Jack was led to his bedroom, and his needs seen to, Dolly Longestaffe sadly shook his head, subsiding into a well-padded armchair.

"It won't work," he said in a melancholy voice, to nobody in particular. "Absinthe makes the heart grow fonder."

23
THE CHALLENGE

In his room at the Beargarden, Jack had finished off the bottle of the Infuriator. He had hoped that drunkenness would bring him release, or at least oblivion. But Jack was a strong young man with an excellent constitution, and since his mother and Aunt Laura had descended upon him at Lochlinter, he had been relatively moderate in his potations. His mother had given him hope, too, that his love for Clarissa Riley would be crowned with success, and her ready acceptance of the girl as a possible bride for him had, along with her assurance that Lizzie Eustace had been muzzled, restored his equilibrium for the trip home from Scotland.

Now, within hours of his return, he found that neither reassurance held true. What Lizzie had not been able to accomplish through the Press, she had achieved through the simple expedient of telling her news to the gossips of London, and allowing them to do her work for her. Worse, he could not give her the lie. He had, in fact, asked her, and had not yet found a way to disentangle himself from her.

Worse still, he had been assailed, not merely by the news that his rash proposal to Lizzie the Liar had been spread throughout Society, but with the appalling intelligence that the beauteous Clarissa was pledged to marry the insolent mongrel pup Vavasor. Lizzie had termed this youth a "cur" in one of her detestably artificial "love letters," in the sole passage that Jack could whole-heartedly endorse. But now even the word "cur" struck him as too generous to the one who was merely an insolent half-breed pup. Insolent half-breed puppy, rather, he corrected himself, savouring the insult.

Jack pulled himself out of the chair, the room momentarily unsteady around him, and then paced the room, building up momentum. For a brief moment he contemplated collapsing on the bed and allowing himself to succumb to sleep.

No! He thought, grasping the green, cut glass bottle, which had been so recently been full of the Infuriator, and draining the last swallow from the bottle's neck. Ah, that was better! The fiery liquid coursed through him, awakening the primal Jack, the man who would not be robbed of his honour by a titled trull and a puppy, respectively. Regardless of that pair, Clarissa was meant for him, and he had to repel those who would, by stratagem or guile, separate them.

He moodily lit a cigar, and sallied forth into the hallway, and then back down to the Club's proper quarters. In the dimly-lit hallway leading to the stairs, the red, glowing tip of his cheroot led him onward, ever onward. As the last bit of absinthe awoke his fires, Jack felt a sudden accession of energy, and a burning desire to right the wrongs that had been done both to him and to poor, helpless Clarissa.

Savrola Vavasor had not found his evening with Finns as pleasant as usual. The dour mood of the party, the acrid taste of defeat, and, most of all, the presence of the Countess of Brentford, whom he sensed viewed with disfavour his engagement to Clarissa, had left him in a rather dejected frame of mind. That mood lightened somewhat after he offered to speak with his mother on behalf of Phineas Finn. The brief moment where his future father-in-law—for it was impossible for Savrola to view Phineas as less than a father to Clarissa—had warned him of the potential risks to his own career in invoking Mother's aid on behalf of Powlett-Jones had touched him, all the more so as Phineas belonged to the Other Side. He could not remember his own father ever considering his son's interests above his own, even for a fleeting moment, and it struck him as auspicious that the family circle into which he was marrying was so much warmer than that which he had known.

His Aunt Kate and his cousin Alice treated Mother with an offhand aloofness, and himself as if he were some sort of half-trained dog—one to pet, on occasion, but also to watch carefully for erratic behaviour. His Uncle John had been good to him, in his way, supporting Mother and himself in that terrible period when, after Father's death, they had abandoned America for England. Uncle John had paid Savrola's school fees, established Mother in a charming house in London, and had opened his home to them. But Uncle John had never quite admitted Savrola to his heart. Oh, that his Uncle was fond of Savrola in his rather dry, humourous way, Savrola had no doubt. But John Vavasor was a better man to discuss ideas with than feelings—comfortable in the abstract reaches of philosophy, the panoply of history, or even the rearing of hounds, his uncle could emerge from his shyness, and flash a canny grin, and share an insight. But as a man dealing with children—especially a fatherless child, as Savrola had been—Uncle John was helpless.

Now, with the smoke from his own cigar rising into the bluish-gray cloud created by Brentford's cigars (which the peer consumed with an alarming quickness) and Phineas's pipe, he felt welcomed, at home. It was a sensation he had never really known before these past three days, attending the Court with Brentford and Clarissa, and participating in what Phineas rather chillingly described as "post-mortems" after dinner.

This evening, there was no post-mortem. Or almost none.

"I shall have to see Barrington," Phineas remarked after a desultory conversation about hunting with the Brentfords at Harrington Hall, when all the dust had settled.

"Shall you?" Brentford asked. "I had rather thought Fitzgibbon put you off that."

Phineas nodded, with the grimness that had vanished during the talk of hunting. "He did. But before I try less common means, I owe Barrington the courtesy of working through more conventional channels."

"He won't care for it, you know."

"I know, Oswald, but what am I to do? Even if he is angry, I nonetheless have a duty in the matter. It was Barrington Erle"—this was directed at Savrola—"who introduced me to politics in the first place."

"I did not know that, sir," Savrola answered.

"Yes, and though we have not always been as close as we once were—for Barrington is first and foremost a party man, and I am not—well, our friendship has survived many differences. If it must wreck on the rock of this confounded case, so be it, but I shan't have it be because I did not speak with him on account of Larry Fitzgibbon—or that tailor's dummy he works for."

"Phineas has ever disliked Lord Fawn," Brentford said with an air of mock wisdom, "but only with the very best of reasons."

"Oh?" Savrola invited further confidences.

"Yes," Brentford continued, "First, they were rivals in love—mind you, he's had a few of those, and Fawn not the most formidable–"

Phineas made a strangled sound that Savrola correctly interpreted as an involuntary snort coupled with a derisive laugh.

"And then, of course, he discovered what I could have told him since boyhood," His Lordship continued, reclining a little further, and sending a smoke ring toward the rafters.

"And what might that be, my lord?" Phineas inquired gravely.

"That His Lordship is far less useful than a tailor's dummy. Your, er, uncle-in-law-to-be errs on the side of charity on that point, my boy," Brentford said, sipping his port, and following that by applying himself once more to his cheroot.

His patter was then interrupted by Elspeth's springing into his lap, purring loudly, and tapping a gentle paw against his cigar, causing the startled Earl to sputter a bit.

"A useful reminder—an emissary, gentlemen, from the Ladies' Side" their host said, knocking the ash from his pipe. "We should not keep the other ladies waiting unduly."

And, as the Earl stroked the grey–and-white cat kneading his vest, the gentlemen finished their port and rose to rejoin the ladies.

Savrola found himself seated opposite his *fiancée* when the gentlemen rejoined the ladies, and, greatly emboldened, took her hand in his own.

"Do not be too sad, my love," he said to the mistress of his heart.

"How can I not be?" Clarissa returned, "with that poor young man in prison for five years, with no hope of respite?"

"There may be hope, dearest. Your uncle and I have been speaking, and I think we may be able to try one more means to free poor Powlett-Jones." And Clarissa never had admired her lover more than now, when his blue eyes, determined chin, and boundless confidence were arrayed on the side of her beloved uncle in a fight for justice.

"Your uncle can brief my mother, and my mother will plead Powlett-Jones's case to the Prince. He does not often intervene, but if she can rouse his conscience in this matter, the very infrequency with which he does intervene will add weight to his plea.

"His plea? To whom?" the young woman asked, perplexed. Her *fiancé* answered confidently.

"As heir to the throne, he can pressure the Home Secretary, or, if need be, plead the case to the font of all the clemency power there is in England."

The young woman looked bewilderedly at her lover.

"He can go directly to the Queen," he said softly.

"Who is your mother, that the Prince would do so much for her?" Clarissa asked, not knowing the rumours that had swirled about that lady's name.

"She is his friend," Savrola replied stiffly. He rose, and made his farewells a little abruptly.

Knowing that he had taken offense where none was intended, Savrola walked his ire off, and, as he passed by the Beargarden, he decided that a game of billiards would turn his mind from his troubles, and turned into the club. He smiled and greeted Hammond, and found a small group in the billiard room. Niven had just lost a game of go-back to Trubshawe, who stroked his extravagant moustache in exaltation at his victory. Vavasor joined the younger men, not noticing an unwontedly serious Dolly Longestaffe staring moodily into a whiskey and soda.

Dolly was, in fact, seeking to determine the nature of a foreign body he espied in the depths of his drink, and wondering whether to order a fresh one, even though this one was as yet untouched. It went against all his principles, but he was older now, he thought, and no longer as straitened in his means as he had once been. Yes, he thought, he would order a fresh drink, and not allow this one to be left on his tab. Hammond's pride be blowed, Dolly thought, waving down a waiter. But before he could implement this momentous resolution, he heard a voice he had not expected to hear again until the morning—and not the early morning, either.

"Now that is what I call cheek," said Jack Standish, surveying the occupants of the billiard room with a jaundiced eye.

Scenting trouble not too far off, Dolly Longestaff rose. "Hallo, Jack," he greeted.

"Hallo, Dolly," the young lord replied in a friendly enough fashion, but then continued: "Look at that devil. Playing billiards with Trubshawe, just as if he had a right to be here."

"He is a member, Jack," Dolly Longestaffe reminded the younger man.

"Oh, a member, is he? I suppose standards really have gone down then, eh. Dolly?" Jack's voice rose a tone, as he swaggered a little further into the room. "Yes, that must be it," he continued, still louder, "Standards are declining, surely. The Beargarden used to draw its members from a higher sphere of Society, and not take in any riff-raff who applied."

"Riff-raff?" Niven interjected, afraid that his Scots ancestry was under attack. "We're all gentlemen here, surely?"

"Oh, most of us are, Niv." The swaggering peer clapped the young Scot on the shoulder. "But not all, I'm afraid," he continued darkly.

"What odd talk for a socialist who talks of renouncing his title," growled Savrola Vavasor, potting a ball neatly in the corner pocket. For the sake of his future bride—aye and of the arrogant youth's own rather likeable parents, too!—Savrola had been prepared to swallow his anger and accept the apology he had been promised, but the arrogant aesthete had a way of getting under his skin.

Jack smelled blood in the water, and moved in for another bite.

"No, we accept dirty money and dirty men in the club these days; not like it used to be, eh, Dolly?"

But that worthy, so appealed to, remained mute, thinking perhaps of a certain baronet who still occasionally infested the club late at night, though generally having the decency to keep to his bedroom until the younger members had retired.

Jack, in the grip of the Infuriator's power, had shed his egalitarian convictions, being far too eager to wound his antagonist. The Chiltern temper, well fed by the liquor, was in its most malignant humour, looking to cause pain, and grasping at any available weapon.

"When I joined the Beargarden, I was assured that my associates would be, at a minimum, gentlemen. Instead, I see playing at our billiards table transatlantic trash –"

"That's enough, Jack," said Dolly Longestaffe with an unwonted firmness.

"No, it ain't, Dolly," the sneering peer answered, as Vavasor struggled with his own temper. "Bad enough that I have to see an American debasing our billiard table–"

"How on earth," Niven wondered aloud, "does one debase a billiard table?"

"Fairly sure you don't want to know, old man," replied Trubshawe.

"—but not just any American, is he? His father went mad, they say. Some loathsome disease, hey? And we all know how those are contracted, don't we?"

Vavasor began to stalk around the billiard table, but Niven restrained him.

"Don't do it, old chap," he murmured, "that's what he wants. He wants you to strike the first blow."

Vavasor nodded, and Niven relaxed his grip.

"And I'm sure we know from whom he contracted it, don't we?" Jack continued, all the bitterness in his heart pouring out now upon the unfortunate Vavasor. Curiously, even as Jack continued his diatribe, he was conscious of a corner of his mind urging him not to do it—a cool, detached observer who knew exactly what Jack intended and what he sought to achieve thereby, and disapproved mightily, but was unable to intervene.

"Yes, we all know, don't we?" Jack, or perhaps the Infuriator, remorselessly ground on. "After all, she's continued in that line of work, hasn't she? Once a trollop, always a–"

But Jack was unable to finish his peroration, for Savrola Vavasor had struck him with his glove across the mouth. Calmly, but with his normally cherubic features twisted into an almost bulldog snarl, he growled, "Lord Chiltern, your insults are beneath contempt, sir, as indeed are you. I demand satisfaction of you—if you have any honour left."

"Left?" roared Jack Standish, although he was exultant at having drawn the challenge, knowing that the choice of weapons now fell to him.

"Left," Savrola replied, quite calmly, now. "It was you, after all, who fled our first encounter, and I was willing to accept the apology which your own mother—since you are so dead to honour as to bring the ladies into it—begged me to accept on your behalf."

"You lie!" Jack roared a second time, sincerely appalled at the double accusation of cowardice hurled at him.

"Mr. Trubshawe, will you act for me?" Savrola enquired. On receiving an affirmative, he then asked his opponent "Who acts for you, sir?"

"Dolly, will you act as my second?" Jack asked, certain of the answer to come.

But Dolly Longestaffe, whose life-long practise it was never to condemn his fellows—"Judge not," he often sententiously decreed, "lest ye find yourself partnerless at whist"—had, quite simply, had a bellyful.

"No, sir, I will not," he said, and a collective gasp was heard at the severity of his tone. "You have behaved like a bully and a cad, sir, and I will have nothing to do with your provocation of a brother member of the Beargarden."

Shocked, Chiltern looked around the room, scanning the faces of his fellow denizens of the Beargarden. His eyes looked interrogatively at Niven, who shook his head firmly, and at Sumner, who averted his eyes. As Chiltern looked about him helplessly, a breathy, wheezy voice came from behind him.

"I'll act for the lad," said Sir Felix Carbury.

He advanced into the room, a gaunt, febrile-eyed specimen of about Dolly's age, with a grin as warm as a skull's, his clothes of the finest, but draped upon the etiolated frame of one in an advanced stage of dissipation. "Aye," Sir Felix reaffirmed, "I'll act for the lad. You can find me here to make arrangements, Mr. Trubshawe," he said to the younger man, with the perfect courtesy that had once marked him before his descent toward elegant ruin.

"Good," said Chiltern. "Make what arrangements you please, Sir Felix. As long as the weapon is a sword, I'll meet you anywhere, anytime, Vavasor. And we'll see how well your affectation of manliness holds when I let some of the hot air out of you, balloon."

"If you don't run a second time—*poltroon*," Vavasor gibed.

Surprisingly, Chiltern did not rise to the bait. He bowed gently to the assembled company, and then to Savrola Vavasor, with a smile no warmer than Sir Felix Carbury's, and passed to his bedroom without a word. He closed the door gently, in perfect silence, and collapsed upon the bed like a puppet, the strings of which had been decisively cut.

GOING THROUGH CHANNELS

The next morning, Phineas Finn sent his card in to the Prime Minister, with a short, urgent request that he have an opportunity to speak with him.

There came no answer.

That afternoon, Phineas presented himself at the Prime Minister's door. The secretary, who knew him, greeted him pleasantly, but then said, "I'm sorry, Mr. Finn, but the Prime Minister simply hasn't the time today. Perhaps after today's session."

And so Phineas subjected himself to a tedious debate about the proper disposition of a charity—an almshouse for elderly woolcarders, in a region that no longer required such residence, as the woolcarders had all long ago been gathered to their fathers—only to see the Prime Minister rise before the debate ended. He quickly followed him out of the Commons, and called to him, "Prime Minister!"

Wearily, and with a resigned air, Barrington Erle turned, and exhaled. "Yes, Phineas, what is it?"

And as Phineas launched into his set speech about the conviction of Powlett-Jones on that one, lowest count, and the boy's deserving a pardon, Barrington Erle's eyes hooded over, like those of a falcon forced to endure the tiresome squeaking of its prey.

The two men walked together, and, to give Barrington Erle his due, he heard Phineas out. But then, as they crossed into a little private room in which the Prime Minister was wont to hold audience, he said to

Phineas: "You cannot expect me to second-guess a jury that gave your client the benefit of the doubt on every other charge, and interfere with the Home Secretary, to boot! Phineas, you have lost your perspective with this case. You did well for the boy, certainly better than anyone expected."

"Expected?" Phineas asked, taken aback.

"My dear chap," Barrington smiled, "when I became aware that you had taken on the defence, I was quite concerned. I know how persuasive you can be," he chuckled warmly. "And you saved your client quite a lot of time in gaol, which I'm sure nobody grudges you. But Sir William McScuttle paid for this prosecution himself, and would have hated to have spent all that money for nothing. Had you convinced Fawn, of course, to recommend a pardon, that would have been different, and I suppose Sir William would have had to live with the disappointment. But I'm sure Larry Fitzgibbon set you straight there, hmm?"

"Oh, yes, Prime Minister. He did."

"Good. Now let's hear no more about the matter, Phineas, shall we? After all, an English jury has ruled, and you did quite well out of it yourself—you pretty much beat the former Solicitor General—and a fine one for you to beat, too!"

"But, Barrington—Powlett-Jones–"

"Is no doubt very well where he is, Phineas," the Prime Minister responded quite firmly. "He's had his day in court, and that is all he's entitled to. No, your efforts saved him a much longer sentence, I am quite sure, so you have nothing to be ashamed of." And with that, Barrington Erle, waved Phineas out of the room, bidding Phineas, "Mind you remember me to Mrs. Finn, and to that lovely niece of yours, Phineas—glad to hear of her engagement—even if the fella is a Tory!"

And the door closed, very firmly, in Phineas Finn's face.

The day was not so far gone yet that he could not catch Lord Fawn at the Home Office, and so Phineas repaired thereto. Lawrence Fitzgibbon was at first obdurate about preventing a meeting between Phineas and the Home Secretary, but Phineas wore him down. Larry had not the heart to be brusque with his old friend, even in his own best interests, and so Phineas was ushered into the Home Secretary's private room.

"Mr. Finn, I had rather thought that you met with my Undersecretary on this matter," Lord Fawn began unpromisingly.

"Yes, Home Secretary, I did. Nonetheless, I have decided to try once more to appeal to you–"

"Mr. Finn, there is a regular process which should be followed in such cases…"

"Yes, Lord Fawn, but I do not wish to appeal to you in the sense of filing a formal legal appeal, but to request that you investigate the grounds upon which the conviction is based, with an eye to determining whether a pardon is in order."

"But you have not availed yourself of all of your administrative remedies! And a jury, which does not appear to have been prejudiced against your client, as they were able to acquit of almost all the charges—why, what basis do you have to request such an investigation?"

And then, realising that Phineas was hoping to answer that very question, Lord Fawn swiftly continued: "No, no; I cannot hear it; you are acting as a barrister, not as an M.P.; it is no concern of mine what has actuated you."

"My client, Home Secretary, is a young man who saved many lives, and now–"

"And destroyed property, Mr. Finn, and struck a superior, Mr. Finn, and is now being made to answer for his deeds, Mr. Finn," his Lordship retorted smugly.

"I see that your Lordship has made up your mind," Phineas said sadly. He had only just recognised that Larry Fitzgibbon had been quite right; Lord Fawn hated Phineas Finn with the special brand of malice that a weak man can bear another human being whom he has profoundly wronged. Twenty years had passed since Chaffanbrass had rubbed Lord Fawn's nose in the ignominy of his over-hasty identification of Phineas as the figure who had followed the late, unlamented, Mr. Bonteen in the night, and no doubt murdered him, and his Lordship at last had the high ground over Phineas!

"I have read the dossier prepared for me by Sir William, who knew that you would—what was his word? Ah, yes, you would try to *nibble* me," his Lordship condescended to smile.

"Ah," Phineas said, with a flicker of a smile on his own face, "I believe Sir William might have intended to say *nobble*, my lord. That, at any rate, is the term used on the Turf. Thank you for seeing me, my lord." And Phineas bowed his way out of Lord Fawn's room, where he met a desperately unhappy Fitzgibbon. The friends shook hands in silence, and Phineas took his leave.

His first two embassies having failed, he set forth to meet Mrs. Vavasor at her home. Here he met with a much warmer reception, but the beautiful widow was herself greatly perturbed, having heard from Savrola a severely edited version of his quarrel with Lord Chiltern—and, as she informed Phineas, she was now deeply concerned for her son's life.

"Englishmen!" She denounced them all, after welcoming Phineas into her ornate drawing room. It was in vain that he pointed out that he was, in fact, Irish. She raged on, "All so proud, so ready to die over a few harsh words! Do they have no idea of death? Of its finality, of the cost it exacts from their mothers, wives—*fiancées?* Is poor Clarissa to be a widow before she is a wife? Am I to bury a son, as I have two husbands? Or shall it be that other woman who mourns—Lord Standish's mother, and his father, too, who were so willing to make peace with me?"

"My dear Mrs. Vavasor," Phineas tried to comfort her, "I know both of these boys quite well—yours only for a few weeks, but long enough to feel that I should be proud, were he a son of mine—and Jack, since he was a boy. I don't know what's gotten into the two young rascals, but we will find a way to let them save their faces without shedding their blood."

"You're sure?" Winifred Vavasor peered deeply into Phineas's eyes, and in fact was comforted by what she found there.

"Quite sure," he replied readily. "I know Savrola well enough to know that this quarrel was none of his seeking, and I know Jack, too. And it's one thing to demand satisfaction, and quite another to try to kill the man standing up against you over a form of words."

Winifred Vavasor had a shrewd instinct, and a mother's quick perceptions. "You have stood in such a quarrel, haven't you?" she asked.

Phineas smiled ruefully. "Once," he answered her. "A long time ago, in a remarkably foolish quarrel brought on by the fact that another young fire-eater challenged me because we both loved the same woman."

"What happened?"

"Very little. We exchanged shots in Belgium—Blankenberg was the name of the town, I recall—and my arm was wounded."

"How infamous!" The widow spoke with true anger. "What if you had died?"

"I quite agree, Mrs. Vavasor, I truly do. It's no good catechizing me nearly three decades after my folly—and I paid for it, I did! That arm ached for months afterward—and worse, I knew myself to have been a fool. Real courage would have been to let the rest of them think I was a poltroon, and not risk everything for a mere show of courage in a meaningless spat."

"And what makes you so sure that this occasion will turn out any better—or at least no worse?"

"I will not allow it. I am too close to both of them to permit the one to slaughter the other. And–"

"What is it; why do you hesitate?"

"I do not believe that either of them has the hard-heartedness to kill. If I can find a way for them to climb down without admitting they are doing so, I believe they will only be too happy to grasp at the olive branch."

At that, Mrs. Vavasor smiled, and her years fell away from her. "You are an Irishman," she said, with a delightful lilt in her voice, "and you know just how the English think. And, before you excuse yourself, and make your departure, I should remind you that I am an American, and therefore can pursue two ends at once. Savrola has already spoken to me about Mr. Powlett-Jones, and your desire to obtain a pardon for him. I am more than willing to help."

"Are you indeed? When you told me about this lunatic quarrel, I had quite resolved to let the legal matter rest, until the unpleasantness between the two young men had been taken care of first."

"Well, it may move faster, Mr. Finn, but I rather think we should begin our work. I quite admire your willingness to fight for your client with any weapon you can find, even if I am chosen as such a weapon. No, no," she laughed a little, "I am quite aware that it was my son who made the running, and not yourself. Prior to this–" and the lady nearly spat the word out "*damned* quarrel, I have heard nothing from Savrola, save for what an angel Clarissa is, and what a paladin you have been on behalf of that poor Welsh boy. So I am, as I say, quite willing to do my part."

"I am most grateful," Phineas replied.

"It is I who have cause for gratitude, Mr. Finn. My son's father was a thoroughgoing scoundrel, as I discovered far too late. Savrola needs a good man to show him how to be a father himself, and I believe he has found that, as well as a truly good girl for his wife."

Phineas cast about for a graceful reply, and signally failed to find one.

"An American stopping the mouth of an Irish politician?" Mrs. Vavasor asked, "I claim a victory then, for my candour. Come, Mr. Finn, make yourself comfortable, so that you may inform me more thoroughly as to what I may say to the Prince. I assure you, I will do my very best to move him."

THE AMBASSADORS

When Phineas returned home, he found his wife and niece at afternoon tea with two gentlemen he did not recognise. The first was a young man, of pleasant, affable demeanour, whose light brown hair was parted in the middle and whose extravagant moustaches, lovingly waxed, protruded beyond his cheeks by an inch or more. The second—ah, the second!

Exquisitely dressed, with a tall, rangy form that must once have been handsome, and the face of a privileged sot, the older man was about Phineas's age, but with a jaundiced, insolent eye, an unflappable air of contempt, and an ineffable aura of raciness that had curdled over time into heartlessness. To be sure, his manners were impeccable as he accepted tea-cake, and he greeted Phineas with a graceful formality that suggested that once upon a time this man might have been somebody. That two such different types should have found their way to his door, let alone cadged an invitation to tea, mystified Phineas. After he shook hands with the men—the younger introduced as a Mr. Trubshawe, the elder as Sir Felix Carbury (a name which to Phineas immediately savoured of old scandal, though he may have been biased by his sudden recognition of the now-spruced up drunkard he had met on the night of the ball), he glanced at Marie, hoping for enlightenment.

Sir Felix, however, took matters into his own hands, and provided the much-needed enlightenment as Phineas drained his teacup.

"My dear Mr. Finn," he explained, "My colleague Mr. Trubshawe and I have come about a delicate matter, each representing the interests of one known to you. I represent your godson, Lord Chiltern."

"And I your future nephew-by-marriage, Savrola Vavasor," put in Trubshawe helpfully.

"I see," Phineas temporised a moment. "Gentlemen, may I invite you to my study to discuss the matter you bring to me? I suspect that it is one that does not warrant discussion before the ladies."

"Oho," said Sir Felix, chortling a little. "You are a fly one, Mr. Finn. Certainly, we will accompany you." And then, with a surprisingly solemn air, he bowed to the ladies, thanking them most prettily for his tea, and the pleasure of their company while drinking it. As the two gentlemen were shown into his study by Meier, Phineas found his arm subtly pulled by Marie. Understanding her import, he begged the gentlemen's indulgence while he spoke briefly with his wife. While Trubshawe stammered his consent, Sir Felix handsomely waved Phineas's apology away.

When the visitors were safely closeted in the study, Marie urgently murmured that he must see Oswald before he met the other gentlemen, as he must speak with him about the same business. Oswald was, Marie informed him, in her private room. Phineas proceeded there and found his old friend.

"Finn, thank heaven!" Lord Brentford sighed when he saw his old friend, and scanned his face. Seeing something in Phineas's expression, he exhaled. "You know then? About the quarrel?"

"I know something of it. That there was one. Not who is to blame, or how to avert the sequel, yet."

Brentford looked Phineas squarely in the eye. "Heaven help me," he said, more agitated under his bluff façade then Phineas had seen him since their own quarrel so many years ago, "my own boy is to blame. How I hate to say it, but I know him, and we both know that d—d Chiltern temper he shares with me! As far as I can make it out, he got some idea in his head that Clarissa was going to marry him—without going to the trouble of asking her, mind you!—and cut up rough with young Vavasor—who's all right as far as I can tell, even if he is a Tory—and all this while, despite the fact that he's taken a notion to your niece, my young scamp has gone and gotten himself engaged to the most unsuitable woman in London."

"What? Who?" Phineas asked.

"Lizzie Eustace, if you can believe such a thing! What could have possessed the boy–" And seeing Phineas's quizzical look, the Earl continued. "All right, Lizzie the Liar's as pretty as she ever was—what price the portrait in her attic?—but she's infamous! And picking a fight over a girl, well, that sort of thing hasn't been done since-since–"

"Since you and I did it?" Phineas asked, in his gravest, gentlest voice. And Lord Brentford's agitation was lifted for a moment.

"Yes," he smiled ruefully, "since then, Phineas, blast you—and bless you for saying 'we' since I'm pretty sure I picked that fight against your will. But listen here—those two men—they're Jack's and Vavasor's seconds, and they are here to ask you to serve as *maître d'armes*."

"Me?" Phineas gasped.

"You. It's to be a duel with sabres, Phineas, and we all know what that means—Jack's a fencing champion, and Vavasor learned a bit in his Army service. They have seconds, but they need a man they can implicitly trust. And so do I," the Earl added, impressively.

"You need…"

"Phineas, we have been friends since our youth, and I would do anything for you. Do this for me. *Do not let my son become a murderer.* With the steel in his hand, if he bests Vavasor, I do not know if he can hold himself back. He's a good boy at heart, but this—this madness in him; I know it all too well. Something is driving him to ever-increasing wildness."

"Oswald–"

"I know you cannot guarantee my son's safety; I do not ask you to try. You must be strictly impartial, and I accept that, of course. But you can, if my son loses control, end the bout and declare Vavasor the winner. I do not care tuppence for this insane quarrel, but would not have my son be a murderer, whether he hangs for it or no. Will you do this for me?"

Phineas could not speak. He nodded his head, whereupon Brentford seized his hand and wrung it in silence. When each had obtained mastery over his feelings, Brentford said simply, "Thank you, Phineas," and clapped the Irishman on the shoulder.

"I had best see Trubshawe and Carbury."

"Aye," replied the peer moodily. "And watch out for Carbury," he added. "He's a scoundrel if I remember him aright. And a toper, too, I'll be bound. And I don't trust the fella, even if I don't remember him aright, Phineas—he's too steeped in liquor and mischief. Trubshawe's all right, though. What a pity my son couldn't find someone like that to stand up with him. Yet more proof that Jack's in the wrong, I fear." And the father turned away from his friend, rather than be seen by him at that moment, and Phineas left the room.

As he crossed toward his study, Meier intercepted him, discreetly murmuring, "The Countess and Lady Laura Kennedy wish to see you most urgently in the parlor, sir."

"Urgently?" asked Phineas.

"Most urgently, they said, sir."

"Right. Thank you Meier. Please explain to the gentlemen in the study that I will be with them in a few minutes, and offer them my apologies—and some further refreshment." That should hold Sir Felix for a bit, he thought grimly, and crossed to the parlor, where he found Lady Laura and Violet waiting for him, along with Marie Finn.

The Countess of Brentford was hiding the extent of her agitation, her handsome countenance strained, but her manner remained serene on the surface.

"Phineas, my boy's vagaries have, I am sorry to say, come to rest at your door. He means to put you to some inconvenience, I hear."

"So Oswald has informed me," replied Phineas, striving to match her tone.

"So very difficult of him, is it not?" She hesitated, her voice near trembling. "Do you–do you mean to oblige the child?"

Phineas answered without hesitation, meeting his wife's eyes. "I rather think I must, Violet," he said using her Christian name for the first time in many years. "After all, I am the boy's godfather, and I must see him through."

"Thank God!" Cried Lady Laura, her eyes moist. "Phineas, what can you do, though, beyond seeing that there is no foul play?"

"I mean to agree on condition that both parties agree that the duel is fought until first blood only. No to-the-death heroics. And, since they must fight abroad, I shall suggest Germany. I mean to require that they use the *schlager*."

Marie's face, tense as he had never seen it before, relaxed somewhat, and she sighed her relief. "*Kluger Kerl*," she breathed.

Violet looked about her in confusion. "I do not understand. If they must stop at the first drawing of blood, yes, that could save life, but–"

"Be calm, Violet," said Marie Finn, her eyes alight. "The use of the *schlager* implies the use of all the protective equipment that goes with it—eyes protected, chest, all the face save for the cheeks—and one can only cut, not thrust."

"The university students all participate in *schlager* bouts," Phineas added comfortingly, "the worst injury they normally receive is a small scar to the cheek, which the young girls find maddeningly attractive."

Lady Laura laughed—not hysterically, but with relief. "Oh, Phineas," she burbled "you have hit upon the answer. Let the boys have their fight–"

"But under conditions that debar any serious injury," added his wife.

"And honour is served, and nobody much the worse off!" finished Lady Laura.

Violet smiled, a little tremulously. "You may have saved my son's life. But afterward we shall have to repair his honour."

"We shall," said Lady Laura firmly.

"We shall," agreed Mrs. Finn, as her husband nodded his agreement.

"My dears, I hate to sound like one of those elderly ladies we used to mock," Lady Brentford sighed, "but I have been so very anxious, and I am so very grateful, that I think I must lie down for awhile. It has been more draining than I dare acknowledge." And rising to her feet, the Countess left the room. As she passed Phineas, she stopped, cupping his chin, and meeting his gaze. "Thank you, my friend," she uttered, "I have no other words but those." And she passed from the room.

Lady Laura, too, stopped a moment before leaving the parlor. She patted her onetime suitor's hand. "You very well may have saved Jack's life with that idea of yours, Phineas," she said. "Be careful, though, in Germany. No plan is foolproof." And with that, she followed Violet out of the room.

"That was Delphic," Phineas remarked dryly, after Lady Laura had gone. Turning to face his wife, he added, expecting a reproach, "I could not say no, Marie."

"No," she agreed, "you could not, and still be the man I married. Still, you have been quite clever. You cannot prevent this fight, but have found a way to reduce the risk greatly. I should be cross with you—but no, you truly had no option. You are what you have always been—unable to watch the struggles of those you love without helping them."

"Then I am forgiven?" he asked.

She laughed, a little hollowly. "At least you have the grace to know that forgiveness is required," she said. "And like you, I cannot watch those I love in the toils without helping them, so—you are forgiven, on condition that you do not get killed." And with that, Marie kissed her husband. They held the kiss, and Phineas pulled her in closer to him. When they parted, Marie mused, "A *schalger* bout can be an unwieldy thing; you couldn't have all the assisting personnel; not without bringing down the Press upon you all, but still…yes, you have made the best of a bad situation."

As he turned to leave, she added, "Brentford and Violet will be staying at Lady Laura's for the rest of their time in London. It is the only support they can give their son without condoning his actions, Violet told me, and they do not wish to make it awkward for Savrola to visit Clarissa."

"I am sorry to hear it," Phineas answered.

"As am I, but I think they are right to do so."

"As do I. I must see those men—the seconds, I mean."

"Do you anticipate any trouble with them?" Marie asked.

"No," her husband replied. "Trubshawe is too good a lad to want blood for its own sake, and Carbury—Carbury is wise enough to know that standing up with Jack may get him back into Society, but not if he comes across as a blood-drinker. Besides, the *schlager* gives Jack an advantage—he's fenced with them at Heidelberg. Carbury won't throw away that edge."

Phineas kissed his wife a second time, and then left the parlor, entering his own study to come to terms with two strangers, fully intending to force terms that would prevent the two young men, each of whom was dear to him, from killing one another, despite their own best efforts to do so.

WHAT THEY ALL THOUGHT ABOUT IT

Bishop Samuel Grantly was seated in the library at his sister's home, reading his colleague Charles Gore's *Dissertations.* As always, he relished the flow of the argument of the Principal of Pusey House, and frankly yearned for the day when he could greet his friend as a brother bishop. He was, however, a trifle disarranged by the learned man's last-ditch defence of the historicity of the virgin birth, and read it once more. "Defend it to protect the teaching authority of the Church?" he muttered to himself, "Why, that was Newman's very error, Charles. Defend it because it is true, not because it supports authority!"

"Forgive me, my brother," came the by now familiar purring tone of Bishop Joseph Emilius, acquaintance with whom had stifled, but not quite extinguished, Samuel's distrust for the American. Emilius was, no doubt, pleasant company, and learned—he had spoken quite well on the subject of predestination, avoiding many of the traps low church theology had constructed around the matter, Samuel recalled, but somehow his presence still jarred, if less so than when first they had met. He replied, "How may I assist you, my friend?"

"It was my impression that as a member of the Catholic party, you were something of a follower of Dr. Newman. Is it not so?"

"The matter is a trifle more complex than that, I am afraid. Dr. Newman's apostasy and his affiliation with the Church of Rome raise not only the question of loyalty to the Crown, and to the vows he took as a member of the Established Church, but that of the excessive love of authority for its own sake. Where we in the Church of England do not presume to make windows into men's souls, and embrace a broad understanding of the Faith, those who followed Dr. Newman into the Roman Church have a distressing tendency to believe that submission to ecclesiastical authority is a positive good, even when that authority oversteps its bounds, or is simply wrong."

"So you do not admire Dr. Newman, then?"

"I did once, very much; and I still believe that we are greatly in his debt and that of his fellow Tractarians, but I prefer the newer generation of High Church thinkers, who have learned from them without imbibing the spirit of submission to man's authority, as opposed to God's."

"Ah," replied Bishop Emilius, casting about for a way to change the conversation from a subject the inherent interest of which (little enough for him in any event) had been exhausted. Then he found one: "Speaking of Papists," he said, "have you heard that Phineas Finn has gotten himself dragged into a duel?"

"A duel? Is this not the same Mr. Finn I met at my sister's ball? A gentlemen of mature years, though younger than myself?"

"Indeed it is, and Mr. Finn is not to be one of the combatants, but the *maître d'armes*, to ensure that no foul play is attempted."

Bishop Grantly scrutinized his colleague with a glance that lacked its usual benignant expression. "I must say, sir, that this profane matter seems beneath the notice of men of the cloth such as ourselves; I am surprised to hear such common gossip–"

"Gossip, my brother, seems a harsh word, and is, I assure you, entirely uncalled for. The two combatants are the very young men who quarrelled in this house, and I had hoped to seek your advice as to whether it behooves me to seek to reconcile these men before any blood is shed."

Flushing with embarrassment, Dr. Grantly stammered out an apology. "I had not gathered from your manner of bringing up the matter that your purpose was a spiritual one, my brother, and I-I sincerely apologise."

"There is no need," the American bishop spoke in his gentlest, most soothing voice. "There is nobody in Great Britain whose spiritual perspicacity I have a greater respect for than yours, and I am troubled by the prospect of these misguided young men killing each other. More, I feel a responsibility, as I was present at the inception of the hostilities."

In fact, Bishop Emilius was growing a little bored with his stay at the Marchioness' home, and, although his meetings with his former wife were giving satisfaction to both parties, he had not yet successfully pressed home his suit. The notion of a flamboyant Christian intervention in this swiftly unfolding drama appealed to his vanity, although his native caution led him to avoid any coupling of his name with that of Phineas Finn. Torn between the prospect of an exciting *divertissement* and the possibility of subverting his plans for the future, Bishop Emilius could not resist at least flirting with the former, which would not, of its own weight, result in the latter. As he was allowing himself to be talked out of his quixotic gesture, his vanity glowed as the Englishman described him as "burdened with an overly active conscience," and "perhaps a trifle too disposed to assume guilt that properly belongs to others."

Meanwhile, the Marchioness herself had exhibited her usual flair for knowing every vibration of each filament of the social web without ever seeming to speak to another about it, and brought the matter up at dinner that evening. She raised it as one who assumed that her spiritually-inclined brother would be in a state of invincible ignorance on the subject, but had discerned that her guest was better informed.

Indeed, the Marchioness had, after a slightly rocky start, rendered a verdict in favour of Emilius. The turning point had been when, some little time after his injuries were inflicted, she had observed Bishop Emilius, in restored health, followed one of the oft-neglected rules of deportment her mother had taught all her children. Shortly after his visits to his former wife had commenced—one of the few vibrations on the web Lady Hartletop had *not* discerned—Lady Hartletop had noticed that Bishop Emilius did not, as so many did in these decadent days, even dear Samuel, rest his person against the back of his chair. Indeed, when on one occasion, his back did so touch the surface of the chair, he had flinched at the solecism, as if the contact caused him pain, and corrected himself. Having awarded her approval to the bishop, she took him a little into her confidence, and began to tell him the story of the duel, only to discover that her brother, normally uninterested and uniformed in matters regarding Society, was unwontedly *au courant.*

"We can only hope," her brother added after flaunting his knowledge of the matter, "that the involvement of Mr. Finn is for the good—perhaps he can effect a reconciliation."

"My dear Samuel," the Marchioness said, "the man's recklessness is well known."

"I have no doubt that he will pay a price in Society for condoning such foolishness, Griselda. Still, if he is as silver-tongued as his admirers report, perhaps he can reconcile these barbarous youths."

"I doubt it, Bishop Grantly," Emilius could not help but interject.

The Marchioness nodded her approval, and made one of her rare pronouncements. "He is an Irishman; no doubt a little blood-letting seems quite innocuous to him."

Plantagenet Palliser, Duke of Omnium, was not in the social swim, though he had the *entrée* to any house in London. He found out about the duel over a glass of wine with his eldest son one afternoon in the House, where they met several days a week. Lord Silverbridge was still youthful enough to declare that he found it all great sport. His father shook his head wearily at his son, and at Frank Tregear, who grinned and added "Perhaps Finn's a tad old for such heroics, Silver, but by George, he don't show it!"

Face long, the Duke said deprecatingly, "The spectacle of two members of the House engaged in an antiquated and savage—yes, and unlawful!—means of settling differences is wholly deplorable. And what of the families involved? Parents, *fiancée*, even Mr. Finn's wife, or the other young man's aunt…"

"Oh, come on, Pater, Mrs. Finn has nothing to fear; Finn's only going to make sure everything is done according to Hoyle."

"Yes, and *schlager*-fencing's awfully tame, what with all the padding, and goggles. No real risk to the combatants, let alone the referee, sir," added the son-in-law.

"No, no. I cannot admit of that," the Duke said. "You can reduce the risk, but any time men are fighting in earnest, the results cannot be predicted with confidence." And with that, he wished his the younger members of the family a good evening, and took his leave.

Rather than turn directly to his daughter's home to dine, the Duke found himself walking in the direction of Portman Square. The evening was cool, and the sun had not yet set. In the twilight, the Duke strode, from St. Margaret Street, to Birdcage Walk, and thence to Marlborough Street. As he walked the familiar streets, from Pall Mall to St. James, Picadilly to Bond Street, the shadows lengthened, and the Duke became unsure whether the impulse which had led him here was wise or no. Still, after having come a trifle over two miles, he decided that, whatever the wisdom of the initial decision, to turn back now would be simple cowardice.

The Duke rapped firmly on the door. A few moments passed, seeming longer than normal in a well-conducted household, but the Duke realised that in this his instincts might be in error. When the door opened, the elderly butler enquired "Your Grace?"

"Is your mistress in?"

Chalmers bowed the Duke into the house, and led him into Lady Laura's private library. The room was much as it had been when her father, the Earl, had lived in this very house. Three of the four walls were lined with overstuffed bookshelves, containing every manner of political treatise and philosophical work, lightened here or there with a tract or a compilation of statistics. The old Duke of St. Bungay, in his last years, had once described Lady Laura as the thinker behind Barrington Erle's premiership, and evidence of the justice of this description was laid out before him.

The only change the Duke noticed from the old days was that the late Earl's heavy, bulbous-legged desk had been replaced with an altogether more feminine affair, a French table with marquetry comprised primarily of tortoiseshell, set off with brass corners. A lighter, more graceful—indeed, one might almost say frivolous, save for the neatly-stacked evidence of serious industry that took place upon its inlaid surface—piece of furniture than Plantagenet would have expected from Lady Laura. He smiled to see her seated behind it.

Glancing up as Chalmers announced him, Laura rose to her feet. She took in his expression, and divined its meaning swiftly. "My one indulgence," she explained with a graceful shrug. Then, to the butler, "Chalmers, you did not warn me–"

"No, milady," the butler said, adding, "quite wrong of me, milady," and disappeared into the corridor, leaving the pair to fend for themselves.

"Lady Laura, I have only this evening heard of the—difficulty—your nephew finds himself in, and came to offer any assistance that I may provide."

The quizzical, amused, look that Chalmers' tactics had evoked left Laura's face. "How very kind you are, Duke. It is good of you. I am desperately concerned, as you can imagine."

"Is such desperation, in fact, warranted? My own son was just informing me that matters have improved, and that the young gentlemen are to fight, yes, but in a foreign country in which their contest is legal, and with almost all the risk of serious injury removed."

"Almost, Duke, being the word that concerns me in the sentence. That, and the question of why my poor nephew is acting so strangely. He reminds me of Oswald at his most wild, and yet is far worse than ever Oswald was—violent, angry, entangled with that appalling Lady Eustace–"

"Not the same Lady Eustace my uncle took such an interest in? The one involved in the dispute over the diamonds? Why, she's old enough to be your nephew's mother."

"Yes, that Lady Eustace." Lady Laura pauses a moment, unwilling to say more, but the sincerity of her visitor's concern lured her to confide in him. "Lizzie the Liar, they call her, and more, too—all bad. I hear rumours of her that I cannot bear to credit, especially since my poor Jack–"

Lady Laura's iron control broke at last, and turning from the Duke, she began to weep. Not prettily, as her sister-in-law would have done, but with terrible sobs, each a concession to emotion that was physically wrung from her.

Plantagenet Palliser stood frozen an instant. His grave face took on a sorrowful mien; he moved as if to go, and spare her pride. Moved by a deeper wisdom, he instead stepped toward her, gently turned her to face him, and held her to him, as she at last gave way to the torrent of emotion she had so firmly suppressed.

At Number 10, Downing Street, Barrington Erle was being catechized, an experience to which he had submitted with a good grace through his political tutelage, but which, as Prime Minister he did not often have to undergo these days.

"The man is obviously unfit to hold office!" boomed Sir William McScuttle, his normally benign face twisted into mask of anger.

"The man does not, in fact, hold office, Sir William, so I do not know why you feel compelled to repeat this assertion to me," the Prime Minister replied, his annoyance beginning to show.

"Very well, then, he does not deserve to represent a constituency in the House of Commons!"

"Surely, Sir William, that is a matter for his constituents, who have voted him in, time and again, over two decades to decide. Two decades in which, I might add, he has backed our party faithfully." He regretted his choice of words almost immediately.

"Faithfully? Pfui! He is the least reliable member of the Party, Prime Minister, as you well know."

The two men were closeted together in the Prime Minister's study. Although the hour was late, the air stale with cigar smoke, and their brandy snifters nearly empty, the discussion had shifted from the pleasant topic of how best to deploy Sir William's money to increase the Party's majority at the next election, to the iniquities of Phineas Finn.

"He's a criminal," Sir William declared.

"Really?" Barrington Erle countered. "Of what crime do you accuse him? Be very careful where you make such an accusation against a member of the House, Sir William, or you could find yourself facing... consequences."

Sir William had gone too far, and, realising it, moderated his tone.

"I do apologise for my zeal, Prime Minister, but surely you do not intend to condone a veteran member of the House promoting dueling, with a younger member involved?"

"My dear Sir William, the affair no longer is a duel, but a perfectly legal fencing match—and outside of the country. Mr. Finn's involvement has, if anything, prevented the crime of dueling."

"Aye, and his seeking to influence the Home Secretary in a secret meeting? The barrister representing a party having a private meeting with the Home Secretary? No impropriety in that, I suppose?"

"Well, Sir William, as you found out about it in a private meeting with the Home Secretary about the same case, in which you were the prosecutor, I am not sure you have anything to complain of. Indeed, as Lord Fawn is in no way disposed to listen to Mr. Finn, but rather swiftly informed you about the matter, if anyone has been badly treated, it would seem to me you have not been."

"Prime Minister!"

The industrialist, formerly comfortably slumping in his armchair, now sat on its edge.

Wagging his finger in an admonitory manner at the Prime Minister, he grated, "If the Liberal Party wants the support of industry, of the companies that are building the future greatness of the Empire - of me, in short—ye'll have tae take our concerns seriously. There are other members of the House, either on t'other side of the aisle or in yer own ranks that'd be grateful for the support I'm prepared tae provide."

"As indeed I am," Barrington Erle answered in his most mellifluous voice, "but you cannot expect me to treat as criminal behaviour that which is not, or to hold a backbencher to a higher standard of conduct than I demand of my own Government." The Prime Minister rose, and walked to a globe, which he spun partway, looking down at all the pink landmasses representing the Empire—his, if only in trust, for the duration of his premiership!—and, gently, the Prime Minister explained the way of his world to the industrialist.

"We do not work in absolutes—black or white—in leading men, Sir William," he mused. "We allow a certain level of informal communication that an outsider might deem unseemly in the abstract, because a Government is a living entity—one must be able to take its pulse, periodically. And so you, in speaking to Fawn, acted entirely appropriately. As did Finn."

Sir William rose to protest, only to be sent back to his chair by a wave of the Prime Minister's cigar. "Similarly, we do not publicly disown or dress down backbenchers for behaviour which, while not unlawful, puts the Party in a bad light. Rather, certain doors just—close. Quietly, but firmly. And nobody is seen to have closed them, but for the member who gets talked about in the wrong way—why, the doors close him out, while welcoming in those who get talked about in the right way."

A smile tugged at the corners of Sir William's mouth. "And the troublesome member?"

"Once the doors are closed, and the member cannot produce action for his constituents, well, they have no reason to return him at the next election. And so a new candidate is found, and a new career begins."

"As simple as that, then," the industrialist breathed.

"It's all a matter of the right people knowing where they stand. And the wrong people learning where they fall."

"And Mr. Finn?"

"An old friend of mine, Sir William; I first brought him to the House, you know. But one who has, perhaps, lost the ability to feel which way the wind is blowing, and has waited too long to come indoors."

"And should he try to come inside now?"

"Once the storm is upon a man, it is too late to open the door. Such a man must learn to fend for himself."

"A DRINK FROM THE SOUP-PLATE OF HONOUR"

Before Phineas's departure for Heidelberg, Marie had suggested he speak to Meier about the niceties of the *schlager*. After the household had retired, a little uncomfortable at invading the butler's private quarters, Phineas knocked at his door below stairs.

"May I help you, sir?" The butler's face was as imperturbably formal as ever, though his coat and tie had been removed.

"I'm sorry to disturb you, Meier," Phineas said, "but, well—I've been reading up on this *schlager* business, and Marie thought I should speak with you about it."

Meier nodded, and invited Phineas into his quarters with a bow. Meier had turned his lodging into a shrine to the glories of the sword. Rapier, sabre, *épée*; each of the three had its place on his wall, mounted but not fixed; these weapons could be taken down for use. At the far end of the long room, Meier had made for himself a fencing gallery, with two dummies, and several targets affixed to the wall. Three umbrella stands, each filled with practise weapons of one of the three primary weapons dotted the corner of the gallery. At the side was a workbench where Meier kept these in good repair, and over the workbench was a photograph of a much younger Meier—with a full head of hair and a Van Dyke, a far cry from his clean-shaven baldness today—in fencing whites, and with a medal depending from a ribbon around his neck.

"So," the butler remarked, a slight smile on his face, "my hobby may be of some use to you, sir."

"Hobby, Meier? It looks like a vocation to me," his employer answered.

Meier's eyes lit at this, and he replied, "Good, good. You understand then. And you go to make sure that these young men do not kill each other, yes?"

"Yes, indeed."

"A good cause, and most honourable. The *Mensur* is not meant to be a brawl, or an end to life, but a test of honour and worthiness."

"The *Mensur*?"

"The proper name of the competition. The *Schläger* is the sword." Meier pronounced it differently than Phineas had heard it said; the "a" came out more as an elongated "ae" sound. "Properly speaking," the butler continued, "it is called the *Mensurschläger*. The contest is the *Mensur*. I have both kinds of swords employed."

"There are two different kinds of swords used? Not just a sabre, or a rapier?"

"Ach, Madame was right to send you to me," Meier smiled. "Come, you leave in three days. I will show you what I can."

In those three days, Phineas was worked fairly hard by his butler. He quickly learned the difference between *Korbschlägern* and *Glockenschlägern*. As *maître d'armes*, he learned, he had the choice of which weapon would be used, and chose the more common *Korbschläger*, with its deep, basket-shaped guard, which felt more natural in his own hand than did the *Glockenschläger*, with the bell-shaped guard from which it took its name. If for no other reason, Meier instructed him, he should select that weapon. "If you must intervene,' he told his employer, "you must have full command of the weapon; a *maître d'armes* who is not comfortable with his weapon is no *maître* but a mere spectator.

When Phineas joked that the *Korbschläger* resembled nothing so much as a dish, Meier unsmilingly told him that this was well known—"That is why, sir, they call fighting a bout 'having a drink from the soup-plate of honour,'" the butler informed him.

Phineas's fencing days were long behind him—he had learned a little single-stick at school, and had fenced sabre at Trinity College, but had not handled a blade since then. Fortunately, somewhere within his body, the memory remained, and he found himself awkward at first, but soon able to parry-riposte with Meier with reasonable form, if not maximum acuity.

The butler's speed and accuracy were dazzling to Phineas, and Phineas felt himself slow and stolid in comparison. He felt the weight of every year that separated him from his college days more than he ever had before. Panting, sweat-soaked, and with his right arm aching, he gasped at the end of the second day, "By heaven, Meier, I had no idea what dreadful condition I'm in. You may have to train me on my return."

"If you wish, Mr. Phineas," the butler replied with one of his rare smiles. "You are not too bad, for a man who has not handled a weapon in far too long. For this affair, at least, you should do."

"Does that mean you'll go easy on me tomorrow?"

"Certainly not; who knows what may happen? But when we finish, you should go to the Turkish steam room, and have them treat you. You wish to be in—what do the English say?—fine fettle? Yes, fine fettle for the day."

Before Phineas's departure, Meier appeared at his dressing room in place of his valet. He carried a long package, broad at one end, narrow at the other.

He unwrapped the package, and held out to Phineas an old *Korbschläger* with three concentric bands of colour—black for the outside band, red for the middle, and butterscotch lapping the blade—coating the basket of the guard.

"This weapon was mine when I fought," the butler explained, "I have set a new blade in it, sir, and made sure it is fit for use. Take it, with my best wishes for a good issue and a safe homecoming."

"I shall return it to you," Phineas vowed, clasping the butler's hand.

The trip to Heidelberg began anxiously for Jack Standish, when he found out that Carbury meant to deny him the pleasures of the Green Fairy, or, indeed, any other liquor.

"Time enough for that on our return, son," Carbury said, with his most passable paternal leer. "Here, content yourself with a pinch of snuff." He leaned forward from his seat in their private compartment on the Boat Train and proffered his snuffbox, on the lid of which a satyr winked.

"Snuff?" Jack was indignant.

"Alcohol is a depressant, Jack," the older man explained, "what you need is a stimulant."

"Snuff," Jack sniffed at it.

"Perfectly legal, dear boy," Carbury assured him. "It's cocaine, which is recommended to tone the nerves, hone the eye, and steady the hand."

Jack accepted some snuff, and in fact felt within a few minutes a glow of well-being, a euphoria, but one coupled with a firmness of purpose and consciousness of powers latent within him.

The journey passed pleasantly enough, especially when Jack slipped away from Carbury for a little tipple of the Fairy. After all, he reasoned, he was feeling so well-bucked by the snuff that he could surely enjoy the absinthe that had become necessary in order for him to relax and to sleep soundly. And Carbury had brought ample snuff to provision them both, and had generously shared it out, so that Jack could use it at his own discretion.

Jack was quite ready for the duel. He had agreed to Phineas's absurd terms—but was quite sure he could, if he chose, kill Vavasor, even within the strict confines his godfather had imposed upon them.

On the morning of the bout, Savrola Vavasor was conscious of just how nervous he was. This hateful peer may have lost the woman he so arrogantly assumed to be his for the plucking, and instead found himself improbably engaged to a harpy adventuress, but Savrola had no such reason to throw away life. He was engaged to marry a woman as good as she was beautiful, from a family he found himself admiring more and more as he was welcomed into its inner circle, and he was finding his feet in Parliament, and even entertaining hopes of office if Barrington Erle fell and the Tories got in, as began to seem not improbable. In short, Savrola reflected, as he was buckled into the absurdly long protective leather vest, descending almost to his knees, he had everything to lose and nothing to gain from this lunatic competition.

And a lunatic game it seemed to Savrola as Trubshawe helped him into the mask, the heavy wire spectacles to protect his eyes and nose, the mailed glove, and all the other accouterments designed to leave only his cheeks and forehead as a target for Chiltern's blade. Finally, when he was fully dressed, Trubshawe led him down to the courtyard where the seconds had agreed the bout was to take place.

"You may cut only, not thrust," Phineas Finn had explained to both combatants at their brief meeting the day before. Chiltern, damn his eyes, had nodded as though Finn were a bore, but then he had done this before, and Vavasor had not. As he saw his rival, along with Carbury, drawing near, Vavasor felt the thrill of fear he remembered from his brief spell in the Army, a physical sensation as of something crawling over him. As he had done then, he dismissed the fear; understandable as it was, it could only hinder him now.

Phineas Finn, dressed as Savrola was himself, and Chiltern, too, except without the helmet, neck-stock, and spectacles, took his position between the combatants. "Gentlemen," he exhorted them in stentorian tones, "I ask you one final time: Will you not put away this folly, and reconcile your differences?"

Vavasor replied, "If Chiltern apologises, withdraws the slurs he passed on both my parents, and undertakes to leave me and mine in peace, upon his word as a gentleman, I will."

Formally, Phineas turned toward Jack. "Lord Chiltern, what is your response?"

"I will not apologise, I will not withdraw, and I will give no undertaking."

With a grave expression, Phineas Finn replied, "Very well. Gentlemen, *en garde*."

Chiltern gracefully assumed the position: knees bent, left hand at the base of his spine, right arm raised, with the blade in a slightly descending curve. Savrola, less accustomed to the position, took it more slowly.

"Fencers ready?" Phineas asked; both nodded.

"Fence!"

Savrola realised quickly that Chiltern was considerably more accomplished than he was, as the peer swiftly launched into the attack, a bewildering series of feints, cuts and slashes aimed at his head, which he only managed to parry because Chiltern was allowing him to do so. From Chiltern's arch grin, Savrola understood that the peer meant to humiliate him, since his own godfather had imposed conditions so unfavourable to killing.

And so Savrola grimly tried to match parry to cut, to discern what was a feint and what a real attack, and the blades clashed again and again.

Chiltern, fueled by the hefty pinch of snuff that he had administered to himself just before heading to the courtyard, was enjoying himself immensely, ready to vindicate his honour, and show Clarissa she had chosen the weaker man. A sudden cut from Vavasor that nearly found its way to Chiltern's left cheek, which it would have been laid open to the bone, transmuted the peer's euphoria to anger, and undammed the depths of rage that had, under the tutelage of absinthe and cocaine, become even more turbulent than in his father's case—had indeed become the bedrock of his character. Knowing it was not really proper in a *Mensur*, he advanced on Vavasor, cutting, disengaging his blade from Vavasor's before the red-haired man could complete a parry, and cutting again.

Vavasor broke ground as Chiltern advanced, the combination of cuts keeping him on the defensive. A desperate feint stopped the raging peer, but opened Savrola up to a cut to the right side of his face, and Chiltern's blade sliced into flesh.

"Halt!" Phineas Finn's voice commanded, as was proper, but Chiltern advanced again, cutting at the other side of Vavasor's face; the wounded man retreated and parried. Worse luck, thought Chiltern, and he advanced again, stabbing at his enemy's throat.

"Halt!" cried Phineas Finn a second time, and a second time Chiltern ignored him, executing a beautiful academic lunge that would have, had

Vavasor not barely parried it, torn into the padded collar at his throat. Overbalanced, Vavasor began to lose his footing, and Chiltern's blade flashed out at the already wounded cheek to do more damage, only to be checked by Finn's blade.

Chiltern roared his frustration as Vavasor, thrown off balance, fell to the cobblestones. Chiltern then turned his attack on the *maître d'armes* himself. It was only Chiltern's yielding to undisciplined frenzy that saved Phineas from being spitted on the younger man's sword. He parried, as Meier had taught him, a cut to his uncovered head, and riposted at Chiltern's protected scalp, crying out his godson's name in the hope that the boy would recover his wits.

But Chiltern, even fighting in a blind rage, had the instincts of a brilliant fencer, and he counter-parried, and slashed at Phineas's face. Phineas sprang back and parried, inelegantly, but just sufficiently, only for Chiltern to spring forward in a superb lunge, which would have reached its target had not Trubshawe, unarmed and unprotected, hurled himself at Chiltern, knocking the young peer askew.

Retreating from his godson's attack, Phineas stumbled against an irregular cobblestone higher than its neighbors, and fell backwards, striking his head against the pavement. The jolt of pain made him cry out, and, although untouched by the blade, he nonetheless experienced a bitter metallic taste in his mouth. He thought of Marie, and tried to rise. For a moment, he felt her physical presence, looking as she had when he first met her. After that, he knew nothing, and collapsed, face up on the pavement, bleeding steadily onto the cobblestones.

End of Volume I

VOLUME II

PHINEAS AT BAY

Volume II

PROLOGUE

From *The People's Banner*, November 30, 189_:

Mr. Phineas Finn, the Member of Parliament for Tankerville, is reported to be near death after participating in a fracas, illegal under English law, but, surprisingly, permissible under the laws of the country in which it took place.

Beyond, then, deploring the barbaric custom of the DUEL still followed by our German cousins, so different from the genteel and orderly behaviour shown by so many natives of that otherwise civil society when they happily visit these shores, we are unable to fasten any legal responsibility for what may well be the deprivation of the House of Commons of a member of long standing. Legal responsibility, we say, and that is what we mean. For it is in no wise doubtful that, should Mr. Finn not recover from his injuries, he will have been, quite simply—murdered.

That the participants in this blood-curdling contest who are answerable for the resultant blood-letting itself should both be men close to Mr. Finn may perhaps tell us more about the Honourable Member from Tankerville than is apparent on the surface. For Mr. Finn has himself, it has long been suspected, participated in at least one such outrage. But THE PEOPLE'S BANNER, although we have often had to chastise the unfortunate Mr. Finn for his occasional fecklessness, and his braggadocio, does not carry grudges against those whom we have had to criticise in the course of our duties as the voice of the Conscience of Britannia. At the close of day, we wish to remember the good in Mr. Phineas Finn.

That he appears, from one eyewitness account, to have met his Nemesis in trying to stem the incarnadine tide for which he bore no little responsibility may, it can be hoped, be of some little comfort to the man's friends and relations. Should, as now seems all but certain, Mr. Finn succumb to his injuries, it may yet be said of him: "Nothing in his life became him like the leaving it."

–Q.S.

1

THE DEATH WATCH BEETLE

It was very wrong of him, no doubt, mused Savrola Vavasor, to think of the Doctor as the "Death Watch Beetle." Oh, he looked the part—big bushy eyebrows like Trubshawe's moustache, corpulent frame housed in a dark gray tailcoat that Savrola suspected might at one time been black in hue, and he was just about as encouraging as the insect he so resembled—boring away at any hope that the little party lodged in Heidelberg could find in a given day, until nothing was left but dust.

In the nearly a month that had passed since the duel, Savrola had spent hours at the bedside of the stricken man. No sign of life, beyond shallow respiration, had been observed by him or any other visitor. The medical staff had apparently gotten enough water and nutrients into the man to sustain life (howbeit Finn was looking frighteningly drawn and gaunt), although Savrola had not stayed to watch the process, and so had no idea how it was accomplished. Did they spoon it into the poor man? Use hoses? He could not bear to ask, let alone see.

Savrola looked down at the older man, and his heart twisted with sorrow. Clarissa would be devastated when—if, Savrola corrected himself, *if*—her uncle died. That he, her *fiancé*, had been a key part of her uncle's destruction, could only ruin their love. He would have to release her, and the whole brightly glittering world of which he had been on the threshold, preparing to step inside with her, was passing away like a boy's castle-in-the-air at an imperious master's summons back to the dreariness of lessons.

Herr Doktor Hans-Uwe Brandt was no more encouraging this morning than on any other. He busied himself around the patient, uttering little Teutonic sounds that made no sense to Vavasor, but which seemed pregnant with meaning to the good doctor. Bustling past Savrola, he nodded with a bare minimum of politeness to the young M.P. and continued on his way.

Left alone again with the patient, Savrola pulled from his pocket a *Commentaries of Caesar*, translated by a once-prominent novelist, found the place where he had left off reading aloud to Phineas, and resumed. He read well, neither too slowly nor too quickly, savouring the writer's turns of phrase, and adding lots of interesting swoops and stresses to catch the attention, if any there might be, of Phineas Finn.

About a half hour later, Marie Finn entered the room. She was dressed more simply than usual, and the silver in her hair was more discernible. With her husband stricken, and removed from Society, Marie had left much of her artifice behind. She greeted Savrola with a kiss, and then, as she always did, she accepted the chair that he had vacated. Savrola left the room, carefully bidding both Mrs. Finn and her husband farewell.

Left alone with her husband, Marie looked deeply upon his features, seeking any sign of the return of consciousness. "Oh, my friend," she said to him, in an echo of long–ago banter, "you have violated your promise, and that means I have not forgiven you, yet. You must redeem your word, and return to me, if you want my forgiveness."

Her only answer was silence.

"You do not know what a muddle things are in, my dear," she told him. "Your godson is in gaol, at least until you decide to live or to die, your niece is weeping herself arid in my hotel when she is not here with you, and poor Savrola is hoarse with reading to you about Rome. And, last of all, your wife—oh, I hear that she misses you sorely!" And with that, Marie laid her head upon his chest, and began to softly weep.

When Phineas's hand stroked her hair, the comfort was so familiar and so welcome that she did not immediately grasp its import. When she did, she froze, with a quick intake of breath. She then slipped from under his hand, taking it in her own, and gazed at his face. He was looking puzzled and worried, and ineffably tired, but he was present.

"Oh, my love," she said, her voice on the edge of hysteria, "can you speak?"

Phineas tried to articulate something, but he was unable to formulate his thought.

"I will ring for help," she assured him, and vigorously shook the little bell on the table until the nurse came.

"Holen Sie Herr Doktor Brandt," Marie commanded the nurse who answered her ring. "Schnell!" The nurse flew off in pursuit of the doctor, and Marie was left alone with her husband for a few moments to savour his return from oblivion.

"Now," she said, "now, my dear, you are forgiven."

The return of Phineas Finn from the threshold of death was a nine-days wonder at the *Allgemeines Krankenhaus* to which he had been brought. The small party that had come to cluster about him was jubilant on that first evening in the bar-lounge of the *Englischer Hof*, where they were staying. They were so exuberant in their hopes that Phineas would be well again that they forgave Herr Doktor Brandt for exiling them until the next morning. Herr Steiler, the bluff and hearty host, on hearing that the husband of the lavish Madame who had filled his hotel these past weeks was on the road to recovery, immediately produced a magnum, and insisted that they feast that night as his guests in fact as well as in name. The room was warm, with a large fire burning merrily in the hearth, and the firelight threw intriguing shadows on the dark wood paneling and on the many heads of game mounted proudly on the walls.

Clarissa Riley, her face still wan from the strain of the feverish journey from London and the agonising weeks of suspense since then, was mute with relief. She smiled, ate a little, drank less, and bestowed far more smiles than words that evening. But the smiles were particularly dazzling as Clarissa gradually took on board that she had not been rendered an orphan a second time. Clarissa had found her aunt somewhat abstracted, a little cooler than was her wont, and very controlled in these weeks in Heidelberg. Had the late Duchess of Omnium been there to observe, she could have informed the younger woman that she was meeting the notorious Madame Max Goesler, who had conquered the old Duke in the Seventies, and not the warmer, more contented Marie Finn, who had lost some of her mystery, but gained indescribably in the transaction.

Upon her husband's return to consciousness, Madame Max began to fade almost immediately, and the more familiar Marie to return. Moreover, Clarissa took heart in the delight of those around her; Savrola was assiduous in his attendance upon her, and in his most sparkling form, waiting upon her, Marie and the Standish party.

All three of the senior Standishes—Lady Laura, the Earl of Brentford, and the Countess—had hastened to Germany when Savrola and Carbury had telegraphed the news of the disaster. Clarissa had, upon receiving a reply from Lady Laura, in which she inquired where the Finns were staying, so that the Brentfords would not trouble them by sharing their hotel, consulted her Aunt Marie.

Marie Finn, grave and sorely tested by her anxiety, had answered her niece, "Let them come, and let them come here. Your uncle will never forgive me if I blame his oldest friends for their son's—their son's..." Marie had been unable to finish that sentence; drawing in her breath and composing herself swiftly, she had concluded, "They shall be as welcome as ever they were. Tell them to come."

The situation was inherently uneasy, with the Standish party's loyalties inevitably conflicted. When their train had pulled into the Heidelberg station, the invaluable Trubshawe had met it on behalf of Savrola and had helped the Standishes to the hotel. Once they were settled, he had seized the opportunity to have a word with the Earl in private.

"My lord, Mr. Vavasor asked me to speak with you upon your arrival."

The Earl had stiffened a little. "Indeed?"

"Yes, my lord. He wanted me to assure you that his quarrel with Lord Chiltern did not run to his family, and that he remembered with great affection the many kindnesses you and the Countess had shown him in London."

"That's good of him," the Earl had replied, a little awkwardly. He had wanted to defend his son, but how could he? The boy had acted dishonourably in an affair of honour; he had continued the attack after winning the bout, and worse, when prevented, he had attacked the *maître d'armes*, who had faithfully performed the mission with which he, the Earl of Brentford, had entrusted him. The Earl was not used to feeling either shame or guilt, and he had felt them both. He had roused himself to reply, nonetheless.

"I am grateful to Mr. Vavasor, sir, and consider that he has behaved like a gentleman throughout this unfortunate affair," he said. "I should ask you to communicate to him, though, that I intend to provide Lord Chiltern with the best possible legal representation, and to stand by him. If Mr. Vavasor chooses not to meet me, or to not speak should we happen to encounter each other, I will understand, and take no offense."

"I am sure he will do no such thing," the faithful Trubshawe had answered, and the two men had shaken hands.

The ladies had been very circumspect with each other, the Countess and Lady Laura asking permission to visit Phineas's bedside, which Marie had granted. The constraint between Marie and Violet had been notable; friendly though they had been for many years, each was careful not to raise any question of Jack or of his fate should Phineas die, or, indeed, the possibility that Phineas might not recover. Their exchanges had had the air of forced conversation at a diplomatic reception between ambassadors of nations that might soon be at war.

Lady Laura had been less circumspect. She had, on their arrival, sought out Mrs. Finn.

Marie, uncertain of what to expect, had admitted her to her suite. In the suite's stark Germanic sitting room, Lady Laura had taken both of Marie's hands, and gazed into her eyes.

"Marie," she had begun, startling Mrs. Finn by her familiarity, "this is a tragedy, however it turns out. When Phineas recovers, as I am sure he will–"

"You cannot be sure of that, Lady Laura," Mrs. Finn began.

"Oh, I think I can be," Laura said with an air of confidence that somehow reassured Mrs. Finn. "Phineas Finn was not born to die so. And if he was going to die, he would have died already."

Marie Finn had always had the upper hand in her exchanges with Lady Laura; bewildered, exhausted, and fighting her own fears, this, for once, was not the case.

"Come," Lady Laura continued, with a little crooked smile, "Who knows him better than we two? I pined for him for a quarter century, and you have lived with him for nearly as long. Do you really believe that he will not come back to you? Have a little faith in the man."

And Marie broke down then, the tears she had long repressed pouring from her, and fell into the embrace of Lady Laura. Lady Laura had been her standby since, and her calm confidence on that afternoon and through these long, weary weeks had helped Marie keep her own faith, in spite of the glum Doktor Brandt.

So it was with some surprise that she heard her own question to Lady Laura. "Laura, that first day you were with me, you said this would be a tragedy regardless, even though you believed Phineas would recover. What did you mean?"

Laura smiled sadly, "Should we not celebrate Phineas's return to life first? We are not yet certain of the completeness of his recovery." Seeing Marie's unyielding gaze, she dropped her eyes, then raised them with calm candour. "Very well. Marie, what happens to my nephew now will be very much a matter in the power of your husband and of yourself. The authorities are prepared to charge him with assault, attempted murder, and more; they are awaiting the moment to discuss it with you, and, now that Phineas is awake again, with him. My brother will not lift a hand to help Jack until the charges are issued—he will not use any influence, nor will he intercede with you or Phineas."

"He could do so, if he chose," Marie said with surprising indifference, "intercede with Phineas, I mean. Why does he not?"

"Oswald asked Phineas to forestall Jack if his temper led him to violate the rules of the engagement. Phineas nearly paid with his life for doing as Oswald asked. Oswald will ask no more of him."

"And you, Laura?" Marie eyed her new friend with some suspicion. "What will you ask of him—or of me?"

"Nothing, Marie. When we first arrived, I was prepared to appeal to you for mercy for Jack, but I am glad I did not have the chance. I will ask nothing of him—or of you, either."

"Why not?

"Because I have suffered with you, and seen you suffer. Jack has brought this all down upon himself. I have no defence to make for him."

Marie relaxed in her chair a bit. "Even if Phineas wishes to undertake no prosecution," she observed, "I am not sure he can forestall it."

Laura shook her head patiently.

"Marie, you know the Continent far better than I do, but I do not believe that a nobleman whose intercession is unopposed by the victim of a crime will plead in vain—if, indeed, he does plead at all."

"And will Oswald plead?" Marie asked.

Laura hesitated. "I do not know," she said at length. "If he believes that neither you nor Phineas objects—perhaps he will. Even then, I am not so sure, though. Of one thing I am sure: Neither he nor Violet—nor I!—will raise a finger or a breath unless you and Phineas allow it, freely. We three dragged him into this; we owe him our loyalty."

"And Jack?" Marie asked in a soft voice.

"Jack is detained at the pleasure of the Kaiser at the moment—and at the pleasure of those whom he wounded, and whom his parents and I love."

It was a night, Marie Finn reflected, for truths.

"For many years I would have thought that you loved me not," she mused.

"For many years I did not!" Laura's laugh was freer than any Marie had ever heard from her before. "Oh, I was an envious wretch, Marie, eating my heart out over Phineas, and jealous that anyone should have him. I hated you—or the woman I supposed you to be."

"I knew."

"All that is changed now," Laura said, a hint of sadness in her tone. "I lived for so long on my grievance that I was wearing it, and myself, quite thin. I should have eaten up my heart in earnest had I not…" She could not bring herself to go on.

"Had you not...?" Marie raised her eyebrows interrogatively.

"Had I not met a gentleman at a ball, and danced with him one night, and seen that the world was only dust and ashes to me because I would have it so. I have released Phineas," Laura said most earnestly, "In my heart, I mean. I have forgiven myself for losing him, and you for winning him."

"And Phineas? Have you forgiven him?"

Laura's smile was shy now, and slow.

"That was hardest of all—to forgive him for taking no for an answer. But yes, I have. When he went off into danger for Oswald, for Jack, for Violet, and, yes, a little for me—I had to forgive him."

For a moment, they each sat in perfect repose, each understanding the other as only a rival can do, and content that their long rivalry had at long last yielded to genuine friendship.

Now, as the ladies rested, the door of the Hotel crashed open, and Herr Doktor Brandt made his ungainly way into the bar. He plowed through the little group of friends, brushing aside the Earl, who had been seated with Clarissa, and made for the settee upon which Marie Finn was perched.

She began to rise as he neared; Lady Laura, in sympathy, also stood.

"Mrs. Finn," the Doctor began, "your husband, he–" the Doctor fumbled for the right words.

"What is it? Has he grown worse?" Marie asked.

"*Nein*, no, he iss much better! He iss speaking now, und asks for you!" And, remembering that Marie spoke fluent German, he embarked on a lengthy explanation that left all the others behind. Whatever he said, they understood the gist of it—its import was reflected in the involuntary clap of Marie's hands, the sparkle suddenly restored to her eyes—and that, *mirabile dictu*!—matched an answering glow in the eyes of the Doctor himself.

Unconscious of the effect that his own pleasure in briefing Mrs. Finn was having upon those who had seen only his dour, forbidding rule in the *Krankenhaus*, he smiled, a peculiarly youthful, charming, smile.

"It iss so sel-dom that one hass the chance to bring such good news, I could not vait until the mornink," he said, to the immeasurable delight of Savrola Vavasor, who filled a glass of champagne, and impetuously strode to proffer it to the "Death Watch Beetle," who took it graciously.

"And vy not?" he said still smiling, "af-ter all, my vatch iss over."

"AS GOOD AS A SHOW"

The return of Sir Felix Carbury to London in the wake of the duel caused no little stir in Society. Sir Felix had decamped as soon as he had done what he perceived as his duty; he had waited until Finn was in the hands of the medicos, his principal—former principal, as he had reminded himself—was in the hands of the peelers, if that was what the Germans called 'em—potato peelers, no doubt—and then, in his own elegant term, he'd skedaddled.

The advantage of being the first home, he knew, was that he could, to some extent, control the way the news would first be received. He was most cross with Jack, really. He had had it in his mind to act as the boy's cicerone—he clearly needed one, mind, so he would have been doing the lad some good, helping him to spend his money wisely, and enjoy being a rich young man in the greatest metropolis in the world. What call had Jack to be picking quarrels with people, when he could be sampling all the delights London had to offer, now that the Old Queen's grip on the scepter was finally loosening, and her pleasure-loving son coming into his own at last?

And he, Sir Felix Carbury, could have schooled the young man into the more … interesting parts of Society—not high Society, exactly, but nevertheless fit places for gentlemen to find their fun.

Yes, yes, Carbury admitted to himself, Jack's money would have been useful to him, as he had precious little of his own left—his stepfather gave him a pittance of an allowance that he would revoke the moment he showed up at his door, and his sister Hetta would do nothing for him (indeed, her husband had threatened to thrash him the last time they'd met, and Sir Felix took that threat quite seriously). So taken all in all, Sir Felix had hoped that he and Lord Chiltern could have done each other a bit of good.

Not now, though. It simply doesn't do to kill the referee in a duel. Can't have it. And the chap was a Member of Parliament, friends with the Duke of bloody Omnium, and married to a rich bint with enough clout of her own to send anyone to Coventry if she chose. No, young Jack was on his own, and that's all there was to it.

With a touch of sorrow for what could have been, Sir Felix drew up his plan of attack for his first day back in London. First, he would call upon the Brentfords. They would have received the news by telegraph by now, of course, but he owed them that courtesy. He supposed he should call upon the Widow Finn, while he was at it—she was a good- looking piece for an older filly, after all, and better a friend than an enemy. No need to call upon that other, younger widow—Vavasor's mother. Or was there? With things being so confoundedly mixed-up, it might do no harm. After all, her son was alive, and pretty well unscathed, so he had only good news to bring to her. The Greeks, Sir Felix hazily recollected from his misspent schooldays, had been in the habit of killing the bearers of unwelcome tidings, but how had noble ladies been wont to reward an attractive messenger who brought good news? And she, too, had plenty of the rhino, and was a good bit younger than Mrs. Finn, as well. A man should never turn down the chance to find a good billet, he reflected.

His first visit, to Portman Square, would have been most distressing to him, had he cared tuppence for any of the inhabitants of the place. The Earl of Brentford, a man only a few years older than himself, had patently been shaken by the telegram sent by Trubshawe, which had merely revealed the serious injuries to Finn, the minor cuts to Vavasor, and the arrest of Chiltern. Shaken though he was, the Earl was formidable. Indeed, his anxiety made him more so than at his first meeting with Sir Felix before the dueling parties had made their departures for the Continent.

In the sitting room at Portman Square, still resplendent with the dark, heavy furnishings of the Sixties, Sir Felix quickly realised that, while he pitied the aunt and the mother, Papa Brentford had the air of a man who was ready to lash out, and with intent to wound. Sir Felix indulged in no mischief or malice; he told the story flatly, with no embellishments, and was clinically precise in his description of events. Quite simply, he did not dare to deviate from bald fact by so much as an inch.

The results were bad enough. When Sir Felix described Chiltern's turning on Phineas Finn, and that worthy's fall to the ground, the Countess and her sister-in-law paled, the latter screwing up her handkerchief in her hands, and the Earl, who had been standing with his back to a floor-to ceiling bookcase, hurled his teacup into the grate with a curse.

Keeping his calm despite the flutter of panic in his stomach, Sir Felix said in his gentlest voice, "I am truly sorry, m'lord, to be the bearer of this news. But Lord Chiltern's instructions to me were quite clear; I was to keep back nothing."

The Earl paced swiftly across the room to the fireplace.

"Poor Finn!" He exclaimed. "I brought this upon him. And my son! What am I to do for him?" He turned his face away from the visitor. His wife rose, and embraced him. Lady Laura, subduing her emotions, thanked Sir Felix with all the poise she could muster, and gently suggested that it would be best if he were to go.

Still on his best behaviour, Sir Felix complied, and took himself to Park Lane. When Meier answered the door, Sir Felix found himself denied admittance, being informed that Mrs. Finn and her ward had already departed for the Continent. The birds had flown. Sir Felix left reluctantly, something in the butler's manner instilling a sense of insult that he could not quite explain, let alone justify. Normally more than willing to play the noble with his social inferiors, Sir Felix found himself a little daunted by Meier's Teutonic iciness.

So he repaired to the Vavasors' home, where he was received by the lady of the house. Shown into her parlor, Sir Felix found her scrutinizing his card when he entered the room. He took heart from the sensuous, feminine atmosphere of the room; redolent with chintz, paisley, and love, he thought comfortably.

"Sir Felix Carbury, Bart.," she read aloud, musingly. "Baronet, it is not?"

"That is correct, ma'am," he said, in his most winning way.

She flipped the card from her hand onto the second cushion on the sofa whereon she sat, claiming the space for herself, and preempting his move toward it. Her gaze was not merely direct; it was piercing.

"My only knowledge of you, Sir Felix," she began coolly enough, "is hardly such as to endear you to me."

"My dear Mrs. Vavasor," the baronet replied, "it is true that I acted on behalf of your son's adversary, but there was no insult from me to him, aye, or from your son to me, come to that! We used each other with perfect courtesy, and indeed, I am come to give you a good report to ease your soul."

And, step by step, Mrs. Vavasor coaxed that full report from Sir Felix. Once again he found himself transfixed by a gimlet eye, one that seemed sure to spot any lies or exaggerations, and he told the tale truthfully, just as it happened. He left out the cocaine, of course, and anything that might redound to his own dishonour, but as to the principals and Phineas Finn, he made a fair report.

Realising that she perceived this, he decided to profit from this enforced truthfulness. "And so, Mrs. Vavasor," he said, "you perceive why I had to come to you?"

"No, Sir Felix," she answered, "I do not."

"But you must!"

"Out of sheer good nature, Sir Felix?"

"Out of respect for your son, who is a brave man, and who stood up well, and is, I am relieved to say, unhurt."

"But I know all these things, Sir Felix, by way of my son's companion, Mr. Trubshawe—yes, and I am pleased to say, by the wife of that poor injured man, Mr. Finn."

"Injured?" Sir Felix shook his head weightily, as a man does when he has heavy tidings to impart. "Dead, by now, I am sure. His wounds were mortal, I am sorry to report."

Sorry though he claimed to be to inform Mrs. Vavasor of this fact, he had been greatly pleased to inform Quintus Slide of the same tidbit;

indeed, Slide had shared his pleasure, adding a handsome little bonus above the amount he had agreed to pay for "The True Story of A Most Criminal Affair, From an Eyewitness," a rather merry little piece Slide had concocted from a conversation over several large balloon glasses of rum the night of Sir Felix's return to the Metropolis. That Slide had been able to keep pace with Carbury at the Beargarden, and to write, not only the article, but the handsomely forgiving eulogy of Phineas that flanked it (which Mrs. Vavasor had only just finished reading), spoke well of his capacity in more than journalism.

"Indeed?" Mrs. Vavasor enquired. "And yet only this morning I had a telegram from my son, saying that, although he has not yet regained consciousness, his doctors do not yet despair of his recovery."

Sir Felix was astonished. "Recovery be blowed," he thought, "that man was at death's doorstep if ever a man was." And then, realising that he had led one of his very few benefactors, and one in the press, worse luck, to make a right Charlie of himself, he blew out his breath in a gust. "Walk-er!" he exhaled.

The sharp blue eyes had missed none of this. "So you *were* the source for the *People's Banner*, weren't you, Sir Felix? Come to tell mamma that her son was brave and true, but first sell a quite contrary story to the rag that hates his *fiancée*'s family. How like you."

"How like me?" the confused baronet repeated.

"But why?" The lady sat bolt upright now. "Why come and tell the mamma what she would have learned by telegram already, Sir Felix?

Sir Felix murmured something gallant about the mamma's beauty, realising that control of this interview too, had been wrested from him.

His failed gallantry told the lady all she needed to know, and she clapped her hands with a laugh. Rising from her seat, she proceeded to a small cupboard, which she opened and peered closely into. Rummaging distractedly through the cupboard, she said, "Oh, Sir Felix, how little you have changed. A good deal aged, I should say, and," she added, placing a forefinger against the side of her nose, "somewhat the worse for drink, I fear—but the essential man remains unaltered by time." She returned her attention to the cupboard.

"Do I know you, Madame?" He asked, standing in his own turn.

"Yes. Well, a little. We met someplace or another where I took a room—Lowestoffe was it? No, no, *that* was by the sea. Islington? Yes, Islington, I fancy. Well, no matter. My landlady had a little niece, a Ruby Rogers—no, blast it, Ruggles, wasn't it?"

Sir Felix paled.

"Yes, you seduced the poor little chit, and enticed her away from her grandfather and her suitor John Crumb—no forgetting *that* name, is there Sir Felix?"

And Mrs. Vavasor turned at last, with a beatific smile and the item she had been hunting in the cupboard.

"And I remember thinking how pleasant it would be," she continued, advancing across the room, brandishing the riding crop, "if someone could but reward you for your abominable treatment of that poor child—and here you are, brought to my very door. So it may be a pleasure deferred, but apparently not one den-"

But Sir Felix was fleeing the room; Winifred Vavasor had not even finished her sentence when his coattails vanished through the doorway.

Laughing in a most unladylike way, she dropped back into the sofa and idly tossed the riding crop onto the chair next to it.

"As good as a show," she said to herself, "and no price to pay."

"As good as a show, and no price to pay," would have been the verdict of the assembled cohort of the Beargarden that evening, though delivered in a manner far more acceptable to Sir Felix Carbury than that previously uttered. Sir Felix Carbury, to give him his due, could tell a tale in such a way as to hold the attention of his auditors, on occasions when he was not constrained by fear, lechery, or both combined. And the fact that the protagonists were members of the Club, and the supporting actors, too, and that the catastrophe had fallen upon one who, while not of the herd, was nonetheless well known to all present, spiced his story with an additional fillip of gossip and *Schadenfreude*.

Sir Felix was not too steeped in liquor to tell his tale, either, as might often have been the case in the past. Cocaine was proving to be a more pressing mistress than the champagne flute, and, at this stage in the old sot's life, he seemed rather buoyed by the change than the reverse – which is, of course, one of the more compelling reasons that a man in his declining years will take up with a youthful and demanding new favourite. It would not have occurred to Sir Felix that his glittering inamorata might prove a fickle jade and would surely one day leave him behind with a shrug and a smile, after having thoroughly wrung dry both his person and his purse. Moreover, he had been moderate in his potations that day, wishing to present himself sober to the Brentfords, to Mrs. Finn, and to Mrs. Vavasor (how the devil was he to have known that the socially prominent American beauty was the same hell-cat who had intruded her pestilent self into his private affairs all those years ago? The Prince was welcome to have her, if he could—for Sir Felix's part, she was still d—d handsome, but the smile on her when she was advancing on him with that whip would've rousted Lucifer. Unlike a baronet who was on his uppers, HRH could at least bellow for help and be sure of getting some.)

So it was with his sense of pique greatly soothed, and his ruffled feathers gently settled back into place that the baronet observed the reactions of his auditors. Niven raised his eyebrow several times—a telling reaction from that phlegmatic chap—Sumner "ooh-ed" and "ah-d" most satisfyingly, and even exclaimed "He didn't!" at just the right moments. Only Dolly Longestaffe, admittedly the best storyteller in the Club, sat there in perfect silence, listening with a grave face. Carbury wondered idly if Longestaffe was jealous, but pushed forward with his narrative until the climax: Phineas Finn, stretching his length on the ground, blood oozing from the back of his skull; Vavasor, struggling to regain his feet; Trubshawe, tackling Chiltern; and Carbury, himself, fetching the *gendarmerie*, or whatever the devil the peelers were called in Heidelberg.

"*Polizei*, Carbury," piped up some young scoundrel at the back.

"How unimaginative," commented Niven. "One would have expected something far more menacing-sounding from the land that gave us Valkyries. Still, a terrible business, taken all in all. Thank heavens Vavasor wasn't badly injured, is all I can say."

"And Standish? He's a member too, you know, Niven," Sumner defended his friend, albeit more out of habit than conviction.

"But for how much longer?" Niven asked. "If he's sent to prison for manslaughter—or murder, even—I don't know that we can maintain him on the rolls. Even if he isn't—well, Sir Felix, did he really attack Finn?"

"Yes, Carbury," asked Dolly Longestaffe, with much more concern than anyone had ever heard in his voice before, even during the Episode of the Mouse in the Orchestrelle of '88, "did he really have a go at Finn?"

Sir Felix weighed his answer. There is no doubt that Sir Felix was, by any measure, a bad man; a wastrel, selfish to the point of cruelty, and indolent. And in the ordinary sense of the word, he had not a whit of honour—he had habitually contracted debts, fully intending not to pay them; he had lived off his mother, until her remarriage had saddled him with a less financially pliable step-parent; he had bullied his sister until her marriage had encumbered him with what he often thought of as a mere junior edition of the objectionable stepfather, and, as Mrs. Vavasor had so vividly reminded him that very afternoon, he had been an unscrupulous seducer of unprotected women. But Sir Felix had not cheated at cards. He had not lied in the Club about another member of the Club—at least, not when his own interests were not at stake. And he would not do so now.

"I am very sorry to report that he did," Sir Felix replied at length. "He took several cuts at Mr. Finn, whose head and neck were exposed."

And Dolly Longestaffe sadly rose, leaving the remainder of his brandy-and-soda, and uttered words nobody had expected to hear from him.

"I believe I am off home, gentlemen. I want to hear what my wife has to say about all this."

In the stunned silence occasioned by his departure, the assembled members of the Beargarden felt a shiver, as of mortality—and promptly ordered up another round of drinks to banish it.

THE PRISONERS

Ifor Powlett-Jones had received a hurried visit from his barrister and solicitor before Phineas disappeared to the Continent. In their brief meeting, Phineas had urged Powlett-Jones not to despair, and to wait with patience to hear from him. Days later, he had heard that his barrister was believed to be dead, and Mr. Camperdown did not appear.

Dressed in shabby, ill-fitting clothes pocked with coarse fabric arrows to remind him of his status as a convict, Ifor was put to labour; sewing mailbags, picking oakum, whatever odd jobs needed doing about the Scrubs. Whole weeks went by without his hearing his own name—to warders and prisoners alike, he was, contemptuously, "Taffy." He was not physically assailed, or, at any rate had not yet been. He was young and strong, and the fact that his conviction was for assault was enough to lead his fellow prisoners to be a little wary of him.

So far, that is.

None of the various gangs in the prison, known as "firms," had decided what to do with young Taffy. Kept himself to himself, but could, if recruited, be an asset. The one prisoner who had tried him on, seeking to steal Ifor's cigarettes, had found himself quickly and mercilessly thrashed—and in a way that left no marks. The other convict did not even bother to "split" on Taffy; no bruises, his word against the young Welshman's, and thus no chance of a discipline for the boy.

For now, Powlett-Jones's life was tolerable, if only just. But seeing only a little patch of blue sky in the exercise yard, constantly linked to men dour at best, cruel—or, what is even worse, completely blank—all these circumstances were leaching the hope and the life from him.

A little over a month and a half since he'd last heard from his barrister, a warder seized him on the way to the workroom. "Not just yet, Taffy," the warder said, "yer brief is here to see you."

And without a further word, the guard and one other led him to the interview rooms. While most such rooms were in a vast cavernous space separated into little cubbies, Powlett-Jones was led into a private room. In that room of bare, featureless cellblock, with a plain wooden table and two heavy wooden chairs –occupied –on one side, Ifor was shackled to a third lonely chair across from the other two. The warders then withdrew, swinging the massive wooden door with its barred window closed behind him.

"Call if you need anything, sir," the first warder spoke to the older of the two men sitting opposite Ifor. That man was not Phineas Finn, but a much older man; one bearing the marks of long illness—pallor, slightly laboured breathing, and a look of fatigue about the mouth and eyes, but the eyes themselves were ablaze with life, and the smile was kind.

"My name is Abner Low," he said, "and you already know Mr. Camperdown. I have come at the request of my colleague, and good friend, Mr. Phineas Finn, who was anxious that you suffer as little suspense as possible."

"Mr. Finn is alive? I had heard–"

Mr. Low raised his hand pacifically. "The press, particularly *The People's Banner*, is not entirely to be trusted. My young friend Mr. Finn"—Ifor smiled at this, for, admire Phineas Finn though he did, he did not see him as young—"was, it is true, injured recently. A result, I am sorry to say, of another quixotic effort to assist a young man in trouble. As in your case, he was mostly successful, but not completely."

Ifor made as if to speak.

"No, no. Mr. Finn was largely successful in your case, you know, Mr. Powlett-Jones. You were almost entirely acquitted, after all. And he has written me to ask that I might inform you that he is not yet done working on your behalf."

"He—has not abandoned me, then?"

"Abandoned you?" The sickly old man looked shocked. "Young man, he is so far from abandoning you that he has already made direct appeals to the Home Secretary and the Prime Minister on your behalf."

"But-but not with any success, sir, as I am still here." Despite his reply, the young man felt a jolt of excitement thrum through his body like a galvanic current; he was not, then, despaired of!

"Not yet." Mr. Low's answer was scrupulously honest. The old man paused. "Mr. Finn desired that I should explain your legal position to you, and I shall do so. As I taught Phineas most of his law, I believe I can set it out as well as he could. Before I do that, though, you should understand that Mr. Finn places his highest hopes in a—well—less formal avenue of redress for you."

"What do you mean, sir?"

"I mean that Mr. Finn has not despaired of obtaining a pardon for you—a full, free pardon, which would set you free and give you your name back. If he can accomplish it, it is by far the best way. He is not sanguine about your legal remedies, and, quite frankly, neither am I."

At Powlett-Jones's puzzled look, Mr. Camperdown interjected, "What Mr. Low means, Ifor, is that neither he nor Mr. Finn can be sure that an appeal—the next stage of the legal proceedings, which I have already begun to put in train, at Mr. Finn's instruction—will reliably result in your being set free."

"Thank you, Mr. Camperdown," murmured the barrister, "for that translation into the demotic. Now, before we move onto those legal remedies, let me assure you of this: Phineas Finn has excellent judgment of what is politically possible—the best of anyone I know. If he believes that a pardon might be obtained for you–"

"Though I scarcely understand how," murmured Mr. Camperdown, "the Prime Minister having already refused..."

Mr. Low's rumbling bass cut into Mr. Camperdown's musings with a little more power than his previous utterances; Powlett-Jones had a sudden sense that, in his prime, Abner Low would have been a formidable advocate.

"If, as I say, Mr. Finn believes the thing is possible, as he does, than I would trust his efforts to bring it off."

"And what must I do?" Ifor asked.

"Nothing," the old man replied promptly. "Wait and hope."

"And pray?" Ifor had heard the three linked together his whole life, and was therefore a little scandalised by Mr. Low's omission in his reply.

"It could hardly hurt, young man," the old barrister answered. "Now let us go over your legal options..."

A little over an hour later, a much more cheerful Powlett-Jones was led back to the cells; Mr. Low, leaning on his stick, was helped into a carriage by Mr. Camperdown. The younger man, his long, lantern-jawed face taut with concern for the old barrister, asked, as he mounted into the carriage himself, "Straight home, Mr. Low?"

"Not yet, Mr. Camperdown. First to St. John's Wood. I have one other appointment this afternoon."

"Are you certain, Mr. Low? You are looking pale, sir."

The old man smiled. "I know. I will be quite all right, Mr. Camperdown. Pass me that flask." The young solicitor did as he was instructed, and Mr. Low drank deeply of its contents. "There," he said collectedly, "that'll set me right 'til I am home again, and Georgiana will be able to cope with me from that point. It does not do to keep a lady waiting, Mr. Camperdown."

"A lady, Mr. Low? In St. John's Wood?"

"A Mrs. Vavasor, Camperdown. A lady to whose son Mr. Finn's niece is engaged, and to whom he has entrusted me with a letter. I am to answer any questions she has after she reads it."

In Heidelberg, jails in the police station, while Spartan, are quite neat. Jack Standish had—enjoyed is not the ideal word, but he had experienced ample opportunity to ascertain that fact over the past month and a half. As Jack had lapsed into a state of utter passivity, he did not appreciably disturb the orderly surroundings so dear to the souls of his Teutonic turnkeys. He refused all visitors, even his parents, and declined to take legal advice. He ate the food his warders provided him, and drank the water they set out for him. He did not ask for, and did not receive, beer or wine. Lady Laura had seen to that, after an interview with Sir Felix Carbury before his departure.

Jack had, upon being knocked to the ground by Trubshawe, come out of the blind rage that had overmastered him. Its power enhanced and magnified by the potent mix of absinthe and cocaine, he had given in to the fury that had unpredictably possessed him from his youth, and upon rising from the cobblestones, he had looked dazedly upon the havoc he had wrought.

It had never been this bad before, never remotely. Sir Felix Carbury—a man whom Jack had known to be a reprobate and a cad—had stared at him with shocked disapprobation; Vavasor had regarded him with contempt. And his godfather—the man he had called "Uncle Phineas" until, upon his coming of age, he had been invited to address him by his Christian name alone, dispensing with the honorific, had lain on the cobblestones, bleeding his life away.

All because of him.

Jack had fallen to his knees in shock. "What have I done?" he had asked, appalled. And then:

"Vavasor?"

"What is it?"

"Is help on the way for Finn?"

"Yes," Savrola Vavasor had answered in a flat tone.

"The police, too, Vavasor. I am guilty of this, and must be taken into custody."

"They are coming, Chiltern."

Jack had nodded in despair. "I cannot cure what I have done, Vavasor, but I will not resist my punishment."

Savrola had made no answer. Trubshawe, binding Phineas's head wound, had made none either; nor did Carbury.

"I am guilty towards you, too, Vavasor. I played you foul just now."

"You had better not say any more about that just now, Chiltern," Savrola had gruffly replied.

"But I must! And more than that, I must say before our seconds that I was in the wrong in both our previous quarrels. Entirely so. I was a jealous cur, Vavasor, and now, see what my damnable rage has done!"

The muscles of Savrola Vavasor's normally mild face had fluctuated between anger and pity. At length he had said, haltingly, "For the injuries you have done me, I forgive you. For Phineas Finn's—let us pray he recovers."

The *Polizei*, tactfully, had chosen that moment to arrive.

The next month and a half, wherein Jack found himself deprived of the Infuriator, or indeed of any brand of absinthe or other alcohol, let alone "snuff"—the cocaine his second had so thoughtfully supplied—was one of absolute agony. When the compulsion came upon him, he would rave, weep, and beg for the drug—the cocaine became ever more important to him as its enforced absence was prolonged—or the liquor. He would threaten the jailers, wheedle, promise them money upon his release, and so carry on that they treated him as little better than a lunatic. Indeed, on the worst days, he had to be restrained to prevent him from dashing his head against the bars of his cell or against the floor.

And when the compulsion slowly faded, his disgust at his own behaviour compounded the guilt for having almost certainly slain his godfather. He could not bear to see his parents, for the dread of seeing the contempt in his father's eyes, and the hurt in his mother's. He ignored their letters—simply could not bear to open them.

His nightmares in those days or nights—for he fell asleep at odd hours, and often was awake throughout the nights—were pitiably vivid. With preternatural clarity, he could see himself being hanged for the murder of Phineas Finn; feel the rough hempen rope being forced about his unwilling neck; turn sick at the sudden, shocking absence of the floor –and then, the fall, the choking at the end of the rope, all the while seeing his own father nod approvingly, his Aunt Laura knitting in the front row of spectators, Clarissa turning coldly away.

Or worse—he could see the tear-streaked face of his Aunt Marie as she stood at the side of a grave, before a stone he dare not look at.

Lizzie Eustace did not figure in his nightmares, now. The threat she presented was far too remote, too much a part of a normal life—a life for which he no longer deemed himself fit. He was no longer afraid that Lizzie would force him to marry her, because he now felt himself to be beneath her contempt. Bitter solace, indeed- to have fallen so low as to be beneath the notice of Lizzie Eustace!

After five or six weeks—he could not be sure—all the fire had burned out of him, and all he was conscious of was a terrible lassitude. He could not be roused to eat, and had to be coaxed out of the bed by the guards and led by hand to the table. "Komm, Graf Chiltern," they would say, and he would obey mindlessly. He ate and drank mechanically, without appetite, but without resistance.

When left to himself he did not read, though he had a Bible in the cell. He did not speak. Herr Doktor Brandt, who had periodically been observing him throughout the weeks, was concerned enough to grant a request that had been made to him several days before. Although the good Doktor had certain misgivings concerning his Hippocratic responsibilities in the case, in the end, his humanitarian side won out, as it always did.

And so it came to pass, in the seventh week of his stay in the Heidelberg cells, that Jack Standish was led to a visiting room. His passive obedience compelled him, though he inwardly shrank from having to see anybody. His jailers had not told him whom he was going to meet, but what mattered that, when there was nobody he dared face? Nonetheless, he obediently followed his guard into the neat, comfortable little office.

There, standing before him, leaning on a walking stick, with grave eyes, but a slight smile, was Phineas Finn. Thinner, indeed, a little gaunt, despite Herr Steiler's and Marie's best efforts to fill him back out, with more gray in his beard and hair than he had had before, but very much alive, and, judging by his bearing, not hostile.

"Hello, Jack," Phineas said in his kindest voice.

"Uncle Phineas…" the young man murmured, and repeated "Uncle Phineas?" Tears welled in Jack's eyes, and began to course down his cheeks. Before Jack or the warders could react, Phineas crossed the room, using his stick to maintain his balance, and embraced his godson. He then pulled back a bit, keeping his grasp on Jack's forearms, and looked the younger man in the eye.

"It has gone badly with you these last weeks, my boy," he said.

"I deserve it, Uncle Phineas. How can you bear to look at me? I have been a murderous brute–"

"Herr Doktor Brandt, whom I have great reason to respect, tells me that you have been a young man under the sway of drugs, of cocaine, of absinthe and of alcohol. Your Aunt Laura tells me that you have also been in terrible trouble, and did not know where to turn for help in your perplexity."

"I do not deserve help; I deserve to rot in prison, and be forgotten."

Phineas smiled gently. "Oh, Jack," he said, "I have known you since your infancy, and you have always been too quick to condemn, root and branch, yourself, as well as others. No, my boy, you will have to accept it; you are forgiven, and that is all there is to it."

"How can I ever look Aunt Marie in the face again? Aunt Laura? My father—or, oh, God!—my Mother?"

"I never said there would be no punishment for you, Jack. This *is* your punishment. You will have to accept forgiveness, and that is no easy thing to do. In Marie's case, you will have to earn it."

"But how can I?"

"You must change. Here; sit down, my boy. I can't rely on my balance just yet." And, delicately lowering himself into one of the chairs in front of the plain wooden desk in the otherwise bare office, Phineas motioned Jack to the chair next to him.

"Now, Jack, to change. My father, who was a doctor in Cork, would prescribe just what my good physician here has prescribed for you: You cannot drink liquor of any kind, nor use any drug. Why some men cannot, while most others can, is a mystery; but it is so. Many of the drunkards of Killaloe were as good a man as my father or me, until they drank. It brought them to a kind of madness. So, too, cocaine, or opium, or any other drug can drive certain men mad, while leaving others unscathed."

"You mean I am too weak in character."

"No," Phineas insisted, "I mean that these substances affect you differently. Doktor Brandt has made a study of it, and has corresponded with Freud of Vienna, who has done more research still. It is *not* that your character is weak, but due to some reaction as yet unknown in your body. You should speak with Brandt, you know; he is very sensible. But everything he says on the subject corresponds to what I used to observe of my father's patients."

"So—I must never drink, or use snuff, or other drugs?"

"That is correct, Jack. But there is more, too."

A very slight smile creased Jack's face. "I thought as much. What else? Give up my socialism?"

"Certainly not!" Phineas rejoined. "If you believe in it, do it. But find a way to do it steadily, make something. Write, put up for Parliament, but don't just carp—get in the fight!"

Jack looked at his godfather with surprise.

"After all this, you would still encourage me?"

"Why not? I may be about to be thrown out of the Liberal Party myself; we could end up going on as Labourites together."

The warder handed Phineas the stick he had dropped in embracing his godson, and he began to walk gingerly toward the far door—the door towards freedom, Jack thought. When he reached the door, Phineas turned and looked quizzically at his godson.

"Well?" He asked, "Aren't you coming?"

Jack's jaw dropped.

"But-but I am in custody here."

Phineas shook his head, smiling. "You *were*," he said. "But your father and I staged a joint raid yesterday afternoon on the *Polizeihauptkommissar*, and managed to persuade him that the matter was a *Mensur* bout gone wrong, and that you had merely gotten over-excited and did not realise time had been called."

"But-but surely Vavasor's complaint–"

Phineas looked calmly at his godson. "Savrola has made no complaint against you. He tells me that he told you on the scene that he forgave you, after you'd begged his pardon. Do you not remember that?"

After a pause, Jack admitted, "I did not believe him. I could not believe that he was capable of such generosity."

"Then you wronged him again. One day," Phineas added, before Jack could succumb to another wave of despair, "I shall introduce the real Savrola Vavasor to the real Jack Standish. I think you will each form quite a different opinion of the other than you have to date. Take my arm, Jack. As I said, my balance is not yet what it should be."

The two men walked together through the door, and through the anteroom, into the crisp, frosty air of a sunny December day.

4

HOMEWARD BOUND

The Finns and the Brentford parties traveled together, although Savrola Vavasor discreetly left a day early. As they said their farewells, Phineas clasped Savrola's shoulder and said to him, "I did not know your father, Savrola, but if it means anything to you, you have acted in this affair exactly as I would wish to have a son of mine behave. I cannot but think that he would share my pride in you."

Savrola flushed with pleasure, and replied, "Coming from you, sir, that means a great deal. I dragged you into this terrible business; I'm sorrier than I can say."

The older man shook his head gently. "You were quite right to do so. And your generosity to Chiltern—that is beyond praise."

Savrola smiled. "I hope one day to see him as you do. As it is, I will put all this behind me, and hope that he and I do not cross each other's paths until he is—until he is well again."

Phineas shook the young man's hand, and bade him farewell.

Upon Phineas's leading Jack from the Police Station, he had taken him to the quay by the banks of the Neckar, where Jack saw his father facing the river. The Earl was gazing into the swift currents, and, for the first time in his life, Jack saw his father as a man no longer young. Phineas walked with him until they were quite near, and called out "Oswald! Here is someone you have long wished to see!" When his father turned around, Jack was startled to see that his eyes were wet. The Earl pulled his son to him, and held him tight. As Phineas began to turn, to leave father and son together, Brentford silently mouthed the words, "Thank you" to his old friend.

The Brentfords dined alone in their room that evening. The Finns, including Savrola Vavasor, dined together, and Phineas soon noticed that Clarissa was troubled. When he asked her the reason, she said sadly. "I know that I am supposed to forgive Jack, Uncle Phineas, but I don't want to. It's unchristian, and wrong of me, but he's caused us all such pain, and he has not been punished for it."

Phineas found himself unable to answer, and met his niece's eyes with difficulty. How could he explain that his oldest friend had borne some of the madness to which Jack had succumbed—the wild, ungovernable Chiltern rage? Or that he had known men—good men— to deteriorate into vicious drunkards, capable of terrible acts?

"It is so hard for the young," he thought sadly, "they have no experience of needing forgiveness." He looked to his wife, who had forgiven him his ancient dereliction in favour of Mary Flood Jones, his long-dead first wife. He had blamed himself for that action for years, as he had chosen Mary, not because he had loved her, but because he had falsely told her that he did, and because he had lacked the strength of character to tell her the truth.

Marie met his gaze, and smiled her little crooked smile, signifying that she understood, but did not entirely sympathise with, her husband's predicament. Then she sighed a little and said, "I think you will find Jack's punishment is only beginning. I imagine Sir Felix Carbury has spread the tale all over town by now. Jack will have a very hard time of it back home."

Savrola nodded. "He may be the first person drummed out of the Beargarden for moral turpitude since the '70s. If he doesn't resign."

"But Uncle Oswald, and Aunt Violet, and Lady Laura—they will just forgive him?"

"Yes," Phineas replied, "but it will cost them dear, and he will know it. And he has a long struggle ahead of him—to regain his health, his equilibrium, and to find a new role in life. He is soiled goods in the eyes of Society, and must build a whole new life."

"But the Brentfords say they love you, Uncle," Clarissa fought back, "and he nearly killed you and Savrola."

"They do love your uncle," Marie answered, "and they are heartbroken at the harm they have done him. But he is their son, and they can no more cast him out than we could disown you."

"Besides," Savrola joined in, "If your uncle can forgive the poor devil the injury he has suffered, I can forgive this confounded scar—though it does itch!"

A thin sally, perhaps, but enough to bring the Finns together in laughter.

Before departing Heidelberg, Jack had submitted to a full examination and interrogation by Doktor Brandt. The Death Watch Beetle had pressed upon the young lord a translation, by his own hand, into English of the 1887 monograph, "Cocaine in the Treatment of Opiate Addiction," by his friend, Herr Doktor Friedrich Erlenmeyer.

"Erlenmeyer says, young man, that the cocaine iss the 'third scourge of mankind,' after alcohol—ja?—und opium. You must learn from his example, and from the stories he tells in his monograph."

"But am I not cured, Doctor Brandt?"

"Nein! No, you are not cured. You only do not suffer any ill effects because you now haf none of that poison in your system. If you ingest it, you vill suffer the same effects as before—and maybe vorse. Addiction does not get better, if you once resume it, *mein guter Jüngling*, it only gets vorse."

"Alcohol, cocaine, and opium—the three scourges of mankind?"

"Perhaps, Lord Chiltern," the Death Watch Beetle said impressively, "it iss sufficient to the purpose if you view them as your own personal scourges. As some men cannot eat strawberries vithout being poisoned, you, at any rate, cannot ingest those three."

"But even a glass of wine?"

The Doctor's glare was unyielding. "Even a glass of vine. Because it will never be enough. And you vill, again, go mad."

Soberly, Jack thanked the Doctor and shook his hand. He would have to resign from the Club, he thought, and then immediately realised he would have to do so anyway. He had dishonoured the Beargarden, hard as that was to manage; he could at least spare it the trouble of drumming him out.

Despite this grim diagnosis, Jack found the trip home soothing. They traveled by train to Bremen, and took ship to Southampton from there. He drank barley-water, fizzy lemonade, orange squash, and tea. His mother was warm and kind to him, pretending the whole affair had never happened. Aunt Laura was a little stiff at first (not unexpectedly; what he thought of as her "pash" for Uncle Phineas had been obvious to Jack since his childhood), but was not overtly hostile. What was unexpected was the way she and Aunt Marie had chummed up. Aunt Laura's cordial loathing for Uncle Phineas's wife had been a byword in the family for as long as he could recall, but now they positively sought out each other's company.

Clarissa was civil, but cold. She avoided Jack's company and spent her time with her uncle or with the Earl, whose endless tramps around the vessel were the only evidence of just how restless and eager to be home he was.

But, rather to his surprise, it was Marie Finn who wrung Jack's heart. She had lost some of her sparkle; she, too, now had a little more gray in her abundant hair than formerly; and, unlike Uncle Phineas, she did not treat these changes as grounds for laughter. When Phineas said to her over tea one afternoon, "I am glad to have left Germany, my dear; I am beginning to resemble a respectable *Bürgermeister*, and would hate to be expected to act accordingly," the sally brought no smile from her, only a sad look.

There was no question that the sea voyage had enlivened Phineas Finn. His sense of balance was not returning as quickly as he had expected, and his own promenades about the vessel were assiduously accompanied by the Earl, in case his old friend should pitch over, or lose his footing. But the salt spray and sea air spoke to something atavistic in Phineas, and every day he gained a little of his old ebullience back.

On the day before last of the voyage, Jack spied his Aunt Marie on her own, bundled in a rug, for the days were becoming cold now. She was reading a novel—*The Picture of Dorian Gray*, again; a favourite of hers since its first appearance in *Lippincott's Monthly*, he observed—and was, he thought, unaware of his approach from behind her deck chair. As he hesitated to speak to her, trying to form a sentence, she forestalled him.

"You are a greedy boy, Jack Standish," she said. "Having received the forgiveness of your parents, your Aunt Laura, and even the man you so cruelly injured, you cannot rest until we have all forgiven you."

Jack scraped the deck with his shoe, and made a strangled sound, as he tried to formulate a reply. She patted the chair next to hers, and commanded, "Come. Sit next to me, so I do not have to crane my neck to see you, and tell me why I should forgive you for nearly murdering the man I have loved these many years."

Obediently, he came around her, sat in the chair next to her, and twisted to face her. She was looking at him archly, but not angrily. "Well?" she demanded. "You have sought me out, and now you have found me. *Erzähle.*" She waited a moment, and repeated, this time in English, "Speak."

"I-I do not even know how to address you anymore," he admitted.

She snorted derisively. "Shall I make you call me Mrs. Finn, then, after holding you on my lap as an infant? I am angry with you, Jack, and have a right to be, but I do not hate you, nor do I disown you."

Tears came to his eyes; he wept all too readily these days, he thought. "I am unmanned by my own sins, Aunt Marie," he said, wiping them away. "I have harmed everyone that I love, and have no excuses to offer, or reasons to give. I hate what I have been, and do not know how to make amends."

Marie's gaze pierced his soul, all of her considerable force brought to bear on him. "You will follow Doktor Brandt's prescription to the letter? For the rest of your life?"

Sadly, he nodded. "I have read the monograph. It is too true of me. And Uncle Phineas–"

"What of him?"

"He told me of the drunkards he'd known in Ireland, whom his father treated. I do not want to be like them. Or like Sir Felix Carbury, come to that."

In her silkiest tones, Marie asked, "Ah, Sir Felix. Tell me what you know of him."

"He is a man younger than my father—or Uncle Phineas, come to that—yet seems much older. He lives on his wits, having driven away every member of his family, and uses cocaine to ward off the worst effects of drink, and drink to ward off the worst effects of the cocaine."

"How do you know this, Jack?"

"He told me, on the voyage to Bremen. He announced it as if he had found the Fountain of Youth, always timing his doses, and carrying about his snuff box, or worse yet, his ghastly needles."

"Jack!" she exclaimed. "Did you not realise what it meant, that he alone, of all your circle, was willing to act for you? Did you not see how you were polluted by his presence?"

The young man shook his head. "I had the engagement to get through, and I was drinking so much absinthe that my hands were losing their steadiness. The cocaine returned it, and so I wanted to believe in the old rogue. I should have cried off, Aunt Marie, and begged Vavasor's pardon on the parade-ground! I was entirely in the wrong, and, worse yet, I knew it, but rage and hate convinced me that I *must* win the bout."

"Then why did you not stop when you had done so?"

"It was over so quickly—I felt no satisfaction; I had not proven myself the better man."

"And why not?"

And at last Jack brought himself to meet his Aunt's gaze.

"Because I was not the better man; I was the worse one. I had degenerated into something terrifyingly like Carbury, but with a bit of ferocity that I called courage."

"Was it not courage?" Marie Finn pressed him.

"How could it be? Vavasor was not my match with a sword, let alone a *Schläger*. He was the one who showed courage, not me. He and my Uncle Phineas. I was a coward, playing a game I was expert in against a novice, and willing to break the rules to hurt him."

"Did you mean to kill him, Jack?"

"No!" The answer was clearly sincere; he was visibly shocked at the question. Jack considered his next words carefully. And then: "But I did mean to hurt him. And then I flew into a rage. I could have killed him, Aunt Marie, had not Uncle Phineas intervened."

"So Doktor Brandt's prescription? How do you view it, then? As a penance?"

He smiled a little then. "No, though it's austere enough for one, in all truth," he said, with a touch of his old spirit, and then added: "I view it as my one hope of not ending up like Sir Felix Carbury."

"Good," Marie Finn replied. She extended her hand. "Then you are forgiven—conditionally, Jack."

He took her hand. "And what are your conditions, Aunt Marie?"

"As long as you make something of yourself. Be Lord Chiltern, be Jack Standish the Socialist—I care not which. But do not be an idle *flaneur*, Jack; my husband did not nearly lose his life for the sake of a charming parasite."

"Agreed. And thank you, Aunt Marie," he answered, his fist striking his breast.

As he got up to leave her, she added, "One other thing, Jack."

"Yes, Aunt Marie?"

"Do not expect too much from Clarissa, and do not press her. As she sees you live a life worthy of you, and as her own happiness surrounds her, her disappointment in you will lose some of its bitterness—and she, too, will forgive you. But in her time, not yours."

Jack nodded soberly, and thanking his Aunt once more, took his leave of her. She picked up her book again, read a few pages, and decided that she no longer was in the mood for a story of gilded youth gone terribly wrong. She rose, and sought out her husband's company.

When they landed at Southampton, the two families prepared to go their separate ways. Jack was to accompany his parents to Harrington Hall until the New Year, and then to go to Lochlinter, to consider, as he told his Aunt Marie in parting, his course. Lady Laura was to travel to London with the Finns, after which she, too, would repair to Lochlinter in the New Year.

Phineas Finn wanted nothing so much as to be home—in his own house, with his books, his cat and his pipe. Moreover, he was eager to see to the affairs of young Powlett-Jones. Low's letter describing his meeting with Ifor and his briefing of Mrs. Vavasor had all been very well, but this next stage of the matter did not call, properly, for a barrister, but for a politician. It needed the personal touch, and it was time he took matters in hand again.

BACKSTAIRS STRATEGY

Mrs. Winifred Vavasor had not been entirely bereft of company in the weeks of her son's German sojourn. She had, of course, received the brief, but not unamusing, visit of Sir Felix Carbury already described.

Previous to that, she had received a visit from young Trubshawe, in his character of Savrola's second. He had called to assure her of her son's courage in the field, and of the slightness of the cuts he had received in the duel.

"Mind you," he had said, in a surprisingly minatory manner for one so young, "Chiltern broke the rules, there—first blood was to have ended it, and he kept on after poor Savrola. Not right, that. Not right at all. Worse, when the *maître* declared a halt, he turned on him, if you can believe such a thing. Hurt Mr. Finn quite badly, too—poor man was unconscious even when I left for home."

"What will become of him?"

"Finn? As a good friend of mine would say, that is on the knees of the gods. As to Chiltern, who knows? The laws in Germany are, well, recondite, I suppose is the word I should use. The *Mensur*—that is, the duel—is legally protected there, as long as one plays by the rules."

"Which Lord Chiltern most decidedly did not."

"True, but who will lay a charge against him? Savrola forgave the chap on the spot, as I told you, ma'am; Carbury fled as soon as he was decently able; and I cannot think that Phineas Finn is the kind of man who would wish to see his own godson prosecuted, even for an assault on his own person."

"You could have sworn out the charge, Mr. Trubshawe."

The young man blushed. "No doubt; but I consider that I was bound by the wishes of my principal in the matter."

"Do you disapprove of my son's not pressing charges?"

Trubshawe considered awhile, before answering. "No-o," he said at length, "not with the chap coming to himself on the spot and confessing his enormities on his knees. It'd take a harder man than me—or your son, come to that—to swear out a charge then."

"I think I do disapprove, Mr. Trubshawe," Mrs. Vavasor said. "But you plead my son's cause admirably, and as his mother, I can only thank you."

With her dark hair, blue eyes, and in a rich blue dress, showing off ivory shoulders and her still-fine figure, Mrs. Vavasor had not lost her power to enchant, and Trubshawe found himself impelled to kiss the outstretched hand. The resultant smile on Mrs. Vavasor's face encouraged him to ask, in a husky voice, permission to call again.

"I am sure you are always welcome to visit my son, Mr. Trubshawe," she replied demurely.

"I-umm, meant—to call upon *you*, Mrs. Vavasor," the young man said. Her smile broadened, and her eyes opened a fraction wider.

"I would be delighted to see you, should you care to call, Mr. Trubshawe," she replied.

Subsequently, some weeks later, a courteous old gentleman, Mr. Abner Low, had called on her shortly before tea-time. That Mr. Low was not in the best of health was evident, and the solicitor who accompanied him had to assist him to a chair.

Waving off Mrs. Vavasor's concerned inquiries, the old barrister asked her to sit opposite him. "My dear lady," he began, "it is very good of you indeed to see me, and, were my old pupil Mr. Phineas Finn back in England, he would have waited upon you himself, of course."

"You were Mr. Finn's pupil-master, Mr. Low?" Mrs. Vavasor could not repress a stir of interest. "What was he like then?"

"Clever. Heedless, imprudent, and not sufficiently interested in the niceties of the law. But the largest heart of any pupil I ever took on, and as keen a sense of justice as any lawyer I've ever known."

"They say he had quite an eye for the ladies in those days," Mrs. Vavasor commented.

The old barrister snorted, and Mr. Camperdown's ears pricked up. "That too. Infernal young pup was always head over heels for some noblewoman or other. Made no end of trouble, I can tell you. Fortunately, he had the good fortune—aye, and the good sense—to marry Marie Goesler—Madame Max, as she was then known."

"You make him sound quite raffish, Mr. Low."

"Then I do him an injustice, Mrs. Vavasor. Since I had to retire from the office some years ago, Mr. Finn has kept my practise afloat, and become a fine advocate in the process. But I did not come to discuss your—ha!—future connection, Mrs. Vavasor, but as an emissary on his behalf. Am I right in believing that you remain willing to join in our efforts to secure Mr. Powlett-Jones a pardon by—well—placing facts before those who may be able to secure a hearing for the lad outside the usual channels?"

"I am willing to place such facts before one whose representations, whether to the Government, or….elsewhere…will at least secure Mr. Powlett-Jones a hearing."

"You know that these channels are, while not unlawful, most unorthodox?"

"Indeed. And I am not surprised by the rash Mr. Finn's being willing to risk his own political fortunes by running counter to his own Party's leadership, Mr. Low—but *you* do not strike me, if you will forgive my saying so, as being one for such expedients."

The old lawyer chuckled heavily. "I am not. I begin to understand the appeal of it for Phineas, though—conspiratorial meetings with beautiful young ladies, all in the name of doing the high justice, when the low and middle have been tried and found wanting…yes, I understand him better now than when he was my pupil. But there is more. I may be a lawyer to my fingertips, Mrs. Vavasor, but I have not lost sight of the purpose of our legal system, you know—and that is justice."

"What is justice, to so consummate a lawyer as yourself, Mr. Low?"

The old man straightened a little in his chair, and his eyes blazed. "Justinian, Mrs. Vavasor, in the very first line of his *Institutes*, called justice 'the constant and perpetual wish to render every one his due,' and I have never seen that definition bettered. Ifor Powlett-Jones has not received his due, Mrs. Vavasor, and I am, at the end of what has been a long life in the law, prepared to reaffirm that justice is the goal, and the law is but a means to that end."

Mrs. Vavasor smiled at the old man, and said, "Yes, you clearly were Mr. Finn's pupil- master. Now be mine. Teach me what I must know to obtain justice for this young man."

He nodded, pleased, and looked over at the solicitor. "The file, Mr. Camperdown. We have much to cover."

The old man kept her at it through teatime, and until supper. When she pressed him to stay for supper, he agreed to dine with her, but apologised that he must then go home and sleep. He quizzed her over the meal, his energy fading somewhat, but rallied enough to eat a little and to persuade himself that she was letter-perfect in her brief.

Mr. Low leaned heavily on Mr. Camperdown on his departure, and nodded off in the carriage on the way home. When the carriage reached his home, Mr. Low needed to be helped out of it and into bed. He slept the clock round, but woke up much refreshed, and feeling more useful than he had in nearly eight years.

His Highness the Prince was known to be one who delighted in the company of beautiful women. The "Marlborough House set"—the circle of friends and advisers, which was growing around him as the Old Queen became in very truth old and began to yield to the ravages of time, became ever more openly a shadow court, one that would form the nucleus of a new generation, though led by one himself no longer young. Nonetheless, that nucleus was dominated by the young and clever—or by the beautiful who were clever enough to create an aura of perpetual youth.

Winifred Vavasor was among the planets that orbited the rising sun, though she circled at a greater distance than most of her sister orbs. If Mrs. Alice Keppel was the Mercury of this nascent solar system, then Mrs. Vavasor might be deemed the Pluto—out on the fringes of the Sun's influence, sometimes coming in tantalizingly close, and yet never entirely in reach to be fully grasped.

As the fall drew on, though, Pluto swooped in closer to the Sun, drawn into its orbit more tightly than in recent years. There were, of course, those who asserted that it was Pluto drawing the Sun into its orbit—but, really, how could one be sure? To put the matter plainly, Mrs. Vavasor was seen among the Marlborough House set far more often then she had been in recent months. Her American accent, and the savour of danger that surrounded her wherever she walked, combined with her undoubted beauty and charm, was a heady mix even for royalty. Royalty, long accustomed to being served, was tickled, frustrated, and bewitched, all at once, by the flower it could not boldly grasp and possess. And, indeed, Winifred Vavasor's thorns could bite deep; apart from her powers of repartee, the persistent rumours that she had—although, as all agreed, no doubt provoked to the deed—made an end of her own first husband years ago, when little more than a girl, received new currency when a distorted report of Sir Felix's flight from her home made the rounds.

For Sir Felix, afraid that she would herself tell the tale against him (thereby displaying his lack of insight into the lady), sought to preempt such a move on her part by telling his own embroidered version of the meeting. In Sir Felix's rendition, he had gone gallantly to call upon the mother of an honourable combatant, to inform her of her son's safety and prowess, even though the account ran to the discredit of Sir Felix's own principal in the affair, and she had declared him impudent in so doing, and flown at him with the whip for daring to visit her prior to her son's return. He had, of course, politely retired, but the lady's propensity to resent courtesies and return violence for them—well, these showed the crude American stuff beneath her varnished English veneer. Or so said *The People's Banner*, at any rate.

When Mrs. Vavasor returned to the Marlborough House set, therefore, those orbs said to be threatened by her approach—a Countess, herself descended from Charles II (through not one, but two, of his mistresses), and a wealthy humanitarian—twitted her about Sir Felix. By contrast, the famous Mrs. Keppel greeted Mrs. Vavasor placidly, and indeed maintained a friendly bearing toward all around her.

Like one of her famous ancestresses, the Countess favoured the direct sally (indeed, so much so that she was oft referred to by the cognomen, "Babbling Brooke"), and asked straightforwardly: "My dear Mrs. Vavasor, how wondrous that you should be with us today! We are all speculating, my dear, if you could be the 'W.V." referenced in that article in the *People's Banner*? The lady who switched a man for calling on her?"

Mrs. Vavasor, to the Prince's ursine delight, answered in song, using a melody inspired by her questioner and addressed to her:

"*Daisy, Daisy, I'll give you my answer true*," sang Mrs. Vavasor,
"*Sir Felix misbehaved, what's a poor widow to do?*
It's proper to disparage
A man not fit for marriage,
So the old roué,
Was sent away
With a box on his ears—or two."

His Royal Highness' roars of laughter set the seal on Mrs. Vavasor's victory in that passage of arms, and even the Philanthropist smiled a little. Mrs. Keppel, friendly as ever applauded with a charming smile of her own and said, "Oh, well done, America! Let it not be said that we can learn nothing from the Colonies!"

The Countess considered pouting, but was distracted by Princess Alexandra, who sought her advice about a present for His Royal Highness for Christmas—*dear* Daisy had such impeccable taste, could she help? Borne off in a wave of royal flattery and solicitude, the Countess' sulk never really had time to set in properly, a fact she would later appreciate when she roundly bested His Royal Highness at bridge—and Mrs. Vavasor, his partner in the rubber, blamed her own "feather-headedness" for the defeat, thereby salvaging both HRH's pride and his good mood.

The Prince's appetite for cards was strong that night, and the rest of the party—even the Marquis of Soveral and Sir Ernest Cassel—had grown fatigued of the game. But not Mrs. Vavasor, who introduced the Prince to "Blackjack" that evening.

The Prince, upon being instructed, declared, "Why, it's merely *vignt-et-un*!"

"Not precisely, sir." Mrs. Vavasor smiled her most predatory smile. "At any rate, not as we played it in Nevada." And the smile that deepened her famous dimples, as she drawled out *Neh- VADD-uh* like the true daughter of the West she was, would have done credit to the most vulpine faro dealer in that fair state.

Whether the cause was the variations between the game as played in France and that as played in Nevada, or Mrs. Vavasor's highly refined card-counting ability (as Mrs. Keppel would later maintain), or the disturbing effect of those panther eyes upon one singularly unused to being marked down as prey, the fact remains that, although the chips flowed back and forth between the two players, the tide was steadily in favour of Mrs. Vavasor.

When that lady had reached what she deemed the precise moment—the Prince was enough in her debt to wish to be let off, but had not yet become cranky and given off danger signals of spoiling the evening—she begged for a respite. "Oh," she sighed, "I must walk along the balcony."

"It is becoming cold," His Royal Highness cautioned.

"I shall wear my wrap, and confine myself to one circuit. I simply must clear my poor head."

"I shall accompany you," His Royal Highness replied.

The two made, in fact, several circuits of the balcony, and were deep in conversation. What form that conversation took, and what was said, is unknown. Mrs. Vavasor never told a living soul whether the conversation took the form of a debate, an argument, an appeal, or a *pas de deux*. Among the ample records of the Prince's dealings with his friends, male or female, no reference is made to this conversation, nor to its issue.

What is known, however, is that the Prince met his mother shortly before her departure for Osborne House, where, as was her custom, she intended to keep Christmas that year. Mother and son were closeted alone together for longer than usual, and the Queen was heard to bid her son farewell with a special kindness. She also delayed her departure for a day, calling for her Secretary, and for some documents she had previously reviewed and approved. She dispatched her Secretary some two hours later.

On a day in mid-December, in fact the last day before he was to depart for his Christmas holiday, Laurence Fitzgibbon received a dispatch box from the Palace. It was the usual end of year business: honours to be handed out, from the Garter to knighthoods, all selected by the Prime Minister and all, as had long been the case, approved by the Throne. Laurence Fitzgibbon, whom age and an anxiety-ridden superior in the shape of Lord Fawn had taught to be meticulous, reviewed them all, and all were approved. So, too, the pardons, which Barrington Erle's Government announced and implemented—not, as were honours, at the New Year, but three days before Christmas, so that the recipients of clemency would not have to spend that most joyous of holidays in prison, with no idea as to their fate. After all, the Prime Minister had reasoned with Lord Fawn, if the Government believes a man to be worthy of clemency, surely the celebration of a last Christmas among the condemned is a needless touch of cruelty?

As Laurence Fitzgibbon perused the short list of commutations, reprieves and outright pardons, he saw nothing unexpected until the very bottom of the list. There, amongst those to be pardoned with full remission, was a name written in, not by a functionary of the Government, not by a scrivener or a secretary, but in the Royal Hand itself:

Ifor Powlett-Jones

The paperwork was included, also in the Royal Hand.

As Laurence Fitzgibbon prepared to bring the pile of directives to the Home Secretary, he whistled once, soft and low. "Oh, Phinny," he murmured to himself, "what have ye done, this time?"

"THE COURSE OF TRUE LOVE..."

Although the autumn had been a mellow one, mid-December decided to remind Londoners that such largesse should not be taken for granted. The delicious snap of each breath that typifies September and October had that year lingered through November, only to turn cruel and biting now that December had arrived. As the year drew to its close, the bitter wind, the short days and the dreary fogs invited all but the most adventurous to stay at home.

By no reckoning was the Duke of Omnium adventurous. He had, all would allow, many virtues, but that of being adventurous—if indeed that be a virtue—had been denied him. Yet, as he sat in his dark-paneled book room at Matching, he bethought him of adventure. Not the kind of adventure his boys had read about as children—idealised depictions of violent times, nor yet again of the buccaneering way in which he had seen some men flash through the political and social worlds. Rather, the Duke thought, as one who must decide soon thinks, about whether to radically reshape his life before he was too old for the reshaping to be of any use.

He thought of himself as old already, and that was part of the problem. In fact, though, sixty had not yet arrived, and his spare frame retained much of its strength. Plantagenet Palliser, as one who had never in truth seemed very young, did not seem much older than he had in those days when his sorely-missed Cora was at his side.

And yet, he knew that he was in danger of sentimentalizing that dear, dead wife of his. Yes, he had loved her—and she had come to love him. Not as freely, as exuberantly as she could have loved that less worthy young man her family (and later the Duke himself) had saved her from—but she had loved him. They had grown together, and if the fit was not perfect—and it was not—she had nonetheless bound him, not only to herself, but to humanity, in ways he could never have foreseen.

That bond had been severed years ago, although he had been reluctant to accept the fact. She was gone, and his memories of her would not prevent him from growing into a sour old man, if he was not careful.

He was disturbed by the surge of feeling he had felt when, in her own study in Portman Square, Lady Laura had broken down, and sobbed on his shirt-front. He had held her then, and comforted her. So strong a woman had been desperately tried before her composure broke, and the Duke could not but feel that the fact that she could accept his embrace in her sorrow and fear for her nephew suggested—perhaps—that she had feelings for him.

The nearness of her, as on the night of the ball, moved him deeply, but very differently than on that earlier occasion. On the first occasion, the Duke had been moved by her charm, her intellect, her—he might was well acknowledge it to himself—her beauty. An eccentric kind of beauty, but of a kind that awoke his own long-banked passions. A face with distinction, clarity of mind, and fierce intellect written upon it, but in feminine form, withal. He found her desirable, he had admitted, and she made the world seem a little more vibrant than it had been in her absence. But on the night he had visited her, and she had shared her sorrow with him, he had discovered more: she touched his heart, so that her ache mattered terribly to him—became, as it were, his own. That he had been unable to help her in her grief, other than to share it with her and hold her, had torn at his heart as it had not been torn in years.

He remembered the last time he had felt the vulnerability of the one who loves to the pains of the beloved. When his little grand-daughter Marie had found a sick kitten in the stables at Gatherum, and run with it to her Grandpapa, he had examined the poor little beast, only to find that it was too late to help. Little Marie had been inconsolable, weeping far more passionately than he could remember any of his own children ever doing. The nakedness of her sorrow had torn at him, and his stiff, ungainly soul had yearned to find a way to bring her comfort. When she wailed that she had done poor Snowy (she seemed to have coined the name on the spot) no good at all, he turned her to him, and told her that Snowy had died cradled in the arms of someone who had loved her, and that animals always knew who loved them.

"But she died anyway, Grandpapa!" the little girl had cried out.

"It is better to die loved and cared for by those who truly love you than alone—or even with those who are kind, but do not love in truth," the Duke had answered.

"Really, truly?" The little girl's look was skeptical.

Remembering the respective death-beds of his uncle, his predecessor as Duke, and of his wife, the Duke's answer was sure, and sincere; "Really, truly," he had said in a voice of utter certainty.

The Duke had overlooked that aspect of love in the years since Cora had died. He had forgotten how utterly vulnerable one was to the internal weather of the beloved. While Lady Laura had gone to Germany, he thought, and meditated on these matters. Could he bear, he asked himself repeatedly, to be so vulnerable again?

The converse question tormented him more: What would become of him, if he did *not* become so vulnerable again?

In the weeks of Lady Laura's sojourn in Germany, he reflected on these things, and even prayed a little. And then he asked the forgiveness of Glencora's shade, if such forgiveness be needed. He had no answer, of course, but dreamed that night, as he had ceased to do, once more of her, as vividly as if she were with him, in all her wondrous, complex and sometimes incomprehensible humanity. So real had the dream seemed that when he awoke, he grieved for her as if his loss was fresh. But he now knew in his heart that Glencora's shade, if such a thing could be, would exasperatedly tell him to get on with the thing, and not leave her in suspense, like the author of a three-volume novel, whose heroine dithers for the whole of volume two, and much of volume three. And, at long last, the Duke was ready to be guided by Marie Finn's advice.

At the Marchioness of Hartletop's marmoreal home in Stanhope Gate, the Right Reverend Joseph Emilius was lost in contemplation. The past months of his stay had, thus far, gone successfully. He had, to use a rather distasteful expression he had heard from one of the Beargarden set, "rubbed shoulders" with many of the highest rank of English society, and, no doubt thanks to his position beneath the Marchioness' aegis, been warmly accepted. He had been invited to preach at St. Paul's by the Dean, and, rather to his surprise, at Barchester Cathedral by his hostess' brother. Thus far, Icarus had not flown too high, nor too near the sun.

He had, less figuratively, "rubbed shoulders" with Elizabeth, Lady Eustace, his wife-as-was, with some regularity since their re-encounter at the Park, and each encounter fed his desire to make her again his wife. What had begun as a craving he could not satiate away from her presence had become, if anything more pressing these last weeks.

As he had pressed his second courtship ever further, the lady had revealed her own wilder streak, only nascent in her youth. Indeed, her boldness startled even him on occasion, as when she invited him to tea with her great friend Lady Wariston and they had improved his education by introducing him to the equines of Berkley. Lizzie's closeness to Lady Wariston might have alarmed him, had she not thoroughly approved of the bishop, and championed his courtship to Lizzie. Lizzie's years among the Decadents, the Pre-Raphaelites (several of whom had painted her in various mythological guises) and the aristocratic pagans who had begun to emerge from obscurity as the Old Queen's grip on the scepter loosened had cultivated Lizzie Eustace's ability to savour both her own sensuality and the power it gave her over those who viewed her as "not quite straight." He had found in her more than a match for his own lust for power, and the pleasures it could bring.

More even than that, he mused in the deep waters of the tub (for Joseph Emilius did much of his thinking in the bath), he had found a troubling level of feeling within himself for Lizzie. When she had, after many encounters over several weeks, finally stood revealed in all her beauty before her husband (*former* husband, a pedantic voice from some buried corner of his mind corrected), he had observed a scar across her lower abdomen that she had not borne in the days of their marriage.

A result of some surgery? Had she conceived, and required a caesarian delivery—or something darker? Or had she merely suffered some injury? Her eyes shone challengingly, even defiantly, at him, awaiting his response. Behind the defiance, though, he had, he was sure, observed apprehension.

He had knelt and kissed the scar tenderly, then risen and embraced her with all of warmth and gentleness that could be found within such a man as he—more, perhaps, than he knew himself to possess. For all of their mutual slaking of passion, there had since passed between them moments of *tendresse* that he had never before experienced. Always he had acted the part of gentle pastor when called upon to play it, and played it quite well. Now, though, he could not see that scar, or any of the other marks that time had laid upon her—subtle thus far, for Lizzie was, by any standards, still a great beauty—without experiencing a curious, haunting yearning for her. He found he cared more for her because of these intimations of time working its will upon her than the reverse.

He could not lose her, he thought vehemently.

And yet, she was no closer to giving up on that absurd young man. She was invested in forcing him to marry her, to honour his commitment to her. In vain, he had suggested practically that such a marriage would be a misery to both of them, that she would not reap the rewards she counted on until she was far too old to enjoy them. In vain, he had pointed out that young Jack was now himself damaged goods, and that the marriage, far from bringing her back into the swim of conventional society, would only send her further into Coventry.

Indeed, on a later afternoon tea, he had heard Lady Wariston making the very same arguments to Lizzie, when she thought that Emilius was out of the room. He had paused at the curtained doorway of the private room where they were sharing tea, rather than in the formal environs of the parlor, and he had heard Lady Wariston urging Lizzie to marry him a second time.

"My dear," her ladyship had said—and, concealed though he was behind the curtain, he could picture all too well the stern look that had come over Lady Wariston's regular features, "you are very hard to please. Here is a gentleman"—Lizzie snorted—"a passable gentleman, then," the older lady corrected herself. "A passable gentleman," she repeated, "who knows you through-and-through, and wants you as you are. You have no need to pretend, to hide or to deceive. Together you could stand against all the world. And instead, you seek to coerce this young blood-drinker to the altar? Within six months, either you or he would most likely be dead. If not, you would be sunk in misery, or separated, on the way to a divorce. You know perfectly well he could obtain one."

Lizzie's voice, fierce, intent: "I will not be trifled with. Do you not see? It is a question of who is to yield in this contest between Jack Standish and myself. It shall not be I."

"And Joseph?"

"Joseph?" Lizzie's voice took on an unusual warmth. "He loves me, I think—but how can I trust him? When he courted me, before, he was just as charming, just as attentive. But once we were married, *he* called the tune, *he* used my money as his own. How do I know he has, as he claims, learned? Will I be at his mercy in Utah? With Jack, I would be a countess—and mistress of the situation—he is not the man to rule over me. But Joseph? He is Society's novelty, now—the Marchioness's curious guest from America. Who would he be when we were in Utah?"

"Do you love Joseph?" The older woman pressed the attack.

A long silence ensued, before Lady Eustace answered:

"Inasmuch as I can love, I think I do love him. I know I want him. But I cannot release Jack unless I know, *know*, that Joseph means what he says in his proffers of love. I have been betrayed by Corsairs before," she added with a touch of bitterness. "Jack is safe, at any road, and no match for me; in any conflict, I must defeat him."

Knowing he could not plausibly extend his eavesdropping much longer, he had rustled the curtain and entered the room, bearing a fresh pot of tea, for the servants were barred entry to what Lizzie called the Nook. Lady Wariston had turned her handsome face, its austere charm accentuated by the gray and black hair piled on top of her head, towards him, smiling quizzically. She had perceived that he had been listening, he realised as he reviewed the experience in his bath, and she was glad that he had been. He had returned her smile with a little bow, and, setting the fresh pot down on the little table between the ladies, had rejoined them. Lizzie, in one of the shows of caprice that he found so perversely enchanting, had commanded him to pour the amber liquor first for herself and Lady Wariston, although convention bade her, as lady of the house, to serve her guests; and Emilius, a cat-smile playing at the corners of his lips, had submitted gracefully to her whim.

Now, as the water drew various aches from his body, and he reflected on his feelings for Lizzie—more complex than any he had thought would afflict him—Emilius knew that this young lordling, as Lizzie was wont to call him, presented an obstacle to his happiness that he could not brook. He must find a way to sever that tie, or Lizzie's surety that she could, at any rate, triumph over young Jack Chiltern, allied with her lingering distrust of himself, would blight the unexpectedly bright future he had found open before him.

He would not lose her.

At that very moment, the object of Bishop Emilius' affections was turning over the situation in her own mind. Elizabeth Eustace had risen from a very precarious position indeed—the sole daughter of an artist favoured by the *demimonde*, but a man who spent commissions as quickly as he earned them—to her current high rank and wealth, but after the affair of the stolen diamonds in her youth, she had found herself relegated to the margins of high society. Nobody quite had the cheek to turn her away, but neither was she quite respectable.

No doubt her connection with the late Lord George Bruce de Carruthers, of dubious memory, had done her no good in the estimation of Society's lynx-eyed warders—ladies of her detested Aunt Penelope's type, though increasingly of Lizzie's own generation. Yes, Lord George had been a naughty one, she reflected; so much the image of the Corsair for whom she had hungered in those long-ago days of her youth. He had, amiably, given her what she could now recognise as good advice when the police were questioning whether she had stolen the diamonds belonging to her dead husband's family. But later, George's monstrous selfishness and indolence had imperiled her very life, left her beauty irrevocably marred, and risked her position in Society. The pain and the scar had cured her of any desire for a Corsair to ravish her, and had strengthened her already quite strong desire to control her circumstances—and those around her.

This was, of course, after her marriage to Joseph, whose sometimes oily social climbing masked the cold steel below. She had learned this the hard way, as he most amiably and pleasantly enforced his will upon her in the early days of their marriage. He had drawn upon her money as though it was his own, and politely, affectionately, rebuked her when she objected to its being pillaged! Not a touch of violence, express or implied; not a word passed his lips that he could not have said before a High Court Judge, in the exact same tones he had employed to her, and not receive the full sympathy and approbation of the Court. And yet, she was quite sure that Joseph had, with equal dispassion, murdered Mr. Bonteen, the politician who was tipped to succeed Plantagenet Palliser as Chancellor of the Exchequer, merely because he was investigating the widespread rumours that Joseph had not been free to marry her, due to the disagreeable circumstance that he was already married. Coolly, he had denied the matter, and, with equal coolness, he had eliminated the man with the power and desire to prove his guilt.

Only the fortuity that the man upon whom suspicion had fallen in Joseph's stead—that rather interesting Irish adventurer, Phineas Finn—was beloved of the absurdly wealthy and determined Madame Max Goesler, who finished Mr. Bonteen's researches, and found evidence that might have even convicted Joseph of the murder itself, had derailed his plan. And even then, in the dock, Joseph had maintained his supercilious calm, and, after hearing sentence pronounced upon him for the bigamy, somehow impelled the first wife to recant her testimony, confounding the law yet again. No, Joseph had many flaws, but his coolness under fire was beyond reproach.

That quality could be maddening, she remembered, but how she had admired it when he was under such pressure as suspicion of murder! And the fact that he was guilty of the murder only added to her admiration of his *sang-froid*. Quite wrong, of course, but how could one *not* admire him?

But admiration, Lizzie reflected, was not trust. And Lizzie could not trust easily—who in her life had given her reason to trust? Even the "honest" men in her life—her cousin Frank Greystock, or her onetime *fiancé* Lord Fawn, say, had not stood by her in her hour of trial, but had advised surrender to those who would tear her inheritance away from her, the lost, wondrous Eustace Diamonds. Lizzie enjoyed power, she admitted, and had since discovering she could wield it in her youth over her then-companion McNulty, but more than enjoying it, she needed it. Jack might—might!—break free of her after they were married, but she had no doubt that unless he did so, she would rule in that household, and at least have security and position. Even if Jack did lack Joseph's rather seductive blend of cool self-mastery and burning need for her.

The only place where he lost that cool control was with her, in their most intimate moments. Joseph's adoration of her physical charms, his willingness to grapple with her as an equal, and his utter lack of the English inhibition which even the most jaded English rakehells of her experience brought to their pleasure, had delighted the *demimondaine* she had been raised to be from her childhood on.

Since his return to woo her, to bring her with him to his preposterous Utah dominion, Lizzie had quite feared whether the traces of time, and worse, the damage caused to her person by Lord George, would have shattered that sensual connection between them –the one thing she had unequivocally cherished from their time together. Instead, when he perceived the harm that had been done her, a tenderness had flared in his eyes that she had never seen before, and his kisses had been healing. Afterward, the passion between them had been, if anything, more intense, and yet that new tenderness had persisted, lingering beyond the threshold of the *boudoir*.

And it was that very tenderness that brought the present frown to Lizzie's lips, curving downward as she gave herself over to contemplation of her situation. For while she took pride in having aroused this unwontedly vulnerable emotion in Joseph, a part of her—ah, ah, how great a part of her!—feared it, as well. Lizzie Eustace was a woman who feared any sensation she had provoked into existence without a calculated effort on her part. What part had tenderness, and its resultant vulnerability, played in her life? None, except that she had play-acted the helpless maiden in her youth, and in later years toyed with the vulnerabilities of others to reassert her own importance. When she had entrusted herself to Joseph before, he had effortlessly asserted the detestable mastery of a husband over his wife in English law. When she had tried again, entrusting herself to Carruthers, she had nearly paid for that momentary weakness with her life.

While she welcomed Joseph's homage and need of her, his tenderness troubled her, calling forth a reluctant stirring of reciprocal feeling in her. While Lizzie warmed herself by the fire of this unwonted blend of passion and tenderness—she dare not admit the word "love" to her mind—in her heart of hearts lurked the half-concealed terror that the tables might be turned; that she, who had so organised her life that she could boast, like the Great Elizabeth, that there was but one mistress in her home, and no master, might in her turn fall victim to this gentle emotion and find herself vulnerable once more through reciprocating the softness she distrusted, and yet longed for, in Joseph.

But herein lay the fascination – and Lizzie was honest enough with herself to concede that indeed, Joseph held a fascination for her, just as she apparently held an inescapable one for him. Joseph was, after all, so unlike poor little Jack. There was no challenge to mastering Jack – and here, Lizzie gave aloud the throaty laugh that Joseph had come to relish, and Jack to fear. No – if Lizzie wanted a foeman worthy of her steel, then surely Joseph was that man. But the ever-pragmatic Lizzie could not allow herself to embrace that feeling—love?—which, if anything, poured oil on the flames she and her enigmatic cleric had stoked, unless he proved his claim to be as utterly hers, as she might one day be his.

Either way, of course, Lizzie could not let go of his little lordship Jack Standish quite as easily as all that. He had offended her *amour-propre*, and she must have satisfaction, and he, at a minimum, must have a lesson. She had been all too aware of Jack's ambivalent feelings for her—the raw, eager desire of a young man who had not yet come into his full manhood, and the revulsion of a young "radical" who professed "free love" and yet was disgusted to see a lady of his own mother's generation and social standing simply avail herself of the privileges for which he advocated. Most of all, she had perceived that Jack's disgust at himself for desiring a woman of his mother's social standing and age had warred with that fierce desire of youth. Lizzie had recognised this war, and had reveled in exacerbating his internal conflict. She had kept him on the boil for weeks, taunting him with his own espoused principles and their conflict with his "honourable" instincts toward women of his own class. She had mastered him, too, she thought, making Jack propose, not once, but twice—and then accepting him!

Lizzie wondered what it was about Clarissa Riley that had shattered the spell that she had woven so carefully about the young man. Was it merely her innocence? Was it that he had always basked in the admiration of the silly young chit, and then, when she had flowered into womanhood, discovered that her admiration was rather more dear to him than he had imagined? Was it the sight of the mongrel pup Vavasor, snatching eagerly at the bland nursery tit-bit Jack had always regarded as his own for the taking – and so had treated carelessly? Or was it simply that he had finally realised that, by affiancing himself to Lizzie Eustace, Jack had cut himself off forever and aye from all the experiences of youthful love, from children, from the sweetness (it had not been sweet to Lizzie, but then, her youth was unusual, or at least she hoped so) of first love?

Whatever the reason, she would not relent, at least not until she had greater clarity as to where she stood with Joseph, and administered the necessary lesson in manners. Let Jack throw himself on her mercy—and she might, she rather thought, be inclined toward mercy; in her heart, she preferred Joseph in any event, if he would but take the initiative and break the impasse. Or let Jack himself find a way to do so. But of one thing she was sure: Elizabeth Eustace would not simply recede. One of these men would be hers. Either the young lord would make reparation, Joseph would prove himself worthy of her, or she would break Jack Standish.

THE CHRISTMAS GREETING

At Wormwood Scrubs, the days passed in an odd limbo of monotony and terror, Ifor Powlett-Jones discovered. As December drew near to its end, he had yet to be impressed into taking a side in the internecine factional struggles among the prisoners, nor yet been targeted by them. Yet he knew that the grace period he had won through the fighting skills he had learned amongst his fellow miners would not last—and that was the source of the terror.

As to the monotony, that was putting it with an understatement that was more English than his accustomed good, hard Welsh frankness. The prison life was seeping away his sense of all that he was, all that he could be. And the visit from Mr. Low, that elderly beacon of hope, was receding into the increasingly unreal past with every day.

Two days before Christmas—Ifor had learned to keep track of the days by scratching notations into the bedstead, and reminding himself of the date, as he had that morning: "Today is Wednesday, December 23, 189_. Tomorrow is Christmas Eve, and Friday is Christmas Day." He had thought the monotony had drained self-pity from him, but the thought of his first Christmas as a convict opened the dam, and it was all he could do to keep his face rock-like, while memories of happier Christmases in Pontnewydd streamed through his mind. Carefully, quietly, he forced them down, and, saying a quick prayer for his family, for Mr. Low, and for Phineas Finn, he resumed work, picking oakum.

He had not progressed very far, though, carefully, painfully trying to unravel the old, heavy ropes, separating the individual fibers for re-use as—what? Fresh ropes, he supposed, if long enough strands could be pulled out of the great hempen mass in front of him. Not too likely with this lot, he thought, with all the tar that had been daubed into the old cordage to extend its useful life. This stuff would, after he blistered himself, cut his fingers, and sweated like Old Scratch to untangle the rubbish, be fit for nothing more than caulking joints of some ship's timbers, with all aboard her unconscious of the wearisome toil of the prisoners that made for such smooth surfaces.

Sighing, Powlett-Jones began to apply himself more diligently; it would not do to fail to meet his daily four pounds' requirement, and draw attention from the warders. Which, somehow, he seemed already to have done, because one of them, Howatch—crusty, but lacking the cruelty that so many of his younger colleagues had—was approaching. His demeanour was, as usual, austere, but he seemed to be fighting an inclination to smile.

"Knock off, Taffy," he said, not unkindly, "I'm to take you to the Guv'nor."

"The Governor?" Powlett-Jones felt a stab of panic.

"That's right, son," the older man said. "Put up your things, and let's not keep him waiting." Ifor complied, and felt a moment's gratitude when Howatch put a pair of darbies around his wrists and locked them in front of his waist, rather than the less comfortable behind-the-back posture he had seen more commonly used. "Let's go, lad," the warder said firmly.

Ifor kept pace with the warder's surprisingly quick step, as they trailed through the halls together. He soon lost his sense of direction in the sameness of the corridors. But after a while, he noticed that the area through which they were progressing was less Spartan and had a few grace notes. Wood paneling replaced cellblock, and soon enough an anteroom warned him that they had arrived. Ifor looked around him in uncomprehending terror, but before he could humiliate himself by pleading for some indication of what awaited him behind the formal mahogany door to the Governor's office, Howatch nodded reassuringly, looked into his eyes, and shook his right hand, saying with a brief, wintry smile, "Good luck, son."

The warder knocked on the door four times, and when it was opened, he led Ifor into the richly appointed office—a beautiful, polished, grand desk with a leather chair behind it for the Governor, a set of three comfortable looking, if plain wood, chairs in front of the desk. A couch, a cabinet. Bookshelves. Dimly, Ifor heard Howatch say, "Powlett-Jones, sir," and, from the corner of his eye, saw him salute. But his gaze was drawn to the occupants of the room. Men, not in prisoners' or warders' garb, but dressed as gentlemen. A stout, bearded cove in black, whose watch chain, dripping seals and masonic symbols, spanned his enormous belly, seated across from Mr. Camperdown, his solicitor at the trial. And, standing by—or leaning against, really—the window frame, with the light at his back, was Phineas Finn.

The barrister was thinner, a bit greyer. He held a walking stick, a common enough implement, but one that Ifor had never seen him carry before. But his smile was magnetic, and his eyes lit up at the sight of his erstwhile client.

"Mr.-Mr. Finn?" Ifor wondered aloud.

Phineas Finn looked expectantly at the heavy-set cove—the Governor, Ifor realised belatedly. The Governor opened a buff-coloured file, extracted a piece of foolscap, and began to read:

"Whereas, Ifor Powlett-Jones is now confined at the gaol at Wormwood Scrubs, having been convicted for grave crimes against the person of one Jasper Tudor, and against the Laws and Peace of the Realm;

"Whereas, the aforesaid Ifor Powlett-Jones's crime having been greatly mitigated by his courageous and selfless acts of heroism on the same occasion as that giving rise to his offense against the Laws and Peace of the Realm;

Know then, all persons by these presents, that: We in Consideration of this heroism, and some Circumstances humbly represented unto Us, are Graciously pleased to extend Our Grace and Mercy unto Ifor Powlett-Jones, Our Free Pardon and Full Remission for his Crimes.

This 15th Day of December, in the Year of Our Lord 189_

VICTORIA REGINA."

Ifor stared wildly around the room. "Pardon? She—the Queen—has *pardoned* me?"

The Governor, with a bit less stiffness than he had demonstrated in reading the document, answered, "Yes, Powlett-Jones. You are pardoned. You will be set free this very day."

"Free?" Ifor asked, hope beginning to kindle in his breast, "Truly?"

Phineas Finn at last strode from his place at the window. He leaned on his stick to catch himself, but recovered, and came forward.

"You are as free a man as I am. The Queen has declared it so, and your liberty is in her gift."

The warder looked inquiringly at the Governor, who subtly nodded, and he released Powlett-Jones's wrists from the darbies.

"You will be issued with a suit of clothes," the Governor said, "and a little money, as well as any of your own effects that were taken into custody."

The reality began to sink into the young man. "Is there somewhere I can go tonight? I am not sure if—whether I can go to Wales straightaway—the sun is going down," he stammered, gazing out the window.

"You will come to us, Ifor," said Phineas, "and keep the Christmas with us, if you will, and then we can help you decide where you are to go from there."

Tears stung the young man's eyes. "May I, then? You won't mind the likes of me, staying with you?"

"My wife has given firm instructions that I am to press you to stay with us," Phineas replied. "You'll get used to being free again, and recover from what you have undergone. We'll telegraph your family so they may know the good news immediately."

Ifor relaxed; the notion of being the center of attention at Pontnewydd at Christmas was strangely dreadful to him. Phineas, remembering his own reaction after being incarcerated, had predicted Ifor's response, and prepared accordingly.

"Thank you, Governor, for all your kindnesses" Phineas said briskly. "Perhaps we can begin the process of outfitting Mr. Powlett-Jones, and take our leave?"

To this proposition the Governor assented, and Ifor added his own inarticulate thanks. He then wrung the hand of the warder, and of Mr. Camperdown. The Governor offered his own hand, and Ifor took that as well. "Thank you, sir," he said, "I shouldn't have dared on my own. And begging your pardon, sir, for I hadn't the time to wash it – Mr. Howatch came to get me that sudden-like."

Looking down at the hand the Governor had released after pressing it kindly, stained as it was with the pitch and clinging fibres of his interrupted task, for the first time Ifor was overwhelmed by the truth – that he was not to leave the Governor's chamber only to return to his tedious prison occupation and the hard bunk of his lonely cell. Tears rose to his eyes, but he blinked them away resolutely as Howatch the warder made offer to lead him away and to assist him in his transformation from prisoner to free man, and the two left the room in amity. The Governor excused himself, leaving Phineas and Mr. Camperdown alone in his office.

"Sometimes," the solicitor observed, "all that we do seems dry as dust—no life for a man. And then there are days like today. I wouldn't have missed this for anything, Mr. Finn. But how did you do it? The Home Office was dead set against us and the Prime Minister wouldn't help, you said?"

"True," Phineas replied. "So I did not go through the Home Office or the Prime Minister."

Mr. Camperdown's whistle was that of an astonished boy. "You went—but you couldn't, could you?"

"Legally? A friend with the right ear? No impropriety there, Camperdown."

"Legally, no, but politically–"

"There will be a cost to pay, Camperdown, and it may very well be high," Phineas acknowledged. "But you were just behind me through that trial, every moment of it. Was what we just saw not worth the cost?"

Camperdown nodded, and took the barrister's hand.

"Merry Christmas, Mr. Finn," he said.

"Merry Christmas, Mr. Camperdown."

Ifor Powlett-Jones slept late on December 24, and when Abigail, the Finn's house-maid, asked if she should wake him for breakfast, it was Phineas who firmly told her to let the lad sleep. "You never properly sleep in gaol," he explained to Marie, who arched an inquisitive eyebrow. "There's always noise, and interruptions, and fear. You sleep, but never wake up feeling refreshed."

Marie nodded, and asked. "What do you mean to do for the boy? You must know he cannot go home."

"But does he?"

Clarissa, resplendent in a kelly green morning gown of India mull accented with emerald ribbon, entered the breakfast room, and kissed her uncle on the head.

"And how are we this morning, Nuncle?"

"Nuncle?" he asked. "Are you flaunting your Shakespeare at me, or suggesting that I've given away my kingdom?"

Before his niece could answer, Marie Finn interposed, "Why not both, my dear? Or do you think Barrington Erle and Sir William McScuttle will not notice your Christmas surprise?"

"Oh, they'll notice. And Sir William will want my head on a platter, surrounded by holly sprigs, I fancy. The real question is Barrington. From what I hear, the younger members are restive and may mount a leadership challenge against him. And if that happens, and if Barrington needs McScuttle—or his money, rather—to fend them off, yes, Barrington just might be inclined to give it him."

"Your head, Mr. Finn?"

Unnoticed by the family, Ifor, dressed in the dark worsted suit that he had been provided with upon his release, had crept down the stairs and had tentatively entered the room. The suit was not an ideal fit, but became him admirably.

"Good morning, ma'am, sir," he said. Then, to Clarissa, who was loading up her plate from the dishes spread upon the sideboard, he added, "Good morning, miss."

"Please help yourself to whatever you would like from the sideboard and join us, Mr. Powlett-Jones," Marie invited the slightly confused Welshman. "I hope you slept well."

"Oh, aye," he answered with a brilliant smile, and followed to the sideboard, where he heaped his plate high in imitation of Clarissa. Joining the family, he bowed his head for a moment, and then, about to tuck in, realised that his initial question had not been answered.

"Mr. Finn, what's this about your head?"

Phineas smiled at the young man's pertinacity. "I had to go around my party—and the Prime Minister—to ensure that your pardon application would get proper consideration. They won't be pleased, nor Sir William, either."

The young man mused for a moment. "He's a bad enemy, sir," he replied. "I hope he does not do you harm."

Phineas scrutinised him carefully. Freed from the fear that had haunted him at every one of their meetings up until now, Powlett-Jones's face reflected an intelligence even beyond that needed to quickly improvise the rescue of his fellow miners. This lad had potential, Phineas decided, and was owed the truth.

"They may force me out of the Party. Possibly even try to take my seat in the House away by running a candidate against me."

"Uncle Phineas, no!" Clarissa exclaimed. Marie nodded sagely. She had expected this, Phineas knew, but Clarissa had not. Remembering only the avuncular guest who had beamed upon her, Clarissa did not yet understand that a Prime Minister in straits of his own could be a ruthless character indeed. And Barrington would see Phineas's resort to back channels—Tory back channels at that!—as a betrayal of the Party: the gravest sin of all to Barrington's mind, even before he had become Prime Minister, and, as such, the living embodiment of the Party.

"I'm that sorry that you are in such trouble because of me," Ifor said. His appetite—a moment before so ravenous—seemed to have deserted him. Phineas caught his glance with his own.

"I am not, Ifor," he replied. "Not a bit sorry. And if they oppose me at Tankerville at the next General Election, I intend to defeat whomsoever they run against me." The lad smiled at this, and his eye drifted to his plate.

"You should eat, Mr. Powlett-Jones," Marie admonished kindly. "We are counting on you to help us finish decorating this afternoon. You must not be weak from lack of nourishment."

The young man grinned, and tucked in with gusto.

The Finns' Christmas Eve "open house" receptions were a well-established tradition. Punch, claret cup, eggnog, a little political chat, and much flirting were the norm. Phineas had been heard to boast that at least six engagements had resulted from their Christmas Eve celebrations, three of them adroitly engineered by Marie.

Part of the fun of the thing was that one never knew whom one would meet, as it was a true open house. Last year, Bunthorne had enacted—all by himself—a scene from the new play he was writing, a farce, and had carried the guests away into gales of laughter at his performance of an imperious dowager, building toward a crescendo with each mention of a handbag that played a key role.

This year, Sir Arthur Sullivan dropped in and played the piano—on condition that Clarissa and Marie sing with him. Clarissa, with the help of Hermione Longestaffe and Lady Mary Tregear, assayed "Three Little Maids," while Marie chose, as a compliment to the composer, but also recognising her own more mature, contralto voice, "The Lost Chord." Always a deft though not a profound singer, Marie poured into the song a passion she normally did not reveal to any but her most intimate friends, and, in the singing, never once looked away from her husband, himself leaning against the mantle, but now without a stick—twice-daily fencing bouts with Meier were helping him recover his balance and his agility.

As Marie sang the final haunting note, the assembled guests received it in profound silence, which hung in the air for a moment, until Winifred Vavasor's soft, still half-American accented voice was heard to say emphatically, "*Brava*," and Savrola Vavasor took it up, as a cry, not a murmur, leading the assembled guests in a round of applause greater than any heard at the Finns' prior *musicales.*

After Marie and Sir Arthur took their bows, the composer kissing Mrs. Finn's hand, the members of the party slowly began to drift into various separate knots of people throughout the reception rooms and the Library. Phineas Finn swept his wife into his arms and kissed her under the mistletoe hung earlier that afternoon by Ifor, so that his uxorious behaviour at least had the sanction of tradition behind it.

The Duke of Omnium arrived a little later than was his wont, and greeted his hostess affectionately. His manner was one of repressed excitement as he sought out those of his children who had come to the Finns—Lady Mary, of course, and her husband, Frank; Silverbridge, over by the fireplace, exchanging banter with Dolly Longestaffe, who had congratulated his wife warmly for her own performance, albeit confiding to Frank Tregear that Hermione was, perhaps, "a somewhat superannuated schoolgirl."

The Duke exchanged greetings with those of his friends who were present—he did not note, as Phineas had, that those currently in favour with the Prime Minister were conspicuously absent. Indeed, of those presently holding office under Barrington Erle, only Laurence Fitzgibbon was in attendance, in what Phineas suspected was an unusual show of solidarity made at no little risk to his prospects.

"How are you really, Phinny?" Larry had asked, looking closely at his old friend.

"How does that Frenchman put it, Larry? 'Day by day, in every way–'"

"'I am growing better and better!'" Fitzgibbon joined him on the last line, and the two Irishmen laughed as carelessly as in their salad days. Which did not prevent Fitzgibbon from whispering a caution into his host's ear: "Beware the Ides of March, Phinny!"

Clarissa Riley and Savrola Vavasor were amusing themselves and instructing Ifor Powlett-Jones by providing potted descriptions of just who everybody was, from John Grey, the essayist and onetime member of Parliament, with his wife Alice, to Lady Eustace, whose appearance at the Finns' raised eyebrows, as she had never before deigned to come, and whose tangled relations with Phineas's godson Jack would have been enough to cause a stir, even absent her reputation for unorthodox behaviour. "The lady with her? That handsome, rather stern-looking one, all in black, even on Christmas Eve?" Savrola answered Ifor's question. "Lady Wariston—an unmarried lady, said to be rather fierce. Surprised she's friends with Lady Lizzie, who's altogether a more social creature."

That Lady herself cast a glance about the room for the Earl or Countess, and, not finding them, sighed imperceptibly. A pity. Still, her presence among the Finns would remind everyone of her incipient place in their circle. She bowed to Dolly Longestaffe, and began to make her way about the room, to show herself to anyone likely to gossip about it all. After all, she reflected, the absence of the Earl and Countess was not entirely a matter for regret, as it gave her the opportunity to bring her left hand, bearing a diamond that had never originated from among the Brentford heirloom ornaments, very much to the fore as she made her rounds and plied her fan.

After himself making the rounds, albeit for very different reasons, the Duke, seeing his host temporarily unengaged, approached him. In a gesture most unlike his normally reserved self, he placed a hand on Phineas's arm. "Finn," he said, "is it possible that we might speak a moment?"

"Of course, Duke," Phineas replied, and led his guest to his study, which had been closed off for the evening. Lighting the lamps, he motioned the Duke to a chair, and took one himself. As he sat, Phineas smiled with relief at being off his feet. Preoccupied as he was, the Duke was always attentive to such things.

"Your injuries," he asked, "are they causing you pain tonight?"

"Not so much pain, Duke, as dizziness and loss of balance. I probably should have agreed to Marie's suggestion that we not hold our evening tonight. But I did not want to disappoint the children—and this will be Clarissa's last Christmas under my roof, as, if you will, my 'child.' And Ifor Powlett-Jones deserves a little joy after his time in prison."

Phineas did not pretend that he expected the Duke to be unaware of this extra guest's identity; indeed, he desired to see if the Duke intended to match the loyalty the Finns had shown the Pallisers over the decades, or to align himself with those who would seek retribution.

The Duke did not fail him. Without any hesitation, he said, "Your loyalty to that boy has been exemplary, Finn. I suspect I do not want to know how you circumvented Sir William, but knowing you as I do, I am sure it was honest."

"Thank you, Duke," Phineas replied. "I can only say that the normal processes had broken down, so I felt justified in adopting a less conventional course."

"But you are recovering your health?" The Duke returned to his prior theme.

"Yes, quite well, I am told. Meier—our butler—was a fencing champion in his youth, and so we have daily bouts, which are speeding my recovery quite well. And neither my godson nor my niece's betrothed was seriously injured. I have much to be grateful for, Duke."

This provided the Duke the opening he desired.

"As have I, Finn. Finn—Phineas—I have this day made an offer of marriage to Lady Laura Kennedy."

"And?" Phineas asked, needing to hear it said outright.

"And she has accepted me, my friend."

Phineas started to jump from his chair, winced a little, and rose more slowly. He walked to the Duke, clasped his hand warmly, then turned and pulled the bell.

"I wish you both every joy, from the bottom of my heart," said Phineas, with his broadest smile.

And when few moments later, Abigail appeared, "A bottle of champagne," he instructed, and then, turning to the Duke, "May Marie know? She will be as eager to wish you joy as I."

The Duke nodded, wordlessly; Phineas added, "Please ask Mrs. Finn to join us for a moment, Abigail." Left to themselves, the two men sat in their chairs, beaming at each other, enjoying the companionable silence. When Marie joined them, she took one look at their scarcely suppressed joy, and said to the Duke, who rose at her entrance:

"You have asked her, then?"

"I have," answered the Duke, in a reasonable simulacrum of his normal manner.

"And she has not been so foolish as to refuse you?"

The Duke, with a little crooked smile, corrected Mrs. Finn: "She has been gracious enough to accept me, Mrs. Finn."

"Ah!" cried Marie Finn, "I am so glad! We must have some champagne, Duke!"

So well had Phineas contrived the matter that at that very moment Abigail entered, curtseyed, and said pertly, "Champagne, mum."

And once Abigail had poured, served, curtseyed yet again, and departed, Phineas raised his glass.

"It seems a pity to drink this toast in Lady Laura's absence," he remarked.

The Duke answered, "She desired to come with me, but felt that tonight her presence was required at Harrington Hall. She left late this morning."

Phineas nodded. "Then let us drink health and joy to you both tonight, and do so again when we may all be together! For tonight, I drink to my two dear friends, who have found each other, and wish you many years together!"

Marie raised her glass, as did the Duke, and they all drank.

"I have detained you from your guests too long," remarked the Duke, "but I wanted you two to be the first to hear, and to hear it from my own lips. Tomorrow I shall tell my children, but I knew," he said, looking at Marie, "that you would share my joy."

"Indeed I do, Duke," Mrs. Finn answered, "with all my heart."

And, clasping them each by the hand in turn, one after the other, and wishing them the joy of the season, the Duke rejoined the party. Left alone with her husband, Marie scrutinised him carefully.

"You look tired, my dear," she remarked casually.

"I am," he admitted. "But I am reluctant to let this night end." He sank back into his armchair.

"Oh," his wife asked, "and why is that, my friend?"

"Because tonight has been magical. I have been sung to," he continued, taking her hand, "as very few husbands ever can hope to be, and as I have not deserved; and then, as if that was not enough, I have seen a great tragedy, for which I bore no little responsibility, come to an end."

"Is that how you view it?" She dropped his hand, and stepped behind his armchair, leaning down and resting her arms on his shoulders.

"Yes. It is as if a long haunting has at last come to an end, and the ghost come back to life."

"And tomorrow?"

"Will be a good day. A day for us, for the children, the Lows—I am glad they accepted for Christmas dinner. But soon enough—no later than March, if friend Fitzgibbon is to be believed—Nemesis will come, and demand the price of some of my felicity today."

"Are you concerned?"

His laugh was a bark. "Of course I am! But even should the worst befall, I regret nothing, Marie."

She came around to face him, and crouching down to allow her gaze to meet his, said, "Then fear nothing. We are not unarmed, or unskilled. We can survive the worst—and we may very well triumph." She rose, and then added, "But not if you tire yourself out with social life. To bed, my love, and I will make sure our guests depart in peace."

Ruefully chuckling, Phineas stood, kissed his wife—and followed her instructions.

HARRINGTON HALL

It had snowed last night, and the night before. Not heavily enough to cut Harrington Hall off from ingress or egress, but enough to reinforce its wild beauty, the beauty that so spoke to the soul of the Earl of Brentford. As Matching was to the Duke of Omnium, so Harrington Hall was to the Earl of Brentford—the one place where he felt truly at home. He could hunt, ride, or even—and this had grown on him with age—merely stroll the grounds, in the one place on earth where every vista welcomed him. Today, he had prowled around the grounds just for the pleasure of the thing. Oh, he had carried a gun, just in case he saw something worth shooting at, but when a white rabbit had poked its head out of a snowbank, and given him what looked to his fancy like a companionable wink, he had waved at the little devil, and strolled on.

Jack worried him still. Poring over books, especially that treatise Dr. Brandt had given him, but also pamphlets about radical politics, trade unionism, and such stuff. Still, the lad had not touched a drop of alcohol since Germany, and was willing to ride out companionably with his father of a morning, as long as the snow had not been so deep that it could ball up in the hooves and endanger the horses. Nice of the lad to think of that, the Earl reflected. He was well aware of the danger himself, and privately thought that Jack was too easily spooked, but seeing the boy's concern for the beasts—well, that was his boy again, not the moody stranger he'd been frightened for, and even a little frightened of, these past months.

Had he ever been as bad, himself? The Earl wondered. He must have been, albeit luckier—yet he'd alienated his own father, d——d near lost Violet over it, and beggared his own sister, Laura, until in desperation she had married that madman Kennedy—

That still rankled; oh, it had ultimately turned out all right—Kennedy's death had freed Laura from his efforts to tyrannise over her. And it was all right for Finn, who was far better suited to Marie in the end, he suspected, than he ever could have been to Laura. But Laura's bloom had been lost, and he regretted bitterly the suffering his sister had undergone, and all in some misguided effort to save him. As he was now trying to save Jack.

The Earl was well aware that his son was struggling to come to terms with his own bad behaviour, and ached for him. Being his son, Jack tried to carry it off lightly, but the Earl knew better. Jack had resigned from the Beargarden, saying to his father, "Least I can do; save them the trouble of chucking me out," and, on another occasion, "After all, Father, if a chap can't drink at the Beargarden, what else *is* there to do there?" The Earl was intuitive enough to know that these flippancies masked his son's ongoing shame, and yet he could not find any way to comfort the boy.

Violet, watching from her bedroom as her husband paced around the front of the house in his evening dress, smoking a cigar—ridiculous man, she thought affectionately, with his shoes and trouser legs in the snow!—knew why seeking out the peace of Harrington Hall had been imperative to him. Violet was concerned, too, though she drew encouragement from her son's increased seriousness—the volume of reading he was doing, the regularity with which he exercised either on horseback, or by practicing his fencing by drilling with a dummy left over from his schooldays. Jack had determined, she felt sure, to rebuild the life and reputation he had nearly completely wrecked, but for the forbearance of Phineas Finn, and of Savrola Vavasor.

Upon their return to Harrington Hall, Jack had written to each of them—a long, detailed letter to his godfather, and a short, formal note to Vavasor, reiterating his apology made on the parade grounds. Jack had shown her both replies. Vavasor had answered by return of post with a surprisingly amiable letter, simply accepting the apology, and saying that he considered the matter fully closed.

Phineas had written a letter that surprised her, too. Violet had always known that he was warm-hearted, remembering his forgiveness of Oswald after the preposterous earlier duel in which Oswald had wounded Phineas's arm. But the letter Phineas sent to Jack was almost fatherly in tone, urging Jack to find some serious matter, larger than himself, to spend his energies upon. The closing paragraph, especially, had moved Violet:

> *I am convinced, my dear godson, that the best cure for all your difficulties is work. Study, yes, but always with the question at the back of your mind: What use can you make of your knowledge and talents, in serving the needs of others? You will, I feel sure, find your happiness, not in the perquisites of your titles, or the wealth that is yours, but in what you can accomplish with both for good. Know that in your efforts you will always have the support of your affectionate godfather and friend,*
>
> *Phineas Finn*

So far, Jack had shown serious application in striving to determine his path upward from his current nadir. His spirits were rising slowly, as each day passed without a drink.

As Christmas Eve dinner was being prepared, the sun had set, and the Earl of Brentford was still ruining his shoes, endangering his trousers, and enjoying a pre-prandial cigar whilst walking about the front of Harrington Hall. A phaeton from the station rolled up the drive, approached the doorway, and pulled up uncomfortably near to his lordship.

"Easy there, Jencks," bellowed the Earl, who only just missed being spattered with slush.

"Sorry, m'lord," the driver called out, hopping off the box to open the top and assist his passenger. Lady Laura Kennedy descended, more athletically than gracefully, but readily enough.

"Laura!" the Earl exclaimed. "You've cut it deuced close for dinner. I'd given you up; I thought you'd decided to stay in London because you had business."

Even in the dim lamplight, the Earl could see that his sister came bearing news, and pleasant news at that.

"Oh, Oswald," she said, in excited tones that he had not heard in years, "I did have business, and I have concluded it. Be happy for me, Oswald," she beamed, clutching his arm.

"I'll be delighted to, Laura, if it be good news," the perplexed peer said. "But what was this business of yours?"

"I am to marry again, Oswald."

At these words, the Earl did his sister a grave injustice. He immediately feared that some mishap had befallen Marie Finn, and that Laura had fallen into her old obsession, as he saw it.

"Are you, indeed, Laura? To whom?" he inquired cautiously.

Divining his fear, she laughed—a loud, silvery, clear laugh that reassured him of her sanity straightaway. In her excitement, she slipped into the nomenclature of their youth and explained, "Plantagenet Palliser has made me an offer of marriage, Oswald. And I have accepted him."

"Has he, indeed?" The Earl required a moment to take the news on board. But then he remembered seeing the pair dancing at the Marchioness' ball, and the rejuvenated air that had clung about Laura since their dance—yes, and he bethought himself of their common fascination with blue books and politics, and her unsung tutelage of their cousin Barrington. Most of all, he saw her shining eyes, her happy smile, and her expectant, eager look.

The Earl whooped with joy, throwing his arms around his sister, lifting her up, and twirling her around. He nearly lost his balance and tossed them both into the snow, but managed to right himself as his sister laughed breathlessly and protested that he must certainly have gone mad. As it was, his cigar flew into a snow bank, where it was extinguished, and Jencks, after he had been paid and the Brentfords' servants had unloaded Lady Laura's luggage, returned to the station with a story to tell.

The Earl led his sister swiftly into the house, his arm across her shoulder. "Violet will be so pleased. Jack, too. The younger boys will pretend to be, but the little rascals have no souls yet; they'll just look at it as a big feed and guzzle, eh?'

And laughing, brother and sister walked into the Hall together.

The Countess of Brentford had observed the scene between brother and sister, and her curiosity was piqued. Still, it would not do to come tumbling down the stairs, she thought, hastening to her dressing table, and whatever it was, it was clearly good news; she would look forward to meeting Laura downstairs, after making the final adjustments to her — And then she heard her husband calling her name, in his hunting-field voice, as if, for all the world, he was running her to earth.

Violet sighed with mock-weariness, catching her own reflection in the triptych-mirror at her little table where she attended to those small adjustments that mattered so much, if only to her own sense of style. Hearing her husband come galumphing up the staircase, still bellowing her name, she stuck out her tongue at her own reflection, then smiled. Oswald would never be entirely domesticated, she thought to herself, and that formed no small part of why she loved him.

As she awaited the inevitable moment when Oswald would wrench the door open, no doubt with a cry of "Sa-ha, old girl!" or some such idiocy, she was distracted by a modest tap on the door instead.

"Come in," she called gently, and Jack opened the door and entered the *boudoir*. He was dressed for dinner and was smiling wryly, in a way she especially loved.

"Mother," he said, "I really think we should go down before Father starts blowing the horn, and releases the hounds."

"And skimp the Great Work?" she said, gesturing at the mirror.

"You look lovely, Mother. You hardly require the rites of the Order of the Golden Dawn to descend to dinner."

"Oh, Jack," she sighed. "You would be surprised. It all goes so quickly, and children grow up to wear evening clothes and drop references to the latest fads."

"And thereby shame their mothers?" The words were lighter than his voice. He was far from healed, yet. She stood, and took his arm.

"Never that, sir," she said. "Now let us go and see what your Aunt Laura has done to cause your Father to take to the field without leaving the house."

As they descended the stairs, mother and son were confronted by a small tangle at the foot of the stairs—Robert and Ronald, the twins, clutching their Aunt Laura's skirts, and Oswald bellowing for champagne—"and something cold for my eldest, too, blast it!"

Laura was administering bewildered embraces to the two little boys demanding her attention—"Will we have to call you 'Your Grace,' now Aunt Laura?" Robert—or was it Ronald?—demanded, while Ronald—or was it Robert?—asked, "May I be a page, please? With brass buttons?"

Violet, with every bit of sang-froid she possessed, said sweetly, "Good evening, Laura. Children, would you please release your Aunt Laura so that she might sit down?"

With the children and their father temporarily silenced, Violet entered the room and gently kissed her sister-in-law on the cheek.

"What is your news, my dear Laura?'

Lady Laura repeated her tidings: "I am to be married, Violet," she said, "to the Duke of Omnium."

"Are you, Laura?" Violet clasped her sister-in-law by both hands, gazing straight into her eyes. "Oh, my dear, do you love him?"

"I do. I truly do, Violet." And the sisters-in-law embraced.

"I say, Aunt Laura!" Jack exclaimed. "No wonder the kids were all in an uproar!"

"And your Father, too," Violet reminded him.

"That goes without saying," said Jack, with a flash of his old humour. "I am frightfully happy for you, Aunt Laura. Many, many congratulations. And he's a lucky man to win you!" And with that, Jack extricated his Aunt from his mother's arms and embraced her in his own turn.

At about half nine, after the dinner was eaten and much celebration of Laura's good news, Jack pushed back his chair.

A trifle embarrassed, he announced to his family, "I think I'd like to go to Lessons and Carols tonight. Would—would anyone care to come?"

Lady Laura's fatigue was catching up with her. She shook her head reluctantly. "I am sorry, Jack, but I am simply too tired." Her nephew smiled understandingly, remembering that her experience with her late husband, a religious tyrant, had given her a distaste for services, one that she had not entirely overcome.

Violet looked at her twins, and at her sister-in-law, and knew it was not to be.

"Well, don't mind me," Jack said in a carefully careless tone, "I'll just be off, then."

The Earl scraped his chair back and rose. "Wait for me, son," he said. "Haven't heard Lessons and Carols in years. Sounds lovely."

Jack beamed, and the two went off together. After they heard the door close, Violet glanced mischievously at Laura. "Lessons and Carols," she mimicked her husband's ursine growl, "Sounds lovely."

Laura giggled—no other word will do—and said, "And Oswald so loves the lessons! The one time Father made us go, he was snoring before they'd reached Isaiah!"

"It is rather sweet of him to keep Jack company, though," mused Violet. "I would have, but with the twins asleep on the floor, and the servants wanting to clear—well, I don't dare leave Oswald alone in such circumstances. He'd have the children re-enacting the Trojan War, or playing bears until they were sick."

Laura smiled fondly. "And Jack? How is he?"

"Calm. Working hard, but with no—well, no appetite for life. He does not drink, uses no drugs, but seems listless when he isn't forcing himself to be active."

Laura nodded her head, and thought a moment. "Patience," she advised. "He is young, and will find his way through."

Father and son had walked amiably through the cloudless night. How the stars shone without the lights and fogs of the City to mask them! Jack loved Lochlinter more than Harrington Hall—its gloomy Gothic sensibility spoke to him in a way that his Father's plain, comfortable Tudor house could not—but a clear, cold night at Harrington Hall was almost as good. The chill awakened him from his post-prandial sleepiness, and, as they crossed a field and neared the little church, he saw a small group of worshippers milling about the entrance. The Earl tossed his cigar into the snow, and they made their way to the Brentford pews.

The Church was older than the Hall—early Tudor, Jack thought, plain and spare. No Anglo-Catholic fripperies here, no ornamentation. There was just wood, dark and light, gorgeously carved, vaunting arches, and candlelight. You could close your eyes and almost believe yourself in the late Middle Ages, and not in the waning years of the Nineteenth Century, an era of bustle and noise, and which promised—or threatened—more of both.

An expectant hush fell upon the congregation. Far away, from the back of the little church, a boy chorister's voice, high, unbroken, with unearthly purity, sang:

"*Once in Royal David's city*
Stood a lowly cattle shed.
Where a mother laid her baby
In a manger for His bed.
Mary was that mother mild,
Jesus Christ that little child."

The Earl was glad that he had come. He understood at a stroke why Jack had needed to return to the church of his childhood; as Jack recoiled from his own violence, his own anger, he needed to experience this ceremony of innocence, and of the goodness that he so often failed to see. The Earl reflected, too, that Lizzie Eustace had done him harm. An older woman with no love in her could damage a good-hearted young man.

As the choristers and the choir processed up the aisle, adding their voices to the carol, the Earl saw his son's eyes, shining with unshed tears. He placed his heavy, age-roughened hand on Jack's and gently squeezed it. After a moment, his son returned the pressure.

The music built, the voices raised:

And our eyes at last shall see Him
Through His own redeeming love,
For that child so dear and gentle
Is our Lord in Heaven above;
And He leads His children on
To the place where He is gone.

Words, however beautifully they were sung, that had never been more than casual pieties to Oswald, Earl of Brentford. But seeing his son's rapt response to the music, the place and the Season, he began, at last, to hope that the boy would find his way through.

THE DUKE'S CHILDREN

On Christmas Day, at his daughter's house in Carlton Terrace (for he had given it to her upon her marriage), the Duke of Omnium had waited until the children had opened their presents, the adults exchanged theirs, and dinner had been eaten before he brought up the matter of his great news.

Thus far, the day had been a more than usually joyous Christmas; the little ones had been enthusiastic with their presents and the festive fare, and had accepted Nurse's edict that nap-time had come with greater placidity than was their norm. Indeed, having roused the house at dawn, the children were exhausted and ready for sleep, and too happy to be really fractious at the thought of bed. Silverbridge's pair put up a token resistance, which even the Duke understood as being mostly offered on a point of honour: the boys could not be seen, even on Christmas Day, to *agree* to nap time. Still, their surrender was quick and painless—that of a garrison which had no will to fight, but must make a show of resistance for the sake of conscience. Quickly quelled, the children went off to the nursery for sleep.

Over a glass of canary in the parlor, the Duke carefully eyed his assembled children. Mary, who in her appearance favoured her mother, was incommoded now by her interesting condition, and preferred to remain sitting as much as possible; she might, her doctor advised, be carrying twins. Still, her fair good looks and overall robust health soothed the Duke's worries for his precious daughter's well-being.

Silverbridge was settling into fatherhood with more enthusiasm than the Duke had expected. The boy was handsomer than in younger days, and steadier, too—a good Liberal of his father's school of thought, nowadays, believing that the role of politics was to gradually improve the lot of those lower than himself in the social scale, and to tend always toward greater equality, knowing that such a goal could never be achieved, but that amelioration of inequality's sting could be.

But Silverbridge wore these beliefs more lightly than did the Duke; he had his mother's sense of humour, and was just as happy romping with the children as addressing the House. The Duke began to feel that his son might prove to be a better leader of men than he himself had ever been, having a greater ability to inspire, if lacking in his father's appetite for detail and hard work. But even there, Silverbridge had grown in the last decade. He felt a quiet pride in his son now, and as for his American daughter-in-law, she had won his heart over the years, proving to be a lively, affectionate addition to the family, a steadying influence on Silverbridge, and a cheerful arbitrator of nursery disputes. Her beauty had come into its full flower now, and she was one of those women who charmed, not by the perfection of face and figure, but by her vivacity, and her sympathy.

Lord Gerald was burlier than in his college days; he had fallen in love with his Scottish estate, and was his own best ghillie, hunting the property with a consummate skill. Indeed, he had become so known for his skill in the preservation and hunting of game that his views were sought from Lochlinter to Ben Nevis' Glenbogle.

Gerald's wife, Agnes, was herself from the Highlands, and had the Highlander's love of the out-of-doors. It had been rumoured, although the Duke did not credit it, that his daughter-in-law had been seen riding astride in jodhpurs, like a man. What the Duke did not credit, Gerald had not only seen, but approved—after initial laughter and some light raillery, which had ceased altogether when Agnes cleared a jump at which Gerald's own mount had thrown him. They had brought, thank heaven, only one of their innumerable dogs with them this year, an aging hound who had decided that she would much rather pad about the house and sleep than continue in the pleasures of the chase. Fortunately, she quite enjoyed the children and their attentions. She was currently curled up in a basket at the foot of the sofa upon which Agnes was seated.

The Duke, seeing that all were served with drink, and that conversation had not yet begun in earnest, decided to seize the moment and share his news. He rose from his chair and strode across the room, where, with his back to the fire, he could see all of their faces.

Mary's quick sympathies told her that some great announcement was in the offing, and in a flash of intuition she immediately recollected her father's dance with Lady Laura Kennedy at the Marchioness' ball, and the pang she had felt at the time. Frank, next to her, sat a little more upright, responding more to his wife's subtle shift in position and mood; she had not shared her suspicions with him, but his own intuitions were strong where she was concerned, and he was wide awake now.

The Duke had prepared a little set speech to make to his children, but it had fled from his recollection, now that he was in a position to speak to them. Never at a loss for words in either house, or in the Cabinet, the Duke became aware that he was perspiring slightly, and not from his nearness of the fire. By his motion, and his silence, the Duke had gained their attention; he must speak now, he realised.

"I do not mean to make a speech," he said, "but I wish to share with you some news of a very pressing and happy nature—that is, I hope you will all feel it to be as happy news. I do."

Silverbridge and Gerald looked at each other in wild surmise; neither had any idea what the old boy was on about, their exchanged glances told the other, and hoped that he was not rejoining the Government as President of the Board of Trade again; Father *would* take on jobs that were beneath his dignity. Mary drew her breath in sharply. In just a few seconds, Father would change all their lives forever.

The Duke, not having had any flight of inspiration, simply announced: "I have, last night, made an offer of marriage to Lady Laura Kennedy,–"

Silverbridge's poleaxed expression nearly halted him in his tracks, but the Duke continued, "An offer which, I am very glad to say, she has been gracious enough to accept. We intend to be married in the coming year, and I hope you will make her very welcome to our family."

Isabel rose gracefully, stepped over to her father-in-law, and embraced him. "Oh, Father," she said, for so he had asked her to call him years ago, "I am so very happy for you."

Frank Tregear also rose, and offered the Duke his hand. "I say, sir, what splendid news! Many congratulations!"

Mary, unable to rise, smiled wanly. "Yes, Papa," she joined in her husband's good wishes, "many congratulations to you and Lady Laura." She felt the tepidness of her words, but could not think of anything else she could say while remaining sincere. Her father crossed to her, and bent down to kiss her.

Frank had, by this point, rung for the butler and ordered champagne and glasses. Agnes followed Isabel's example, and so the Duke was surrounded by his children's well-wishes. Except, that is, for those of his sons. Silverbridge rose, and Gerald followed his lead. When champagne came, he accepted a glass, as did Gerald. The family all looked to Silverbridge, as the heir, to propose a toast.

Stiffly, uncomfortably, Lord Silverbridge raised his glass, saying, "To Father and Lady Laura: the Duke and Duchess of Omnium."

All drank, except for Gerald, who set down his glass untasted. "I am sorry, Father," he said, "I cannot congratulate you on this marriage. Pray excuse me."

And, without another word, Gerald left the house.

The day was cold, and snow was lightly falling. Gerald had stormed out without a coat, hat, or scarf. His initial impetus took him several streets away from his sister's home, striding through the snow, thinking of his mother, long gone now, but whose warmth and humour he missed to this day. Gerald had always respected his father, always admired him, but Mother—Mother, he had simply loved. She it was who had comforted him after childhood injuries, and after his adolescent escapades had come to light. Mother had always secretly sympathised with all her children, and especially her youngest son, in their misdeeds. Father could be so remote, so austere, as to seem inhuman on occasion. But not so Mother—and now, she was to be replaced! Another woman would be Duchess of Omnium, sit at Mother's place at the dining board, and it would be as if Mother had never been! Heartsick, Gerald paused in his headlong rush through the streets.

He had been walking for some little while, and though the snow was light, the wind was cruel. He pulled out his watch, and saw that he must have been plowing through the streets for a little over a quarter hour. "Almost halfway there," he thought to himself, realising that his path had not been so purposeless as he had supposed. For in the irremediable absence of his mother, he had been seeking the closest substitute he could find: her closest confidante, Marie Finn. A little more than ten minutes' walk would see him to Park Lane, and it was either that, or return to Carlton Terrace, which he knew he could not yet do, or, at least, not without provoking a quarrel with his father. Indeed, his sudden departure and unkind words might have already brought a quarrel with his father upon him. No, Gerald thought, the Finns would take him in, and let him warm himself, if nothing more—and put off the evil hour when he had to confront his father.

Gerald was feeling the cold more keenly by now, the tips of his ears raw, his hands jammed into pockets to protect them. Still, he had been more uncomfortable while stalking deer, and had counted the day well spent. No, what made him feel this cold so much more acutely was how well it reflected his internal state. Matters had been so deucedly fragile since Mother's death! Other people's fathers mellowed with age, came to be referred to jocularly as "the Guv'nor," or some such name. But the Duke of Omnium—no, the flaw was not in the title, but in the man, Gerald realised. Plantagenet Palliser, then, was so shy and so awkward in expressing feeling that one could never quite believe in his love.

And yet, even there, Gerald knew he was being unjust to his father. Gerald knew that his father loved him, and Silver, and Mary. But Gerald did not feel that love as a reality in the day-to-day of ordinary life, because Father kept it all so buttoned up within him. More likely than not, Father would try to express his affection for a chap by reading him a lecture about monetary policy, or duty. That made the affection hard to detect, but did not deprive it of substance. Ah—here he was. He trudged up the steps and seized the knocker.

As he rapped on the Finns' door, the thought occurred to him that he might be intruding on their Christmas Day celebration. He thought of slinking away into the deepening shadows, but no, Meier was already opening the door.

The butler's normally imperturbable face displayed an unusual indication of surprise—a barely lifted eyebrow—as Meier murmured, "Lord Gerald? Won't you come in, sir, and I will see if Mr. and Mrs. Finn are at home?" Meier showed Gerald into the anteroom, and then asked, "Would you care for a brandy while you wait, milord, to take the chill off?"

"Thank you, Meier, I would," Gerald answered. Good old Meier, he thought, you can come bursting into the Finns' home uninvited on Christmas Day itself, but d—d if he'll let you take a chill. And, in fact, Meier poked the fire into renewed vigor before he disappeared. He returned with a glass and decanter, and left the latter on the sideboard after pouring a generous tot into the glass and handing it to Gerald.

"One moment, my lord, if you please," Meier intoned, and was off again. The first glass of brandy and proximity to the fire took the chill off Gerald. He felt better, at least in his body, and trusted that Marie Finn would see him through the tangle of feelings he had not worked out how to domesticate.

Instead of Meier, Mrs. Finn herself came bustling into the room.

"Lord Gerald!" she greeted him, "What a pleasant surprise for us on Christmas Day. Would you care to join the family," she continued, scrutinizing him closely, "or would you perhaps like to speak to me first?"

Gerald smiled, a little sadly.

"That obvious, am I?"

"Oh, Lord Gerald–"

"Please, Mrs. Finn—just Gerald. We are too good friends for formality."

"Very good then—Gerald," Marie Finn had never been one to take a liberty with any member of the Palliser family, and was not about to start now.

"Mrs. Finn –"

"I thought that we would abandon formality, Gerald," Mrs. Finn smiled, and motioned him to a chair near the fire. They both sat. Gerald abandoned badinage.

"I take it you know my father's intentions?"

"You mean, that he is engaged to be married? I do."

"Yes; and to whom—to Lady Laura Kennedy!"

"I know this, Gerald; your father told me himself."

Gerald stood, and strode to the fireplace. "Can you see that this puts me in a devilish hard place? Another woman in my mother's place? A new Duchess of Omnium?"

Marie Finn rose, and joined the young man at the fireplace. She gently laid her hand on his shoulder.

"Whether your father remarries or no, there will someday be another Duchess of Omnium, no? Isabel shall sit in your mother's place one day, will she not?"

"That's different, Mari-Mrs. Finn, and you know it is."

"Tell me how it is different, Gerald."

"Isabel is my brother's wife. My brother's, not my father's."

"So it is your mother's place as your father's wife that you cannot bear to see filled, is that it?"

"Yes."

"Does it not matter to you, my friend, that your mother is no longer here to fill her place, and that your father has been very lonely for many years?"

"But Mother was irreplaceable! How can Father even think that, of all women, Lady Laura Kennedy, could fill her place?"

Marie let the question hang in the air a moment, and then replied: "Perhaps it is not her place that he wishes Lady Laura to fill."

Gerald's confusion was evident. Marie continued, "Your father loved my friend the Duchess very dearly. She cannot be replaced, as you so rightly say, and for all these years, your father took that to mean that he must be alone, with only memories to comfort him. Could you live happily that way, Gerald?"

The young man's face was troubled; he saw the justice of Mrs. Finn's argument.

"Gerald," she went on, "Lady Laura is so different from your mother as is night from day. There is a reason for that, my dear boy; he does not want a substitute. He wants a wife, but not an *ersatz* Glencora."

"Then why Lady Laura?"

"Think of how much she has in common with your father! Politics, policy, weights and measures–" Her examples drew a reluctant smile from Gerald, who chimed in irresistibly with Mrs. Finn on the obvious next example, "Decimal coinage!"

That made them laugh together for a moment. Then another thought struck Gerald, and he asked, "Will she make him happier than Mother did?"

"Would you hate her for it if she did?"

"Quite possibly," he said, with a serious undertone. "I do not know if I could bear to see Mother surpassed."

Marie laughed, a sad little laugh. "That will not be. Glencora taught your father to peep out every now and again from behind those walls he has built to protect himself from the world. She made him love—herself, first of all, and then her children. He is not the man he was before they married, and cannot be that man again. So he does not need a new Glencora to help him reach out to those he loves. Lady Laura could not play that role, and need not even try."

"What role will she play, then?"

Marie thought for a moment. At length she answered, "Once Lady Laura and I found that we had become friends, she told me of an old French maxim that had frightened her for many years; that in every love, there is one who kisses, and one who is kissed."

"Why did that frighten her?"

"Because the maxim assumes that love will never be fully mutual—that one party or the other will love more than he, or she, is loved."

"How does that apply here?"

"Assuming Lady Laura's French maxim is true," Marie said, "who was the more loved in your parent's marriage?"

"Mother," Gerald answered certainly. "She loved Father, I have no doubt, but he was famous for yielding to her needs over his own career."

"And if Lady Laura had been previously in the same position?"

Gerald began to grasp her argument. "Then both she and Father would have been more loving than loved. How tragic for them both!"

"But now?" Marie could lead a witness as well as her husband, and do it without wig or gown.

"Now," Gerald exclaimed, "they have a chance for a more equal love."

"In large part, because Glencora made your father the man he is today. And, Gerald, for what it is worth, I believed that by the end of their lives together, your parents were both kissed as much as kissing. And I reject the French maxim utterly; it merely is used to resign those who are *not* loved as deeply as they love to their lot in life."

Gerald thought a moment. "Still, for a long time, Father must have been very unhappy."

"He bore it. Because he knew that she had love for him, and that it was growing. That was enough for him, then.

"And now?"

"Now, he may be ready for a different kind of love—thanks to your mother, in very earnest."

Gerald took her hand, pressed it warmly, and said simply, "Thank you for helping me understand. I must get back."

"Of course. Let me have Meier fetch you a coat and scarf. And take the carriage. It is getting cold out there."

When the carriage left him at Carlton Terrace, Lord Gerald entered the house cautiously. The children were not yet in sight, and the party was going on, if rather haltingly, in the parlor. Gerald came in, still wearing Phineas Finn's borrowed coat and scarf.

His father rose, and was about to speak. Mary began to struggle out of her seat, ready to play peacemaker. Gerald raised his hand to forestall them both.

"I have been a fool, Father," he said with obvious sincerity. "I apologise for my rudeness, and my unkindness, and wish you and Lady Laura every happiness."

The Duke's eyes softened, and his son took his hand.

"Merry Christmas, Father," Gerald said, and embraced him. A little stiffly at first, the Duke very gingerly, and very gently, returned the embrace.

NUNC DIMITTIS

The New Year had passed, and January turned to February, the latter giving way in its turn to March, and yet no move had been made against Phineas Finn. In the House, a sort of fragile truce held; Phineas behaved as if he had no suspicion of any hostility between himself and his colleagues, and they treated him with cool civility. He was not invited to welcome the New Year with the Prime Minister, but then, he had hardly expected to be; Barrington was a notoriously poor dissembler and, if he intended reprisals, could not bear to eat or drink with the intended target thereof.

Phineas spent much of this time at home, at Chambers, or at the law courts. Mr. and Mrs. Low came in for their share of visits, and the old barrister was delighted to have been a part and parcel of Ifor's release. The Earl and Countess of Brentford each sent an affectionate letter, giving the Finns joy of the New Year, but then went silent. Lady Laura sent Phineas a more important letter, which, in view of the many each had previously written the other, may stand as the conclusion of their long correspondence; any future letters would see them cast in very different roles.

Mrs. Finn, who received the family correspondence from Meier early in the day, handed it over to him after breakfast. Viewing its thickness, and the return address, he looked over at his wife.

"This letter," he observed blandly, "you have not steamed open."

"I am quite sure that I have no need to, my dear. But you may wish to read it in the library."

"Oh?"

"I suspect that Lady Laura is making up her accounts, if you understand me. Unlike so many of the English, she is not one to let matters lie without comment."

"Do you wish to read it?" he asked in dead earnest, this time.

"No," she replied without a moment's hesitation. "It is for you, and you only."

Phineas withdrew to the library, and opened the envelope.

My Dear Phineas, wrote Lady Laura,

For so I must still address you, after all these many years. I write to tell you, not what you already know—that I am to be married again, and will be married this time for love, and for no lesser reason. No, I write to tell you how I have come to be free of our old love—for you did love me once, Phineas, and, had we married, I believe you would have been true to me, and loved me as much as I, for so very long, loved you. You were mutable, but not fickle, in those days—you had the double gift of loving easily, and of healing from love's shafts just as easily, then.

Phineas's eyes pricked when he read this line, and he admitted its justice.

I had neither of those gifts, Phineas. I clung to my love for you long after it was clear that you had released yours for me, and in so doing I did us both a very great wrong. You were loyal to our friendship, but I set all my passions on you, to my poor husband's great harm. He was just enough of a man to perceive the state of my soul, but too small a man to respond with generosity, and essay to win my esteem and my friendship, let alone my love, to him. And then all those years after his death, and your second marriage—for that poor girl in Ireland never truly had your heart, my dear Phineas, had she? What to say of them? Byron has been in my mind for so long, now—his verse that runs

For the sword outwears its sheath,
And the soul outwears the breast,
And the heart must pause to breathe,
And love itself have rest.

I thought I understood those lines, Phineas, and found comfort in them. I was a fool; it was my heart outwearing my breast, a sword of my own making hollowing me out, and my own heart becoming so sunk in endless, self-inflicted misery, that it would only have rested in the grave.

I was beginning to realise how hollow I was wearing, how divided from all I had once loved—Oswald, Violet, Jack—by the Idol I had made of my one great love (for so I thought it) when Plantagenet Palliser and I encountered each other. To my surprise, he saw me—not as a political tactician, or as a sister, as an aunt, nor even (as you have long seen me) as a friend—but as a woman.

And I found myself not quite ready to let the sword wear out the sheath after all, and at last ready, instead, to release the love whose resting time had come so very long ago, and at my own hands. It is so very easy, Phineas, to delude ourselves, and to refuse to see the death of love! And, not unlike our poor Queen, I have spent many years doing just that, until Plantagenet found a way to awaken me.

We will read many blue-books, and white papers together, he and I, and will spend much time discussing the means and ends by which good policy can be enacted, and of what it consists. We will, no doubt, be thought the dullest Darby and Joan ever to appall the aristocracy. But you, who know us both so very well, will not be fooled by the surface appearances others see, and will recognise that we are, in very truth, a-roving by the light of the moon.

God bless you, my onetime love, and may I be as happy in my new love as you have been, and remain, in yours.

Laura

On a day in the middle of January, Ifor had asked to see Phineas in his study.

The young man sat gingerly on the sofa, as if afraid he would damage the green upholstery, shot through with gold and red threads. His question, though, was not delicate at all.

"I can never return to Pontnewydd, can I, Mr. Finn?"

"I would not say 'never' quite yet, Ifor," Phineas began to answer, and at the lad's skeptical look, internally awarded Powlett-Jones full marks for perspicacity. "Sir William will not always have it his own way, you know. But yes, I am afraid that for the foreseeable future, Pontnewydd is too dangerous a place for you to visit."

"Sir William has not had it his all his own way, Mr. Finn, and please don't think me ungrateful. But for you, I'd be in gaol, and that's a debt I cannot repay. But I want your advice: what should I do, now that I am stranded among the English?" The boy's grin did not hide the very real concern that underlay his question, and Phineas decided to broach a scheme that had been maturing at the back of his mind since he had learned that the pardon was likely to be granted.

"What would you think of my own profession? The law, I mean, not politics. I think you've courage enough, and sense enough, to make an advocate. Mr. Low was taken with the quality of the questions you asked at your meeting with him, and you withstood a very vigorous cross-examination from a first-rate barrister. You could do it, you know."

"The law, Mr. Finn? I'm no University man, to be studying the law."

"You do not need to be. Oh, it would cost a little more, increase the required deposit to whatever Inn you studied at, but a university degree is not required to become a barrister."

"Is it not?" Ifor was astonished, and for a moment, his eyes gleamed with hope. "But there'd be schooling, surely?

"Yes, at the Inn. And there would be an entrance examination, and, after your schooling, you would have to sit the bar examination."

"How could I do all that, Mr. Finn? And how am I to afford the schooling?"

"I would pay your fees, Ifor, if you truly wish to do this. I would welcome the chance to set you up in life."

"After doing so much for me already? Why, Mr. Finn?"

"Because of all the men whose lives you saved. And also because I know a good man, who is a dedicated lawyer, and a born teacher, too, who can no longer work to earn his bread at the law, but who could train you up for the examinations, coach you through the schooling, and would make a good lawyer of you, if anyone could."

Powlett-Jones thought a moment, and he grinned cheekily. "Two good deeds for the price of one, Mr. Finn? Mr. Low helps me, and by helping me–"

"You in turn help my old pupil-master. Just so, Ifor. And you each do me a good turn by helping the other."

"And what happens after, Mr. Finn?"

"You shall join me in Chambers, and be my pupil. I can help you build a practise of your own. Interested?"

"Interested, is it? Grateful it is that I am, Mr. Finn, and you have no idea how grateful!" Ifor's flushed, taut face demonstrated just how excited he was at the plan.

"Oh, I rather think I do, Ifor," Phineas replied, "Remember that once I too was a young Celt with very little money, trying to make his way in an English world, and there were friends who opened doors to me, too."

In the weeks following, Ifor's life had been radically reshaped. He had always been one for reading, so was not completely put out when Low gave him a pile of books—poetry, Greek drama translated into English by Mr. Gilbert Murray, Shakespeare, and, of course, the Bible.

"Learn to love words, lad," the old barrister had growled at him affectionately. "Savour them like a good meal. You're a Welshman, after all. Here, try some of this." He handed the young man a translation of *The Mabinogion* into English.

"I know them in the original, Mr. Low," Powlett-Jones told him, "Da was right proud of the old stories."

"Good. Read them in the English, and tell me how they differ—what's lost? What's added? A true barrister is no mere plodder. He needs to have a touch of the poet about him, as well as knowledge."

Powlett-Jones's days became filled with books, and discussions with Mr. Low—and sometimes Mrs. Low, who joined them whenever he read Shakespeare aloud to his pupil-master.

He found he had a flair for reading aloud, and found himself encouraged to give the characters different voices, and to write lists of the words he did not understand, and report back to Mr. Low with them. He suffered with Lear, schemed with Cassius, played the demagogue with Mark Antony. Low had him read that speech every week, on Friday.

"See how you have grown into it?" he asked, the fourth Friday evening. "You're putting more meaning into it, beginning to see the shifts of mood and irony."

Meanwhile, Mrs. Low taught him the rules of etiquette, and began instructing him in the conventions applicable to a lawyer—one solidly rooted in the middle class. "You can't go too far wrong," she said, "if you model yourself on Phineas Finn. Watch how he treats ladies, yes, and women, too. Watch how he handles his cutlery, and his napkin. You're to be a gentleman, my dear boy, not a coal miner."

As she had, many years before, conceived a motherly attachment to Phineas, so now Georgiana Low found herself doting on Ifor.

He spent most of his days at the Lows', but occasionally joined in the daily fencing bouts between Phineas and Meier. The Austrian butler, at least his employer's age, was still terrifyingly quick with a lunge, and parried, like d'Artagnan before him, like a man with a healthy respect for his own skin. Phineas lost almost every bout, but Ifor occasionally, by dint of his youthful speed, here and there snatched a victory from the older man.

Phineas had, after consulting Marie about the appropriate amount, begun providing Ifor with an allowance. He had taken Ifor to his own tailor, and opened an account for him at several stores, including Henry Sotheran's and Hatchards bookshops. The young man luxuriated in books and words, in history and literature, and practised his writing with ever-longer letters to his family in Wales. The new knowledge fermenting within him could not be kept to himself—he was forever running to Phineas, or Marie, or Clarissa, with some newly found treasure that he simply had to share with them—a figure from mythology, such as

Croesus or Medea, appearing as a real person in Herodotus, say, or his discovery that Macbeth had been a real man, and not just a character in a play.

Meanwhile, no sign of any reaction from Barrington Erle or Sir William appeared. Powlett-Jones's brother wrote that Jasper Tudor was aching to come to grips with Ifor himself, although he did not trouble himself or the other miners—his own sense of fairness, rough-hewn but not non-existent, would not allow him to quarrel with a man because of a grudge with that man's brother.

The blow at last fell in mid-April, when, at the end of an evening's session of the Commons, Phineas found himself summoned by Lord Fawn into the Prime Minister's briefing room. A small, handsomely appointed room with a long oblong table, surrounded by wooden chairs, dark mahogany-paneled walls, and at far end of the table, the Prime Minister himself seated at the head, with Sir William McScuttle standing behind him, at his shoulder.

"Finn, Prime Minister," Lord Fawn announced, with a pleased, anticipatory tone. His Lordship marched to the end of the table, and took a position behind the Prime Minister.

Sir William smiled broadly, ready to savour what was to come next.

"Phineas," said Barrington Erle, with a solemn, unhappy mien, "I wish to hear the answer to this from your own lips: Is it true that you have circumvented the Home Secretary's and my own refusal to recommend a pardon for your client, Powlett-Jones, by conspiring with a member of the other party to directly approach—I can hardly believe I am forced to ask the question—to directly approach the Queen through unofficial channels?"

Phineas listened to the question and paused for a moment, formulating his answer to protect Savrola.

"Of course he did!" burst out Sir William. "Why do we care what story the man tells?"

"Be silent, Sir William," Barrington rasped out angrily, "I will have Mr. Finn's answer, not yours."

"Prime Minister, I did arrange for representations to be made to Her Majesty through unofficial channels," Phineas answered calmly, "and, yes, I was aware that in so doing, I was circumventing the Home Secretary's determination."

"And my own?"

"I will confess that I took our conversation to mean that you would not overrule the Home Secretary—not that you agreed with him."

Lord Fawn sniffed; Barrington Erle searched his old friend's face and nodded, accepting the answer.

"Would it have made a difference, Phineas?" he asked wearily.

"I should have acted in the same manner, Prime Minister, though my heart would have been heavier."

"Would it, indeed." The Prime Minister paused, but found himself unable to leave the matter there. "Why, Phineas?" he asked gently.

Before Phineas could answer, Sir William did: "Because Mr. Phineas Finn knows better than do his superiors! Because–"

"Sir William." Erle's voice, improbably for so feeling a man, sounded more like the cracking of ice than human speech. "Please leave the room, if you are going to continue to interject." The coal magnate flushed a dark, winy red. Phineas had not previously understood the level of hostility between these two men, and that Barrington Erle hated being driven by this money-scattering petty autocrat. That put-down might have just cost Barrington his premiership, thought Phineas. But Barrington was waiting for an answer, an answer he had every right to.

"The verdict was unjust. Lord Fawn's resistance to my appeal seemed to me rooted in personalities, not in the merits of the case–"

"That is not so!" Lord Fawn's pained bleat seemed curiously sincere. Did the man not even know how he bristled at their every encounter? Phineas asked himself.

"If I have done you an injustice, Lord Fawn, it was unknowing. But we have been chalk-and-cheese for decades, and the merits of the case are so clear–"

Barrington Erle waved away this digression.

"And your confederate?" He asked.

"I cannot say, Prime Minister."

"You mean, of course, that you will not," the Prime Minister corrected.

"That is so."

Barrington Erle leaned his chair back a little bit, and interlaced his fingers over his small stomach. He began to speak quite deliberately, quite calmly.

"I acknowledge that you believed an injustice had been done your client, Phineas." His tone was almost gentle. "But you knew that you were defying a decision made by the Home Secretary and affirmed by the Prime Minister, both of your own party, by exerting—pressure—on the Throne itself."

"That is so, Prime Minister."

"That is simply not good enough, Phineas. I had hoped to find some—understanding on your part of the enormity of your action, some comprehension that the Throne cannot be severed from the people's Government without undermining the very essence of parliamentary government."

Phineas remained silent a moment. Barrington was correct, of course, in the abstract, but this case had not been abstract to Phineas—it had been terror and near death in that mine, and vindictiveness on the part of the mine owner, seeking to destroy a young man who had, in the process of saving most of those at risk, failed to defer to authority, even when that authority was not able to act appropriately. In a sense, Phineas had committed the same crime. For a moment he thought of trying to explain it all to his old friend, but he quickly realised that the gulf was too wide. He remained silent.

"Phineas," Barrington Erle said, a firmer note in his voice than previously, "I warned you once, years ago, that a man who defies his Party will one day reach the day when it says to him: *You shall never more be officer of ours.* You did not profit from that warning, and now that day has come. The Liberal Party Executive and I have conferred, and I speak not only as Prime Minister but on behalf of the Party, Phineas."

"Yes, Prime Minister?"

"You are this day expelled from the Liberal Party. In acknowledgement of your many years of service, I will allow you to apply for the Chiltern Hundreds, and spare yourself much of the public reprobation your conduct would otherwise draw."

So it had come to this! Phineas smiled, and met Barrington Erle's eyes.

"Thank you, Prime Minister—but no."

"No?" asked a puzzled Barrington Erle.

"No? How 'no'?" a perplexed Lord Fawn inquired.

Sir William, though silent, began to grow red again. The smug smile that had spread over his face as Barrington Erle had announced Phineas's expulsion faded, replaced by a wary look.

"No, Prime Minister," Phineas repeated. "I remain the duly elected Member for Tankerville, and will continue to serve my constituency in any way that I can."

"But you were elected as a Liberal, man!" expostulated the Prime Minister. Lord Fawn bore as shocked a look as if Phineas had proposed overthrowing the Monarchy. Sir William glowered.

Now that it had come to the fight, Phineas felt free. "True, Prime Minister. But I did not resign the Party; it expelled me. It is for the Electors of Tankerville, at the next General Election, to decide whether they wish for me to continue as their representative."

"Rubbish!" Sir William's answer was almost a shout. "What good can ye do them, Finn? Once it's known you've been expelled from the Party, there's nowt you can do for them, other than jaw at us."

"They may feel that is enough, Sir William," Phineas smiled cockily at the coal magnate, hoping to infuriate him. "At any rate, Prime Minister, as I am no longer affiliated with the Liberal Party, I will take my leave of you." As he turned, he nodded to Fawn and McScuttle. "Gentlemen," he said, and left the room.

As he left, McScuttle demanded, "Surely we can force a by-election!"

Lord Fawn shook his head ponderously, hoping to hide the fact that he did not know the answer. "Deplorable," was his only comment.

Barrington Erle, emotions warring in his breast, said only, "We can discuss the best response to Finn's effrontery tomorrow. Excuse me, gentlemen."

Lord Fawn bowed himself out of the room. McScuttle left, as well, casting a puzzled look back at the Prime Minister.

BARCHESTER TOWERS

On "Low Sunday," the Sunday after Easter, the Cathedral Church of St. Columba, which has achieved a certain notoriety under its more common appellation, Barchester Cathedral, traditionally has had a guest preacher. The roots of the tradition date back, it is said, about forty years, at which time the bishop's chaplain gave a sermon that split the diocese for a decade, the harbinger of an internecine battle between the incumbent Archdeacon and the newly-appointed bishop that lasted until the bishop's wife, and then subsequently the Archdeacon's father-in-law, died. When those two blows fell, it was the bishop who stretched out the hand of peace (an enfeebled hand in his case), but, having taken it, the Archdeacon honoured the implicit cessation of hostilities the gesture entailed, and peace was restored. The overture of peace had, by chance, also fallen on Low Sunday.

And so the Dean reigning at that time had endowed a memorial series of sermons in the name of the onetime Precentor whose funeral rites marked the end of the Barchester Chapter's schism, but had conditioned the endowment on the sermons being delivered on a clergyman not resident in the Diocese. The endowment had but formalised and perpetuated the practise of the Dean during the years of schism, so that, although the sermon to be given this year was technically the thirtieth Harding Sermon, it was in fact slightly over forty years since the practise had been implemented.

Low Sunday, or *quasi modo* Sunday, as it has been called, was a time when the people of Barchester gathered to see a new thing—a new face, a clergyman who had no connection with the Diocese, who might bring the stimulating ideas of the Metropolis, or the exotic accent of the Antipodes. This year, Bishop Grantly had invited his sister's houseguest, the Right Reverend Joseph Emilius.

Even that audacious gentleman was impressed with the setting for his sermon. As he entered the choir, he passed through a screen of metal and coloured marbles, designed by Sir Gilbert Scott. The organ, in the triforium, has been famously described, by an unfortunate young scholar, as both "massive" and "classical," which words, while true, do not quite capture its brooding presence, seemingly awaiting the opportunity to bass forth the trespasses of the inadequate performer on its keyboard, or to shiver the spines of the congregation. Likewise, the stalls—"massive" and "classical" were again the words chosen by that scholar, in his meticulous setting out, over a century ago, of the cathedral's contents. How rightly he described too the baldacchino of wood over the altar, with urns upon its corners, and the solid altar screen to the east, classical in design, of wood, with a pediment, festooned with a triangle surrounded by rays, enclosing certain Hebrew letters in gold. This unfortunate young man (for he was mad, and thought he was describing Barchester Cathedral as it had once been, and not as it was at the time he wrote and as it remains today) acutely noted that the cherubs were rapt in contemplation, seemingly of the Hebrew letters.

Joseph Emilius strode to the eastern end of the stalls on the north side to inspect the pulpit, with its great sounding-board. Yes, he thought to himself, it should do quite nicely. The Archdeacon's stall was curiously carved, Bishop Emilius noted, with three curious statuettes at the far end of the prayer-desk. The first was a rather charming figure of a supple, vigilant cat, while at the other end, the figure of a demon—their king, in fact—was kept at bay by the watchful cat; a ghastly figure of Death in monk's robes separated them. While the exterior of the Cathedral has its fair share of *grotesquerie*, this prayer desk was almost the only, and certainly the most prominent, example within. As he inspected the statuettes, the American bishop stretched forth his hand to stroke the cat—and then stayed it, a bare inch away.

The bishop shook his head with a rueful chuckle, and walked away, sparing the adjoining bishop's throne, at the south-eastern end of the stalls, but a glance. Had he looked more closely, he would have perceived upon the sides of the throne the motif of the patron saint of the Cathedral, smiting upon the nose a sea-serpent, an allusion to a well-known adventure of the saint. Instead, he turned to look out upon the pews, across the expanse of black and white marble pavement in a chess-board pattern. Even in his ripe middle age, the bishop retained a playful side; the pattern of the pavement invited hop-scotch, and, alone as he was, he had an impulse to skip across the tiles. Gravity prevailed, of course, and he instead continued his tour of the cathedral. He, Joseph Emilius, would on the morrow, preach a sermon to the dignitaries of Barchester, and to many of those highest in the Church, who had come specifically to hear him deliver this thirtieth Harding Sermon. Icarus had, indeed, soared very high, he thought—immediately then asking himself: Too high? Had he drawn such notice to himself that the tongues of scandal would reignite, and, like the Sun, melt his waxwork wings?

"Extemplo Libyae magnas it Fama per urbes,
Fama, malum qua non aliud uelocius ullum:
mobilitate uiget uirisque adquirit eundo
parua metu primo, mox sese attollit in auras
ingrediturque solo et caput inter nubila condit..."[1]

---

1 "Straight through the mighty Libyan folks is Rumour on the wing
—Rumour, of whom nought swifter is of any evil thing:
She gathereth strength by going on, and bloometh shifting oft!
A little thing, afraid at first, she springeth soon aloft;
Her feet are on the worldly soil, her head the clouds o'erlay."

–Virgil, *Aeneid*, Bk. IV, ll. 173-177 (William Morris, trans., THE AENEIDS OF VIRGIL DONE INTO ENGLISH VERSE, at pp. 95-96 (1876)).

He murmured the lines to himself, rolling Virgil's resounding phrases about Rumour running rampant through Carthage to proclaim the dalliance of Aeneas and its queen upon his tongue, as though they were a particularly well-aged Madeira.

Too late for such thoughts, the bishop reflected, and, in any case, Lizzie was no Dido—one could hardly envision her, even at her most dramatic, flinging herself upon the funeral pyre for love's sweet sake. No, a more martial allusion was called for here.

Alea iacta est! He thought, switching briskly from Virgil's paean to Empire to Caesar's military campaigns. If he backed out now, the scandal in the clerical world would be sufficient to dash him from the heights he had achieved, even if it did not awaken memories of his previous English sojourn. No, the die was indeed cast, and he must continue to trust in his star, and to hold his course. In the end, he knew, virtue would triumph.

The music of the Cathedral of Barchester is glorious, and if the choir is not quite up to the standards of the long-ago precentor and sometime warden commemorated that next day, it and the organist at least had the benefit of his wisdom and musical taste, using on these occasions as it did *Harding's Church Music*, an exquisitely bound, sumptuous volume that contained all that its author had known on the subject to which he had dedicated much of his professional life. The *Introit* was all it should be, the hymn after the reading superb. The Gospel lesson—"Doubting Thomas"—was read with appropriate gravity, and the emphasis on the skeptical apostle's finally convinced exclamation of "My Lord and my God!" delivered with solemnity worthy of Beerbohm Tree at his most oracular; Emilius bethought him of the actor's granting of Magna Carta, in a scene added to *King John* for spectacle's sake. And then it was time for him to take to the pulpit and preach.

As the organ murmured darkly, Emilius mounted the steps, laid the text of his sermon on the slanted ledge built into the pulpit, and began.

"My brothers and my sisters," he greeted the clerical and other dignitaries and worthies of Barchester, and those who had traveled to hear this anniversary sermon, "Thomas the doubter may stand for us all as typical of the age in which we are living, of the way we live now." He paused. Good, he thought, gauging the reaction—provoked, but not yet shocked.

"Unwilling to believe, unless we meet, ourselves, with indisputable proof, blinded by skepticism, fueled by the revolutions in science, in politics, in archeology, which seem to tell us that the beloved stories in our Bible are just that—stories—we, like Thomas the Doubter, stand before the Risen Lord with no idea of what to affirm, what to deny.

"And yet, is Thomas's message to us only one of dubiety reproved, of skepticism routed? Let us not forget the answer given by this same Thomas, when Our Lord determined to return to Jerusalem, even though his disciples warned him of the common report that the authorities intended to stone him. When Jesus resolved to go into danger—nay, into certain death!—it was Thomas, the Doubter who said unto his fellow disciples simply, 'Let us also go, that we may die with him.' Surely it is thus that we may best meet this new age in which we are living. Though the rocks of certainty appear to be clouds of unknowing, we go forward, regardless, trusting in the will to believe, the desire..."

He had them.

Bishop Samuel Grantly sat enthroned, all of his misgivings about the American bishop rising again as Bishop Emilius preached his sermon. Griselda had wanted it, and, as was almost always the case, she had gotten her way—she had renewed the endowment in their grandfather's name long-ago established by the Dean at the time of his death, and, in truth, Samuel had no great desire to oppose her. But something in the sermon—well-phrased, excellently delivered though it was—stirred those old misgivings. Perhaps it was the man's emphasis on the importance of the will of the individual, and of that will's strength; perhaps it was his casual assumption that posited the incompatibility of knowledge and belief. But Emilius' message, reduced to its essence, was one of courage in the face of a world without God, or order of any kind. Without saying so, the American bishop suggested that the law of the Universe was Chaos—not Order, not Strength, not Love. His teachings were less redolent of Christ Jesus than of the German Anti-Christ Nietzsche.

All this, Bishop Grantly thought, without actually saying any one thing that the Bishop of Barchester could point to as clearly contrary to orthodoxy! The American might be steeped in sin, or guilty of only profound error, but he, Samuel Grantly, had licensed the use of his pulpit for this persuasive, unhealthy exaltation of human self-assertion. Looking in the congregation, he saw mostly enthusiastic faces: some, such as those of Lady Eustace and her older friend, Lady Wariston, positively rapt, while others were merely engaged with a perspective they had not encountered before and found it intriguing. What his late Father would have said, he could only too easily imagine; he could hear those gruff tones in his mind: "Good heavens! Drag the mountebank from the pulpit, Sam, no matter what the scandal—just shut him up!" His grandfather, in whose name the sermons were being given, would have reacted more gently, but his reproach would have carried the more sting as a result. "Perhaps, my dear," he could hear those soft, well-remembered tones, "perhaps a less controversial choice might have been better. The poor fellow does not seem to understand that not everybody is ready for Peitsche. Oh, Nietzsche? Well, whatever his name is, I'm sure he means well." But seeing, as others would not, his carefully suppressed shame, his grandfather would have comforted him: "Oh, don't worry, Sam—look, he's finishing up now, and the anthem is coming soon, and that will make everything better. No better rebuke to extreme thinking than good music–"

The bishop's fantasy of his grandfather faded away as Bishop Emilius left the pulpit, his lambent eyes expressing self-satisfaction. He had delivered the sermon well, Bishop Grantly conceded ungrudgingly. His quarrel was with the matter, not the manner. Emilius bowed to him, and took his place in the apse. The service went on to the Creed, and then the prayers and then the anthem, an old favourite of Bishop Grantly's, who had, as a young boy, first heard it being scraped on his grandfather's violin-cello.

When it was all over, Bishops Grantly and Emilius went to greet those of the congregation invited to the reception afterward in the

Chapter House's largest room. As the two ladies from London congratulated Emilius warmly, Grantly noted the fervent eyes of the younger one, while even the harder features of Lady Wariston registered aloof approval. He thought for a moment that Griselda and Lady Wariston would be well matched, and then at once realised his error. Griselda was aloof, true; icy, still, a frozen lake that could chill, or freeze. If that freezing was unto death, Griselda would be indifferent, but she would not triumph in her power to chill or kill. Lady Wariston was something different—cold, he thought, but predatory, too. He felt a profound aversion to her, quite unlike the sadness he felt when he remembered the solemn, but not unfeeling, "Grizzle" of his childhood.

As Bishop Grantly excused himself, and drifted away from his guest of honour to those who had come to meet one or the other bishop, he discovered the event had been a success in almost everyone's eyes. The Bishop of Cambridge seemed to have entirely missed the undercurrent of Emilius' sermon, for he congratulated Samuel Grantly with genuine enthusiasm. "Well done!" he said unequivocally, "A splendid note of resolution for the thirtieth anniversary!" Indeed, none of the clergy present seemed to have been put out of sorts by what they had just heard. Only Aunt Eleanor, a clerical widow as well as a cleric's daughter, seemed critical. He saw her lingering at a table with a glass of hock, and joined her.

"I don't like that fellow, Samuel," she said, with an asperity he could not remember ever having heard from her. "Too fond of the sound of his own voice. Too fond of himself. Hadn't you spotted it?"

"No, Aunt Eleanor, I hadn't," he replied. "And yet, I think I disapprove of my choice even more than do you. I am glad to be home in Barchester once more; and gladder to be saying farewell to the Right Reverend Joseph Emilius."

"Is he not staying, Samuel?" The old lady's eyes were compassionate, understanding.

"He returns to London on the morrow, to my great relief. I will not say with my blessing. Barchester will be the sweeter for his departure, and London the worse for his arrival."

"You have lost your taste for your new acquaintance?"

"It took returning home for me to realise fully that there is something unhealthy about the man. His sermon, here in the old pulpit from which my father and both my grandfathers preached, awoke me to the meaning of all the stray comments and sly remarks that I had heard without understanding." The bishop looked around cautiously, and, lowering his voice, went on, "I believe him to not be what he seems."

Aunt Eleanor smiled, a little tremulously. "Does he return to Griselda?"

"Yes; she finds him an admirable clergyman, I gather, as she has renewed her invitation for him to stay with her, although he had suggested that he return to Claridge's when he goes back to London."

"Do you—do you fear for her safety with such a guest?"

The bishop considered.

"No. No, I do not. Griselda is more than a match for any clergyman, and in any case has only done him good. Bishop Emilius strikes me as spiritually unhealthy, a possible corrupting influence on the unwary, but Griselda—Griselda–" But the bishop could not complete his thought without speaking ill of his once-deeply loved sister to his deeply-loved aunt, and so he remained silent.

But Aunt Eleanor did not. "And Griselda is no longer susceptible to any influences other than her own will, is that it, Samuel? That is why he horrifies you, is it not?" she continued, with a flash of the insight that had taught him early not to try to lie to her. "He horrifies you," she continued, "because his philosophy leads to something very like Griselda's state of life."

Samuel considered. "Yes," he said. "Yes," he repeated, "and that is why she has nothing to fear from him. She has imbibed his teachings direct from the source."

Eleanor Arabin nodded sadly. "Poor Susan!" she exclaimed. "How she grieved for her girl as she became ever more remote, and was ultimately lost to her. We feared you might be, too, once, you know."

"I did not. But I am glad to hear that your fears were not fulfilled."

The old woman smiled. What she might have said next cannot be known, for before she could say or do anything, a young man stood before them.

"Excuse me, Bishop Grantly," the young man said, "I know it's bad form to button-hole you at a tea party, but if I could have a word –"

The young man was familiar to Samuel Grantly; he closed his eyes and whirled through his memories. After a few seconds, he rose, excused himself to his Aunt—he saw his cousin John, her son, making his way over, in any event, so she would not be entirely deserted—and then turned to his interlocutor.

"How may I serve you, Lord Chiltern?" he asked.

The young peer standing before him met the bishop's gaze evenly, although his own eyes betrayed a lack of serenity and many haunted nights. "I have been told that you are a good man," Jack Standish said.

"I try to be," the bishop answered.

"So do I," said Jack with a laugh that sounded like it might crack at any moment. "But I do not succeed all that often, for all my good intentions. I am quarrelsome, I am a drunkard, I have hurt those whom I love, and *I cannot find my way*."

The bishop knew at once that the young man was utterly sincere—and quite desperately afraid.

"Come and tell me all about it," he said, and abandoned his other guests altogether.

CONFESSIONAL

The Bishop led Jack into his study, and the two men sat opposite each other. The bishop's study was a large, airy room, with mullioned windows at the back behind the bishop's desk. Although Dr. Grantly's predecessor had left the room as it had been in the day of Bishop Proudie, who had made no changes after his wife's death, Dr. Grantly had shown no such respect for Mrs. Proudie's chintz and cushions. While the room was not quite as it had been in the days of his grandfather, Bishop Samuel Grantly had restored much of its atmosphere. If anything, the study was a bit more Spartan, a little less the room of one given to gentle contemplation and edifying conversation, and more that of an active scholar and administrator. Samuel Grantly did not delegate half as much to his archdeacon as had his grandfather; if pressed, he would say that no archdeacon comparable to his own father could be found in these days.

Despite this, Bishop Grantly managed to keep a steady stream of articles, essays, and books flowing from his pen. He wrote in fits and starts—becoming enamored of a topic, researching it in depth at the Cathedral library, or sometimes the British Museum when in London, and publishing what he found. Often, what he found had been different than what had been his expectation on going into the subject. He had a high opinion of the value of evidence, and was known to quote the maxim of the Autocrat of the Breakfast Table: "Not to take authority when I can have fact." Despite his sincere horror at Emilius's sermon, or, rather, at the foundational world view that underpinned Emilius's sermon, ostensibly a call to courage in the Christian journey in a hostile world, Dr. Grantly embraced in earnest the credo once championed lightly by his predecessor Dr. Proudie: *Magna est Veritas.*

But despite all of his literary and intellectual efforts, and in addition to the administrative work of the diocese, Dr. Grantly firmly believed in the duty to help those who are struggling. Jack Standish had not been prepossessing the first time they had met; never mind, the bishop thought, any man who needs help and owns up to the fact is my brother, and deserves my best efforts on his behalf.

As Jack squirmed a little in the deep, brown leather club chair the bishop had replaced Mrs. Proudie's by-then ancient reclining couch with, the bishop asked him, "What led you to seek me out?"

"You were there that night." Jack forced out after a long silence.

"At my sister's ball, you mean?"

"Yes."

"What of it? Other clergymen were there as well, some of them resident in London."

"Like Emilius, you mean? That humbug?"

The bishop paused a moment, unsure if this slight truculence was a sign of mental aberration or of insight.

"A gentleman to whom you nonetheless owe an apology, surely."

Jack laughed hollowly. "True enough," he conceded, "but that sermon—was that even Christian, what he was saying, underneath all the window-dressing?"

The bishop was startled; this unhappy young man was, other than his Aunt Eleanor, the only person who had shared Dr. Grantly's instinctive recoiling from his guest's unspoken premises.

Dr. Grantly smiled thinly. "I am not entirely sure, myself. But again, why do you seek me out?"

"When I fled the room, I turned back at one point—I was so frightened at what I had done that I could not stay, but to leave was so cowardly!—and I saw you looking at me."

"Yes?"

"You looked sad. Not angry, not contemptuous, not anything but sad. And sad for me, as well as sad at what I had done. I remembered that in Germany, when I had made things worse yet." And then, more tentatively, "I believe I can tell you what I have done, and that perhaps you can help me not to do it anymore. I have seen what will become of me, if I do not stop what I am doing—it is like being on a railroad train at night, and the wheels strike a spark against the track, and for just a moment the path ahead is brilliantly clear."

"And?"

"And I am afraid, bishop. I am afraid, because, though I have not had a drink in six months, I long for it every day. I cannot settle myself to any work, I cannot wish myself well. I cannot go on as I have, by my own will alone, as that—that mountebank Emilius would have it, but I do not know any other solution."

The bishop sighed. "Tell me everything, in order. Let us see where the facts lead us."

Jack told his story well, informing the bishop truly of all that had passed between himself and Lady Eustace, between himself and Savrola Vavasor, the role of alcohol and "snuff" in the story, and mentioning (without excusing himself) Sir Felix Carbury's introduction to and provision of the latter. He described clinically the duel, the wounding of Phineas Finn, and the diagnosis of Dr. Brandt. At last, he slouched in the chair, exhausted by the recital. His eyes were downcast, not daring to meet those of Dr. Grantly.

To his surprise, the bishop laughed a little, a gentle laugh, not cruel. Jack's eyes met those of the bishop.

"Why are you laughing, sir?" he asked, the blood flooding his cheeks, the anger, still there, still so damnably close to the surface.

"I was only thinking how good it is that you are making this difficult confession to me, and not to my late father. He would not have understood. I do not know that either of my grandfathers would have understood better, but they were both men of great compassion, who would have tried to understand, and would certainly not have judged you."

"And you, Bishop?"

Samuel Grantly collected his thoughts. "When I was a young man," he said at length, "there was a doctor in Barchester named Thorne. He retired from doctoring after he married—his wife was wealthy—but he told me a tale I have never forgotten. He had known, and tried to rescue from drunkenness, two men, a father and son. The father was strong in body and in mind, the son weak in both—but young, and with the resilience that youth brings. Both died of drink, though the father was strong enough that, if anybody could have shaken off the chains of drunkenness by force of will, it would have been he. And yet, he failed."

The two men sat in silence a moment.

"Why did the doctor tell you this story?"

"Because I had been to see him over my own inability to stop drinking, and the harm it was doing me."

Jack sat bolt upright in the chair. "Your own–?"

"Yes, Jack," the older man said. "I, too, have seen the spark that lights the way to disaster—a good metaphor, if I may say—and have known that I must stop myself, while knowing that I could not. And we are not unique. Think of St. Paul."

"St Paul?" Jack's mouth screwed upwards in his perplexity.

"For the good that I would, I do not: but the evil which I would not, that I do" the bishop quoted. "Perhaps St. Paul was not thinking of alcohol, but it is very apt, is it not?"

"Yes. Too apt, I think. But what is the answer, then, if not strength of will?"

"Surrender," the bishop said. Jack's panic-stricken look moved the bishop to clarify his answer. "To God, I mean, not to alcohol. Prayer, meditation, service to others. Understanding that your strength of will is irrelevant, and only God's grace will keep you sober. And that you, in turn, must live a life that is productive and good—for others, not just yourself, Jack!—for that grace to take hold."

"But that is just what I want, bishop! I don't use my title because I want to be part of a more egalitarian, better England. I just have not found the way to serve."

"Your title is neither the problem not the solution. I know some men who I think can help you—a community built on monastic lines, but of men living in the world. An old friend of mine, a younger man than I, but a good one for you to know, leads the community. Would you like me to give you an introduction to him?"

Weary, but with a glimmer of hope for the first time in months, Jack said merely, "Yes."

The Community of the Resurrection, in these days, was still located in the little village of Radley, five miles outside of Oxford. The members, clergy sworn to celibacy and sharing all things in common, did not take permanent vows, rather renewing their vows annually. While they followed the Daily Office in a fashion that would be familiar to other Anglican (or even Roman Catholic) monks, they were known for their involvement with the social issues of the day, advocating on behalf of the poor and dispossessed, and seeing their ministry as rooted in educating the wider church and the World to the needs and rights of the poor. So committed were they to this ministry that they were contemplating leaving the beautiful little village in favour of a less idyllic setting—in Yorkshire, perhaps, but certainly in an industrial section of the North.

The superior of the Order was no longer resident among his brethren at this time, however, having recently been named a canon at Westminster Abbey. And so Jack Standish came to London and not to Radley, and thus face-to-face with Canon Charles Gore. In his mid-fourties, Gore's early slenderness had filled out a trifle, but he still presented an ascetic figure, with piercing steel-gray eyes, light hair only slowly graying, and a truly formidable beard.

The Canon was able to set Jack quickly at ease, to the younger man's astonishment. It helped, of course, that he was what the Countess of Brentford would call *one of our set*; with his late brother having been the Earl of Arran, and his grandfather the Earl of Bessborough, Canon Gore instinctively understood Jack's *milieu*. Irish Ascendancy peers, both of them, of course, but still: English to the core, and, more importantly, *one of us*, he could hear his mother saying.

Moreover, Jack's quickly revealed socialism, far from leaving Gore nonplussed, roused his enthusiasm. Before Jack knew it, Gore was describing the Christian Social Union, an outgrowth of the Order, through which he himself was a key proponent of Christian socialism. He knew several of Jack's Fabian friends, and, even better, shared Jack's admiration for the trade unionists who were contemplating building on the tentative success of the Independent Labour Party, and replacing it with a true Labour Party—one that would not field a few independent candidates, supplemented those jointly supported by the party and the governing Liberal Party, but would be a force in its own name and its own right. Gore, who had scandalised Oxford by having a dockworker's union leader address Divinity students during their strike, quoted with approval the union maxim, "not charity, but justice."

Having set Jack at ease over a very pleasant tea in his scholar's rooms at the Cathedral—a book-crammed warren with good old Georgian furniture from the Gore family seat—the Canon invited Jack to tell him how he could be of service. Having confessed his trouble already to the Bishop of Barchester should have made it easier for Jack to confide it to this cheerful, sympathetic figure, but somehow it did not. Jack had conceived a liking for Gore, and wanted the Canon to like him in return.

As if sensing the difficulty, Gore prodded Jack a little bit. "Bishop Grantly has informed me, in his letter of introduction, that you are here seeking my help. I am a priest"—that choice of words jarred the younger man; he had forgotten that Gore belonged to the so-called "Catholic Party" within the Church, and was notable for combining a devotion to what he called "sacramental religion" with his socialism and good works—"and I am here to assist you in any way I can."

Jack struggled to find the words with which to begin. Canon Gore sighed deeply.

"It is hard, is it not," he said gently, "to have to make so humiliating a confession twice. I know a little—I have heard of the scene at the Marchioness' ball from my sister, who was present, and who knows your mother well. I have heard of the fight in Germany from my mother, who had it from one of her friends, and know that you injured a Member of Parliament who was there to referee. What I do not know is why so promising a young man as yourself would act in a manner so inimical, not only to his own interests but, as I perceive from our conversation today, to his own best self."

And Jack told him everything, dry-eyed and competent until the very end, when tears, scalding in their shamefulness, would be put off no longer.

Canon Gore passed the younger man a handkerchief. "Do not blush for your tears, Jack," he comforted, "for they do you credit. They mean that the real Jack Standish is still there, despite all that you have suffered." He changed tack suddenly: "You are an old Harrovian, like myself, are you not?"

"Yes," Jack answered, composing himself.

"Too late to have studied with Westcott, I think, though. A pity. He'd have been just the man to set you on your path. He once said to me, and I have never forgotten it, that 'a life of absolute and calculated sacrifice is a spring of immeasurable power'—and that power can free you of alcohol, Jack."

"As it freed Bishop Grantly?"

If Canon Gore was startled to discover that the bishop had been so forthcoming, he did not reveal it; he merely murmured, "Even so."

"But how? I do not know what I believe about God, so to whom am I sacrificing, and how do I make the sacrifice?"

"You are sacrificing the escape alcohol provides, and that part of yourself that delights in it—the part that lusts to tear down, rather than build up. As to God, wait and see what you believe; it's hardly surprising that in your current state, you should not feel His presence."

Jack nodded thoughtfully, but then asked, "All this sounds logical, Canon Gore, but how am I to do it? I mean, what steps do I take?"

"You have lived quietly for four months now, you have told me. So I will not advise a retreat at this time. You need to engage the world now, I rather think. So I will ask you this: Have you ever done any relief work? Actually spent time assisting the poor, in a soup-kitchen, or bread-line, or at a school for their children?"

Ashamed that he was unable to answer affirmatively, Jack shook his head.

"I thought not. No, no; don't take it amiss. I mean no criticism by that, only that the best way to clarify your path is to try something in order to see where your gifts lie. Will you try what I advise?"

"Yes," Jack answered.

"Good. I am sending you to my friend Morrell, who is much of our mind as to politics, and he will put you to work. But I would ask you to see me on a weekly basis, and let me know how you are getting on. And you must promise me that you will come and see me, no matter the time of day or night, before you take any drink. On your honour. Agreed?

Jack nodded. "Agreed."

Canon Gore strode to his desk, and sat down. "I am writing Morrell's particulars, and my own, so that you may be sure of finding me in any emergency—or if you just need to speak to someone who is holding you in his prayers. Because I will be, you know. And if you feel that you are likely to take a drink, you must not be afraid to seek me out under any circumstances." Gore's smile was kind, and his eyes seemed almost blue. "After all," he continued, I have your promise, and I am on the telephone exchange, and you can call me at need," he added, taking a sheet of paper from his desk, removing a pen, and, as it scraped a little on the paper, frowning. "Bah," he said, "these confounded pens are worse than the ones at Harrow." The ink started flowing then, and the Canon finished writing the telephone number, and where he could be found at various times. He surveyed the paper, made sure that all was as it should be, then blotted it gently and handed it to Jack.

He rose, shook hands with Jack, and saw him to the door.

"I will see you in a week's time, my friend?"

Jack nodded, and impulsively seized the clergyman's hand again. "Thank you," he said earnestly. "I will try my hand at whatever work Reverend Morrell thinks me fit for."

"I shall call him as soon as you are away. He is a good man, and his associates are worth knowing, as well."

And with that, they made their farewells, and Jack ventured out into the street, to find a cab that would bear him to the northeast suburbs of London, toward Victoria Park near the outer end of the Hackney Road, and St. Dominic's Parsonage.

PHINEAS AT BAY

Although Phineas Finn had maintained an even demeanour throughout the unpleasant interview, as he left the Prime Minister's briefing room, he was conscious of an anger rising in his bosom. Not against Barrington Erle; Barrington had tried to be fair, had ensured Phineas of an opportunity to be heard, and had, quite clearly, believed what Phineas had told him. The gravity with which Erle had approached the matter, too, acted as a firebreak to Phineas's anger. It was very hard to be angry at a man who had, as Barrington reminded him, warned him of the limits of independence in the past, had listened to him, and had acquitted him of dishonesty. Also, Barrington had clearly taken no joy in his decision to expel Phineas—unlike Sir William McScuttle.

He could forgive Barrington, and did so. Lord Fawn was hardly worth his anger, although that peer had always detested Phineas since the former's disastrous appearance as a witness at the trial of the latter. A weak man like Fawn could not bear to have his rectitude questioned, let alone to be shown up for a hasty, vacillating fool in public, and that indignity had clearly rankled within Fawn's breast for decades.

No, Phineas's anger was reserved for the smirking, smug industrialist, the man who declared that Ifor was a criminal for exercising initiative and saving the lives of his fellow workers, rather than deferring to the master's agent, and letting them die needlessly. The sheer remorseless folly of it all had galvanised Phineas into action in a way that he had not been motivated for far too long.

In the months between Ifor's pardon and the falling of the blow, he had come to believe that his entry into the gilded circle of society had blunted his once-keen perception for injustice. When living men and women were nothing but pawns to be sacrificed in return for profit by their employers, the casual assumption that progress was gradual, but irresistible and perpetual—that, as Coué had made common parlance, day by day, in every way, we are growing better and better—could not be treated as an axiom. No, progress had to be fought for, wrested from those who, either in well-meaning complacency, or in hard-fisted cupidity, would resist it to cling to unjust privilege and power.

Phineas now felt that, after a promising start, he had fallen into the former category. He remembered now with embarrassment a turn around the gardens of Matching with the Duke of Omnium, in which he—Phineas Finn, the Doctor's son!—had deplored the doctrine of equality. Yes, he had made a fair point, of the danger of mob rule, but he should have known better of the courage and wisdom that those who did the labour in Britain could bring to its deliberations. But it had been the Duke who had made the point that the diminishment of class distinctions over time was imperative.

His journey into the bowels of the coal mine, and the private prosecution of Ifor Powlett-Jones, simply to reinforce the dominance of the owner and his agents, even when they were making catastrophic mistakes, had re-awakened Phineas to the indifference of many even among those whom he loved to the conditions under which the working class lived. His own Party—or rather, his former Party—had likewise fallen into the trap of assuming that their precedence and power were worth sacrificing the lives of those who did the hardest, least rewarded toil.

He had always been a Radical at heart; Mr. Monk and he had fought together for Irish tenant-right, and he had supported disestablishment in an evanescent moment when that had seemed possible. It was time for him to be once more a Radical.

And so, in the weeks before the summons from Barrington Erle, Phineas had been laying his plans. He had eased out an elderly Party stalwart as the agent for Tankerville, replacing him with his own man. He had relied, quite surely, on his old friend Lawrence Fitzgibbon—and on Lord Fawn—to let the story of how Ifor's pardon was obtained make the rounds. Not that he included Larry with his Chief! Rather, Larry, fond though he was of Phineas, was incapable of keeping a good story to himself, while Fawn, knowing himself to have been yet again thwarted by Phineas, must needs blazon forth his complaint to the world.

Phineas's initial steps had accomplished two goals: Control of the election machinery for Tankerville was quite solidly in his hands, and the Independent Labour Party members had sat up and taken notice, and had been cultivating Phineas these past three months.

Leaving aside the members whose seats were held in an uneasy equipoise as they were both members of the Liberal Party, but with support from the ILP (as it was called to distinguish it from the more militant Labour Party, which had yet to elect a member)—only three members were solely backed by the ILP. Those three members, however, included James Craig Laurel, a self-educated, nonconformist Evangelical lay preacher, who had once been a miner himself, though in Scotland, not Wales.

Laurel had been watching Phineas longer than Phineas knew. Finn's taking on Powlett-Jones as a dock brief had saved the Labour member from having to try to find him counsel, and his efforts for the boy had been applauded by Laurel, who had feared a lazy, disinterested defence, as indeed sometimes happened in such cases. He had introduced himself to Phineas after Christmas, and the two men had genuinely taken to one another.

Though a little younger than the Irishman, Laurel looked older, with his receding hairline, greying, bristly beard, and habitual expression of worry. But he was shrewd, charismatic, and could laugh quickly, showing a fine set of teeth, albeit discoloured by his frequent pipe smoking. Alone among the members of the House, Laurel did not wear the traditional frock coat, topper and wing-collar, but rather sported tweeds, a red tie, and a deerstalker. His flouting of the conventions of the House earned him some raillery within, and was the subject of striking caricature without, but also made him a household name.

He intercepted Phineas now, noting the Irishman's quick steps and slightly heightened colour. It pleased him to note that Finn was now recovered enough from his wounds to stalk past at his old, impetuous pace, yet somehow sensed that all was not well.

"Finn!" he called. "Finn!" He had raised his voice a little, but not so much that other members would be drawn, he hoped. Phineas stopped, and wheeled to face him. Laurel was relieved to see his face composed, but suspected that the appearance of calm was but a veneer. He had not known Phineas Finn long, but knew enough to see that the man before him was very angry.

"Hallo, Laurel," Phineas greeted the Labour member. "Care to accompany me home for tea?"

"Is it not late for tea, Finn?" Laurel asked.

"Well, I know you do not care for spirits, and–"

Laurel's look of perplexity faded to amusement. "Finn," he laughed, "Have you dined? No more than I. And while I do not drink spirits, I am quite partial to my dinner. Shall we do so here, or repair elsewhere?"

Phineas smiled, and answered, "I am sure I can accommodate that taste, if you wish to join us at Park Lane."

Laurel accepted, and the two men left the House together, and in so doing provoked a certain speculative curiosity in more than one member. Especially intrigued at the sight was the lynx-eyed Frank Greystock. "Well, well," he murmured to himself, "Barrington Erle's majority seems to have been whittled down by yet one more."

Upon arriving at Park Lane with his guest, Phineas discovered that Marie was entertaining Savrola Vavasor and his mother. If that last-named lady, resplendent once more in her trademark blue, was startled to see Craig Laurel join her at dinner, and to be taken in to the table by him, she gave no sign of it. Instead, Winifred Vavasor simply left off enchanting Ifor Powlett-Jones, and set out to charm the Labour member, clearly enjoying his willingness to be charmed. Clarissa and Savrola each tried to speak with Phineas before dinner was served, but he deflected them, attending to his guests. Only Marie was telegraphed an answer, in response to an interrogatory look, which earned her a nod. She, on her part, shook her head, and resumed discussing wedding plans with Clarissa and Savrola.

After dinner was served and Meier had bowed himself out, Phineas answered the question that was uppermost on the minds of everyone at the table. "I should let you know that you are eating at the table of someone worse off than Everett Hale's 'Man Without a Country,' for I am now a politician without a party," he said with a jaunty smile.

"Oh, Uncle!" cried Clarissa.

Savrola shook his head gravely. He had known that such might be the result, but the actuality was more perturbing than he had anticipated.

Ifor's troubled look betrayed the state of his own feelings more vividly than could have any exclamation.

Winifred Vavasor, by contrast, was stimulated. She loved nothing better than being at the heart of things, and had been brought into the present imbroglio by her son (whose prospects could not be directly affected by those of Clarissa's uncle), at the request of the man who had knowingly risked his own political career. She was curious as to how he would take this disaster, and was so far favourably impressed by his slightly jocular bearing.

As for Marie, her look of polite interest gave nothing away.

Craig Laurel, his generally suppressed Scottish intonations coming through, gruffly said, "Not if ye dinna wish tae be, Finn."

And so the hare broke cover—or was it the hound?

Phineas smiled gently, ready for the next stage of the game.

When the ladies withdrew, and Ifor excused himself to return to his studies, that next stage commenced.

"Finn, ye know that we of the ILP are feeling ta'en for granted by the money-men who are controlling the Liberals. Erle was just this side of acceptable tae us, but he's a marked man. And whoever follows him will need the blessing of Sir William McScuttle."

Phineas's smile became grim indeed. "Not a good augury for the Party, Laurel," he remarked, and drew in a mouthful of smoke from his old briar. Elspeth, who had been cleaning her paws, recognising the established signal, nimbly leapt into his lap, and began padding around to nestle for a nap. Laurel's features softened a bit.

"A lovely wee beastie, that, Finn."

"Yes, she is."

"I have two, myself. Most of my friends prefer dogs, but I like the independence of a cat. And independent," the Scotsman continued, "is what we of the ILP have intended to be, but we have taken the easy way out for too long, relying on the Liberals. It's time we formally organised our own self-standing Party."

Savrola Vavasor watched with fascination. Here was a development indeed!

"Aye," Laurel continued, "I willna pretend it would be easy, not will I pretend it will be soon that we hold power. But the working man—and woman, if I have my way—is not represented as things stand now by either Party, and that must change."

"Go on," said Phineas Finn.

"Finn, we need men. Good men, men of principle—yes, and who know the ways of the House and of government! We dinna have a man among us with anything like the experience and knowledge of the ways of governing that you could bring to us. And you would do well to be a man with a party; independent members often find themselves unable to do anything for their constituents."

"And thus soon cease to be independent members?"

"Precisely," Laurel agreed. "Our members now are few, and most are beholden to the Liberals, but if Erle falls—and I think he will, and that soon—they willna wish to be governed by McScuttle or his catspaw."

"And so?"

"And so the time is ripe for us to declare our independence, to caucus amongst ourselves only. We would be more respected, with you among our ranks; ye have held office, ye are known to be honest, and honourable, but know Government from the inside. Will ye think on it?"

Phineas took a pull on his pipe, and stroked the cat gently. She purred, a surprisingly loud sound from so small an animal.

"I will do better than think on it, Laurel: I accept."

"Good man!" He stood up, walked over to Phineas, and shook his hand. "I'll leave you and young Mr. Vavasor to rejoin the ladies, if I may; it is a bit late for me."

Phineas motioned to rise and dislodge Elspeth, but Laurel held up a minatory finger.

"Don't disturb that kit for me," he said. "I'll see myself out. Goodnight, Finn. Yes, and you too, Mr. Vavasor." And Mr. Laurel left the room.

"Uncle Phineas," said Savrola Vavasor, who had come to style his soon-to-be relative-in-law so, "wasn't it unwise for you both to have a Tory in the room for that discussion?"

Phineas shook a little bit with silent laughter. At length, he said, "Not at all, Savrola. You were meant to hear every word. And feel free to let Frank Greystock know what you have heard tonight—but don't let him think that you are betraying me! He would think less of you for it."

"But why do you want Frank Greystock to know that the ILP members are thinking of bolting the Liberals?"

"You tell me," Phineas replied.

The younger man took a pull at his cigar, and all that could be heard in the room was the crackling of the tobacco and the little cat's wheezing snores. The firelight and the dim lamp flickered, and one could see in the dancing shadows a glimpse of Savrola as an older man, as his jaw clamped down on his cigar. At length he replied:

"You want Frank Greystock to know about the Labour members so that he will understand that the Liberal Party's strength is reduced."

"Correct."

"He already knows that Erle is in trouble."

"Yes."

Savrola's eyes danced; he pulled in a heady draft of smoke, and rolling it out intoned:

"You want Greystock to demand a General Election."

"That's it."

"You won't be fighting a by-election in which your expulsion from the Party is the only issue; you'll be fighting a national referendum on the role of labour and the rights of the working man."

"Which ought to go down well at Tankerville, eh, Savrola?" Phineas agreed with a broad smile.

The Tankerville constituency had grown steadily more industrial in the years since Phineas had been elected to Parliament as its member. The coalmines that surrounded it were not as prosperous as they had once been, but gave plenteously enough that the town remained one in which labour and management had not yet gone to absolute war. In part because the individual mines had not yet consolidated, although Sir William had made a bid for one family-held property, the mines were small enough concerns that they were run by those who lived cheek-by-jowl with the miners, and attended church with them. Penny-pinching and autocracy of the kind Sir William practised had not yet found a foothold in Tankerville.

One reason for this, of course, was the fact that Sir William had been repulsed. The Tennant family had fallen on hard times, to a large extent because the son and heir had become the worst sort of absentee owner, gadding about the globe and leaving the mine to its own devices. Still, the young man had a conscience, and had resisted the blandishments (such as they were) of Sir William, selling out instead to a corporation headquartered in Vienna, and owned by the former Madame Max Goesler. That corporation confounded Sir William by appointing a local manager, investing in new equipment, increasing wages, as well as promoting safety, and nevertheless, despite Sir William's dire prophecies of ruination for both the corporation and its labourers, managing to turn a profit.

The same corporation had purchased a significant percentage of the shares of two other mines in the district that included Tankerville, and had improved the miners' quality of life in those mines as well. While the ownership of the corporation was not a secret, neither was it generally known outside the mining community, which viewed their M.P. as a "downy cove" for investing his money (or so they thought) amongst those whom he represented. The miners appreciated that Phineas Finn did not chuck his weight about at election time, but respected their independence, and also appreciated that their brothers at Tennant's had not lost their livelihood, or become subject to Sir William, thanks to the Goesler rescue of the mine.

Indeed, the expansion of the suffrage meant that Phineas's margins of victory had increased since his triumphant re-election after his trial, and he had great confidence that his switch from Liberal to Labour could be survived, especially if the reason for it came out. Phineas rather hoped that his Liberal opponent, would be foolish enough to raise the matter.

"A General Election, Uncle Phineas, gives you a fight that you can win."

"Just so, Savrola. A fight I can win."

RUSHFORTH & BINDTHEBOY

Lady Eustace had been patient, by her standard, for the past four months. But when, at the reception following the Harding Memorial Sermon, which Joseph had delivered so satisfactorily, Jack Standish had simply brushed by her without a word, buttonholed the Bishop of Barchester, and then disappeared, she lost all semblance of patience. Nor had Joseph taken any kind of measure to provide the reassurance that she (in her heart) craved, and that might persuade her that she could enter into a more lasting relationship with him. Both the game she played against Jack Standish as a second, and, increasingly, lesser string to her bow, and that with Emilius were in stalemate. And, like many an aristocrat before her whose patience has been frayed like a bit of picked oakum by the misbehaviour of others, she consulted her solicitor.

Not, of course, the long-vanished (but well-remembered) firm of Mowbray and Mopus, a pair who, for all of their ethical slipperiness, had served Lady Eustace well. A pity that Mowbray and Mopus were both gone now: Mowbray to prison for malversation, and Mopus to the asylum for—well, polite society did not speak of the cause of Mopus' disorder, but he had, seemingly, convinced himself that he was, not a man, but a sheep, and like that gentle herbivore would eat nothing but grass and some oats. Occasionally, when he had nightmares, a panicked bleating would bring an attendant running, but he would soon be comforted, wrapped in a warm woolen blanket and return to sleep. *Sic transit Gloria mundi.*

In view of the seemingly permanent non-availability of her former legal advisors, Lady Eustace had found a newer firm, a pair of solicitors specializing in the representation of ladies of a certain rank, of a certain disposition, and, often, of a certain age. For a reasonable fee, they would so safeguard Lady Eustace's property that she need not fear the claims of the bank, the Inland Revenue, or the angry housemaid alleging that her former mistress had used her shamefully. In sum, her new firm of solicitors accepted responsibility for protecting Lady Eustace's capital from the various predators who longed to carve off a slice of it, as well for as extricating Her Ladyship from any little imbroglio she might fall into as a result of her own whim.

Only once had these paragons been sorely tested, on that unfortunate afternoon when Lady Eustace, returning to England after a sojourn in France, had been found to be carrying a great load of what at first glance appeared to be a quantity of rather valuable *point d'Alencon* lace. The customs officer at Dover had found the lace, secreted in a false bottom in one of Lady Eustace's bags, and had desired to arrest Lady Eustace for unlawfully seeking to evade paying the duty thereon. She, keeping her head and holding her tongue most admirably, had sent for her solicitors, and Mr. John Rushforth had confounded the customs officials by demonstrating beyond peradventure that the lace was not French, but was of English manufacture, and had even waxed quite brilliant upon the differences between the tightly woven hexagonal patterns of a traditional *point d'Alencon*, and the airier open-work hexagons of the Bedforshire masters, also known as "English Lille." Therefore, Mr. Rushforth submitted, no duty was owing.

The Superintendent of Customs at Dover, a Mr. Hawthorne, had sulkily threatened to prosecute the matter under the law of attempts, on the theory that Lady Eustace was guilty of trying to buy French lace in France, and smuggle it into England without paying the duty, contending that the mere adventitious fact that she had been gulled by the lace-dealer into the purchase of spurious French lace that happened to be English did not absolve her from her criminal intent, which she had done her level best to effectuate.

Mr. Rushforth had laughed merrily at this, countering that Mr. Hawthorne had better give the matter up, because how could he prove that the English lace had not been in the bag when it left England, journeyed to France, and then returned to England?

Mr. Hawthorne had then pointed out that ladies did not customarily carry non-contraband goods in false bottoms of bags, and what of that, hey?

Mr. Rushforth had then replied that an Englishwoman's baggage was her castle, and if it had a false bottom, why hadn't she the right to use it, and since the lace *wasn't* contraband, but good English lace, and none of that inferior French stuff, hadn't Hawthorne better shut up about it, since he could neither prove an offense nor an attempt?

And, with that, Mr. Rushforth had led Lady Eustace triumphantly out of the Customs office, and to a waiting hansom, leaving the apoplectic Mr. Hawthorne sputtering that there was more than one false-bottomed baggage in the case—an insult that Lady Eustace had marked, but found it politic to overlook at the time. That Mr. Rushforth had freed her from the toils of the law was much, but that he had convinced the customs man that her French lace (as it in fact was) was in fact *English* lace by pointing out its obvious superiorities to foreign rubbish satisfied her that she was dealing with a student of human nature who would not often go far wrong. That conclusion was solidified by the fact that Mr. Rushforth never mentioned the nationality of the lace to Lady Eustace, or ever suggested that she was guilty of anything more than common sense in availing herself of the extra compartment in her bag.

Several years had passed since then, and now Lady Eustace was heartily weary of the impasse in which she found herself. She decided, at length, to find a mechanism by which she could bring matters to a head, and see which, if either, man could rise to the occasion. If she could not have what she wanted, if Joseph's protestations of love were mere empty rhetoric, she would at least seize the enhanced social position and money Jack owed her by plighting his troth to her. She needed, in short, to force both their hands, and to see if the tenderness the former evinced to her was anything more, and, if not, to get what she could from the latter. So on a cool morning in late April, she betook herself to the offices of Rushforth and Bindtheboy, to see whether her counsel's astuteness could provide the means of testing the mettle of her men.

Rushforth and Bindtheboy's offices are not palatial, nor even commodious. They have several little warren-like rooms on Limeburner Lane, appended to a large rectangular room facing the front—a room lined with chipped bookcases containing unopened volumes of law reports that repine like once-youthful widows at a ball, and where motes of dust cavort in the few beams of sunlight that penetrate the grimy windows and graying curtains. It was in this large front room that Lady Eustace met her counsel.

Wilfred Bindtheboy, a small, dapper man, flicked a handkerchief on the cracked leather cushion of the ancient wooden chair offered to Lady Eustace that morning. His poorly-dyed moustaches were more purple in hue than the attempted black. Still, he knew his law, if not his tonsorial tonics, and concisely explained the concept of breach of promise to Lady Eustace.

"Now, then, milady," the little man said, "breach of promise, milady, is a form of action—a type of proceeding, that is, in court, milady—in which the law recognises that an engagement is not merely a sentimental attachment, or perhaps"—and here, the lawyer chuckled as one not in the know might imagine one in the know might chuckle—"a dynastic alliance, hmm?"

Seeing Lady Eustace's flat expression and unresponsive eyes, he hastily resumed:

"In any event, milady, an engagement, whatever motivates it, milady, is also a contract—a contract binding in law, provided there is consideration."

Impatiently, Lady Eustace brushed aside this potential obstacle.

"Well, of course there was consideration, Mr. Bindtheboy! We are adults, Lord Chiltern and I, and though passion no doubt played its role, calm deliberation informed us at every step of the way."

One must, perforce, admit that Lady Eustace's soubriquet of "Lizzie the Liar" may have lacked the elegance appropriate to its subject, but did capture the lady's ability to dissipate to shimmering ether the stark angularity of fact, whenever she deemed it useful.

"Oh, not that kind of consideration, milady! No, no, consideration in the legal sense, milady."

Even Lady Eustace, who delighted in her title, and had no objection to what she charitably thought of as the "lower orders" scraping and bowing to her to their hearts' content, was beginning to weary of the blizzard of honorifics. Mr. Rushforth, leaning negligently against the bookcase, shifted his bulky frame, transferring some of the dust from the shelves to his person. His partner's mixture of fanfaronades and groveling were a sore trial to him.

"And just what is consideration in the legal sense, Mr. Bindtheboy?"

The little man eagerly explained, "Consideration, milady, means some object of value, which changes hands along with a promise to form a contract. The value of the consideration is unimportant—it may be as worthless as a peppercorn, milady, which is why your ladyship might have heard of a 'peppercorn rent.' The value of the object is unimportant, as I say—as long as it changes hands along with the promise."

"Why is that?" Lady Eustace asked.

"Because without consideration, all you have is what in law is called *nudum pactum*. Which means, milady, naked promise."

Lady Eustace, who had her own private opinions as to the value and enforceability of *nudum pactum*, nevertheless thought that Mr. Bindtheboy looked a little over-excited at the opportunity of using the phrase in conversation with a beautiful woman.

"*Nudum pactum*," Mr. Bindtheboy pronounced again, with relish, "is unenforceable in law—of no effect. Traditionally, of course, the exchange is of an engagement ring–"

"Like this one?" Lady Eustace removed her glove and displayed the engagement ring she had received from Sir Florian Eustace in the days when Jack was still teething.

"Why, yes, milady, that would suit very well, milady. And so, you see, milady has all the requisites for a legal action against Lord Chiltern."

Mr. Rushforth, who had a good eye, not only for lace, but for stones, as well as a keen appreciation of the changing style in rings since the 1870s, broke in, unable to bear it any longer. "Of course, some authorities opine that the exchange of mutual promises is itself sufficient to establish consideration, and so the matter need not be one which we go into very much detail on."

"But what would a lawsuit get me?" Lizzie, ever practical, wanted to know.

"At a minimum, money," Mr. Rushforth answered. He stroked his chin, fingers rasping against his close-cropped beard. "Damages for your injured feelings."

Lizzie mulled this over, unsure of how pathetic a spectacle she wished to present in court. On the one hand, she certainly desired to punish Jack Standish quite severely, and to force her other lover into proving his worth, if any. And, to be frank, Lizzie enjoyed attention and notoriety, as long as it was of the right kind. And she certainly knew—nobody better—the value of money, so mulcting Jack for a large sum would not be unpleasant to her. Still, she reflected, for all of her love of the stage, this might not be the ideal venue in which to draw the kind of attention she enjoyed.

"While the court cannot order the defendant to make good on his promise, milady, the disapprobation of Society and of family often may force him to do so, milady." Lizzie's ears pricked up at Mr. Bindtheboy's interjection, and her lips crooked into a rather disconcerting smile.

"And, of course, there are the social costs, themselves," Mr. Rushforth smoothly added.

"Social costs?" Lady Eustace murmured demurely.

Mr. Rushforth smiled, revealing nicotine-stained teeth. "Oh, yes," he replied. "No gentleman, having been found guilty of jilting a lady, and it having needed the law to coerce him into showing the barest requisites of honour, could expect to be other than a pariah."

"So, if I understand your meaning, gentlemen, Jack would have either to marry me, or to pay me money, and could find himself socially ruined, unless the matter was settled out of court?"

"Yes, milady," the ever-eager-to-please Bindtheboy answered.

"That is substantially correct," Mr. Rushforth confirmed.

Lady Eustace pondered a moment, thinking—who knows what? Did she reflect on the fact that her own conduct with respect to her former husband might give Jack a means of defence? Did she balance her bruised *amour-propre* against Jack's youth and relative innocence? Is it even possible that she bethought herself of his erratic conduct since his coaxed proposal, and asked herself whether she bore any responsibility for his troubles? Perhaps; Lizzie Eustace was, for all of her flaws, not entirely without human insight, and could, on occasion, be kind. But this was not such an occasion; if the thoughts crossed her mind at all, they did not long linger.

"Prepare the papers," she instructed her counsel.

And with that, Lady Eustace rose, accepted Mr. Bindtheboy's flustered compliments, wreathed in a parting cloud of "miladys," took Mr. Rushforth's hand, too, and, with a captivating glance into his eyes, murmured to him "Do not fail me in this matter"—an entirely unnecessary admonishment to the lawyer, who was already anticipating his fee. Cupidity, not Cupid, was always the road to Mr. Rushforth's heart.

THE END OF THE LINE

After their meeting with Phineas Finn, Lord Fawn and Sir William McScuttle left the Prime Minister.

"Fawn?" The industrialist caught the Home Secretary's ear.

"Yes, Sir William?"

"I think it is time you and I had a talk. Things are in a pretty way when Mr. Phineas Finn can snap his fingers at the Prime Minister of Great Britain."

"Indeed, yes. Deplorable," answered Lord Fawn. Although Lord Fawn owned Fawn Court, his inability to find a wife of sufficient means to renew his family's prosperity had left Lord Fawn with seven hungry sisters to support, and teetering precariously at the edge of an overdraft. Barrington Erle had given him office, and employment, but the emoluments of office were but a sprat to catch a whale. Sir William had been subsidizing the Home Secretary in so lavish a manner that Lord Fawn was, for the first time in his life, free from anxiety over losing his ancestral home, or failing his sisters in his duty as their provider.

Sir William had presented his largesse as his patriotic duty in enabling a great minister of State to function free from the drab, workaday cares that men such as himself were made for; he flattered Lord Fawn, asked his opinion, and pretended to weigh it. From his combined good offices and laudation, he had obtained Fawn's absolute devotion, as being the one man who genuinely understood what His Lordship could be, if given half the chance to show his true mettle.

Although subtlety was not his natural *métier*, Sir William had mastered the art of issuing his dictates to Lord Fawn so dexterously that the latter did not even realise he was being correspondent to command; he sincerely believed that that Sir William was his admiring, invaluable agent, who executed Lord Fawn's behests from sheer admiration of the latter's statesman-like qualities.

Lord Fawn, having narrowly escaped thralldom to Lizzie Eustace so many years ago, had fallen into a very different kind of subservience. He often tried Sir William's patience, but the mercantile knight had been preparing him for a contingency that he believed had now arrived.

Barrington Erle, he reflected, as Fawn followed him toward a quiet nook, one which was generally untenanted, was proving too obdurately wedded to the old ways to suit his purposes. For all of his willingness to accept the money Sir William provided, he refused to reciprocate in his own coin—power. As Prime Minister, Erle had, no doubt, been good for business. But Sir William was not interested in policy, but in profit, and in power. And as to the latter, Barrington Erle had been remarkably chary of yielding any. Without the Duke of Omnium's devotion to policy, and his painfully acute ear for falsehood, Barrington Erle had nonetheless striven to steer a middle course—to recognise the new politics of money, and use them to retain Liberal hegemony—but had not given Money, in the form of Sir William, its due. Barrington Erle stubbornly insisted that the party's manifesto was its policies, and not those actions that inured to the benefit of those who made the Liberal majority possible through their generosity.

Even the relatively small matter of Phineas Finn demonstrated Erle's unsuitability—the Prime Minister had, incredibly, been reluctant to banish the errant Member for Tankerville, and had clearly resented his own forcing of the issue, despite Finn's arrogant flouting of the will of the Party. In short, Barrington Erle was no longer useful, and would have to go.

But a new Prime Minister would have to be one who would sing to McScuttle's hymnal, take his dictation, and who could be counted upon to do so without the stubborn pride of Barrington Erle. Ideally, a man who wanted exactly what his patron wanted, and for his reasons.

Sir William was determined to make Lord Fawn Prime Minister, and to govern through him. It was time to explain to his friend the necessity—the stark, inexorable need—of the Nation for a Fawn Government.

Sir William did not foresee much difficulty in persuading his friend that his unique gifts must now be put to the service of Queen and Country.

The House was closely divided in those days; of the 670 members, three hundred and forty-one stood with the Liberal Party; under Frank Greystock, three hundred and twenty-nine owed allegiance to the Conservative Party. The nine Independent Labour Party members were jointly sponsored by the Liberal Party (Savrola Vavasor had reported this to Dolly Longestaffe, who promptly christened these members the "Lib-Labs" and, between Savrola reporting the term to Frank Greystock, and Greystock's using it scornfully in several speeches, the name had taken hold.) As to the three purely Labour–supported members, they voted with the Liberals, and so they did not count as a separate force.

So, on the next day, when Phineas Finn did not take his traditional seat, but rather joined the three purely Labour members, a ripple of comment was heard, and those Liberals not in favour with the Prime Minister were startled, but nobody was too perturbed. The balance was much as it had ever been, and Phineas's changed seat spoke more to his exile from the councils of the party that had brought him into the House than to anything else. While some members—Savrola Vavasor, as a matter of course, and Mr. Monk, now grown very old, but still fond of and loyal to his former *protégé*—groaned in spirit for him, the majority of members took it in stride.

Two weeks later, at almost the very end of April, the Naval Funding Bill was due to be debated and voted upon by the Commons, and, as the most recent version of the bill incorporated Phineas Finn's lifeboat bill, at long last broken free of the chains of committee, Marie Finn and Clarissa Riley had come to see the debate.

Clarissa had been warned the night before that Frank Greystock had ordered a three-line whip to oppose the bill, and that the bipartisan triumph that had marked the opening of the session would not be repeated. At dinner with the Finns, Savrola had been glum for a moment, and then had brightened.

"Still," he said, "Greystock said that while we could not vote for the bill *in toto*, because of the over-expenditure involved, we could, if we chose speak up in favour of specific provisions. He especially gave me leave to speak up for the Lifeboats Clause, and told me to make sure you knew it."

"That was good of Frank," Phineas said gravely.

Clarissa asked, "Uncle Phineas will the bill pass?"

"It should, Clarissa, since we"—and here he blushed, and corrected himself—"I mean, the Liberal Party, that is, has a majority, especially with the Lib-Labs voting."

The conversation turned to other things—the forthcoming wedding, most of all, and the opening of Marie's old house in Surrey a few weeks early to accommodate the affair, especially the arrival of Phineas's surviving sisters, Clarissa's aunts—and eventually the suggestion was made that the younger generation take a turn about the garden to look at the moon (Savrola had a few new constellations to try out on Clarissa, and was hoping to persuade her of the existence of some as yet unnamed ones he had discerned).

After Savrola had led his *fiancée* into the garden, Phineas chuckled a little bit.

"Poor Savrola," he said, laughter still in his eyes, "It is hard to remember being that young."

"The bill will not pass, then?" His wife joined him on the sofa, and he twined his arm about her shoulders, as she snuggled up to him. He leaned his face against the back of her head, the dry, slightly spicy scent he had associated with his wife's hair all these years wafting itself into his nostrils.

"It should," Phineas replied, a little drowsily. "It should, but something is up, I fear."

"Why is that, my dear?" Her hand, cool with underlying warmth, lay against his cheek.

"Because Frank Greystock is paying his respects; he's respecting our family tie to Savrola, and letting me know that he is doing so. Incidentally, he's also getting Savrola's maiden speech out of the way on a bill he opposes, but let's not tell the boy that."

"I see. But does that Mr. Greystock's paying his respects imply that he believes you remain worthy of respect—that you are unlikely to be unseated, and so will remain a force to be reckoned with?"

"Perhaps," Phineas answered thoughtfully, and then added, "Of course, he could just be trying to protect Savrola from a falling out with us over his vote. He's not a bad chap when it comes to the *personalia*, you know."

"This I did not know," Marie said, in her best teasing mock-serious voice. He turned her a little bit toward him, and kissed her lips, gently at first, and then more passionately. At length, he pulled back.

"Mrs. Finn?"

"Yes, Mr. Finn?"

"Shall we withdraw for the evening?"

"Oh, yes, Mr. Finn," she replied, "an excellent suggestion. I believe the view of the night sky is *much* finer from my boudoir than it is in the garden."

Phineas had not, prior to the debate's beginning, communicated his unease to Savrola, an unease that only increased when he spotted Sir William McScuttle in the Visitor's Gallery.

Phineas spoke once more on behalf of the whole bill, but with special reference to the Lifeboat Provision. He adverted to the critical importance of Sea Power, quoting Mahan and the newer volume, *The Naval War of 1812*, and then sat down. Savrola Vavasor rose some minutes later, and made his maiden speech on behalf of that same provision. Phineas watched the young man, remembering his own nervousness, and ultimate failure, upon attempting his maiden speech.

After a good start—echoing Phineas's own sentiments about the Lifeboat Provision, claiming that it bore the hallmarks of Tory Democracy, as he quoted his own Leader's original endorsement, Savrola then turned to the reasons why he could not vote for it.

"But the bill as a whole," he said, "encompasses too much expenditure on wasteful, er, expenditures, for naval vessels we do not need any more of," he faltered, eyes drifting toward Clarissa, who watched him lovingly, but sadly.

"That is, the wasted money spent on vessels we do not need is a—er,"

"Waste, perhaps?" A Liberal member jeered at him.

"And therefore, I must vote against this bill–"

"Seems rather a waste," quipped a Lib Lab.

"With the hope that a clean bill on the Lifeboat Provision will be separately introduced as soon as is practicable." And with that, Savrola Vavasor sat down.

At the luncheon recess, Phineas sought out the younger man, who had a pint of beer in front of him.

"Never mind, Savrola," he said, "you were splendid on the important part. For a maiden speech, not bad at all."

"That's what Greystock said."

"I'll bet he said more than that," Phineas smiled.

"Yes," answered the Conservative leader himself, arriving with his usual admirable timing, "I told him to be less convincing on the merits when he can't support the bill, blast him. How are you, Finn?" And the two older men shook hands.

"Well enough, Greystock; and you?"

"Oh, fine, fine. Just getting ready for the last leg of the debate. Good to see you, Finn; you must visit us when we're all down in Surrey, eh?"

And with that, and a smile and a nod from Frank Greystock, they all made their way back to their places. "Too confoundedly cheerful," Phineas thought, as he resumed his place.

The second part of the debate turned to more technical things. Barrington Erle made a short, carefully prepared speech about the necessity of the expenses budgeted for the Navy, and the vital importance of an up-to-date, large navy in the defence of Empire. He did not mention the Lifeboat Provision. Phineas thought that the Liberal benches were a little restive, yet another indicator of danger. Lord Fawn had come to join Sir William in the Visitor's Gallery.

When at last it came time to vote, the recipients of Sir William McScuttle's bounty—"McScuttle's members," as Quintus Slide had pithily phrased it—stood, and looked to Lord Fawn. Seeing him impassively nod, they walked out in a bloc with the Tories.

Phineas, who had been concentrating almost exclusively on the Lifeboat Provision, saw this at first as an oblique thrust from Sir William, so oblique that not even Phineas understood what was happening, as he and Craig Laurel walked into the lobby with the Government side.

Barrington Erle, noticing the defections, and the reduced knot of men surrounding him in the lobby, realised what had happened at the exact same moment as Phineas did.

"Loss of supply," the Prime Minister whispered to himself, his face turned ashen behind his still-dark beard.

"Loss of supply," said Phineas Finn to Craig Laurel.

"Loss of supply?" The Scotsman, a less experienced Parliamentarian, did not know the phrase.

"A supply bill is one for the appropriation and spending of funds," Phineas explained, "When such a bill fails, it is called a 'loss of supply.'"

"From your expression, Finn, I gather there is more weight to it than just that."

"I am very much afraid so, Laurel. It means that the Government must resign; that Parliament must dissolve. It means a General Election."

And Phineas Finn, who had known that it must happen, and indeed, had prepared for it by prompting Savrola Vavasor to share what he had heard with Frank Greystock, felt a surge of anger, nonetheless, for those who had walked out at the behest of Sir William McScuttle, and a corresponding empathy for Barrington Erle, whose Premiership was almost certainly lost beyond recovery, even if the Liberals were returned.

Barrington Erle caught Phineas's eye, and walked toward him.

"Betrayed, I see," said the Prime Minister, "and I think we all know who orchestrated it, eh, Phineas?"

For a dreadful instant, Phineas was afraid that Barrington's sharp political wits had deserted him, and that the Prime Minister suspected him. Barrington's next words set his mind at rest, however.

"Sir William McScuttle has paid a great deal of money to arrange this petty triumph," Barrington Erle said. "I wonder whom he will try to elevate to my place?"

Phineas laid a comforting hand on his old friend's arm, but said nothing.

"And yet you walked out with us, Phineas, after we expelled you. I am sorry for that, my friend; though I felt in truth it was required, it saddened me more than you can know."

"That may be why Sir William has turned on you so quickly," Phineas rejoined, "I suspected something of the sort would eventually be tried, but I did not envision it so soon."

The Prime Minister (for so we may call him for yet a little while) smiled wearily. "Nor did I," he admitted. "Though I was quite sure I heard the sound of sharpening knives. Still, we must do our duty to the end, mustn't we, Phineas?" And then, in a loud voice, Barrington Erle called to his loyal members:

"Gentlemen, it is time we go back into the House, so that Mr. Speaker can declare Parliament dissolved. From that moment on, the Government has fallen."

As Barrington began to walk toward the Chamber, a youthful smile tugged at his lips. "Phineas, Mr. Laurel," he said, "shall we walk in together, at the very end?

Craig Laurel's face grew dour, as he fell in to Erle's left, with Phineas flanking him on the right. "'Tisn't the very end for Labour," he grumbled.

"No," said Erle, "but it is the very end for me. Let us show them how men face such things.

And they entered into the Chamber, where the Speaker, in dissolving Parliament, dissolved as well the reign of Barrington Erle.

The General Election season was about to begin.

TIME AND TIDE

The Duke of Omnium pulled his watch from the pocket, and opened the hunter case, carefully depressing the button at the crown atop the stem. The watch, massy and thick, had belonged to his uncle, his immediate predecessor as Duke, and was dear to him, not so much for the old man's sake, as for the occasion on which his uncle had presented it to him—his wedding to Glencora. The watch was antiquated now; its small, round crown, lacking a winding knob, its escapement and chain movement, something he had been told was no longer used in watches, and as for winding them with a key? Hardly ever seen, except in very old watches, normally worn by very old men.

But Plantagenet Palliser was, above all, loyal—loyal to old possessions, and even more so to his memories, until quite recently, when he had chosen to strike out in a new direction—to marry again, and brave his children's disapproval, and his own inability to release the past. He had, when Gerald stormed out on Christmas Day, known fear of a kind he had never experienced before: The fear that, in finding Laura, he might lose his sons. Silverbridge's manners, and his basic good nature had held his disapproval in check, but his brother's *demarche* had tested that forbearance to the limit. The Duke had taken out his watch, time and again, examined it closely, and yearned for his younger son to return and make it up with him. He had twiddled with the key, thinking to wind the watch, only to find it had not yet wound down. They had sat, all of them, miserable, nearly silent, until Gerald's return.

That reconciliation had eased the tensions, if not totally eliminated them. On New Year's Day, however, when Lady Laura had dined with the Duke and his children, her bearing and her simple, unaffected kindness to them had done more.

Laura had not tried to charm them, nor to propitiate them, he had observed with approval. Rather, she had been matter-of-fact in her approach.

"I knew your mother quite well," she had said to Mary, Silverbridge and Gerald. "And I would never dream of trying to fill her place in your family—what I must learn to call our family, now. Because, you see, although we were only middling-good friends in her lifetime, I have come to love her, in learning to love your father. She helped make him the man I love today."

Gerald, endeavouring to make a jest, but falling flat, asked "But what are we to call you?"

The Duke groaned inwardly, afraid that the fat would now be in the fire. But his *fiancée* smiled brightly, youthfully.

"Would 'Laura' do? I should like that best of all, I think."

Silverbridge, his soft heart touched by her humility, and her lack of presumption, rose, crossed the room, and embraced her, kissing her forehead.

"Then Laura it shall be. But you will have to learn to be a grandmother, you know. We need one in this family, as my wife's mother can seldom be in England."

"Yes," Gerald joined his brother, "and my wee bairns" ("Oh, Gerald," groaned his wife, only half in jest) "need all the grandmothering they can get, so we look to you—Laura." Her name sounded well among them, and peace was restored.

Later, Lady Mary Tregear had privately approached her stepmother-to-be, leading her to her own private study, which had been her mother's special room, and embraced her.

"I was unsure how I felt about Papa remarrying," she confided in Lady Laura, "but I remembered seeing how alone he usually is, and then I remember how he looked waltzing with you at the Marchioness' ball, and then I was glad—no, I *am* glad that he has found you—Laura." And the younger woman kissed Lady Laura, and fled the room, for fear that she might cry.

Left momentarily alone among so many memories of the late Duchess, Lady Laura felt her own eyes sting with unshed tears. "Oh, Lady Glen," she thought, "I will be good to them! And to him!"

A Duke of Omnium, however late in life he marries, cannot simply plight his troth in a Registry Office, as might a simple Mr. Palliser. Society has its legitimate expectations, as does the Crown as well, and a certain level of ceremony is required of any Duke on such an occasion, let alone of a former Prime Minister.

Neither the Duke nor his intended bride had a great love for the ceremonial aspects of their rank, but both bowed to tradition. The Duke drew the line at the Abbey, however, preferring Barchester Cathedral. He wrote a letter to Bishop Grantly, whom he had known since their Oxford days, and requested him to take the service himself, "one old Oxonian seeing another through a complicated occasion," as he had written the bishop.

Bishop Grantly's more effusive reply to the Duke's warm but formal letter eased the Duke's nervousness that, in marrying again at his age, he was being an old fool. He remembered his own uncle's proposals to the then-Madame Max Goesler, and although his match with Lady Laura was much more suitable in every way (not least because the old Duke had been over eighty the first time he proposed, and the lady less than half his age), he had feared that his own proposal would be seen as folly. Of course, Laura was much nearer to his age than had Madame Goesler been to the old Duke's, and he himself was not yet an old man—of that, he felt almost sure.

The wedding would have to be in the late summer, if not the fall, they had decided, especially as the political winds began to sweep the land. Neither the Duke nor Lady Laura wished to exclude the Finns, and as of now, Phineas Finn was *persona non grata* at any gathering with a Liberal Party flavor. While the Duke had sympathised with Finn's loyalty to his client, he could not begrudge Barrington Erle his wrath. Laura, Erle's cousin, was considerably less sympathetic.

"Really, it is too bad, Barrington," she had chided him when he announced to her over tea in Portman Square his decision to expel Phineas from the Liberal Party.

"It is indeed, Laura," the Prime Minister observed severely, "but Phineas knew what I had decided, and that I would not countermand Fawn in this matter. He owed me loyalty, not subversion."

The Duke of Omnium's silence was a pensive one, as he sipped his tea, watching Barrington with a reflective eye. Barrington had ever been one for order and loyalty, he thought—the watchwords of his functionary's life—and had not ever quite learned the value of grace when confronted by the moral qualms of one's supporters.

The Duke felt a little cursed by his ability to see both sides of the case that evening. When he had spoken approvingly to Phineas of the latter's post-conviction efforts on behalf of the young miner, he had not quite envisioned their involving a beautiful woman's suborning the Prince to act as an emissary directly to the Queen. The audacity of the move both affronted and amused the Duke, who had deplored the dubious tactic for himself, but could hear in his mind Glencora boisterously applauding the Irishman's ingenuity.

Laura had been notably reticent on the matter, no doubt not desiring to inflame her cousin's ire any further. After he left, Laura turned to him and said, "Oh, Plantagenet, it is a shame for the Party to lose Phineas Finn! Barrington is right to be cross with him, but does not expulsion seem...heavy handed?"

The Duke paused a moment, knowing as he did that Laura had for many years passionately loved the Irishman, and still counted him among her own friends. At length, he replied, "Of course it is. Finn may have been wrong in the way he chose to help the young man, but he believed—as he told me, Laura—that Fawn was biased against his client by the fact that it was Finn who represented him."

"I, too, can believe that," Laura said reflectively.

"As, I am afraid, can I. Erle is not wrong to defer to the Home Secretary—or would not be, if he had a Home Secretary with judgment worthy of deference. But he has Fawn, a man of fundamentally good intentions, but lacking in precisely that quality—judgment."

When they next saw the Prime Minister, a few days later, neither the Duke nor Lady Laura mentioned Phineas Finn. Nor did Barrington Erle. They had not reached agreement on this matter, but they had not openly quarrelled either.

Laura was glad of their mutual forbearance when, only two weeks later, the "Fawn faction," as they had been named, had betrayed Barrington, voting down the Naval Budget Bill, and causing the Government to collapse.

"It's McScuttle!" Barrington had roared his outrage in her drawing room in front of Plantagenet—a level of temper that she had never seen in Barrington before. In that single, almost animal cry, Barrington Erle's entire sense of frustration, betrayal, and rejection by those whom he had previously led to success, if not quite triumph, momentarily flashed out of him. He gathered his resources, and calmed down.

"By heaven," he continued in a more reasonable tone, "He is trying to dominate the Party, and to make his own puppet Prime Minister, and that simply will not do. And yet, if they will choose that poor fish for a leader, who is to stop them?"

And the two men who had each held the office of Prime Minister looked helplessly at each other, both knowing that the office could not but be debased by being ceded to a man who would rule in name only, a pawn not even to a statesman behind the throne, but to an avaricious man dedicated merely to advancing his own interests.

By May 15, the warrants had gone out, and it was known that the General Election would be conducted in July. With no Government, and with the looming vote, the House stood empty. On that day, fourteen men gathered to meet in the Vestry Room of St. Dominic's Church, lent them by the sympathetic rector.

The Vestry Room itself was oblong, paneled with dark wood where not covered by matching bookcases, freighted under a load of theological volumes, including the Ante-and Post-Nicene Fathers' writings in thirty gilt-decorated, blindstamped maroon octavo volumes, jostling against *Lux Mundi*, as well as a complete set of Browning's poems and Maurice's *Theological Essays*, *Fabian Essays*, *A Dream of John Ball*, and some ponderous looking concordances, including one from America. The sole off-key note in the symphony of book titles lining the walls was a complete, and clearly much read, set of Thackeray in red leather.

The Vestry Room's mullioned windows were narrow and tall, letting a diffuse light in from the little churchyard. Today, that light was none too strong, a watery gleam barely discernible in the varnish of the once-fine, but now scored, chipped, and worn surface of the long lozenge-shaped table that ran much of the length of the room.

At the head of the table, Craig Laurel sat, with Phineas Finn at his right. On his left, taking notes in shorthand, sat the Rector's secretary, generously loaned to the meeting. The secretary, a brisk little woman of about thirty years old, was neatly but inexpensively dressed in a black merino skirt and bombazine blouse. Her pencil moved quickly, sometimes even violently slashing the paper, as she strove to capture the deliberations of the meeting and its members talked vigorously over one another.

When the discussion became particularly heated, the secretary, Miss Proserpine Garnett by name, scrawled arcane symbols across the paper with even more than her usual ferocity, her tongue peeking out of the corner of her mouth.

Not that the conversation thus far had warranted Miss Garnett's faithful recordation. Each of the members gathered had expressed the same concerns, albeit with differing emphases: their dread of losing their seats against a well-funded McScuttle candidate, or, what would be even worse, watching such a candidate split the vote, and assist Frank Greystock to a majority. Indeed, the notion of following Fawn as pilot fish to McScuttle's shark was distasteful, to say the least, and while the Lib-Labs had been able in good conscience to caucus with the Liberals under Barrington Erle's leadership, to place themselves under the leadership of a man like McScuttle would simply be impossible.

As the anxiety in the room built, Craig Laurel brought his fist down upon the table with a crash that made the teacups nearest him dance.

"All right, then!" he roared. "Be quiet a moment, because Mr. Finn and I agree wi' ye!" As ever in moments of high emotion, the Scots burr that he largely suppressed re-entered his voice.

The room fell silent. Miss Garnett waved for more paper, and Jack Standish, behind her, stepped forward to bring her a sheaf, taking away the pile of notes she had compiled. Jack had, in his nearly two months of working at the Rectory, found himself tasked with all kinds of work, from the menial—preparing and serving meals in the soup kitchen—to writing book reviews for Jack Tanner's *Revolutionists' Journal.* Today, he was here to observe for the Rector, assist Miss Garnett, and to keep order if the panic of these men—none of whom had long purses to spend on a contested election—broke loose in the room. As Morrell had told him, his first order of business was to "see to Prossy's safety."

Jack had come to love the work Morrell gave him, and indeed, to love the man himself—other than in what Jack privately thought of as his cavalier treatment of Miss Garnett. Granted, she was middle class (if that), but she was pert, kind, and fearless. She deserved better, and Jack was always impeccably polite to her, causing her to semi-facetiously style him "milord," even though she knew nothing of his origins or class, other than that he was an Oxonian. That anonymity had prompted in him a level of confidence that her amity, often garbed in irony as it might be, was directed to the man, and not the title. He enjoyed watching her strong, skillful hands fly across the paper so competently.

As the silence stretched on, Phineas looked at Laurel, who nodded. Phineas rose, and leaning with both hands on the table, looked up and down the table, meeting the eyes of each of his companions. He saw anxiety, but not panic. They would do.

"Gentlemen," he began, and caught himself. "No," he corrected himself, "my friends. Yes, my friends, because we are about to undertake something together in which we will have to trust each other implicitly, and each one of us must do his share, or the whole thing collapses. If Craig Laurel and I tell you that we believe we can influence this General Election in such manner that we can prevent either Lord Fawn or Frank Greystock from becoming Prime Minister, that we can bring the Independent Labour Party out from under the shadow of the Liberal

Party, and obtain a recognised role in the next Government—will you join us?"

The men around the table did not know Phineas Finn well, though they liked what they knew of him. That he had imperiled his political life for a young miner (a fact that Laurel had shared with them, unbeknownst to Phineas) earned their respect and some level of their trust.

The two academics in the room were prepared to follow Phineas, whose experience in Government and in the House gave him the intuitive understanding and a sense for what was possible that they knew they had not yet acquired. For the other nine men around the table, that rationale was insufficient. But Craig Laurel was one of them, a man who had laboured in the mines as a boy, had his lungs torn at by the dust, and known the hazards and pains of that life himself. The men around that table, almost all of them, had come up from similar backgrounds—men who had risen through their own efforts, or, in several cases, the children of labourers who had found a means to attain education and membership in the Mother of Parliaments. That status alone represented a victory over the odds, and now, here they were, contemplating becoming players in the Great Game. They respected Phineas, but would follow Craig Laurel to the Gates of Sheol itself—and further.

At Phineas's invocation of Laurel, they bayed their assent. Laurel stood with Phineas at the head of the table, side by side. When the men had quieted, Phineas Finn began:

"It is all," he said, "a matter of numbers, and the power they can provide. Let me explain..."

When the meeting was over, Phineas was able to have a quiet word with Jack, who quickly recounted his meetings with the Bishop of Barchester and with Canon Gore, and his work for Morrell.

"You look well on it," Phineas said, clapping his godson on the shoulder. And indeed Jack did—he was enthusiastic but not febrile, calm and restful in a way that Phineas had never observed in the younger man before. With a friendly farewell, Phineas went off to see Morrell and Laurel in the rectory.

Left alone in the vestry room, Jack sat down, exhausted and exhilarated. Exhausted by the passion that had been the room—the raw panic that had building before Craig Laurel had taken the floor, and cleared the atmosphere enough that Phineas could be given a hearing. The simplicity and audacity of the plan exhilarated Jack—Labour would take a seat at the table by asserting its right thereto.

And he had been present for the beginning. He realised that, in his role at the meeting, he had brought nothing but the most humble assistance, but now he did—money! There would be expenses for all thirteen of the men, and Jack could assist in defraying them. He jumped out of his chair and began to stride through the church toward the door nearest the rectory, on the north side of the aisle. As he walked by, a small, shabby man stopped in front of him.

Miss Garnett, up at the High Altar, finished her devotions, crossed herself in a manner that would have given apoplexy to her Evangelical mother, and turned around to descend. She saw the small, shabby man, with a large protuberant nose tinged a gentle red approach Jack, clinging to his arm.

"What is it you want?" she heard Jack say. "Who are you?"

To her astonishment, she heard the little man answer with a question of his own: "Yer Lord Chiltern, ain't yer?"

Jack's answer was too low for her to hear; Miss Garnett, unthinkingly advanced a step toward him.

She took another step, heard the little man say, "Service o' papers, melord. Eustace vee John Standish, Lord Chiltern, melord. Breach o' promise," with a leer that she thought was meant to be ingratiating. Jack silently took the proffered packet.

"No gratuity, melord?" the little man said with a nasty, insinuating smile.

"I'll give you a gratuity, you—you rodent," Miss Garnett said vehemently, "be off with you, or I'll box your ears for you—with no charge!"

Miss Garnett was a small woman, with somewhat drab brown hair, although she had kind eyes, and fine features. The blaze in those normally humourous eyes was enough to frighten the little man—hardly any larger than Miss Garnett herself—and he scurried off into the shadows. Jack's nerveless fingers dropped the packet, and he walked, dazedly, back to the vestry room. Proserpine Garnett picked it up, and followed him there, only to be confronted with his back, shaking as though he was holding back some terrible convulsion.

"Jack?" she called gently.

"No, please, Miss Garnett." His voice was a wounded cry. "I had thought I could start fresh..." He swayed, shaking, not with anger, as she had first thought, but with self-loathing, and pain.

Miss Garnett was not as well-read as Jack. She was, however, far more learned in the realm of feelings and self-hatred, having known both in the context of an unrequited love—a love for her employer that had only expired when, a few years prior, his wife had come close to deserting him for another, younger man. The convoluted waves of feeling that had swept the rectory at that time had broken her fever, and taught her that Morrell had nothing for her but affection, and that even his affection came liberally laced with a patronising, well-meaning superiority. Miss Garnett recognised in Jack a sorrow and a loss of confidence like unto her own, and believed she now understood why the young man was so quiet, and why he never drank wine or spirits. She, too, had tried to drown her sorrows in the bad old days.

Dry sobs racked Jack's throat. He could not abide that a woman, especially this woman, should see him break down. He had hoped, prayed, that he would be spared this, and yet had it come. But not in front of Miss Garnett. He tried to turn, drowning in his anxiety, and ask her to leave, but the shame and sorrow struck him again, like a wave engulfing a spent swimmer, almost at shore, but just far enough out to drown, if the wave caught him. He fell into a chair, and tried to turn away from her, to hide the unmanly tears.

She sat in the chair next to his, and drew his unresisting body to her. She cradled him against her, his head to her bosom. "There, there," she said softly, "I'm here, I'm not going anywhere." Looking down on him tenderly, she held him gently and firmly, comforting him by her simple presence, and acceptance of whatever trouble had fallen upon him.

The tableau lasted—who shall say how long? A minute, ten? Long enough that Jack felt whole, restored to himself by her comforting presence, and able to think again. He moved free from her embrace, and, taking her hands in his own, met her eyes.

"I should be ashamed that you saw me behave in so unmanly a way," he observed.

"Are you?"

"No." He paused a moment. "There is nobody else who could have comforted me as you have."

"Nobody? That is sad, Jack."

"Not if you meant what you said. That you are not going anywhere..." His eyes questioned her.

"Not if you want me..." Her own eyes and her sudden blush gave him the reply he sought. He drew a deep breath; and suddenly, in spite of everything, Jack Standish marveled to find that the sense of peace that had eluded him for so long had come upon him in that meeting of the eyes.

"Then I am safe. But this lawsuit—it is for breach of promise."

"I do not believe it of you."

"It is true," he said. "There were reasons, but I did the thing."

"Did you love her?"

"No." He was quite sure, now. "I did not. I desired her, and she knew it, and made me think that was love."

"And now?"

"Now I know better." His arms closed firmly about her, and he kissed her. "My godfather, Mr. Finn, is in with Morrell, even now. He is a barrister, and will know what can be done, if he has not yet left."

"I understand," Miss Garnett said. "Go to him."

Jack rose, and walked, a little shaken, to the door.

Now it was Miss Garnett's turn to feel shame. She had, she felt, humiliated herself—mistaken the boy's need for comfort for something more—a kindling of passion for herself, drab little church mouse though she wa—

"Proserpine," she heard his voice, and slewed her head to see him, absurdly handsome, serene now, framed in the door, hand extended to her in mute invitation.

"Come with me?"

"To see your godfather?" She heard the hope in her voice and cursed herself for it.

He grinned openly. "Well. That'll do for a start."

She rose, thinking to herself, *so this is joy*, and went to meet his godfather properly.

THE OPENING SKIRMISHES

A June wedding date had been chosen by Clarissa and Savrola in consultation with Marie long before there was any reason to think that the summer would be notable for anything other than the normal London torpor. Now, of course, the Finns found themselves engulfed in war on two flanks—Jack's breach of promise suit, and the General Election. The latter would take place in July, and, Phineas reflected, the campaign season would be like life in Thomas Hobbes' state of nature: Nasty, brutish and short.

The Conservatives, perhaps scenting potential division in the voters of Tankerville, had sent in a promising young man by the name of Despard-Smith to get blooded in his first campaign. The Liberals, officially headless now, and with Lord Fawn (or, rather, Sir William McScuttle) making his play for dominance within the Party had sent a serious man, one of McScuttle's own lieutenants, to retain Tankerville for the Liberals. That lieutenant, a former naval officer named John Rowland, had clearly been sent with instructions to wrest the seat from Phineas Finn by means fair or foul. His speeches suggested that Finn was an enemy of Capital, and would dissipate the resources of the Nation in a well-meaning but ultimately fruitless effort to reward the idle, the shiftless, and all those who expected to eat without working.

Rowland waxed biblical in one speech, declaiming, "Mr. Finn has forgotten the word of the Apostle to the Gentiles, who said 'This we commanded you, that if any would not work, neither should he eat!' But

Mr. Finn would reverse this age-old precept, encouraging the idler, the ruffian, the one who takes, rather than he who makes!"

On another occasion, in front of the Yellow Hotel, Rowland attacked Phineas as unstable, saying, "What worse can be said of a man than that he has participated in not one, but two duels! A man of violence, Mr. Phineas Finn has shown himself to be, a man utterly lacking in bottom, a traitor to his Party and to his class!"

Mr. Quintus Slide, ever on the lookout for a good story, and delighting as ever especially in any which were deleterious to Phineas Finn, sought an interview with Mr. Rowland. Ensconced in the saloon bar, with the staff McScuttle had provided and Tankervillians who had come to his banners, Rowland was at his ease.

"You have used strong words, sir, of Mr. Finn," the journalist began. "Traitor to his Party. Traitor to his class. Can you justify them?" Slide's ingratiating grin reassured the aspiring politico that the question was asked in the hope that indeed Rowland could, and Mr. Rowland was intelligent enough to perceive this.

"Indeed I can, sir," he answered. "Mr. Finn's departure from the Liberal Party was the direct result of his subverting, in the interests of a client of his, the procedure by which pardons are considered. When the late Government declined to forward his client's application to Her Majesty, why, Mr. Finn side-stepped the Government, and approached the Throne directly."

"And what sort of man was this pardon for?"

"Oh, a common enough criminal," Rowland answered airily, "a young Welsh tough who attacked his foreman in a mine. A socialist rioter"—Rowland's flight of fancy had now caught wing—"a despoiler of property and violator of order, who did not know his proper place! Just the sort of man a radical like Finn would break all the rules for!"

Quintus Slide wrote all this up, and featured it on the front page of *The People's Banner* at the beginning of June. He fully expected some response from Phineas Finn, but not the one he received.

On the first Monday of that month—June 7, as it happened—the editor was eating his elevenses at his chipped and battered rolltop desk, trying to decide between two stories for the lead—one, an industrial accident story, which he had titled "Sons of Toil Buried Beneath Tons of Soil," and the other a description of the latest triumph of Marshall-Hall down the Old Bailey, in which he cast the Great Defender as an agent of social decay. When Miss Allen looked in, her sharp-featured face surmounted with auburn hair, and framed by the crisp winged collar of her pure white blouse, her usual air of severity had left her.

"A Mr. Finn to see you, Mr. Slide," she informed him, a touch of unwonted mischief in her face. "Will you see him?"

And before Quintus Slide could respond, his old enemy breezed in, quite as if it were his office, and not Slide's. Slide was about to expostulate with her—or with Finn, he really was not sure—when the Irishman took his hand, shook it, and claimed a chair.

"Of course he will, Miss Allen!" Phineas Finn cried cheerfully. "After all, the *Banner* does not bear malice towards those it criticises, eh, Mr. Slide?"

"All right, all right, Finn. Leave us, Jean." And when Miss Allen had complied with her employer's request, Mr. Slide scowled at Phineas and asked: "What do you want, Finn?"

"To reassure you," answered Phineas, quite pleasantly, "that I have no intention of bringing an action against you, Mr. Slide."

"An action!" the Editor nearly shouted. "What kind of action could you bring?"

"For defamation, of course, Mr. Slide."

"Defamation?" The Editor's veins stood out at his temples.

"My dear Slide, calm yourself. I did say that I am not bringing an action, did I not? You should be pleased. Perhaps even a little grateful, I should have thought. After all, you would not want to be embroiled in a defamation suit. Very nasty things, they are—especially one involving His Royal Highness."

Quintus Slide looked bewilderedly at Phineas. "His…Royal… Highness…?"

"I am informed it was the Prince who urged Her Majesty to pardon poor Mr. Powlett-Jones, and your article does rather suggest that Her Majesty was ill-advised on that score. Of course," and Phineas's tone now grew severe, "I cannot guarantee that as things stand His Royal

Highness will not conclude that you have defamed him, and bring such an action."

"The Prince? Bring an action?"

Now, Mr. Slide was happy to carp, in a purely amusing way, at the Palace from a safe distance, but he knew one thing about his readers: they were, by and large, devoted to the Throne. And *The People's Banner* could ill afford to differ too much with the loyalties of its readership.

"Of course," continued Phineas, as if working through a problem with a client, "if you were to do another story, one that set out the truth of poor Powlett-Jones's circumstances—why, I cannot imagine the Prince would pursue the matter. After all, it behooves him to be magnanimous, and you weren't to know, if your informant passed on inaccurate information."

"No, no, that is true, Finn—Mr. Finn—I only can print what they tells me, as you know."

"Of course, Mr. Slide. Who could do more? Though I doubt the Court would see it that way—you know how conservative judges are. And no doubt *The Jupiter* would enjoy the spectacle—you are, after all, a major competitor...I believe the Germans have a word for it—*Schadenfreude*, is it not?"

"What would you have me do?" Slide asked, near panic.

"Why, write another story. Meet Powlett-Jones yourself. And tell the truth about him. After all, Mr. Slide, does it not occur to you that we may be near a great re-alignment of the electorate?"

"What do you mean, Mr. Finn?"

"If the Liberals are trying to represent the same business interests as the Conservatives, and we now have expanded the suffrage—well, does it not occur to you how well placed you are?"

"How well placed I am?"

"*The People's Banner*, I mean. As the people's right to vote is recognised, and their voice is heard, the party that seeks to represent them is likely to grow—and that right quickly. While those parties that seek to divide the wealthy classes between them—well, they are fighting over a pie which is largely eaten, and ignoring the new voters, who are the mass of England."

"The Labour Party?" Slide was skeptical.

Phineas nodded. "The party of the people," he said quite simply, "and the party of your readers, once it declares its independence. Oh, it will take a decade or two before Labour is equal to either Conservative or Liberal as a party—but that's where all the growth will be."

Quintus Slide stared at Phineas. "You really believe that, don't you?"

The Irishman smiled and rose to depart. "If I am right, it will be the story of the Century—and I mean the Century that is about to begin. The first reporter to get that story—well, as I say, it will be a sea-change in English politics. Let me know if you wish to see Mr. Powlett-Jones, in any event." He glanced at the two articles on Slide's desk, and, catching one up, extended it to the Editor. "Ah. I shall look forward to seeing this on the front page of *The People's Banner.* It was a similar mining accident, you know, that was *prevented* from reaching a similar level of tragedy, precisely by the heroic actions of Ifor Powlett-Jones. Perhaps you can do a series."

"That I would like to do, Mr. Finn. As to the other—I will consider what you say. Most carefully, I do assure you."

"Good day, Mr. Slide."

"Good day, Mr. Finn."

And with that, Phineas Finn took his departure. Slide heard his voice speaking to Miss Allen on his way out through his office door, and her velvet laughter in response, but could not make out his words. He wondered whether he was being handed a thumping great opportunity, or used with greater skill than the Irishman had displayed in their prior dealings. Ultimately, he realised, the answer could very well be—both.

In the last two weeks of May, and the first two weeks of June, Phineas Finn seemed to be constantly in motion. Sir William McScuttle had ended support to the Lib-Labs, and brought forth challengers to each of them. Thus, in addition to his role in making arrangements for the wedding, Phineas was busy disbursing funds and advice to his fellow Labour members to assist them in staving off the assault on their seats from both the Liberals and the Conservatives. The Liberal candidates chosen by Sir William for the boroughs currently represented by Lib-Labs were men of his own stamp, many recruited from the ranks of his own enterprises. Some were popular locally, and in at least three boroughs, it would clearly be touch-and-go. For Phineas's strategy to work, Labour must hold all the Lib-Lab seats, and its three independent seats. There was no margin for error.

Marie Finn was in charge at Tankerville, as her husband busied himself with the races scattered across the country, including that of the newly declared ILP candidate, the youngest Mr. Camperdown, standing in a borough in which the Lib-Lab member declined to run due to some financial irregularities, which he feared Sir William would bring to light.

But Mr. Camperdown was not the only new recruit. An elderly Lib-Lab in Ireland announced that he simply could not stand for re-election —his health would not permit it. Phineas quickly moved, and recruited his old friend Sinclair Yeates, a retired army officer who had become popular as a resident magistrate in the borough of Skebawn, to stand for election. He had lost precious time travelling to Ireland, and met the Major and his wife for tea in Shreelane House, the Major's slightly ramshackle but comfortable residence.

"Me, a Labour candidate?" Major Yeates had laughed. His wife Philippa had looked interested, however, and Phineas had pressed the point.

"Craig Laurel says we need men of education, of experience, and he is right, Yeates. The Conservatives and the Liberals are both chasing the money-men. Surely you don't want them ruling everything, do you?"

"Well, of course not, Finn, but I doubt the lads down at the local exchange would think of me as a champion of the working man, you know."

"Would they not?" Phineas smiled. "Yeates, this is Ireland. You know what we Irish say, don't you? That the Irish and the English know each other like the fox and the hound?"

"Ah, but which is which?" Major Yeates enquired.

To his surprise, it was his wife who answered the Major's question. "That depends on whom you ask, surely," Philippa Yeates replied surely, with a small smile. "You must do it, Sinclair."

"But as a Labour member, Philippa. What would they say in the Regiment?"

"Congratulations, if you win," she replied pertly enough, and they all three laughed.

"All right, Finn. You can count on me. As long as you don't expect me to dress as a navvy, that is," he added with a subfusc smile of his own. After tea, Phineas returned to his hotel, where Mrs. Rafferty managed to put together a meal that was unusually palatable by her standards. He was joined by another old friend, Mr. Florence Knox.

"As a Labourite?" Mr. Knox was amazed. "Yeates is willing to stand as a Labourite?"

"I would have asked you to stand, Flurry," Phineas said, sipping his rather indifferent port, "only I knew you wouldn't have touched it on a bet."

"Would I not?" The younger man was unsure whether to be amused or offended.

"Half the year in Westminster? With no pay? Or expenses? When you could be left as factotum by Yeates, and could organise his victory."

"Something in that, Mr. Finn, something in that."

"And if you stood—as either a Labour or a Liberal candidate—the Conservatives would be bound to ask Yeates. And with the suffrage limited as it is here—why, he might very well have won, and hard feelings between you, then"

Mr. Knox pursed his lips, and thought. "Then you've dealt us a hand that will suit us all, Mr. Finn. I'll see the Major through, and serve in his absence, if he wants me."

"Good man, Flurry. You'll need money of course, for expenses."

"That I will, Mr. Finn. Where will that come from?"

"The ILP will be advancing you reasonable funds. Reasonable, mind. Remember the goose and her golden eggs, Flurry."

Mr. Knox grinned broadly. "Reasonable is it I'm to be? Very well, I shall be, Mr. Finn. Who will the Conservatives get, anyway?"

"Well, having nobbled the candidate they wanted, Flurry—I'm not sure I care."

Mr. Knox clinked glasses with Phineas, and after a little desultory talk, they parted. Phineas Finn began his trip back to England the next day.

In addition, Phineas had to take steps with respect to the affairs of his godson. He had referred Jack to the youngest Mr. Camperdown, and, after Camperdown had been retained, he in his turn instructed Phineas as Jack's barrister. Phineas and Mr. Camperdown met several times, and, when Mr. Camperdown filed the answer to Lady Eustace's claim, it included, in addition to the rote denials, demurrers, and exceptions, several affirmative defences intended to non-suit Her Ladyship. One defence in particular caught her eye; that "Upon information and belief, the defendant says, that after making the supposed promise and undertaking in the declaration mentioned, and prior to any intermarriage with the said ELIZABETH EUSTACE, he received notice and information that the plaintiff was not free to marry, being the lawful spouse of one JOSEPH EMILIUS; and that the defendant does therefore demand judgment dismissing the action."

"Scoundrel!" Lady Eustace exclaimed upon reading the copy of the Answer forwarded to her by Mr. Rushforth. (Mr. Rushforth was far too intelligent to deliver it himself, and even Mr. Bindtheboy's adulation of the Lady gave way here to a prudent respect for his own skin.)

"Who is that, my dear?" Joseph Emilius, lounging in a settee, inquired casually.

"The young Mr. Camperdown," said Lady Eustace, "is every bit as bad as his father was before him. He claims that I am legally unavailable to marry—that I am still married to you."

"Indeed, my dearest? Yet here I am, ready to go through it all again, just to make sure the thing is done properly."

"This wretched man Camperdown is spreading lies about me so that his cowardly client will not have to face up to the wrong he has done me. And all you can do is jest?"

"What would you have me do?" Bishop Emilius' voice was unusually gentle, lacking its normal music.

"You, living with the Marchioness, what would you do? You say you want me for your wife, but what risk have you taken for me? What sacrifice will you make for me?" Lizzie's rage died down, and, all fret and affectation exhausted for the moment, she looked, just for an instant, every day of her age. Almost plaintively, she added, "How on earth can I trust you, Joseph? Even if I love you enough to marry you a second time, how can I believe it will be any different than it was before?"

"These past months…" he began to offer.

"Prove nothing," she rejected the suggestion. "Nothing, other than that which I already knew—that you and I are, in some very real way, compatible. But trust requires more than that, does it not?"

He thought a moment. "And you need more than our … compatibility, to engender trust sufficient to return to me?"

"Oh, Joseph," Lady Eustace sighed, and his heart rose within him for an instant, only to tumble back to earth when she continued, "of course I do."

His eyes flared, and he stood, his languid demeanour replaced by a sudden access of energy.

"Then of course you must have it, my dear." He took her hand, raising it to his lips, and kissed it. He then turned, and left.

HASTE TO THE WEDDING

Clarissa Riley awoke earlier than she would have liked on the day of her wedding. She was conscious of the servants stirring below, making the final preparations for the event itself. Pulling on her dressing gown and her slippers, she tip-toed to the stairs and descended just far enough to look into the parlor.

There was Meier, fully dressed, confident-looking, not a hair (of the few he sported) out of place, re-grown military mustache at the ready. The servants were lined up for his review, and he paced up and down, inspecting them.

"*Also*," he said—not the English conjunctive, but the German word that had no exact parallel in English, but could be approximated by "so" or "well" as an introduction to a sentence—"*Also*, my friends, today our Miss Clarissa leaves us. Madame and Mr. Phineas will have eyes only for her today, but we will do better, yes?"

"Yes, Mr. Meier," Frau Forstmann, the housekeeper, replied, also scrutinizing the staff closely.

"We will do our young lady the honour of a send-off worthy of her—and of the love we bear her—will we not?"

Thomas the Boots nodded especially hard at this; his infatuation with the young lady of the house had been evident for some time. Meier stalked along the line one more time, and, catching a glint in a highly polished sideboard he added, "Yes, we will give a send-off befitting a proper lady, because she is *not* a mischievous girl who would spy down the stairs in her dressing gown, is she? Well, is she, staff?"

"No, Mr. Meier!" The staff roared with one voice, several cheeky grins breaking out among the parlor maids.

"Meier!" Clarissa wailed, and came down the steps to confront her old friend.

He whirled, his face a total blank. "*Guten Morgen, gnädiges Fraulein*!"

She tried to look disapproving and lady-of-the-house-ish, but *protégée* of the former Madame Max Goesler though she was, she had been Barbara Riley's daughter for far longer. The slight twitch of Meier's lips betrayed his amusement, and she walked over to him, and embraced the major-domo. She then kissed Frau Forstmann, and, grinning, said to the staff:

"How very kind you have all been to me, and how very grateful I am to you all. You make me so confident that everything will go swimmingly today. And I will miss you all so very much when I go away..."

"We'll miss you, too, Miss," said Thomas the Boots, only to be lightly cuffed by Jenkins the under-butler.

"And so we all shall," Meier said, patting Thomas on the shoulder. "Any last instructions for today, Miss?"

Clarissa fondly smiled, shaking her head. "I wouldn't presume, Meier."

"Breakfast in half an hour, Miss Clarissa?" Frau Forstmann enquired.

"Yes, please Frau Forstmann—and thank you all so much!"

And with that, Clarissa Riley went upstairs. On her way up, she heard Meier's voice once more. "All right, then. To your stations. And—make me proud today."

Last night she had been distinctly nervous about the wedding, but somehow the bustling, cheerful staff put heart in her. She returned to her room, trailed part of the way by her lady's maid, who began to run her bath. As Clarissa heard the splash of the water against the porcelain of the tub, she thought back on her rashness in accepting Savrola on such short knowledge of him.

She had been, she reflected, greatly curious about life, and conscious of a profound desire to participate in every experience that might fall to the lot of a woman. She felt impelled to hurry to meet life and its challenges, to join the stream of life, whether or not she fully comprehended her role therein. She had seen herself as just one drop in a turbulent, ever moving, bubbling stream. But Savrola had, when she mentioned this conceit to him, simply smiled.

"Ah," he replied, "but some of the drops sparkle."

Now that the day itself had begun, Clarissa felt keyed up, but not exactly anxious. Excited, that was the word. Early on in her engagement, she had been fearful that she had plunged too quickly, leaped before sufficient looking. Words in her mother's old copy of Elizabeth Barrett Browning had driven her to her uncle's study late one night for comfort. Finding him at his desk reviewing a brief, despite the lateness of the hour—had it been for Ifor, whom she was starting to think of as the brother she had always longed for, but never had? Perhaps—in any event, she had not hesitated to interrupt him.

Wordlessly, she had showed her uncle the passage:

Unless you can think, when the song is done,
No other is soft in the rhythm;
Unless you can feel, when left by One,
That all men else go with him;
Unless you can know, when unpraised by his breath,
That your beauty itself wants proving;
Unless you can swear "For life, for death!" —
Oh, fear to call it loving!

Uncle Phineas had read the poem carefully through. He looked at her over his reading glasses, and said to Clarissa, "Mrs. Browning was a gifted poet, no doubt, but she puts things forcefully, simply, as poets often do. Look here, at the next stanza." He pointed, and Clarissa read:

Unless you can muse in a crowd all day
On the absent face that fixed you;
Unless you can love, as the angels may,
With the breadth of heaven betwixt you;

Unless you can dream that his faith is fast,
Through behoving and unbehoving;
Unless you can die when the dream is past —
Oh, never call it loving!

Uncle Phineas had waited until she had looked up from the page, and said, in his gentlest voice, "My friend the Duke of Omnium did not die when the dream was past—and his love was not perfect or idyllic, but tempestuous, and with all the contrarieties and squalls of life. Yet he loved, and she loved, as truly as ever a couple did. Do not let Mrs. Browning frighten you, my dear."

"Uncle Phineas, you were married once before, Mother told me."

"Yes, Clarissa, I was."

"Did you love my Aunt Mary?"

Phineas had then paused a moment. "When I first told her I did, I thought that was the case. I later came to realise that, although I cared for her, I did not love her as I could best love a woman, and I married her nonetheless. In doing so, I did us both a great injustice—she was a lovely girl, and could have found someone who would have loved her as she deserved."

After a little while, Clarissa had asked, in a small voice, "Did she know?"

"I sincerely hope not, Clarissa. She died so soon, you see, that she may not have." The pain in his voice startled her. "I lost not only Mary, but the son she bore me—he died only a few hours after his mother."

"What was his name?" she asked.

"Malachi. After my father, your grandfather, my dear girl. How he would have loved you."

She leaned up against him for a moment, and then murmured:

"So I should not let Mrs. Browning frighten me, then?"

"Do you love Savrola—in your heart, truly, as far as you know your heart?"

"Yes."

"Then be at ease," he had said, "and trust to your heart."

In the months since, her feelings had become ever more clear, and ever stronger. Her love had been confirmed by a barrage of experiences—the suspenseful ordeal of viewing Ifor's trial together, Savrola's willingness to assist her uncle, and then later his assiduous care, not only for her, but for her uncle and for Aunt Marie when her uncle had been injured, his regular letters sent from the House when speeches were dull, enlivened by little drawings of the long-winded speakers, and of Savrola himself, as a little be-suited pig, snoozing in his seat. All these things had endeared him to her, and the terrible fear that she had undergone when his own life was endangered had taught her that her uncle had been right. She knew, on her wedding day, that she loved and was loved, and could acknowledge it without fear.

Her bath ready, Clarissa prepared to meet the day.

The day was, thank heaven, fine. Nary a wisp of cloud disturbed the pale egg-blue of the sky, and the warmth of the day was caressing, not stifling. The chapel on the property had been long disused, but not deconsecrated, and, as a gesture to Phineas, the Reverend James Morrell had agreed to conduct the service. Clarissa had been raised Church of Ireland by her mother, which Phineas had respected, but Marie Finn suspected that Morrell would have found a way through, had that not been the case.

Of the wedding service itself, there is little enough to say; it is quite short, and the Prayer Book's vows are universally known. That Savrola recited his vows steadily, with a bit of a boom to his voice that was not usually present, and that Clarissa said hers without trembling, but with happy confidence, is true, as is that Phineas gave the bride away with due gravity. Clarissa's aunts wept, but not so much as to embarrass themselves, their husbands shook Savrola's hand, and clapped him on the back amiably enough.

On seeing Clarissa surrounded by a phalanx of uncles, Dolly Longestaffe was heard to remark that the Finns' house would be the safest place in London one could wish for in the event of a Fenian uprising.

Hermione Longestaffe giggled and swatted her husband's arm gently with her fan, suggesting that Dolly's new policy of spending time in the company of his wife was paying dividends; on their arrival, Mrs. Longestaffe had described him to Marie Finn as having "become positively uxorious, my dear!"

"Oh, dear," replied Mrs. Finn, "I do hope you can bear the imposition."

"It is too, too bad," Dolly himself had interjected, slyly smiling, "why, I have discovered that Hermione actually has *views* on things. Most refreshing views they are, too."

"Are they?" Mrs. Finn was amused.

"Considerably more entertaining than watching old Felix Carbury try to count cards, at any rate. And the old girl gets in a better class of port for me than what we get at the Club."

And so the Longestaffes seemed to have found a new *modus vivendi*, and one which continued the Longestaffe policy of moderation, as their family was soon to be, Mrs. Longestaffe blushingly informed her hostess, moderately larger come the New Year.

Morrell limited his sermon to the joys of matrimony, to the disappointment of Philippa Yeates, who had been hoping for a good Socialist diatribe with which to tease Sinclair about his comrades-in-arms. Alas, the good Reverend spoke only of the interdependence of husband and wife, of their making possible through their love the full flowering of each partner to the marriage, in terms that brought nods from the handful of "New Women" in the congregation, while the older stagers (such as Sinclair himself) looked slightly dubious.

During the sermon, Dolly Longestaffe had commented to Mrs. Longestaffe that Morell "seems to put his wife on a bit of pedestal, old girl," only to be pleasantly surprised by her arch reply, "As long as she gets a good dusting every now and again, Dolly."

The Duke of Omnium sat next to his own *fiancée*, less stiffly than was his wont, and Lady Laura watched the proceedings with open satisfaction. A little toward the back at the chapel, the Earl and Countess of Brentford beamed at the young couple. The Earl could be heard to whisper at one point "Be piping my eye next, Vi—our little orphan girl looks like a princess!"

As indeed she did, for her Aunt Marie had exercised her notable taste to good effect; and while it is axiomatic that all brides must be beautiful, Clarissa bid fair to outshine them all on this happiest of happy days. The ivory silk of her bodice fitted her slender waist to a nicety, flaring out gracefully into a skirt which trailed into a four foot train that Savrola was at great pains not to tread upon. The gown's sleeves and its over-skirt were a cascade of snowy Irish lace that frothed and bubbled like Clarissa's own joyous laughter, and about her milky neck was clasped the double strand of the famous Vavasor pearls her *fiancé* had given her as a wedding gift. Her little hand, clad in a white kid glove, through which a slit on the glove's third finger afforded a glimmer of the wide golden band Savrola had so recently slipped onto the finger itself, held an intricate bouquet composed of orange blossoms, maidenhair, noisette roses, trailing ivy and – the ultimate tribute to Clarissa's place of privilege in his affections - several of Meier's finest white orchids.

On the groom's side of the congregation, Frank Greystock himself, and his wife Lucy, grown even prettier with age, if perhaps a little plumper, honoured the spirit of truce that the Finn nuptials represented. More notably, perhaps, the mother of the groom was dazzling in a peacock-blue moire Paquin and escorted by a clearly doting Trubshawe. When they had come in together, Savrola had rolled his eyes, and muttered to Phineas Finn, "Lord help me, sir, I think that chap could end up my stepfather."

"Do you indeed?" Ifor Powlett-Jones, whom Savrola had asked to stand up with him, was transfixed at the spectacle.

"I dread it. He's a good fellow, and I'm grateful to him for Heidelberg, but one doesn't want a stepfather who's a year one's junior. I'll be the laughingstock of the Tories."

Powlett-Jones put in, "Aren't you already in trouble for having a Welsh socialist as a best man?"

Savrola grinned, "No, you don't, Ifor. No escape for you. Greystock's put it down to my family connections. Besides, he thinks we need to start courting the working man's vote, too. Can't leave it all to your lot."

Phineas shook his head, smiling a bit. "Greystock," he said, "has got his head properly screwed on. Which is more than can be said for Lord Fawn, so life at Westminster could become very interesting come the new Parliament."

And so the service went smoothly, and the connubial knot was securely fashioned.

As the guests spilled out of the chapel and onto the sward where refreshment tents were set up in various ranks of splendour, the happy couple made their way toward the central one. Across their path was Jack Standish, and with him Miss Proserpine Garnett; uncertain of his welcome, it had taken all of Jack's courage to accept Savrola's surprising invitation. Heart filled to overflowing, Savrola called out quite as naturally as if they had been lifelong friends, "Hallo, Standish! Missed you in the chapel!"

Jack, a little uneasily, came forward. Miss Garnett moved with him, her nearness making this awkward moment just a little less so.

"Hallo, Vavasor," he began, adding, "You've never looked lovelier, Clarissa. I'm happy for you."

Clarissa relented; how was she to be unforgiving on her wedding day? She smiled at her courtesy-cousin, emboldening him to kiss her on the cheek, and to take Savrola's outstretched hand. Relieved beyond measure, Jack brought Miss Garnett a little closer.

"Vavasor, Clarissa, I'd like you to meet my intended, Miss Proserpine Garnett."

Clarissa was surprised; the woman—she doubted if Miss Garnett could be called a lady—was thirty if a day, and, even in her festal best—a sturdy, snuff-coloured poplin, enlivened by a nosegay of violets—undeniably dowdy. Yet Jack looked at this Miss Garnett as if he had made up his own soul in finding this woman. The strained look had left his eyes, and he seemed, now that he was sure of his welcome, more at ease than Clarissa could ever remember him.

Savrola was in that state of happiness that only wants to see the rest of the world as contented as himself. He exclaimed delightedly at Jack's news, and shook his hand again.

"Well done, Standish!" he cried, and then, taking Miss Garnett's hand, added, "I am delighted to meet you, Miss Garnett, and wish you both every joy."

Clarissa smiled warmly, more at her husband's—and the unaccustomed word warmed her heart, even as the thought crossed her mind—spontaneous rejoicing with he who rejoices, and took Miss Garnett's hand, too. Thinking to herself, "In for a penny, in for a pound," she invited the other couple, "You must go in with us."

"Oh, no," Jack demurred, "it's your day."

"Not at all; I insist," Clarissa replied. Unsure of their ground, Jack and Proserpine looked at each other, only for Savrola to settle the matter.

"Come along," he said smiling, "You can't deny a bride her wish on her wedding day, can you? Bad form, to say the least."

And the two couples walked forward together.

Behind them, the Finns and the Earl and Countess of Brentford saw the whole thing.

"Is that young woman with Jack one of us?" the Countess asked.

"Doubt it," her husband answered. "Don't know that I'm prepared to make an issue of it, though, if she's good for him. Not after all he's been through."

Violet looked outraged for a moment, and then smiled a little ruefully. "No. Well, it's my side of the family coming out in him, no doubt."

"Eh?"

"We are willing to take matrimonial risks that most would balk at, you know."

Behind them, the Finns formed the rear of the impromptu procession toward the tents.

"Savrola is wise beyond his years," Marie Finn remarked, watching the two young men enjoying an animated discussion.

"Oh?" Phineas asked.

"Yes," Marie replied. "He has learned already one of the great lessons."

"And that would be?"

"In victory, magnanimity."

THE LOST LEADER

Marie Finn was stretched comfortably on the settee in her parlor, the broadsheet tented over her head, concealing her visage from observation. Unusually for her, she was perusing *The People's Banner* with relish, her contralto laughter bubbling up from within. Across from her, reading the same newspaper with a more muted, but effectively identical response, Lady Laura Kennedy was astonished. Finishing the piece, she let the broadsheet pages fall from her grasp, wafting gently to the floor.

"Astounding," Lady Laura said.

Marie also let the *Banner* drop to the Axminster.

"Remarkable," she agreed with her friend.

"If Phineas had been able to manage that twenty years ago…" Lady Laura mused.

"Or even last year…" Marie Finn agreed.

Meier, having left the tea for the ladies, plucked the discarded copies of the journal from the floor and removed them for incineration. On his way to the incinerator, however, he re-read the article, with a quiet, wry smile. How he wished he had been present for the discussion that had led to it!

Come the Age, Come the Man

This page noted last year, in reporting the injuries of Mr. Phineas Finn, the Member for Tankerville, a new maturity and purpose in his efforts to avert bloodshed caused by a violent quarrel between a Tory and a Socialist peer. That a member of the aristocracy should espouse such principles is a sign that the voice of labour is beginning to make its voice heard, and that the long night in which those who toil remain voiceless in the political councils in the nation is at last drawing to an end, and the first lambent rays of dawn begin to warm the Earth.

In such a time as this, old alliances fail, and old enmities prove to have outlived their usefulness. So it has proven when the Liberal Party candidate for Tankerville provided us with false information, purporting to demonstrate that error was the basis for the pardon Her Majesty so graciously bestowed on that sorrowful son of Wales, who, after saving the lives of his brother workers in the Stygian depths of the coal mines, was cruelly persecuted by the owner of that mine, a grasping Gradgrind without pity or ruth.

But THE PEOPLE'S BANNER *has conducted its own investigation (see page 4), and can now reveal the* TRUTH*—that Ifor Paulet-Jones was the victim of foul play, an injustice brought to light by his barrister, and remedied swiftly, decisively, by the* QUEEN HERSELF.

Worse even than the foul play attempted by the aspirant to represent the Good People of Tankerville, THE PEOPLE'S BANNER *has also uncovered the unpalatable truth that* MR. JOHN ROWLAND, *the Liberal candidate for Tankerville, has been and remains in the pay of that very Gradgrind—Sir* WILLIAM MCSCUTTLE, *notorious for the Legree-like cruelty of the mines he runs, slum owner, and partner in Sir Horace Bodger's rum-pots and distilleries. (See page 5)*

In all of these inquiries, Your Editor has been forced to recognise that the Liberal Party is not what it was in the days when Barrington Erle took office, or when the Duke of Omnium held sway. LORD FAWN *no doubt means well, but is a mere titled understrapper, propelled by a richer man's lucre, what these days cry out for? Rather, in turning to join his lot with that of the Working Man,* MR. PHINEAS FINN *has, at long last, reached out to grasp the bright destiny which we have long hoped that he would seize, breaking from a senescent party to add a Voice of Experience to a new and untried one, bright with hope, but needing the tempering of practicality to transform its Castles-in-the Air into the Many Mansions of Tomorrow.*

Meier sighed expressively. He sincerely hoped that the change in tone would not induce Madame to take in *The People's Banner.* His gloves already needed changing often enough, and the poorly set ink smeared almost as greasily as the words they made out.

Journalists, thought Meier, *Always at your throat or at your feet.*

The *volte-face* of Quintus Slide was well-timed, and the resultant confusion of the forces of Rowland bade fair to turn the election in Tankerville to a rout for them. Phineas was regularly in the borough, addressing meetings, answering questions about his changed affiliation, reassuring the business interests of Tankerville—of whom, after all, he and his wife numbered themselves, he was not slow to point out—that he was no foe of profit. At one meeting, where the merchants of Tankerville were predominant, he drew a laugh by challenging greed as the enemy, not entrepreneurship: "A friend of mine in the City reminded me of the great slogan of our American cousins: 'Bulls may thrive, bears may thrive—but pigs are marked for slaughter.'"

The businessmen of Tankerville were somewhat satisfied by Phineas's proclamation of the reasonableness of his goals; to the extent that they were not, Phineas was unapologetic. "I refuse to treat my fellow citizens simply as tools," he answered one questioner, "as a means to my own profit and as nothing more. And if that answer is not sufficient for you, why, your remedy is to vote for one of the other candidates."

But it was among the working men and women of Tankerville, not all yet enfranchised, but more of them able to vote than at any prior time in the borough's history that Phineas enjoyed his greatest success. Listening to their complaints at his constituency "surgery," entering their pubs to share a beer, answer questions, and make his presence felt, Phineas found himself as always enjoying the company of his constituents. Like the men his father had treated in Ireland, his constituents' hard-headed bluntness sometimes hid their good nature to those who had not come to know them, but in his decades as their Member of Parliament, Phineas had known them too long to be unsure of their welcome.

In the pubs, especially, the men and women felt free to ask their questions, and Phineas soon found himself surrounded. Most of the questions were friendly, though the occasional die-hard Liberal accused him of apostasy, or the odd Tory truculently declared his loyalty to "t'other side." When old Aysgarth the Gardener had growled that, Phineas had laughed, and ordered the man a pint.

"With my compliments," Phineas said. "And no hard feelings." Phineas offered the old man his hand, and Aysgarth accepted it. Phineas was later not a little put out, though, when he went into the Fox and Hens, a miner's pub, only to discover that Ifor Powlett-Jones was at the center of a knot of workingmen and their wives, sisters and daughters, regaling them with a blush-making account of Phineas's defence of him.

Their eyes met, and Powlett-Jones grinned happily. Not wishing to embarrass the lad, Phineas raised his hat gently and left. Later that evening, having tea at the Lambton Arms, the hotel at which he always stayed in Tankerville, having won his long-ago surprise victory while using it as his base, he raised the matter with his wife, who had come up with him for these last few weeks.

"Did you know Powlett-Jones was going to be here?"

"Do you disapprove, my dear?" asked Marie Finn in her turn.

"I don't want the lad feeling he's a performing animal, Marie. He's not under any obligation to–"

Phineas stopped, as his wife, who was not prone to such things, was in fact snickering.

Seeing his perplexity, she explained: "Oh, my dear, of course he is under an obligation to you! You are giving him the *entrée* to a life beyond what he ever dared hope for himself, are you not?"

Phineas's face grew still. "We are," he said softly, "everything that I am endeavouring to do is possible because of you—not just your money–"

"Our money," Marie corrected gently.

"But because of how you have seen what we would need to wage this campaign, and how you prepared for it years in advance. Anything we accomplish in these next three weeks will be as much your achievement as mine—but how on earth did you know it would come to this?"

Marie laughed prettily. "Ah, such a feminist you have become Mr. Finn! I am glad!" Then, more seriously, "No, I am glad that I could anticipate the needs of this campaign, my dearest, but how did I know? You have never run easily in harness, and Barrington Erle, good man though he is, could not abide that. And I knew that one day it would come to a conflict between you and he, however much you both wished to avoid it. And so, like the ant in the fable, I prepared to defend Tankerville against the assault that might never come—but that now has." She spread her hands in a charming gesture of satisfaction. "And so we are well garrisoned."

"And Ifor?" Phineas asked.

"Ifor is making a down payment on his debt to you."

"To us," Phineas corrected.

"And he is feeling more like a man than he has at any time since his arrest, and, no doubt, he is doing you considerable good with the voters. What would be immodesty in you, is perfectly acceptable in him."

"How very cynical," Phineas exclaimed in an unconvincing tone of shock.

"Fortunately, you have always enjoyed my more cynical moments," she said, casting a coquettish look upon her husband.

He sat beside her, took her hand, and raised it to his lips.

"I enjoy all your moments," he replied, kissing her soft, white palm.

On the night that the final results would be tabulated and certified, Barrington Erle was ensconced in his sitting room at Number 10. The telegraph office installed in the room was now augmented by a telephone, and the Prime Minister (for so he remained for now, at least) was receiving up-to-the-minute information. Barrington sat in his armchair, moodily smoking a cigar, while his cousin, Lady Laura, tried to divert him with a running commentary about the various local elections as the returns were certified and telegraphed.

Barrington Erle was well aware that the revolt within his Party bade very fair to end his own premiership once and for all. Indeed, he had treated the matter as a foregone conclusion in the Lobby when the Naval Funding Bill went down to defeat. But now, in the last week of the General Election, he began to hope for a recrudescence. Barrington Erle knew himself to be both much more competent and much less thin-skinned than was Lord Fawn. Moreover, while members of the Upper House could and did serve as Prime Minister—why, the Duke of Omnium had done so, two decades back!—the Prime Minister who ruled from the Lords was under several disadvantages, not the least of them being the need of having a deputy as Leader of the House. Finally, Sir William McScuttle had, Barrington's spies reported, been lording it over those members who had not flocked to his banner, and might have sufficiently antagonised them that they would prefer a return of the *ancien regime* to the puppet regime of Lord Fawn. Barrington had been carefully reaching out to his friends within the caucus, and to potentially disaffected members of the Fawn faction, and he was, he thought, making progress. He had not much time for campaigning, but then a Prime Minister seldom had a serious challenger, and the Tory candidate, a fellow named Barthwick, was a young barrister, who had only recently defected from the Liberals. No bottom, Barrington Erle decided, and no threat.

"Here's one of Phineas Finn's successes," Lady Laura commented. "Who would have thought that silly Major Yeates would have stood as a Labour member? The man's a natural for the Tories if ever I've seen one."

"A good man for all that," interjected the Duke of Omnium. "And I did not find him silly—he has made rather a good fist of things in Ireland."

Barrington chuckled a little. "Yeates was one of your appointments, wasn't he, Duke?"

"Oh, no!" exclaimed Lady Laura humourously. "My dear Plantagenet, I am sorry. It's just that Major Yeates always struck me as a well-meaning little boy, hoping to be made hall monitor."

"And who better to make hall monitor, Laura?" her cousin returned with a smile. The Duke waved the whole matter off with a casual gesture and a smile at his *fiancée*.

A little silence fell, as Lady Laura sought to find a new conversational gambit. The Duke inspected his former acolyte carefully. The weeks of anxiety had told on Barrington Erle, who looked unhealthily pale, and a little bloated from his usual trim self.

Barrington checked the complex map he had made, with two-thirds of the results known already.

"So far, it looks like the ring is holding—some new faces added, some old stagers seen off—but the balance will be the same—with the Lib-Labs, and the Labs, we should still have a working majority."

A respectful knock sounded at the door. Bidden to enter, the butler at Number 10 did so, and advised the Prime Minister that Sir William McScuttle would be grateful for a word.

"Would he indeed?" Barrington Erle snorted. "Send the man in, Grayson," he agreed ungraciously. "No," the Prime Minister interrupted the Duke and Lady Laura's motion to vacate the room, "Anything Sir William has to say to me, I prefer to have witnesses to."

"Sir William McScuttle, Prime Minister," announced Grayson, and the little man bounded in amongst them.

"Sir William," Barrington Erle bowed, and added: "You know my cousin, Lady Laura Kennedy and her *fiancé*, the Duke of Omnium, I believe."

"Of course," the industrialist said, pleasantly enough, "Milord Duke, Lady Laura. Prime Minister, are you sure you would rather not be alone for this conversation?"

"You can rely entirely on the discretion of Lady Laura and the Duke, Sir William."

McScuttle smiled, with the air of one who had tried to do the decent thing but had been prevented. Now, he would do the less decent thing.

"So, Prime Minister, most of the results are in, I believe."

"Two-thirds, Sir William."

"With a few surprises, I think."

"Yes," Barrington said, with an unusual touch of malice, "I know that you went to great efforts to reclaim Tankerville for the Party. Bad luck, that."

Sir William scowled for a moment. "Yes, Finn has survived to fight another day."

Lady Laura smiled. "Oh, Plantagenet, isn't that good news? I am pleased for Phineas and Marie."

Sir William started, and glared at Lady Laura. The Duke smiled, and said, "You will excuse my *fiancée* and myself for placing ties of affection and long friendship over party loyalty. Mr. Finn is an old friend, and we are glad to hear of his good fortune."

"Well, he appears to have been lucky in Ireland, too—Yeates has squeaked in," the magnate grudgingly added.

Walking over to his map, Barrington Erle pondered. "The numbers should remain about where they were, I should think—most of the outstanding seats are safe enough, I believe."

"Most of them, yes," said Sir William.

Lady Laura had ceased to be her cousin's mentor in politics some time ago, but all her hackles were raised.

"Yes," the Prime Minister continued, "I believe we Liberals will have sufficient numbers to put together a majority."

"How good of you to care, Prime Minister." The savage note of pleasure in Sir William's voice rang every alarm bell in Lady Laura's finely honed political mind. Something was very, very wrong here. She glanced at Plantagenet. Even he seemed puzzled by the industrialist's tone, and was suddenly on the alert.

"My dear fellow," Barrington Erle's eyes were tired, but unvanquished, and his face sagged with the fatigue incurred over the past months, propping up endangered candidates while functioning as a caretaker Prime Minister. But his voice rang out with clarity and force. "I may lose the leadership contest, but at least we will be having it, and not the Tories."

"You won't lose the leadership contest, Prime Minister," Sir William said, but with an almost indecent elation, and emphasizing Barrington's title a second time, with an even rawer edge than before.

"Oh?" Barrington alone seemed unaware of the emotional currents in the room. "You've come to sign articles, then?"

"You won't be in the leadership contest, Prime Minister." Again, McScuttle's voice took on that raw edge on the title. Barrington turned away from the maps and faced the industrialist.

"And why do you say that, McScuttle?"

The coal magnate smiled almost beatifically like a clergyman about to bless a battleship. But instead of blessings, a hoarse laugh came from out his mouth.

"So sure of yerself, Erle," Sir William McScuttle cackled. "Runnin' all over England tae help the lads in trouble, to preserve the majority. And all the while not lookin' over yer shoulder at young Barthwick. And ye should have, Prime Minister, ye should have!"

Barrington Erle studied the man in front of him. The Duke rose from his chair, and stepped closer to the Prime Minister.

"Aye, ye should have because I funded him! He had money and tae spare, running about the borough, declaiming 'Time fer a change!' and 't'awd man's lost his touch!' And with you nae around tae answer him, well—he did for you!"

"He did for me?" Barrington Erle asked the question softly.

"One of those safe seats was nae so safe, Barrington Erle—and ye've been turned out of Parliament altogether!" Sir William's voice reached an almost hysterical pitch of exultation on that last phrase. Finding a more normal tone, he said "So you'll not be in that leadership contest, *Mr. Erle.*"

Lady Laura took several steps toward the industrialist, but Barrington Erle's upraised hand stayed her.

"Be so good as to leave my house, Sir William," he said, in a voice of unutterable weariness.

"It's your house no longer—*Mr. Erle,*" Sir William spat at him.

And for one moment, Barrington Erle's fatigue, the pain of this newly revealed, latest betrayal, and his resignation left him.

"It is until I am formally relieved, sir," he roared, with such ferocity that the little mine-owner stepped back in fear. "D'you think I'll treat as official any malicious tidings from a little scoundrel such as yourself? You think you can put in my place—aye, or his before me"—gesturing to the Duke—"a tailor's dummy, so that a crawling little guttersnipe like you can rule England? They won't have it." Barrington's calm had returned, but he still seemed rejuvenated, empowered by his anger.

Half-cowering, half defiant, Sir William shot back: "And who's they?"

"Imbecile," Barrington Erle contemptuously replied. "The Labour members, you jack. They might have stomached me. You? Not a hope. And they'll know it's you, of course, not Fawn, who would rule."

"And how will they know that?"

"Because we chucked out a man who witnessed you leading Fawn by the nose. Because Phineas Finn knows, and, in no small part thanks to you, he's one of the thirteen votes neither side can form a government without. Imbecile." And, suddenly weary again, the Prime Minister sat down.

"You heard the Prime Minister. Go," commanded the Duke, with a look that had quelled better men than Sir William McScuttle.

Backing toward the door, Sir William was halfway out of the room, and then he shouted "I'll be back!"

Before he could leave, though, Barrington Erle's derisive laugh reached his ears, as did the erstwhile Member of Parliament's parting words: "You'll be back? Only to deliver the coal you underpay those poor wretches to dig out of the ground."

The Duke walked to the door to make sure that Sir William had left, and then returned to the sitting room. Laura met him at the door.

"Could it be true?" she asked. Before he could answer her, a tired voice answered her from the chair.

"'Course it is, Laura," Barrington said in a heavy voice. "He's not going to explode that bomb, only to have me to deal with again." His breathing was raspy, laboured. His face was gray.

"Barrington!" Lady Laura, suddenly ashen, rushed to her cousin's side. "Help, Plantagenet!" she cried out.

The Duke pulled the bell. When Grayson appeared, the Duke ordered him: "Fetch a doctor, quickly."

"Yes, milord," Grayson, flew out of the room, to use the other telephone and get help.

Lady Laura crossed over, and bent over, helping the Prime Minister to remove his collar, which seemed to be strangling him. The Duke poured water into a glass, and proffered it to Erle, who drank greedily.

"Thanks, Palliser," the Prime Minister murmured. Unsure what to do next, the Duke rose, and strode to the 'phone. Even though he knew rationally that help was on the way, he picked up the phone, and started to put through a call to his own doctor. Perhaps there were things that they could do to help the Prime Minister while that other doctor was on his way!

Laura remained crouched over her cousin, whose breath was coming in gasps. She chafed his hands, more out of desperation than out of any belief that the action would be of any use. "Hold on, Barrington," she whispered fiercely into his ear, "help is coming." He closed his eyes in pain for a moment.

"He's—an—imbecile—Laura," Barrington Erle gasped.

"Yes, Barrington," she answered unsteadily, trying to communicate to her cousin a calm that she could not feel, "but don't let's worry about him now!"

The Prime Minister gave a ghastly little grin, all the more horrible for the blue tinge of his lips. "Now or never, Laura," he breathed out, "Tell Finn"—a convulsive shudder interrupted him.

"Yes?"

"Tell Finn"—but the Prime Minister's face contorted a second time. Laura's heart lurched within her; she had loved Barrington since their shared childhood. If she must lose him, she must not fail him in his last moments.

"What, Barrington, what?"

An almost beatific smile passed over Erle's face. "To drive a hard bargain," he gasped out.

"To drive a hard bargain?" She repeated his words uncomprehendingly, as tears streaked her face.

But Lady Laura was speaking to the clay only; the soul had departed. The Prime Minister was dead.

IN THE MIDST OF DEATH, WE ARE IN LIFE

The death of a Prime Minister, especially one who has expired in the very hour of his defeat, does not go unnoticed. The Palace had to be notified, a funeral organised—and this in the sweltering depths of July—and a Government had to be formed.

When the Finns found out, they came at once to Lady Laura, and heard from her own lips the story of what had transpired, and Barrington Erle's last charge to Phineas. Phineas's aspect grew ever darker as she unfolded the tale of her cousin's last hours, and when he heard of McScuttle's behaviour, he jumped up and stalked about the room in fury.

"The scoundrel!" he exclaimed once, as Lady Laura faithfully described McScuttle's insulting behaviour, and then "Good for him!" upon her description of how Barrington's wrath had cowed McScuttle, effectively blowing him almost out of the room, like a leaf carried off in a gale.

The Duke of Omnium stood protectively over Laura, his hand on her shoulder, a gesture she reciprocated by covering that hand with one of her own. Even in her surprise at Erle's death and her—yes, her grief for him, Marie Finn could not suppress the thought: How natural, how right, those two look together.

When Laura completed her account, and described Barrington's final message to him, Phineas Finn gave a smile the likes of which she had never seen on his face. "Drive a hard bargain, is it I should do?" he said softly, in a voice that betokened no good for Sir William McScuttle. "Oh, I will. I most assuredly will."

But first there was the funeral to be gotten through. At the request of the dead man's closest living relation, Lady Laura, the Duke organised the memorials, in consultation with Frank Greystock. The funeral was a fitting remembrance of Erle's life in politics—or, as was said again and again at the obsequies, his life of service to the Nation.

On coming up to London, the Earl and Countess of Brentford had to hear the story themselves. Oswald bridled at the tale, and stormed out of Laura's house in Portman Square, once their father's home. There, the boy Oswald had played with Barrington Erle, had been minded by the older boy, and had been initiated into many of the ways of the world. And Barrington had always stuck by Oswald, even in the years when his own ungovernable temper had pushed him to the margins of Society.

Yes, and Barrington had been loyal to Laura, too, when scandal had been cast upon her by that wretched man she had married! Barrington had stood by them both in their vicissitudes, and now was their time to repay that loyalty. Oswald was thinking of how best to deal with Sir William McScuttle—he was leaning towards a good old-fashioned horsewhipping—and decided to consult Phineas. After all, for all their falling out at the end, he thought, Barrington and Phineas had been d—-d thick for many years. Oswald was so far sure of his friend as this: He could not believe, would not believe, that Phineas's no doubt justifiable anger at his expulsion from the Liberal Party would embitter him against Barrington, especially after the latter's death.

When Oswald arrived at Park Lane, and was shown into Phineas's study, he found that he had not, in fact, been mistaken. Phineas wrung Oswald's hand, and before Oswald could say anything, the Irishman grew reminiscent.

"I miss Barrington already, Oswald. We walked into the House together after that last vote, did you know? For all that passed between us, he was still my friend."

"I'm glad to hear that. I am sure Laura was, too."

"He was my first sponsor in Parliament—Loughshane would not have fallen my way without Barrington's help. And then, after poor

Mary died, it was Barrington who put me in play for Tankerville. He was loyal to me as long as he could be—and even then regretted when he could no longer be."

They sat a moment in silence. And then Oswald raised the question of how to deal with Sir William McScuttle. Again, his friend did not disappoint him. Phineas, it was true, deprecated the notion of physical violence in this case. Instead, he gave a grim smile and said, "I mean to serve out Sir William far better than that, Oswald. Barrington himself gave me one suggestion, and your sister's account gave Marie the other."

"What do you mean, Phineas?"

"The numbers are much as they were in the last Parliament. With Barrington—gone—and not counting the Labour members, there are 328 Liberals and 329 Tories."

"So Frank Greystock will try to form a Government?"

"And he will, at least in the first instance, fail. The Labour members are now 14—the nine Lib-Labs, the four Labour members, and one new Labour member, Major Yeates from Ireland."

"So the fourteen of you–"

"Will vote against Frank Greystock's attempt to form a Government, and against Fawn's. Barrington knew that the Labour members are needed for whichever side wants to form a Government. Without us, as long as we stay together as a group, neither Lord Fawn nor Frank Greystock has a working majority. That is one weapon we have against Sir William McScuttle."

"And the other?"

Marie Finn, sitting decorously on the sofa, answered the question.

"Laura said that Sir William boasted of funding Barthwick. I do not believe that spending funds in a General Election to defeat the Prime Minister of his own party will endear Sir William to the Liberals in the House."

"D'you think Fawn would care about that?"

Marie remained silent a moment.

"My husband thinks so," she answered, and left it at that.

"Fawn's a narrow, petty man in many ways—we both know that, Oswald. But that's largely because he is desperate to be respected as a man of honour, and to do the right thing, if he could but know what that is. He spends half his life in a muddle over what honour requires of him, and the other half resentful that people see his muddling. But he has a sense of honour, and I don't think he'll take this from McScuttle."

The Earl pondered a moment. "I think you're right, Phineas. Yes, that's Fawn to the life—not a bad man at heart, even though he is a bit of a tick. So what?"

Marie smiled gently. "We have Meier looking for proof of what Sir William's maneuvers regarding Barthwick were. If we can find that Sir William did what he admitted to Laura, then we would not have to bring her, or the Duke, into it at all, but we still could–"

"By thunder, done right, it could finish him in Society!" the Earl exclaimed. And then, as an afterthought, he added: "And the majority? Who shall be Prime Minister?"

"Not Fawn," Phineas answered firmly. "I have other ideas, but they are still—developing."

Sir William McScuttle moved aggressively forward with his effort to cobble together a Government with Lord Fawn at the helm. He fairly quickly consolidated the majority of the Liberals; even those alienated by his high-handedness during the elections did not wish to fall afoul of the new Prime Minister and thereby deprive themselves of all hope of preferment. A decent respect for the passing of Barrington Erle required, of course, that some delay be incurred before the announcement of a new Government. And so it was mid-July before the first meeting to form a Government was called by Sir William McScuttle.

The meeting opened with Lord Fawn paying tribute to the late Prime Minister, after which he asked the Party Secretary if there were any administrative matters to be resolved prior to addressing the leadership.

Mr. Rattler, the now elderly Party Secretary, rose arthritically and walked stiffly to the podium.

"Milord," he announced in a wheezy rasp, but with sufficient power to fill the hall. "Milord, I do."

"Well, what is it?" Lord Fawn's anxiety to be selected betrayed him into discourtesy here, and he realised it himself. "I mean, Mr. Secretary, please state your business."

"Yes, milord. I regret to inform Your Lordship that I have received communications from nine members informing us that they wish to disassociate themselves from us, and will no longer recognise the whip."

"Eh?" asked Lord Fawn.

"Yes, milord. The nine members are Mr. Bunce, Mr. Jenkins, Mr. Doolittle, Mr. Swann, Mr. Camperdown, Mr. Harker, Mr. Robinson"—

"What?" expostulated Lord Fawn, "Not Sherwood Robinson?"

"No, milord, Mr. Octavius Robinson."

"Ah, I see. Carry on."

"Mr. Somerville, and Mr. Ross."

Sir William growled, "The Lib-Labs."

"What, all of them?"

"Aye. Still, they'll come home in the end. They've nowhere else tae go. They'll nae wish tae support Frank Greystock, now will they?"

Nobody could answer that seemingly logical conclusion. Comfortable that he had locked up sufficient votes from the active Liberal Party members, Sir William bludgeoned the rest into submission. The leadership competition resulted in a lopsided vote in favour of Lord Fawn. Ultimately, the losing side fell in line, and Lord Fawn had secured the support of 328 members.

In a similar hall, also in Westminster, Savrola Vavasor had the opportunity to participate in his first Conservative Party Conference. It did not delay the Vavasors' wedding tour long; Frank Greystock was nominated by acclamation, and quickly secured the support of 329 members of the House.

Greystock addressed the Conference: "I am informed that the Labour members have unequivocally split off from the Liberal Party, which means that we have a numerical advantage."

"A majority!" The cry went up "A majority!"

Greystock motioned the crowd to silence.

"A majority of one, my friends, with fourteen unaffiliated members who accept the whip from neither party? No, no; that is no working majority, no basis from which to govern." Greystock's confident expression, the broad smile beneath his moustache, belied his reasonable words. "We have a bare majority, but one that can be blocked on any measure that the Labour Party and the Liberal Party agree should be blocked. In other words, we have no majority at all, but would, if we try to govern with only our own members, govern only on sufferance."

He waited, like a skillful conjurer—for he was, after all the chosen *protégé* of that master wizard of the House, the late Mr. Daubeny—until the buzz reached its peak. Then he roared out his solution, cutting through the confusion of the crowd.

"We should, in my opinion," Frank Greystock shouted, "approach the Labour members and invite them into a coalition with us, to provide England with a stable government."

Savrola Vavasor started. Here was Tory Democracy indeed! Bypassing the Liberals, seeking to find common ground with Labour!

The rest of the Conference was less enthusiastic, but acquiesced. After all, what else could they do?

As Phineas Finn had remarked some weeks before, it was a matter of numbers.

ILL MET BY MOONLIGHT

On a Saturday in late July, the Labour Party Members of the House met at Phineas Finn's chambers on the early evening. They discussed the recent informal approach through Savrola Vavasor, implemented shortly before leaving on his wedding tour with Clarissa, to form a coalition with the Tories.

"To his credit," Phineas explained, "Greystock did not ask Savrola to be his messenger; he volunteered."

"For family reasons?" asked Craig Laurel, a little perplexed at the notion of such a coalition.

"In a sense, but not because of my family. At the end of his life, Savrola's father spoke of something he called 'Tory Democracy,' which Savrola has built into a philosophy of reform for the benefit of the working classes."

Craig Laurel sniffed. "Hardly the majority view in that party, though, is it?" The Members who had risen from the hardest backgrounds, especially Bunce, laughed out loud at this sally.

"Perhaps not," Sinclair Yeates interjected, "but if we seize this moment, we could make it so. The Tories are, I know, not our natural allies, but there is such a thing as *noblesse oblige* in the minds of many of them. What we would demand as a right, they would extend as grace."

Craig Laurel bristled a little at this, but before he could speak any words that would be difficult to retract, Yeates went on:

"I do not mean we should accept these things as a grace, but whatever their motives, there might be common ground upon which we could build. Perhaps we should meet with them, and explore Greystock's suggestion."

The men discussed a little. "Tavy" Robinson was distrustful, as was Laurel, most of the others were undecided, but not willing to run counter to Laurel. As the discussion ground on, and the last golden beams of the sunset slanted into the conference room's windows, Phineas finally raised a hand to speak.

"I think Yeates has raised a fair point," he commented, "how can we know whether the Tories will meet our concerns if we do not speak to them? How can we determine how we can be most effective in securing change if we refuse to speak to one of the two parties? And besides," he added, a thin smile on his face, "when the Liberals hear that we are meeting with the Tories, they will realise that they cannot assume we will fall in line."

Laurel barked his hard laugh at that, and said, "Aye, that alone makes it worth doing, if ye ask me. McScuttle seems to think we've nae choice but tae back his puppet."

After some little discussion, it was agreed that Greystock's suggestion of a meeting to explore a possible coalition would be accepted, and that Yeates ("He speaks their language, after all") and Craig Laurel ("He'll be the hardest one to convince, in any event—might as well have him asking the difficult questions") would make up the Labour deputation.

The sun had fully set by the time these conclusions were reached, and dark had fallen. After the last of the members had departed, Phineas went back to his own room, and looked at some of the correspondence he had neglected due to the shuttle diplomacy he had been forced to conduct throughout the General Election, and then due to the funeral of Barrington Erle.

As he lit the lamps in his room, and tackled the letters, he saw nothing that needed immediate handling—although the case against Jack was coming on quickly—it was set for the beginning of August, and would be almost the last of the session. Phineas had expected the case to be slower in wending its way to court than this, but realised that it was, after all, a simple case in which no motion practise had taken place, nor had any matters arisen to slow it down. And, of course, in such cases, especially with titles and noble families on both sides of the "v.", the Clerk's Office had a tendency to expedite the proceedings. Still, two weeks was very little time to prepare—not that there was much for Phineas to prepare.

He had, on the one hand, a client who would admit his promise and his breach thereof. He also had a plaintiff who was renowned as a persuasive and skillful liar, but whose testimony would be confirmed by his own client in all of the legal elements she was required to prove. Why, then, fight the case at all?

First, because Lady Eustace's demand for damages was extortionate. Yes, the Brentfords could afford it, but were disinclined to do so—after all, Violet had reasoned, the immorality of Lizzie Eustace working her poor boy into a lather of lust such that he did not know what he was saying, and then demanding payment for him to be released from her clutches, was patently obvious.

This excellent moral argument, however, gained almost its entire force from the personalities involved. Absent a nuanced understanding of the circumstances leading up to the promise and breach, Jack was entirely in the wrong. Indeed, even with such an understanding, it was far from clear to Phineas that any of the feelings and emotions that had swept his godson mattered a farthing.

Not to mention Jack's troubles with alcohol, and the duel! These matters had finally begun to recede, but if Phineas called his client to the stand, they would be eminently fair matters for cross-examination.

Phineas and Mr. Camperdown had placed their faith in the expectation that the threat implicit in their filed answer to the complaint—that they would rake up all that unpleasantness with Emilius again—would deter her from proceeding any further, or lead to a quiet negotiation. Neither had eventuated.

Not that the argument was utterly lacking in foundation; the basis for the court order dissolving Lady Eustace's marriage to Emilius had been the conviction, and the conviction was utterly undone on a basis that implied that the divorce had been improvidently granted.

But even if that were the case, did that provide a basis for invalidating the later court order on the grounds that the prior court order upon which it had relied was invalid? Mr. Low was openly skeptical, though he acknowledged it so thoroughly muddled matters that it might be worth a try.

As Phineas was beginning to try to puzzle his way through the matter, he slowly became aware of another presence in the chambers. He was not aware of having heard the latch of the door to chambers open, nor did he consciously hear the faint creak of a floorboard in the hallway leading to his room. Nonetheless, some atavistic instinct made him look up from his papers.

Other than the yellow nimbus of light creating a brightly-lit area around Phineas's desk, the room was illuminated only by the splendid, pallid shafts of moonlight admitted by a high bay window. Just at the fringe of the pool of silvery light, a cloaked figure, a man with saturnine features, a close-cropped beard and dark hair stood, in absolute silence. When Phineas rose, the figure took a few steps into the room, and, carelessly flinging back his cloak, revealed the black clerical suit beneath.

Insouciantly letting his cloak settle behind him, as he lowered himself into the chair, he made himself comfortable, and, meeting Phineas's eyes, asked politely, if belatedly, with eyebrow raised interrogatively, "I may be seated?"

The gentleman in front of Phineas Finn was one he had never met before—although he had seen him somewhere—if only he could recall.

"You were at the Marchioness' Ball, were you not?" Phineas asked, resuming his own seat.

"Very good, Mr. Finn. Most astute," the clergyman said in a mellifluous voice. The gentleman was about his age and height; a little grayer, perhaps a little heavier, although the cloak and the cassock beneath it made the question a little unsure.

"But we have not met, have we?"

"No, Mr. Finn. We have not met. And, yet, our paths have crossed."

Phineas cocked his own eyebrow now, and patiently waited for his visitor to state his business. The two gentlemen looked at each other quite calmly for a few moments.

Stalemate.

The clergyman laughed, seemingly with genuine amusement.

"I am the Right Reverend Joseph Emilius," he began, "a name you no doubt recall."

Phineas frankly stared at his interlocutor. He experienced the eerie sensation of having conjured a demon out of his own past by his very musings on the man's role in the ugly *contretemps* between his godson and Lady Eustace. If all he had heard—aye, and believed!—about this man was true, he was in the presence of the murderer for whose crime he had himself stood trial. And yet that man's guilt was no better proved than the guilt others had laid upon himself. Phineas was not sure what to think, but as to feeling, he was most conscious of an intense curiosity regarding his visitor.

And, of course, Phineas was conscious of the fact that he had threatened to rake up a past which this man—a probable murderer—was presumably anxious to keep safely buried.

"Yes," Phineas heard his own voice say, calmly, lightly—if a touch dryly—"I believe I recall the name."

Emilius's feline chuckle gave way to a heartier laugh. He clapped his hands once.

"Ah, Mr. Finn, you are no doubt wondering what brings me to call upon you so late? And perhaps the fact has not escaped you that you have interposed yourself in the affairs of one who is dear to me?"

"I do wonder—at your purpose in calling."

"I am not here, Mr. Finn, to place any obstacles in your way, or to try to change your course with respect to Lady Eustace."

Phineas remained silent. The bishop, in the face of the barrister's silence, continued.

"I see that you require me to make the running, Mr. Finn. Very well, I must make allowances for all the suspicions you have no doubt harbored of me all these years."

"Do you think me unjust in harboring suspicions of you?"

"Ah, Mr. Finn, which of us, like Caesar's wife, is truly above suspicion? But you, of all men, must know the folly of judging by appearances. Still, none of that is to the point now, Mr. Finn. The fact is that circumstances have brought our interests into alignment."

"Have they, Mr. Emilius?"

"My title is quite genuine, I assure you."

Phineas coloured a moment, and then said, "My apologies, Bishop. Whenever I have thought of you, over all these years, it has always been as 'Mr. Emilius'; I do not believe that I even knew before this evening that your Christian name is Joseph."

Emilius waved away the apology, although his pleasure in receiving it was evident.

"I quite understand, Mr. Finn. For me, it is always 'Mr. Bonteen.' Never just 'Bonteen,' nor his Christian name, nor even his full name. Always that oddly formal way of thinking of the man. I did hate him, you know. For coming between me and Lizzie—my wife."

Somehow, Phineas could not but return confidence for confidence with this man with whom his own fate had been so singularly linked. "I hated him too. He viewed me as a parvenu—as a stage Irishman who might pick his pocket, or sneak his watch at any moment."

Emilius' eyes flared in understanding. "Yes," he agreed, "His opposition to one's interest was one thing, but that lordly contempt, directed at one by such a—such a—But that no longer signifies, does it, Mr. Finn?"

Phineas looked carefully at his visitor. Gently, he said, "What does signify, Bishop Emilius? Why have you come to me, of all people?"

Emilius smiled, his composure quickly recovered. "As I say, our interests run together, Mr. Finn. You do not want Lady Eustace to win her suit for breach of promise against Lord Chiltern. Neither do I."

"No?" Phineas's curiosity was aroused.

"No. Lady Eustace believes that she can shame Lord Chiltern into surrender. If she does so, she will marry him—not for love, but to seal her victory. I will lose her—and the only reason I have returned to England is to win her back."

"Is that even possible, in view of what has passed between you?"

"Oh, yes. She understands me quite well, and I her. But she requires me to prove the depth of my feeling."

"And you?"

The bishop shrugged. "What choice have I? Her price is that I make a sacrifice for her—take some risk. And so, I come to you."

"And how can I assist you?"

"It is I who shall assist you. I will testify for you that my marriage to her was valid. In so doing, I will risk everything—my status in Society, my career as a preacher of some repute—because cross-examination will reveal the extent of the scandal at the time. Society will hear that I was charged with and convicted of a crime, and that the authorities believed—and no doubt still believe—that I was guilty of a blacker one still."

"I do not see the point."

"Do you not?" The clergyman was surprised. "If she chooses that I be cross-examined, as she may, and if the right questions are asked, I will be spurned by the Society that has embraced me. My name, which I have slowly, painstakingly built up from the dirt into which it was trodden, will be cast back into the mud again, to be trodden even deeper than before. I will return to America, alone, and humiliated. All at her choice, because I will have given the choice to her."

"And you are prepared to undergo such risks for that? At the whim of a woman of whom—forgive me—Society speaks quite ill."

Emilius' smile had a little sorrow in it; for a moment, Phineas felt a shaft of empathy for the cleric. And yet he felt in his heart more sure than ever that Emilius had, indeed, murdered Mr. Bonteen.

"For her, I will do all this, in the hope that I may win her."

"You must love her very much," Phineas heard himself say.

"Yes, Mr. Finn, I suppose that I must. I did not understand that twenty years ago, but I know better now. So," he said, resuming a brisk, business-like tone, "will my testimony help your case?"

Phineas cogitated. "Yes," he answered. "Even if the cross-examination damages you heavily, there is no escaping the fact that the testimony against you regarding your alleged first marriage was recanted. Your presence in the courtroom as Lady Eustace's husband, desirous of taking her back, cannot but help the defence."

"Good. I am again at Claridge's, so you can reach me there. I was the guest of the Marchioness for some months, Mr. Finn, but when I conceived of this plan, I knew I must withdraw; I would not have her shamed by her guest, and forced to expel me."

The clergyman offered his hand. Phineas could not refuse to take it, and so they clasped hands for a moment.

"Together, Mr. Finn," the bishop said with a return of his theatrical aplomb, "we will free that young man—and, I hope, that for myself, at any rate, virtue will not be its own reward."

With those words, Joseph Emilius withdrew, quickly swallowed up again by the darkness from whence he had come.

22

THE PARLEY

Frank Greystock very much desired to be Prime Minister. In the previous Conservative administration, he had held high office, but this was his first chance to grasp the nettle himself, and to be the first man not only in his Party, but in the Councils of the Nation. Because the Tories had the single largest bloc of members of the House—albeit only by one vote—it had been he, Frank Greystock, who had been summoned to the Palace, and tasked by the Queen herself with the great task of forming a Government.

He would still be young for a Prime Minister these days—rising forty-five, and still looking a bit younger than his age. Hunting and riding had kept him reasonably fit, and though he had put on a little flesh since his youth, it was not as yet too noticeable. To a casual glance, he was still the dashing M.P. who had married Lucy Morris, then a mere governess, albeit a well-bred one, for love. He had never regretted that decision, and he was among the most uxorious men in the House, where members often stayed late in order to, as one member had put it, "avoid the cold supper at home." Frank Greystock had chosen a harder path in some ways, declining opportunities to marry for money; his reward was that now, the partner of his hearth and lady of his house was always as glad to welcome him home as he was to see her.

That morning, as he breakfasted with his wife and youngest children, he knew that the task before him was a heavy one. Lucy had jollied young Jolyon into eating his toast soldiers, leading little Lydia to demand one for herself. The aspiring Prime Minister turned crossly to his daughter, and was about to rebuke her, but her pleading eyes, and sad mien melted any annoyance the arduousness of the day to come had kindled within his breast. Sighing, he rang the bell. A maid flounced in and curtseyed, only to be told, "We need more toast soldiers, Mary Anne. And eggs, I suppose, to allow for their sacrifice."

From across the table, Lucy smiled at him.

"After all," he said, shrugging his shoulders, "a Prime Minister must keep an adequate Army to allow reinforcements."

"Is it decided, then?"

"Hardly," he answered. "There are only fourteen of them, but the Labour members hold, just this once, the balance of power. If we can bring them into a coalition with us, we can govern. If Fawn can, then the Liberals maintain a majority."

"But the Labour members have always voted with the Liberals before, haven't they?"

"True, my dear. But Barrington Erle had the knack of keeping them all around the table, and he's dead now. They knew Erle would give them something for their constituents, or make sure the manifesto reflected at least some of their priorities. He'd built up some goodwill with them. But Fawn? He thinks a labourer has no place voting, let alone legislating. And he's in the grip of a rather nasty industrialist who I rather suspect has no concept of making concessions, even when it's in his own interest to do so."

"And you, Frank? What can you offer them?" Lucy asked.

"Right now, I can offer them a hearing—find out what it is they need for a coalition to be acceptable to them. And then I'll decide if the thing can take place."

"You want it to, surely?"

"Very much, old girl." For a moment, his usually pleasant smile hinted of the wolf. "But not at the cost of transforming our party into something it was never meant to be."

"Is that likely, my dear?" The question was skeptical.

"Lucy, I believe in bettering the lot of the lower classes as much as anyone—Phineas Finn included. But the way to do it is gradualism; let loose an uneducated mass of workers into the House, and they'll either pass wildly impractical schemes, or, worse, be led astray by some cheap demagogue who promises them the moon, but just uses them for his own aggrandisement."

Lucy's laughter rippled sweetly as she fended off Lydia's efforts to reach across her mother's plate to the newly-replenished toast rack. She gently slid the toast rack to where Lydia could reach it, and the child seized a slice and began happily smearing jam on it.

Frank shot an interrogative look at his wife, who answered the unspoken question, laughter still bubbling within her.

"I'm sorry, darling, but you just put me so much in mind of Coriolanus—'For the mutable, rank-scented many, let them/Regard me as I do not flatter, and therein behold themselves.'"

"I knew there was good stuff in Shakespeare," her husband rose, chuckling, walked around and kissed the top of Lucy's head, "but it takes a former governess to hunt it out. Shall I try it on the Labour members, d'you think?"

"Well, we have no Tarpeian rock for them to tumble you down, but I doubt you would get any more votes that way than did Coriolanus."

Kissing the children goodbye, and leaving Lucy to supervise the immolation of the toast soldiers, Frank Greystock left his house to meet with the Labour delegation.

Meanwhile, in Park Lane, Phineas Finn was reviewing the evidence gathered by Meier's efforts. He felt himself ready to move. Phineas made sure that the word got out about the meeting between the Labour members and the Tory leader; he then awaited results.

Craig Laurel was, despite his humble origins, or perhaps because of them, a man keenly sensitive to condescension. He could detect contempt in the raising of an eyebrow, the inflection of a voice, even in the sometimes overly-hearty jollity his social superiors were wont to assume with the working class.

To his credit, Craig Laurel thought, he did not detect the faintest whiff of condescension from Frank Greystock. Polite, matter-of-fact, cheerful, the Tory leader was clearly aware of what he had to gain from this meeting's success, and did not try to hide that awareness. On the other hand, he was a genuine Tory, a firm believer in privilege and the perquisites thereof. It was, Craig Laurel meditated to himself, a perpetual surprise to him—both how charming the upper classes could be, and how uncomprehending, too.

The other members of the Tory delegation were less inspiring. Mr. Thomas Roby, a short bald old man now, was, it was true, a consummate political professional, and one not averse to coalitions. Indeed, his close association with his opposite number in the Liberal Party, Mr. Rattler, had always been a means by which necessary legislation passed the House even at times of the gravest division. All this, of course, was to the good. But Mr. Roby, like his Liberal friend, was a man whose convictions could be boiled down to one precept: England was best served when his Party held sway. All else—all policies, all measures, were subordinate to Mr. Roby, so long as what he termed "steady hands"—that is, Tory hands—held the tiller of the ship of state.

Major Yeates quickly engaged Mr. Roby, and was clearly doing his best to make the meeting "go." With a slightly dyspeptic gaze, Laurel watched the Major set the old man at ease, inquiring after the shooting at his spinneys, speaking of the poor quality of the shooting at his own Shreelane Lodge, but discoursing knowledgably about the high quality of the hunt in his borough. Mr. Roby's frosty demeanour, as though he had been summoned to dine with Jacobins melted quickly, as he began to perceive that the Major, at least, was a man one could do business with.

The third member of the Tory delegation, young Despard-Smith, who, having missed Tankerville, was nonetheless found a place when a Tory member unexpectedly died, was of a clerical family. At first, hesitantly, Despard-Smith and Craig Laurel began to find common ground, on the subject of the prohibition against usury. Despard-Smith deplored the ruinous rates of interest charged the poor, and the practise of employers in the outer counties of using the "Company Store" to hold workers in debt. With this, Laurel could keenly agree, and did.

As for Frank Greystock, he dropped in and out of both discussions, watching to see if these wildly disparate men could establish enough common ground to run together in harness. If so, a functional coalition could be achieved, and his premiership begin.

The auguries were good—the men were discoursing amicably, tea was being consumed, and party lines breaking down. But now, alas, the difficult part was at hand: the specifics of what the Labour members would require to caucus with the Conservatives. Frank Greystock knew that there was no subtlety, no technique that could postpone the setting of terms indefinitely.

As the general conversation died down, Greystock smilingly addressed the small gathering. "Gentlemen," he said, "I am most pleased to see that we have had an opportunity to explore informally our common interests and common ground. But of course, we are meeting to see if we are able to together form a Government, since neither we Conservatives nor the Liberals alone have sufficient numbers to create a working majority."

Craig Laurel noted, "You have a numerical majority, Mr. Greystock, do you not?"

"That is so, Mr. Laurel, and, accordingly, I do not mean to lead this discussion from a position of weakness. But a numerical majority of one is not a working majority, and our party would greatly prefer to lead from a position of strength. We believe that if we join with you to form a Government, that Government would be solid enough to run for several years, and would do the Nation a great deal of good."

"Aye, but how? Your priorities are not ours, are they?"

Patiently, Frank answered, "Certainly not in all things, Mr. Laurel, but it seems to me that there are many goals your party has been unable to pass into law as allies of the Liberal Party; perhaps you can do better with us."

"Aye? How d'you feel about limiting the hours of work? Or the age of employment for children in mines, or as chimney sweeps?"

Sinclair Yeates immediately poured oil on the troubled waters, while supporting his chief.

"The point is, old man," he said, "you know our priorities, and the issues that have brought us to declare our independence from the Liberals. The real question is, how far are you prepared to go to meet us? In terms of legislation, or of the manifesto? In terms of positions in the Government?"

Greystock considered both questions carefully. At length, he replied, "Which matters to you most? Legislative priorities, or office?"

Yeates looked to Craig Laurel.

"Legislation," the Scotsman said firmly. "We've nae objection to promotion, and I think one position in the Cabinet as a gesture of good-will would be appropriate, but we care more about the legislation."

Roby sighed audibly. "Are you sure?" he asked politely. "Office is so much easier for us to give than legislative priority, and a sympathetic administrator can accomplish a great deal."

"Why is office easier?" Laurel asked.

Roby replied, "The Prime Minister has office within his gift. Legislation requires a majority of the House to pass, and, as you know, while we have some areas of agreement, I cannot guarantee that every bill we agreed to put forward would be enacted."

Laurel nodded. While the answer did not please him in one sense—the power to legislate was the power to make lasting change, while the discrete decisions made by one administration could all too easily be reversed by its successor—it did convince him that the Tories were dealing in good faith, not promising more than they could perform.

"Will there be any legislation that ye will advance for us?" Laurel asked.

"The Lifeboat Measure we can commit to moving even now; it was bogged down in the last Parliament, but I do not think that was because of entrenched disagreement with the substance of the bill." Mr. Roby answered promptly.

"Any others? Worker safety, in particular"

Frank Greystock answered this question: "We would need to caucus amongst ourselves for a few days, to be sure that any answer we give you would be a promise we feel reasonably sure we can perform. Might I suggest we meet again in a week's time?"

"Aye," said Craig Laurel, "That seems fair enough."

"And, remember, do consider looking more closely at the benefits of office," Mr. Roby interjected, "The Prime Minister's ability to deliver in that area is considerably more, and we could accordingly meet more of your priorities that way."

"We will," promised Major Yeates, "and in this week, we will apprise our caucus of what progress we have made, and of what you have communicated to us."

"Good," said Greystock, shaking hands with first Laurel, then Yeates.

As the Labour members left the building, they glanced at each other.

"They'll be waiting for us at St. Dominic's," Laurel remarked.

"'Myes," Yeates replied, "seems odd to be meeting at a Roman church."

"St. Dominic's isnae Roman," Craig Laurel informed the Major.

"No? Sounds Italian, though," Major Yeates shrugged.

"Aye, well, St. Dominic was Spanish, though he died in Italy, right enough."

"Unusual name for an Anglican church then, isn't it?"

"As he died in 1221, he's still on the calendar—and don't blame me, son; I'm a Dissenter, myself."

By this time, the Major had hailed a hansom cab, and they were on their way to the Church. When they arrived, they were met by Miss Garnett, who led them into the vestry room, where tea was laid out, and the other dozen members were awaiting the news.

After they were seated, and had an opportunity to take a little tea and a sandwich or some tea-cake each, the assembled Labour members drew silent. Craig Laurel set out the discussion accurately, without comment, detailing all that had taken place. When he finished, he turned to his companion.

"Anything I left out, Major?"

"No," the Major replied decisively. "My impression, for what it is worth, is that they are willing to give us some positions and some sway in how the laws are administered, but much less in terms of making the laws."

"So we could ameliorate the laws that exist," Mr. Camperdown said, "but not formulate new ones."

"We do not know this for sure, of course," Yeates answered, "and we will know much more in a week's time. But, yes, that is what I believe."

"Not an entirely unreasonable opening bid," said Tavy Robinson, "But what are we to expect from the Liberals?"

"Can we expect anything from Lord Fawn?" asked Bunce.

"You mean McScuttle," corrected Mr. Camperdown.

"Which itself suggests the answer," Craig Laurel added in a dour tone.

Phineas Finn, who had been notably silent all through the discussion, spoke up at last.

"Actually, gentlemen, I have received a note from Laurence Fitzgibbon."

"Fawn's understrapper?" Yeates asked.

"For his sins." Phineas confirmed. "Lord Fawn would like to meet with a delegation from our Party to discuss the possibility of our caucusing with them."

"Would he, now?" Mr. Camperdown asked in a silky voice. "And what terms will his Lordship propose?"

Phineas smiled grimly. "That is just what I intend to find out. And, of course, to address some issues on behalf of our own caucus."

Craig Laurel looked intently at his friend. "Ye've something in mind, haven't ye?"

"Yes. I plan to make sure we can obtain the best offer we can get from the Liberals—and that does not include taking the whip from Sir William McScuttle."

A murmur of assent was heard from around the table. Phineas pressed his advantage to go on.

"And so it behooves us to discuss what terms we will require to caucus with the Liberals, and to make sure that their offer is better than that of the Tories. So, gentlemen, with your consent, I would suggest that Laurel, Yeates, and Robinson meet with the Tories in a week's time, as they suggested, and that I, Camperdown, and Laurel meet with the Liberals as soon thereafter as practicable. Are we agreed?"

"Why d'ye want me in both delegations, Finn?" asked Laurel.

"You are our leader. And—I think you will want to see what happens at our meeting with the Liberals."

"Will I?"

"Very much so, I suspect. And Sir William will be glad to see you, I am sure."

The Scotsman looked intently at Phineas, and said dryly. "Aye, belike he will be."

"Does my suggestion meet with the approval of the members?" Phineas asked, and it was agreed by acclamation.

On their way out of the vestry room, Camperdown murmured to Robinson, "I'm that glad I'll be going to that meeting."

"Are you?" The younger man was surprised.

"I don't think Finn cared for Sir William at all. And I suspect that he has something planned to get that point across."

"And?"

The young solicitor grinned. "I don't care all that much for Sir William, either. And I've seen Finn in court. I'd hate to miss the re-match."

THE END OF THE AFFAIR

At the very end of the High Court session, the matter of *Elizabeth, Lady Eustace v. John Standish, Lord Chiltern*, was called. Most of the other judges and barristers had departed for the Long Vacation, but a handful remained and came to the Court to see the proceedings. The public had, after a glut of political news, turned to this sensational trial, titillated by the spectacle of a woman, born a *demimondaine*, perhaps, but an undoubted aristocrat, suing for breach of promise a nobleman of even higher birth, young enough (if only just) to be her son.

The trial, in short, promised to be a great show, the best since the Tranby Croft matter. That case, one of cheating at cards amongst the nobility, had been diverting, but really was rendered sensational by the involvement as a witness of the Prince himself, whose participation in the gambling had been deplored by the mocking press, while earning him popularity among the commoners for his human frailty and jovial manner. *The People's Banner's* joining in the raillery had cost it dearly, and had made Quintus Slide all the more susceptible to Phineas Finn's warning during the General Election season. Now, as he sat in the courtroom watching Finn himself awaiting the judge's entry, he wondered if he had, in fact, backed a winner.

It was true that the story on Powlett-Jones had been a *succès fou*; Slide had published it solely in the hope of avoiding unpleasantness and possibly alienating some portion of his readership, but it had done far more. Readers had written in, praising the *Banner* for taking up the cudgels for the poor innocent lad; some had sent gifts intended for the young miners (and, under the gimlet eye of Miss Jean Allen, Slide had forwarded those gifts—at least, such as were not of value to himself to himself—to the care of Mr. Phineas Finn). And Finn had been triumphantly re-elected, by an absolute majority, even with another Liberal threatening to split the vote. So, taken all in all, Quintus Slide was reassessing his old foe, and leaning toward a longer-term tacit alliance with the Irishman—if, that is, Finn was right in his prediction that Labour would rise. Thus far, Labour had held its own, for the first time without the support of a major party, and that was as good enough an augury as could reasonably be expected.

So far, though, Slide was not too impressed with the trial. Oh, old Nathaniel Spiderwort was good enough an advocate for the plaintiff in his opening; Finn's cautious reservation of his opening was no doubt good tactics, but what the deuce was a chap to write about this tedious, muted scandal?

Slide brightened when Lady Eustace took the oath. Her Ladyship was, he reflected, as handsome as ever, despite the passage of the years. Her features were firm without sharpness, her voice retained its music, and her charm had not worn thin. But even with all her beauty, she was clearly considerably older than the slim, grave young defendant, and it was hard to see the twice-married Lady Eustace as a maiden wronged.

Cleverly, she did not present herself as such. She testified to herself as one who had married—for love—a handsome, titled, gilded youth, only to have him snatched away from her after bare months of connubial bliss by a cruel fate, and who then had married a second time, in good faith, only to see her beloved husband torn from her arms by the law. After such anguish, she testified, she had resolved never again to wed, never again to open her heart to love, save only for the highest form of love a woman could know—that of a mother for her son.

This point in Lady Eustace's testimony had a pretty effect on the jurymen, particularly the elderly foreman, who reached for a handkerchief to offer Lady Eustace, as tears welled in her eyes, and as her voice hoarsened slightly—oh, how wondrously slightly—on the note of mother-love.

The effect on Quintus Slide was less edifying; the journalist snorted, not quite audibly for the bench and bar, but certainly loudly enough that Lord Chiltern could hear. He was not foolish enough to draw attention to himself by turning around to discern the offending party, but he wondered nonetheless as to his identity. Slide himself contemplated Lizzie's performance as might a discerning critic of the theatre; Corno di Bassetto himself could not fault her.

False, as they used to say, as dicers' oaths, of course—the late and distinctly unlamented Sir Florian Eustace had been dying of drink, dissipation, and heaven alone knew what resultant maladies when Lizzie Greystock (as she had then been) married the man; Sir Florian's son and namesake saw his mother perhaps twice in any given year, and found her perplexing and frightening. According to Miss Allen, whose network of informers was formidable enough that she had become aware of Mrs. Finn's, without knowing to whom they owed loyalty, young Sir Florian was studying at Oxford, so terrified of his inherited predispositions from both parents that he was seriously contemplating taking Holy Orders as a means of avoiding temptation. Still, false though every word delivered from those beautiful lips might be, the performance rang with the powerful conviction that can transmute poor melodrama to Shakespearian heights. Or, put in terms more akin to the thoughts of Quintus Slide, she had the poor jurymen "eating out of her hand."

Lizzie then moved on to meeting her young beau.

"I was at a tea, with Lady Wariston," she testified, "and Lord Chiltern helped me to tea-cake. He sat down next to me, and was so kind—I could not believe that a woman whose best years had flown could know love again—and with a man so pure, and good—for so I thought him then."

And the tears began to flow.

Lady Eustace described how she had been woken from the placid, if drab, life of a mother whose only chick had flown the nest.

"I was lonely," she admitted, emotion bringing her voice just to the point of cracking, "and missed my poor Florrie dreadfully. And then Jack—Lord Chiltern, I mean, began calling. Only on occasion, at first, but then regularly. And then," she testified, "he begged me to marry him. I was at first shocked—how could this be? I was no longer in my first youth, how could one so good, so kind choose to tie his life to mine, blasted and lonely as it was?"

"So you refused him?" Spiderwort asked. Phineas thought for a moment of objecting to the leading question, but realised it would play as pettifoggery.

"I did. But—he persisted, avowing that he loved me, and could only be happy if I said yes. I told him it was cruel to trifle with a woman's heart, but he knelt again, and bade me love him."

"And did you?"

"Oh, yes," said Lady Eustace, and she let one of those looks fall upon the foreman which make a slave of a king. "How could I not?" And she subsided, exhausted, into the witness chair.

"Lady Eustace," Mr. Spiderwort addressed the witness simperingly, "I do not wish to prolong your ordeal. But let me ask you this clearly: Did Lord Chiltern unequivocally ask you to be his wife?"

"Yes." The answer came out as wrung from the lips of a dying woman, but was clearly audible throughout the courtroom.

"Did you accept him?"

"I did, I did!" The witness was bravely drawing upon her last reserves of strength.

"And has he refused to honour his promise?"

"Oh, he has, he has…why, Jack, why? How have I failed you, my love?" The plaintiff addressed the defendant directly, in heartbreaking cadences. Lord Chiltern turned an ugly shade of red, the result of his shame at the fact that he had, in fact, breached his engagement with no provocation, mixed with his anger that one so utterly false could mime the appearance of truth so convincingly.

His Honour Sir Archibald Dowson, pendulous cheeks wagging in sympathy, cautioned the witness. "My lady," he said, in fatherly tones, "you must not address the defendant, no matter how great the temptation to do so."

Pulling herself together with a visible effort, Lady Eustace apologised prettily for her breach of courtroom decorum, her very posture bespeaking exhausted virtue. Here she sat, she seemed to communicate; she could do no other.

"Nothing further m'lud," said Mr. Spiderwort, and behind him, Mr. Rushforth looked on with stern approval, while Mr. Bindtheboy seemed drained utterly of life, so fervently had he suffered with his client.

"Mr. Finn..." Before the Judge could interject, Phineas was standing, and, having noted the time, gave the judge what he wanted most of all.

"My lord," Phineas stated gently, "It is clear that the witness would benefit from an opportunity to compose herself, and, perhaps, take some refreshment. Might I suggest that the Court adjourn at this time for luncheon?"

"A very sensible and—hrmmph—humane suggestion, Mr. Finn. Shall we say ten past two, members of the jury?"

As the jurors filed out of the box, the look of sheer indignation and contempt which the foreman bestowed upon Jack Standish would have chilled a more experienced litigant even more than it did Jack. That look might have lost some of its force if the juror could have seen the instant rejuvenation of Lizzie Eustace, and the cheerful look she bestowed upon her counsel, once they had left the courtroom and were sequestered in a little conference room.

"That was hard work," she said, smiling contentedly at a job well done. "Is there anywhere one can get a tolerable beefsteak near here?"

As Phineas Finn tore into his own beefsteak, the younger Mr. Camperdown—indeed, the youngest Mr. Camperdown, as Phineas had taken to calling him, in the course of their defence of Ifor Powlett-Jones—asked him, "What on earth can we do, Mr. Finn? He's tied our hands, he has."

"I know, Camperdown," replied Phineas. "He won't let us raise unchastity, although Meier and Polteed have brought us some evidence there; he won't let us raise her undue influence and his own youth. I respect my godson," Phineas continued, "for his sense of honour, but he is not an easy client."

They were seated in the Bar Mess, along with Ifor Powlett-Jones, who had been eagerly watching the proceedings, and was hanging on their conversation. Not that conversation was plentiful; the youngest Mr. Camperdown, whose dour look spoke volumes, was now the third generation of his name to be vexed and harassed, and to have to have his luncheon ruined, by the wiles of Elizabeth Eustace.

"Now I understand what Burton meant," Ifor volunteered in a conversational lull. At the blank glances he received from Phineas and Mr. Camperdown, Ifor struck a pose, and declaimed: 'He that marries a wife that is snout fair alone, let him look, saith Barbarus, for no better success than Vulcan had with Venus.'"

Phineas laughed aloud, and drained his tankard. "That's Low's influence!" he exclaimed, clapping the young Welshman on the back. "Where's it from?"

"His *Anatomy of Melancholy*," answered Ifor, "don't you know it?" The young Welshman seemed disappointed.

"No, Ifor," Phineas replied, "but it seems I should make its acquaintance."

"Who the deuce is Barbarus, anyway?" asked Mr. Camperdown, put out by all the literary talk.

"A man who knew all there was to know about melancholy, it seems," Phineas replied, his eyes shining with amusement.

"He must have had Lady Eustace in a case, then, is all I can say," Mr. Camperdown muttered disconsolately.

"Come!" Phineas stood, and gathered his gown around him, "We're not dead yet. We have one last hope."

"And what is that, Mr. Finn?" Powlett-Jones asked.

"A witness."

"A reliable one?" asked Mr. Camperdown, with a flicker of interest.

"One about as reliable as Lady Eustace herself, in fact," Phineas replied. "But as far as I know, he's breaking the habit of a lifetime and telling the truth."

"You seem very confident, Mr. Finn, for a barrister relying on an unreliable witness."

"I don't think this case is about the facts, Ifor. I think it's about breaking an impasse. And besides," he added, as he headed out of the Mess, "What else do I have?"

The Earl of Brentford resumed his seat in the courtroom. Violet had wanted to come, but he had persuaded her to remain at home. Persuaded being the operative word; time was long past when he would have ever tried to order Violet to do or not do anything. But this courtroom was no place for a mother to hear her son traduced. It had been hard enough on him, and worse for that little church-sparrow of a woman who'd accompanied him—she was ashen, but determined, all through the morning. And she'd not strayed from Jack's side through the luncheon interval, making him eat a little, making sure he had that fizzy water he liked nowadays.

She was common, right enough, but Oswald liked her. He liked the way she looked at his son, clearly knowing the worst, but seeing the best. He liked the way his son looked at her, too—solicitous, warm, adoring—and strong. For the first time in he could not say how long, Jack looked like a whole man.

No more fence-sitting for him; Vi would come around. When Jack had to go off to sit with Finn and the rest, he called her over.

"Miss Garnett!" he hissed. "Keep a chap company will you? I'm as nervous as a fox with the horn sounding in his ears."

Miss Garnett slowly, warily, drifted over toward him, and hesitantly took the seat he patted on the judge's bench. He smiled at her suspicious, frightened gaze. When had he transformed into the terrible old man who frightened his future daughters-in-law?

"It's all right my dear," he said reassuringly, "if Jack's for you, so am I."

Proserpine Garnett had, although she did not know it, a sweet smile. Thirty she may be, and of common stock, the Earl thought to himself, but she'll make a countess in her day.

When all the players in Lizzie Eustace's courtroom drama were in place again, Sir Archibald Dowson asked if Phineas had any questions for Lady Eustace.

"None, my lord." The Irishman's answer was as unexpected as it was mandatory. Jack had made clear that, as he had given his word, and violated it, no cross-examination of Lady Eustace was to be allowed. Jack's instructions were binding on Phineas, of course, but then Jack did not know what was to come.

After Mr. Spiderwort rested, Sir Archibald asked Phineas if he had any evidence to call.

"Only one witness, my lord," Phineas said, with an insouciance he did not feel. "Call the Right Reverend Joseph Emilius."

The seconds it took for the bailiff to go out of the courtroom and bellow the clergyman's name in his stentorian voice seemed endless.

They ended, however, and the bishop, resplendent in his episcopal uniform of apron and gaiters, walked sedately into the courtroom. He bowed to the Judge, and was escorted to the witness box, where, disdaining the chair, he stood. The clerk asked him to state his name for the record, and, in his most mellifluous voice, he recited "The Right Reverend Joseph Athanasius Emilius, Bishop of the Territory of Southwestern Utah, in the United States of America."

Lizzie had been thunderstruck by his name being called; she was even more so by his appearance in the flesh. Most of all, she was astonished that a man standing at the very edge of an abyss could be so calm, and resolute.

"Mr. Finn," Sir Archibald said, "you may examine."

"Thank you, milord. Might I ask the plaintiff to please rise for a moment?"

Lady Eustace did so automatically, before Spiderwort could object. She met her former husband's eyes, a small curl forming at the left corner of her mouth, her mien completely unreadable.

"Bishop Emilius," Phineas Finn asked, "are you acquainted with the plaintiff?"

"I am." Emilius' answer demonstrated the same coolness Lizzie remembered him exhibiting when arrested so many years before.

"And how are you acquainted with the plaintiff?"

"She is my wife."

"Bishop, was not that marriage nullified by judicial decree, approximately two decades ago?"

"That is correct."

"Then how can you state under oath that the plaintiff is—not was, but is—your wife?"

Before the bishop could answer, Spiderwort was up. "Is my learned friend cross-examining his own witness, now, m'lud?"

"Overruled, Mr. Spiderwort. The question is compound, but not leading." Then, leaning toward the witness box, the judge posed a question of his own. "Does your lordship follow the question?"

"I do."

"Then the witness may answer it," the judge ruled.

"I say that the plaintiff is my wife, because the nullity was obtained on the basis of false testimony, subsequently recanted, and is therefore itself null and void."

"Have you moved to vacate the decree of nullity?"

"The matter is in train. I have retained counsel to do so."

Phineas Finn was not, and had never been, the legal expert his own tutor Mr. Low was; nor did he possess the combination of aggressive effrontery and cunning that had marked Mr. Chaffanbrass, his own defender. What he brought to the fray was his keen insight into human nature, honed over the years to the level of intuition. Sometimes that intuition led him into risky gambits. His next question was one such: He was going to ask a man whom he had excellent reason to distrust—whom he, in fact, believed to be almost entirely bad—a question that was not legally relevant, but which could play havoc with his case. Phineas's only defence to the reproachful shade of Chaffanbrass was that the question would be asked by Lady Eustace's barrister, in any event—that, and his intuition that the question could end the case, cried out for him to ask it.

"If that is so, Bishop Emilius," Phineas posed the question carefully, "why, then, have you waited for so long before seeking to vacate the decree absolute?"

In the pause that followed, Phineas either saw the cynical eyes of the bishop soften for a moment, or was deceived by a trick of the light. The moment passed; the bishop formulated his answer.

"Because I did not want my wife restored to me by the force of law," he said, "but to return to me of her own free will and accord. Because I would not chain to me by duty, she to whom I am bound by love."

The atmosphere in the courtroom grew heavy. Phineas did not know if the testimony given was true, half-true, or all false—but he had a terrible suspicion that the feeling behind it was true. An image flashed through his mind, from a traditionally staged *Oedipus Rex* in his student days, of the moment when the actor portraying the ruined king put aside his mask, and revealed the living flesh beneath it.

If there was a dollop of truth in the old rascal—and Phineas doubted it mightily even now—some glint of true gold that lay beneath the tinsel, then Phineas felt that he had caught a glimpse of it.

"Nothing further," Phineas Finn said, and sat down.

From her seat, Lizzie had seen—something; how she interpreted the same phenomenon as Phineas had observed cannot be known. Now she saw something else: Joseph was utterly vulnerable to her. She wondered, quite seriously, if he had lost his reason. Was he mad? Cross-examination on the case leading to his bigamy conviction could strip all the sympathy his testimony earned him from the jury—yes, and ruin him socially, too! More, cross-examination about the murder of Mr. Bonteen could do even more—Mr. Rushforth had told her about the wondrous discoveries of M. Bertillon, and Joseph could yet be tied to the club that had killed Mr. Bonteen, if Scotland Yard had kept it. Perhaps he would not be convicted, as the method was still relatively untried in England, but he would have to fight to keep the rope from around his neck.

And it flashed upon Lizzie, quite clearly, that if any man knew and had weighed all those factors before going into the witness-box, it was Joseph Emilius. This was no madness, but a deliberate decision—a gesture of trust that she would not choose to have those questions asked, or, rather, that if she did so choose, her spurning his love would matter far more than the attendant catastrophe. Far from seeking to compel her, he had placed himself completely in her power, trusting her to understand the gift, and to value it accordingly. This was his response to her challenge some weeks past—his *beau geste* was to quite literally place all his life into her hands.

In comparison, the wrongs done her by Jack Chiltern, and the money she could wring from him, or the trumpery social advantages she could obtain in a second loveless marriage, were small beer indeed. She needed to act, and that right swiftly.

Mr. Spiderwort was about to pose his first question, when Lizzie Eustace pulled at his gown. He turned to her.

"We need to speak."

"M'lud," the barrister obligingly reported, "might the Court take a brief recess for me to confer with my client?"

Sir Archibald sighed heavily. "Very well, Mr. Spiderwort," he said. "Fifteen minutes, members of the jury."

Only when the judge, the jurors, and Lady Eustace, along with her legal advisors, had left the courtroom, did Joseph Emilius subside into the witness chair. He looked every day of his age, and possibly more.

After only a few minutes, Phineas, Jack, and Mr. Camperdown were called into the judge's robing room. What seemed an eternity passed. Oswald looked with fascination at the man who, he was sure, had literally gotten away with murder. Ifor could not help but pity the man's isolation in the box; still under oath, he could speak to nobody.

The plaintiff and her champions, Jack and his lawyers, returned to their respective places. The jury trouped into their box again.

"Members of the jury," Sir Archibald announced, "the parties have reached a negotiated settlement, and your service is hereby concluded. You are dismissed, with the thanks of the Court." A murmur arose among the spectators, as the baffled jurymen were quickly led out of the courtroom.

The judge then asked if there were any applications prior to closing of the proceedings. Hearing none, he declared the session closed, and rose.

"Over so soon?" murmured Proserpine Garnett. "But how?"

She was immediately reassured when Jack Standish turned to her, with his most dazzling smile. He strode to where she and the Earl sat, and, as she rose, embraced her.

"Free!" Jack declared. "Action withdrawn, no imputation on my character, no costs, even."

"My dear boy!" the Earl exclaimed.

Quintus Slide moused his way over to Phineas Finn.

"How did you do it?" he asked the barrister, a question Ifor had only just articulated himself. To both, his answer was to subtly gesture to the witness box. The bishop painfully rose, and stepped out of the box, walking a few paces away—only to be halted in his progress by Lady Eustace.

"So you wish to annul our annulment?" she asked, coolly enough.

With a good effort at his usual *diablerie*, Joseph Emilius answered, "Or, if you prefer, to marry you a second time. I am entirely at your Ladyship's service."

She smiled, quite warmly. "No doubt. Let us discuss the arrangements tomorrow. For tonight—I should like to celebrate."

"Monico's?" the bishop asked, "the Cavendish?"

"I was thinking Green Street. Just off the Park," the lady suggested, and the bishop's weariness began to leave him, if his gradually expanding smile was anything to go by.

"Just like the Cheshire cat," breathed Ifor Powlett-Jones.

The happily re-coupled couple left the courtroom arm-in-arm, with Lady Eustace bowing ironically in the direction of Jack, the Earl and Proserpine Garnett. It is possible, though unclear, that the bishop's own slight inclination of his head was intended as a salute to Phineas Finn, but Ifor Powlett-Jones ever afterwards maintained that it was so.

Soon thereafter, Lady Eustace became once more Elizabeth Emilius. If the wedding was not attended by those of the highest rank (indeed, the Marchioness of Hartletop did not deign to respond to her invitation, showing that the bishop had paid a high price for his determination), enough of their circle were present to make the occasion festive. Dolly Longestaffe, who never refused an invitation except upon the ground of potential boredom, reported that the event had been especially fraught with interest, as the attendees were evenly split between the *demimondaines* and the ecclesiasticals. Dolly was heard to say that he was tempted to make book on which faction would convert the other, but he was the only attendee without a rooting interest.

Before that date, however, Jack Standish received a note in an all-too familiar, fine italic hand. Heart sinking, he opened the envelope, and found inside a short note. It read as follows:

Jack,

You have never begged my pardon, as a gentleman should who has not kept faith with a lady. You should have done, you know—I rather think I would have let you off sooner, had you done so, because you would have treated me with the respect you owed me. I admit I might have made you squirm a bit, but I think I was due that, don't you agree? You can, if you will, repay that debt, and in a way that will not impair your honour: Keep a friendly eye on my living Florian. He is naïve, and idealistic, and fears me rather, but I confess I have a fondness for him. Try to see that the world is not too harsh with him, if you can. Especially if he mistakes—as you once did—desire for love.

Do not make that mistake a second time, Jack. That woman who sat in the public gallery and then accompanied your father upon the bench may be a common little church-mouse, but her eyes were boring into me throughout the whole time we were in court, and she clearly loves you.

Love is a strange thing, Jack, and for all my past suitors and my long-ago marriage to the first Sir Florian Eustace, I know only this of it: Do not reject it lightly. If you love this woman, marry her—even if it is, in the eyes of the world, a mésalliance. I know I shall be renewing one in the eyes of the world—and yet, I think we shall suit.

As I hope you and your church mouse shall. Farewell, my little lordling. I forgive you.

ELIZABETH EUSTACE

How strange, he thought upon re-reading the note, I believe she is trying to be helpful—kind, even. And he wondered what had made her so charming, and yet so selfish, and how he could have wanted her so badly. And for all that, he kept her last note among his things—somehow comforted by the fact that, at the end of it all, Lizzie Eustace, of all people, had sought to urge him to follow his heart. It almost reassured him that she had one of her own.

In any event, Lady Eustace and Joseph Emilius were once more sealed together, and after a brief sojourn in London, the Bishop returned to America and his flock with his wife. Word has come back from the States that she does indeed style herself Lady Emilius, and is occasionally so named in the newspapers describing her good works there. She, and her bosom friend Lady Wariston (who joined the happy couple in America), were at last report deeply involved in the education of young ladies and gentlemen, who no doubt benefit mightily from such moral, if occasionally severe, influences.

That they do not confine themselves only to the Western United States is to be understood, and occasionally, they have, all three, returned to London for the season or a portion thereof. The Bishop does sometimes preach while in London, but only seldom; he has been heard to say that his London visits are "fallow periods" for him, not times of labour. Still, from time to time, he has been known to accept a special engagement.

He has not been invited, however, back to Barchester.

THE HARD BARGAIN

As the dog-days of August wore on, negotiations with the Tories were reaching their culmination. As a result of Yeates's, Robinson's, and Craig Laurel's patient negotiations with Frank Greystock and his team over a three-week period, the parameters of the Conservative offer were becoming firm. The bargain proposed by Greystock remained, effectively, what it had been: Labour would have a seat at the table, and a voice, but could not insist on its own agenda. Both parties would work together in good faith to find areas of common ground, where the lot of the working classes could be ameliorated without violating the Conservatives' core principles. Laws that were slackly enforced could be tightened, and Labour could have one Cabinet member, and one sub-Cabinet officer, in different departments.

When Craig Laurel protested that this was not so very much, Frank Greystock evenly and calmly explained that Labour was, after all, providing only fourteen members. Yes, it was those fourteen who would make the majority a working one, he conceded readily enough, but if he gave more than his own members could stomach to Labour—why, there would be no Government at all.

Greystock made his case to Laurel and Yeates, saying. "You are a bran-new party, now that you have split from the Liberals. Even though you are numerically small, you will be able to boast a Cabinet minister, and an Under Secretary in your first year as a Party. And you will be able to call our attention to injustices that our side of the aisle does not perceive, but would be ready to remedy."

Within the caucus, Craig Laurel privately admitted that Greystock was being fair in his offer, and that, in fact, the Tory Leader's continued refusal to promise more than he could perform reinforced his belief that Greystock meant to keep his pledges.

"This may be," he wound up, around the now-familiar lozenge-shaped table at St. Dominic's, "as good as we can do." Major Yeates nodded his assent. Robinson unhappily agreed.

"Perhaps," said Phineas Finn. "But before we agree, I should point out that Lord Fawn is at last returned from the country—and our meeting is set for tomorrow. Let us see what our former colleagues have to offer."

Lord Fawn had, Phineas was sure, meant to show security in his own position, and perhaps even respect for the seriousness of the negotiations, by setting the meeting in the Prime Minister's briefing room. He had, no doubt, forgotten that this was the very chamber in which Phineas had been brought before the late Prime Minister and had been ejected from the Party.

Phineas found that he had no objection whatsoever to holding the meeting in this room; in fact, the surroundings added savour to the occasion.

The Liberal delegation was made up of Lord Fawn himself, Lawrence Fitzgibbon, and, inevitably, Sir William McScuttle. When the members entered, Fawn nodded civilly enough at Finn and Mr. Camperdown, and did not appear to know just how to greet Craig Laurel. Fitzgibbon shook hands amicably enough with the other Labourites, but grinned broadly at the sight of Phineas, and pumped his hand as McScuttle scowled.

After everyone was seated, and refreshment served—Phineas recognised the wine as a favourite of Barrington Erle's—McScuttle opened the meeting.

"All right, we've aye heard about these meetings ye've been havin' wi' Greystock. And we know full well that he'll give ye no say in any real policy, and only window dressing in office. So what are ye'r terms tae return where ye belong?"

Lord Fawn made a deprecating motion, his large, greying whiskers bouncing with disapproval. "Yes," he said, at length, "I think Sir William puts it bluntly, but why should we not be blunt amongst friends?"

Phineas answered, "Ah, but are we?"

"Are we what?" Lord Fawn asked in his own turn, confused.

"Among friends."

"Oh, come, Finn!" his Lordship expostulated, almost disappointedly. "I would not expect you to be petty about a matter of Party discipline under the late Prime Minister. I had thought rather more of you than that."

"I did not mean my expulsion from the Party, Lord Fawn. I voted with the late Government to the very end, you may recall."

"Then to what do you refer, Finn?"

Phineas opened a buff-coloured folder, and pulled out the first fruits of Meier's work. With his usual efficiency, the major-domo had put together a dossier of documentary evidence that established beyond peradventure that Sir William McScuttle had funded the successful campaign of young Barthwick to unseat Barrington Erle. Meier had employed an efficient, if less than savoury, detective, and Mr. Polteed had come up with the goods.

These reports, and page after page of supporting evidence, Phineas now lay before the three men gathered. As Lord Fawn grew pale, Sir William grew red. Finally, Phineas made a brief peroration.

"The fact that a leadership contest was triggered by a pre-arranged loss of supply is, while close to the bone, within the rules."

"What rules?" sneered Sir William.

"The informal rules that govern dealings between members of the same Party who are drawn into competition," answered Phineas, "the rules that make it possible to air our differences without resorting to unrestricted internecine warfare."

McScuttle would have replied, but he saw Lord Fawn nodding seriously.

"Quite a different thing," Phineas continued, "for a member of the Liberal Party's inner circle to fund the Conservative challenger to the late Prime Minister, all while Barrington was working to expand the Liberal majority. Or, to put it another way, deliberately sacrificing a long-standing party leader and his seat while accepting the benefit of his hard work for the Party as a whole. That," Phineas said in his severest tone, "is simple treachery."

"D—n you, Finn, I won't be lectured at by you!"

"But the worst has not yet even been said of you, Sir William." Phineas opened a second buff-coloured folder. Meier had obtained a full, sworn statement of Sir William's behaviour from Grayson, the butler at Number 10. The young detective had thought it would be difficult to extract that account, in view of the tradition of confidentiality sacred to British household staff, and had come prepared with blandishments, from money to employment. But Polteed had underestimated his man, and when Meier met Grayson in the Twelve Bells pub of a night, he had no need to offer any inducements but one.

"Bring it home against that wretched man," Grayson had entreated, his eyes pooling with unshed tears. "Mr. Erle was a good man, kind to the staff, hard-working. And to see him bully-ragged by that—that–" Words failed the servant, but the duty of discretion that had formed the old man's code during his many years in service broke before the imperative of avenging his last master. The affidavit demonstrated the old man's acute memory, as it was almost verbatim as Phineas had had it from Lady Laura and the Duke of Omnium.

Phineas simply read the affidavit aloud, and passed a copy to Lord Fawn.

"Do you see, my lord," he asked, "why our confidence in the Party has been shaken?"

"I knew nothing about this," Lord Fawn said, with unusual vigor for him.

"About the money, or about the gloating?" Camperdown asked the question.

/

"Neither," Fawn replied. "You must believe me, Finn. I would never condone this sort of behaviour."

"What sort of behaviour? Successful behaviour?" Sir William could stomach no more. "It is nearly a new century, gentlemen," he said, casting a harsh emphasis on the last word. "You will need to be ruthless to thrive."

Fawn gestured toward the affidavit, and toward the reports spread out across the table. "Not like this. We must not abandon honourable standards."

The other men were silent. Lord Fawn grew visibly more uneasy. "You are very quiet, Finn. You cannot believe it of me that I knew of these actions."

Phineas met the troubled gaze of the weak, but well-intentioned, man whose pomp and self-regard had so often vexed him.

"No," he answered at length. "I do not believe it of you, Lord Fawn. We have never been friends, but I know that you would not be deliberately dishonourable."

The peer breathed more easily.

"But you have allowed this man to try to buy and sell seats, and you have not seen the extent of the mischief he has done. Sir William—do you have any response to this evidence?"

The industrialist's anger had left him now. He was quite, quite calm.

"Honour, you say. Mischief, you say. But how are you any better, Finn? You have your wife's money, you fought me with my own weapons."

"But within the rules, Sir William." It was Lord Fawn who spoke in Phineas's defence.

The industrialist's laugh was genuine. "Rules? There are none, deny it as you may. My money will be good enough for the Conservatives, if you don't want it, and for Labour if they don't. Your Lordship took it happily enough, when I was making you Prime Minister."

"You said you wished to enable me to concentrate on matters of State…" the peer began to justify himself, but a loud laugh from Sir William cut him off.

"You, concentrate on matters of State? Oh, Fawn, I had you doing whatever I wanted you too—licensing a plant here, trading a favour there! What a good, obedient, Prime Minister you would have been. And still will be, I think, with all the money you owe me."

"I don't think so." Mr. Camperdown's voice carried a quiet authority.

"Oh? Why not, young-feller-me lad?"

"Because demanding the provision of money or services with menaces is a felony, and you've just done it in front of four witnesses." The solicitor was superbly confident. "And the avowed attempt to corrupt a holder of public office? That won't stand you in good stead either."

McScuttle, unsure of his ground, was struggling to formulate a response. Phineas prevented him from doing so by adding, "I have not yet made these reports available to the press. But I will. No party will trust a man willing to betray it for a fleeting advantage. And your name will be odious throughout England. The resultant scandal will be easier to survive back in Wales than here."

Pointing at Fawn, the industrialist cried out, "But he owes me all that money!"

Phineas smiled grimly. "You will be repaid. Lord Fawn will secure a private loan, and be quit of you. Now go."

As McScuttle left the room, he turned and said, "Ye've won today. But me and my kind? We're coming for you 'gentlemen.' And we learn from our mistakes."

In the silence after this departure, Fawn stared disconsolately at the table. Sadly, slowly, he admitted, "I have been a fool."

"But not a knave," Laurence Fitzgibbon replied, comforting his fallen chief.

"I shall never find a private loan, Finn. I am too much embarrassed. I will owe that blackguard money my whole life."

"I know a good man," Phineas said, "who will make you a loan on terms you can afford. You need not be McScuttle's creature. Ezekiel Breghert will see to it that you are not."

Lord Fawn looked up, and sadly muttered his thanks. Then he added, "I shall never be Prime Minister now, shall I?"

"No, Lord Fawn," Phineas said gently. "But I have some suggestions that you and Fitzgibbon could take back to the caucus. I believe a creditable solution can be found."

"What's that, Phinny?" asked Lawrence Fitzgibbon.

"That Lord Fawn, as the leader of the Party, upon discovering financial irregularities and malfeasance within the Party, selflessly sacrificed his own promotion to form a coalition with the Labour Party to root out corruption, and restore the public trust in Government."

"But who could lead such a coalition?" Lord Fawn asked, almost in a wail.

"It would have to be a man who could command respect across the political spectrum," Phineas said. A light began to dawn in the eyes of Laurence Fitzgibbon.

"And one who could untangle whatever other financial messes McScuttle has made," Fitzgibbon added, beginning to be enthusiastic.

"Someone who would be willing to legislate against abuses, even when such legislation would go against powerful interests," Craig Laurel observed severely.

"Yes," added Camperdown, "and someone who could carry things with a high enough hand to shame the other fellows into voting his way."

"An elder statesman," said Lord Fawn.

"And one who has built a coalition government before, and knows that both parties' agendas must be advanced as far as possible," Phineas added. "In short," he continued, "there is only one man who could bring together the kind of Government we need as a result of McScuttle's misdeeds."

"Planty Pall!" shouted Larry Fitzgibbon, carried away by his enthusiasm.

"You mean, of course," Fawn said, with a faint revival of his minatory manner, "the Duke of Omnium."

"Yes," Phineas Finn said, "the Duke of Omnium."

And with one accord, each took his glass, and they raised them as one.

"The Duke of Omnium," they toasted.

THE WEDDING GIFT

Late August in Barsetshire can be bucolic indeed—sun-dappled days, brimming tankards of ale, as the rippling fields of wheat in Farmer Hedgepath's boundaries begin to mature, ripening into the stalks and flowers that will soon enough be bound into sheaves, the Cathedral choir singing its best beneath itchy ruffs and starched surplice, but grateful for the cool airiness of the stone fastness in which they sing. Dark and blessedly catacombed with little areas in which even the less godly can find rest for their bodies, if they prefer it to refreshment for their souls, Barchester Cathedral especially does not let the high summer concern it.

Still, a wedding in late August is an optimistic thing, even as weddings go—aye, even as second weddings go. The sun that today playfully makes a kaleidoscope of the ripples running in a stream through the grounds of Plumstead Episcopi may tomorrow scorch and weary the elderly, and transmute the bridal repast to spoilt, deflated mockeries of what once were delicacies fit to grace a Duke's table.

August, in short, is a month in which only a bride as indifferent to Society and a groom as unaware of its mores as Lady Laura Kennedy and the Duke of Omnium would willingly have selected. Lady Mary, too busy with her new-born Glencora to remonstrate, failed to provide her father and step-mother with appropriate guidance in this matter. And Lady Agnes? Agnes was herself now the proud mother of Donalbain Plantagenet Palliser, whose bright thatch of red hair honoured his mother's forbears, and, as the even prouder Papa Gerald declared, whose appetite honoured his father's. No, there was no help to be found in Lady Agnes.

Perhaps Lady Silverbridge could have sounded the warning gong, but, as an American, albeit one who had lived for some years now among the English, Isabel had never believed herself to be sufficiently adroit in the ways of her adopted people to warn those who had been born to those shores what was, and what was not, feasible in Society. Isabel's shyness was exacerbated by the fact that the happy couple comprised her father-in-law, a Duke (albeit one who had embraced the solecism of his son marrying an American) and the daughter of one earl and the sister to his successor. And so Isabel remained mute, though most assuredly not of malice, and the Duke and his *fiancée* were not warned of the perils of their course.

Marie Finn, of course, would have counseled, warned, and, if necessary, stage-managed the affair brilliantly, but between her behind-the-scenes work with Phineas's campaign and those of several other Labour members now triumphantly ensconced in the House, and her guiding of Meier in his investigation of Sir William McScuttle, Mrs. Finn had, just this once, lost sight of the Palliser family's affairs.

And so it was, a bare week before the wedding, that the Duke was presented with a telegram along with his morning coffee at Matching Priory. It read, simply, "MOST URGENT MEET WITH YOU STOP MAY WE DESCEND ON MATCHING MORNING STOP," and signed FITZGIBBON/FINN.

The Duke's reply was likewise concise. "EXPECT YOU MORNING STOP OVERNIGHT IF NECESSARY STOP LUNCHEON CERTES STOP."

The next morning, a swelteringly overcast day that had the Duke uneasily picturing his guests either scorched by the sun or oppressed by a downpour, was one in which he welcomed distraction of any kind. There was, quite simply, nothing further for him to do before the wedding; all the arrangements were made, and all of the variables which his careful, precise mind could address had been dealt with. Only that great imponderable, the weather, which could only be ameliorated, not cured, lay outside of the Duke's domain. Lady Laura, now with her family at

Harrington Hall, would be installed at Omnium two days prior to the wedding. Her dress and trousseau were ready, as he had been reliably informed by the lady herself—for there was nothing shy about Lady Laura, now that she loved and was happy in her love.

His own clothes were prepared, and his bags packed, for their first trip together as man and wife—not to the Continent, but to Scotland, where Lady Laura wished to banish her unhappy memories by bringing her new husband to the Highlands, and, ultimately, to Lochlinter. The Duke, as was always his custom in non-essential issues, was perfectly happy to give way to the wishes of others. Lady Laura wished to show him the beauties of Scotland? As long as he was not expected to stalk a deer, ride a horse, or throw the caber, he was perfectly amenable. Besides, Lady Laura had suggested including a visit to Gerald and Agnes, as an opportunity to look in on young Donalbain in his natural habitat, a suggestion the merits of which were obvious to him.

So the Duke was more than usually amiable when Finn and Fitzgibbon were shown into his study. He shook hands with both men, and even showed them the newly installed telephone that Lady Laura had persuaded him to accept as a most characteristic wedding gift from his bride-to-be. After they were served with coffee, he asked almost jocularly, "So, gentlemen, what brings you to see me by special appointment, less than a week before we are all to meet again?" And Fitzgibbon's solemn answer took the Duke entirely by surprise.

"The Queen's service, Duke."

"The Queen's service?" the Duke repeated blankly.

Phineas interjected, "We know that your wedding is but a few days away, but we are here in an official capacity, on the Nation's business."

"And what capacity and business is that, Finn?"

"We are here as delegates of the Labour and Liberal parties, respectively, Duke, and come here to ask you to lead us in endeavouring to form a coalition government."

Such was the modesty of the Duke that he did not draw the obvious inference; instead, he asked "And how may I assist you, gentlemen? I have been out of the swim for some years, but if I can be of some service to you..."

Fitzgibbon looked at his old friend Phineas, hoping for some assistance in enlightening the Duke; he need not have worried.

"You can best assist us, Duke, in agreeing to lead us, and to join our discussions as we try to reach agreement on a coalition between our parties."

A lesser man might have been staggered; the Duke of Omnium merely sipped his coffee reflectively. "What you are in effect asking me, gentlemen, since the two of you represent a working majority of the House, is whether I would be willing to become Prime Minister a second time."

"Yes," said Phineas Finn, "should our discussions prove successful, we would anticipate Her Majesty asking you to try to form a Government." Fitzgibbon nodded his assent.

Putting down his coffee, the Duke rose, and paced a few steps.

"You ask very much of me, gentlemen. I am about to be married, and my *fiancée* would lose her wedding tour."

Gently, Phineas said, "I believe Lady Laura would be proud to delay the wedding tour for so happy a cause."

"But will it be happy?" the Duke shot back. "My previous tenure in office entailed a great deal of work for my—for Glencora, and could have a similar effect upon Lady Laura."

"'The labour we delight in physics pain,'" quoted Fitzgibbon in a rare flight of fancy.

"Eh? What have Ferdinand and Miranda to do with this situation?" The Duke sounded almost querulous at Fitzgibbon's frivolity.

"But—it's from *Macbeth*, Duke," Fitzgibbon stammered, shocked to have caught the Duke in an error.

The Duke's face was set resolutely against them—literally, not figuratively, as he had walked the length of the room once more, and was staring out the mullioned window into the rose garden designed by Lady Glencora so many years ago.

"Larry," Phineas heard himself say, "would you leave us a moment?"

Fitzgibbon nodded his assent, and rose. After Phineas heard the click of the door closing, he rose and joined the Duke at the window.

Phineas Finn was, by nature, a warm and affectionate man, and, in his youth, no small portion of his charm had come from the spontaneity with which he expressed his likings; it was not by coincidence that men who had addressed their closest friends by their surnames for decades thought nothing of addressing him by his Christian name, and of being so addressed by him.

The Duke of Omnium, however, with his formidable carapace of reserve, had never been such a one.

Despite this, Phineas lay his hand gently on the other man's shoulder.

"Plantagenet," he said softly, using the Duke's name for the first time, "what is troubling you?"

The Duke turned to face Phineas, breaking the momentary physical contact, and raised his eyebrow, unsure whether to be offended at Phineas's presumption, or to accept the familiarity as a reciprocation of his own on Christmas Eve. Even in his unsettled mood, the Duke was anxious to avoid an injustice.

"Sir?" he temporised, in a manner that strove to be freezing but could not quite succeed.

"Surely you must want to be Prime Minister once again, my friend, and this time with a coalition designed to go in the direction you desire, at heart, to lead, not restricting you to pabulum measures. So why do you react as if I brought your death-warrant?"

"It was a death warrant for—for her," Plantagenet Palliser answered, too churned up in his feelings to resent the question, or the questioner.

"Was it?"

"She was so proud of me, Finn, so devoted to making the thing go, that she worked herself into a weakened state. And then, when I failed–"

"You failed?" Phineas's tone was puzzled.

"You must know I did, Finn—I gave the Garter to those who earned it, not those who expected rewards; I did not charm Sir Orlando, or promote his useless hangers on—and it all ended, and then—Glencora lost heart, and blamed herself, and–-died."

The Duke sat in the window seat, with the air of a man who was too exhausted to stand any longer. Phineas drew up a chair, and met his friend's eyes.

"That is not so, you know."

"What do you mean?" the Duke asked in a leaden voice.

"The Duchess knew it was in the nature of a coalition that it could only run a short while. As soon as normal conditions returned, it must collapse. She worked so hard because she hoped to prolong it until the last minute, for your sake."

"Yes!" the Duke denounced himself, "for my sake. Because I had got so fond of office, so greedy that I could not just let go. Because I—what is that makes you smile, Mr. Finn?"

"You will blame yourself, won't you, Duke, no matter what the facts are? Greedy? You clung to office—like most Prime Ministers do, by the way—not out of greed, but out of hope."

"Hope? What hope?"

"That you could accomplish more than just keeping the Government running—that you could make real some of those policies you had spent so many years developing and advocating. And, instead, it was a government of stand-patters you were asked to lead—not willing to do anything but the bare minimum necessary to keep things just as they were, until it was time to go back to business as normal. You never gave up the hope of being more than a caretaker Prime Minister."

"And yet, that is all I was. And Glencora paid for it; I was harsh and rebarbative, and unthankful to her."

"So don't do it again."

"Don't be Prime Minister again?"

"No. Don't be harsh, unthankful or rebarbative to Lady Laura. And don't stand pat. It's Labour that wants to make you Prime Minister, not Mr. Roby and Mr. Rattler. You'll have to take some chances this time around."

The Duke's eyes gleamed a little at that, but a question remained.

"And Laura–?"

"As poor Fitzgibbon was trying to say before, she'll thrive on it. She loves policy as much as you do, and she'll be better than you at knowing just how far you can go. Nobody knows the Liberal Party as well as she does, and she'll know whom you can rely on and whom you must watch for treachery."

"I will have to speak with her before I answer."

"Of course. Harrington Hall is on the 'phone, you know."

"Ah." The Duke pondered a moment, and then a smile, surprisingly boyish, broke through.

"Finn?"

"Duke?"

"How did you know something was troubling me?"

Phineas snorted. "Larry Fitzgibbon catching you out on Shakespeare?" he said. "That was cause for alarm, not merely concern."

The Duke's smile remained in place for a second longer. "Will you make my apologies to Mr. Fitzgibbon, while I telephone Harrington Hall—Phineas?"

"Of course," the Irishman replied, "After all, if 'twere done when 'twere done, 'twere better it were done–'"

"That will do, Mr. Finn," the Duke reproved the younger man, but did so with another smile, and in a mockery of his normal minatory tone.

As the Duke strode to the instrument, Phineas left the study. When the operator picked up, the Duke requested to be connected to Harrington Hall.

Lawrence Fitzgibbon hunched in an armchair, the very picture of misery.

"I've dished us, haven't I, Phinny?" he inquired when his old friend came out of the study and joined him in the library.

"Never say die, Larry," Phineas answered. "His Grace is on the 'phone, you know."

"Oh?" The news did not appear to cheer Mr. Fitzgibbon.

"So, too, is Harrington Hall," Phineas remarked.

"Ah." Lawrence Fitzgibbon grunted. A moment passed. "Did you say Harrington Hall? Isn't that Chiltern—oh, hang it, Brentford's, place?"

"Yes."

Lawrence Fitzgibbon looked hopefully at his friend. "I don't suppose somebody might be spending time at her brother's country seat."

"So my wife informs me."

"Ah!" The Liberal politician looked hopeful again. "What now?"

"Wait and see, Lawrence. Wait and see."

A little time passed. Bored, and yet still anxious, Phineas began following the titles of the volumes along the wall. The classics, of course, even the historians; Suetonius, Tacitus, Dio Cassius—even Flavius Josephus—giving way to Gibbon's great synthesis, and a myriad of books on economic policy that the Irishman's eyes skipped over. He would not have expected, though, to see literature—and modern literature at that—so well represented: Tennyson, Thackeray, Tolstoi, Tro-

"His Grace will see you now, gentlemen," the butler informed them, and led them back to the study. On returning, they found the Duke behind his desk, an air of quiet satisfaction about him. Outwardly serene though he appeared, Phineas nevertheless detected his inner excitement.

"Gentlemen," the Duke said, "I take it you need an answer as soon as practicable?"

Nervously, Lawrence Fitzgibbon began to backpedal. "Ideally, Duke, yes, but if Your Grace needs to sleep on the matter…" He trailed off as he saw the smile on Phineas's face.

"Or," Larry continued, "you could tell us now. That might be quite helpful, too."

The Duke returned Phineas's smile, and included Larry in his response. "Gentlemen, I will return to London with you to wait upon Her Majesty. It seems we are to be in harness again."

"And the wedding?" Larry could not but ask.

"Will continue as scheduled, of course, Fitzgibbon. Since my *fiancée* has assembled her trousseau, it seems I must assemble my own."

"I don't believe I have ever heard Her Majesty's Government so described before," Fitzgibbon said, with a laugh.

"No," Phineas replied, "But I can think of no better wedding gift for Lady Laura than a private box at the creation of the new Government."

SHE STOOPS TO CONQUER

"My dearest Jack," Proserpine Garnett said firmly, "it simply cannot be."

"Why not?" Jack Standish was laughing at her, now; affectionately, but still, he could not be serious.

"Jack, this is a society wedding. The Duke of Omnium is marrying your aunt. Your Mother and Father, the Earl and Countess of Brentford, will be there."

"Well, yes, my dear, that would follow."

"And all of their friends, and associates."

"I believe that is traditional, yes," Jack replied a trifle smugly.

They were at the Half Moon, where Jack had found a warm, if wary, welcome. Miss Garnett, of course, was well known there, and their taking a table together had caused a few eyebrows to lift.

Not, however, that of Ezekiel Breghert, who observed them from his own customary table. He continued his discussion with young Marchbanks, but, when Jack made a little bow to the old banker, returned it with a wink and a nod. When Jack ordered soda-water and Miss Garnett tea, the wariness dissipated, and a few old friends drifted over to the young peer's table.

"Hallo, Standish," greeted the youngest Mr. Camperdown, who raised his hat and bowed, "Miss Garnett," he said politely, and moved on.

"You do not understand, Jack. This is a wedding in your family. If I accompany you, I will be paraded in front of the entire English aristocracy as your intended."

"Just so," Jack replied.

"Do you still not see? They will judge me there, whether as fit or unfit. They will drive me away, as one unworthy."

Jack's jaw set firmly. "They would not dare," he said, adding, "You were willing to attend Vavasor's wedding with me."

"Of course, my love—only to help you through that terrible first meeting with them all. And then – the first great social occasion since you'd put aside the drink, with all the others there drinking, and the wedding toasts – oh, my dearest, of course I felt that I must be by your side. I hope that my being there helped give you courage—"

"Oh, it did, Proserpine. It meant everything, having you with me—and not just because you are a kindred spirit who was also *not* joining in the toasts, as you say. And it's true—without you, I couldn't have faced 'em. Not that Vavasor wasn't anything but handsome, and even Clarissa thawed out a bit—but having to parade yourself, as you put it, in front of everyone who knows every dreadful mistake you've made, to see if they can take you back…"

"Take you *back*—you see?"

"What do you mean?"

"You belong in their world. I don't."

"You do, if you marry me. And we're trying to change that world, anyway, Proserpine—so why are you afraid?"

"I'm thirty-two. I'm plain, I'm common, I'm–"

Jack stood up, walked to her side of the table, and knelt before her, even as she spoke.

"You are vibrant, you are beautiful, and you are the only woman alive who sees all of me—and loves me anyway. I am the fortunate one, to have won your heart." He kissed her gently, and swiftly (though the Webbs noted it from their nook, as they noted everything), and rose.

Although only the Webbs had seen the kiss, the acoustics of the common room at the Half Moon were such that almost all present heard Jack's declaration. As the young poet with Breghert started and looked at the couple in open astonishment, the old banker placed a firm hand on his shoulder, preventing him from rising. Breghert grinned broadly at the young lord and nodded his approval. The Fabians, socialists, Bohemians all present applauded the young couple, even the youngest Mr. Camperdown. Jack, flair for the dramatic at the fore, bowed to the crowd. Miss Garnett, recognising the young man staring at her, made a decision.

"Very well, Jack," she said, "I will attend this wedding. But I think that it is time we re-ascend to the streets, and make our departure."

"Very well, my love," Jack answered. "As they say in storybooks, 'your wish is my command.'"

Looking at him over her spectacles, a trick of hers that somehow brought his heart to his mouth, she replied with mock severity, "See that it remains so, sir," and gently led him by the hand to the stairs leading up and out. Her old acquaintance, a man who had known her only as a lovelorn secretary and was anxious to investigate the change, was impeded by the crowd, and by the elderly banker. And so Proserpine led the ascent back to earth, her swain trailing devotedly in her wake.

In the fresh air of the night, her fears seemed exaggerated—but not entirely so. She believed that the Earl would make her welcome, after their shared experience in court, but still, in her heart, she feared the Countess, with her perfectly-maintained beauty and her habit of enquiring casually of any new name or face, "Is he" (or "she," as Miss Garnett's own case warranted) "one of us?"

A sparrow among the falcons, Proserpine felt herself; she would never be one of them.

The Duke of Omnium consulted his old watch to verify the time once again.

"It won't do, you know, Father," Gerald laughed. "It has only been three minutes since you last looked, and they are not yet even late." The Duke looked over at his other son and heir, and saw the same grin reflected back at him—their mother's smile, and her habit of gibing at him.

"The Cathedral is more full than I had expected," he remarked, hoping to change the subject.

"The wedding of a Prime Minister, conducted just before he puts an administration together? Can't see how that would be a draw," Dolly Longestaffe drawled as he entered the room. Bowing his head to the Duke, he added "Sorry to intrude, Your Grace; they wanted someone to let you know that they are here."

"They?" The Duke found himself confoundedly nervous; his collar was far too tight, and the Cathedral far less cool than he thought it would be, at least in this back room where he and his sons were waiting.

"The bride and her attendants, Your Grace," Dolly helpfully supplied. "We are ready to begin. Or, as they say so much more impressively in the theatre," clapping his hands, "'Places, everyone, please.'"

The Duke's wedding had indeed drawn quite a crowd. The family and friends tended to cluster in the central seats, while the political elite of both parties dotted the Cathedral, with Lord Fawn off to one side and Frank Greystock off to the other.

Fawn was a different man these days; Ezekiel Breghert had, indeed, taken pity on the hapless peer, and paid off Sir William McScuttle. Fawn was finding Breghert a much more congenial creditor than McScuttle. The old banker had reviewed the documents McScuttle had induced Fawn's to sign, and discovered that McScuttle had been effectively making himself master of Fawn Court, Lord Fawn's family seat for many generations. With Mr. Camperdown's assistance he had bought the loans, albeit at a heavily discounted price. The discounted rates would themselves have stretched Fawn's resources, but Breghert found a compromise: Fawn would sit on the board of a company Breghert owned and would provide a little prestige, and perhaps in that capacity occasionally host an event, at the company's expense, at Fawn Court. In return, Breghert would pay Fawn a reasonable director's fee, out of which Breghert would forgive the loan in installments while providing Fawn, for the first time in his life, with genuine security, as opposed to the illusion Sir William had cast even as he filched Lord Fawn's patrimony.

Breghert's explanation of the swindle that had been perpetrated by McScuttle and his solution to the problem had earned Fawn's earnest admiration and affection. Wooly-minded and petulant as he could sometimes be, Lord Fawn was nonetheless capable of gratitude, and would happily have married any of his remaining maiden sisters to Breghert if the fancy had struck them. As Breghert confessed to Phineas Finn, he was not really making any money from Fawn, but neither was he losing any. "It is not business, my friend," he had said, "but seeing such robbery as that makes my blood boil."

"And the sisters?" Phineas had asked, laughing.

"Ah, well—the eldest—she has possibilities, Phineas—a warm smile, and she seems to favour me. Who can tell, eh?"

With Lord Fawn's economic woes finally and truly resolved, and his career developed in the City (as he came to see it), his interest in politics had waned, and with it, his desire to serve in office. Still, he was present at the wedding, as all of them were—nearly the entire Liberal constellation, all of the Labour members (no longer Lib-Labs), and not a few Conservatives, including young Mr. and Mrs. Vavasor, now back from their wedding tour and clearly relishing their first Society event as man and wife.

"He wants to take up painting, Aunt Marie," Clarissa whispered to Mrs. Finn as they waited for the ceremony to start, "and he wants to begin with a portrait of me, if you can believe such a thing!"

"And what more suitable subject, my dear?"

Clarissa's response to her aunt's question would never be known, as the Cathedral organ roared its opening notes, and the service began.

All brides, of course, as we have noted before, are beautiful, though whether this comes from canon law, common law, or Act of Parliament has been debated at length since as long ago as 1328, when the issue was first raised in *The Mirror of Justices.* Lady Laura Kennedy, as a woman of mature years, might have, one would have expected, qualified only under such law, but one would have done the lady a grave injustice. Her face, once ascetic and sad, was now noble, and even serene. Her tall, rangy figure had aged well; her step was still elastic, her movements free. Most of all, Lady Laura knew how to make the most of her assets—an ability enhanced to an even greater extent by a short visit from Marie Finn as Lady Laura was dressing—and she did not make the capital error of seeking to capture the innocent freshness of youth. Lady Laura looked neither young nor old, as she and her brother processed toward the groom, and many of those who had been apt to write her off as simply a blue-stocking were heard to draw in their breath.

The classic simplicity of her pearl-grey summer silk gown, astutely tailored with an eye towards stressing the elegance of her long-limbed frame, became her as no youthful furbelows could. Lady Laura smiled as she passed Lady Mary, glancing at her soon-to-be stepdaughter and touching her finger to the only ornament that relieved the almost nun-like severity of the gown – a magnificent sapphire brooch, bequeathed to Lady Mary by her own mother, and which the younger woman had insisted upon lending the bride for the occasion. "Something old, something borrowed, *and* something blue," Lady Mary had said whimsically, pressing the brooch into Lady Laura's hand with a kiss and a suspicion of tears in her eyes. Lady Laura, her own eyes misty, had replied, "Thank you, my dear. And the something new would be…?" "Yourself," Lady Mary had answered softly, embracing the older woman.

Certainly the Duke of Omnium was taken with his bride, and received her hand almost reverentially. The Duke's responses, those of his bride, and their vows were spoken clearly, firmly, and with a solemn joy that became both them and the setting.

Bishop Grantly and the Dean had suppressed their Anglo-Catholic tastes in favour of the simplicity favoured by the couple, but made up for it with a closing cloud of incense that threatened to obscure the path for the closing procession.

And then it was done. Phineas and Marie Finn remained in their seats through the postlude, a Bach fugue dear to Marie, and then

Phineas excused himself for just a moment, leaving Marie with Savrola and Clarissa, and retreated to the St. Columba Chapel.

"Why is Uncle going to that little chapel now?" Clarissa wondered aloud.

"To pray a moment, my dear," Marie Finn answered. And indeed, because of an innovation only introduced to the Cathedral by Bishop Grantly and Dean Peterson, Phineas Finn was able to kneel at the little altar, light a candle, and give thanks for the easing of his friends' loneliness, and the easing of his own soul. The long haunting was over.

Before the wedding feast at Gatherum Castle, the Countess of Brentford had retired to her room, one of the lovelier guest suites whose massive windows faced the lawns of the Castle. She was bathing her temples in eau-de-cologne when her son's familiar knock sounded at the door. "Enter," she called. When Jack stepped in, he had with him Miss Garnett, nervous but determined in brown silk.

"Mother," Jack said without preamble, "I wanted to tell you, before we all go in to dinner: I have asked Proserpine to be my wife, and she has done me the honour of accepting me."

"Has she, indeed?" the Countess raised her brows. "Perhaps, Jack, a family wedding is not the ideal moment to announce this engagement—it would seem to be—upstaging, I think the term is—your Aunt Laura."

"I don't intend to make a speech, Mother, but neither do I wish anyone to have the wrong impression." Jack had the mulish look the Countess had long associated with attempts to deprive him of a coveted sweetmeat in his infancy.

"Of course not." the Countess sighed. "Well, then Jack, you had better leave myself and Miss Garnett to become better acquainted. You might wish to find your father, as well—you know how he hates to be the last to know anything."

"Oh, I told the Pater long ago." Jack looked as though he were preparing to brazen it out, but at the sight of the delicately arched eyebrows soaring still higher, and the pressure placed upon his instep by the foot of his betrothed, he wilted a trifle. Casting a dubious look at Proserpine, he nodded, and left the room in search of the Earl.

"Shall I ring for tea, Miss Garnett?" The Countess suited her words to her actions without waiting for a response. In the slightly uneasy interlude before the arrival of the tea, the ladies sat opposite one another, politely discussing the beauties of the wedding service and of the Cathedral.

When tea arrived, the Countess poured, and made use of these moments of quiet to determine her attitude toward the initial skirmish. She observed the be-spectacled, thirtyish woman in front of her, clad in a dress of which neither the colour nor cut suited her, and whose mannerisms that betrayed her middle-class origins as she drank her tea in the artificially refined way of one determined to commit no solecisms.

She also observed that Proserpine Garnett was acutely frightened of her—and frightened, she suspected, of letting Jack down. And she remembered the older women who had tried to browbeat her, Violet, out of marrying the former Lord Chiltern, now the Earl and her husband of many years.

But then she thought of her husband, who held himself out only as a judge of horseflesh, not of his fellow human beings, but who in fact possessed quick, intuitive sympathies. Oswald had met Phineas Finn, she recalled, under absurdly unpropitious circumstances all those years ago—men from widely disparate backgrounds, with Phineas as an eager young politician and Oswald as—no other word would do—a wastrel; rivals in love, even. And yet, Oswald had conceived of a liking for the young Irishman almost immediately that had flowered into a life-long friendship, despite a lack of interests, background, or experiences in common. Oswald had known, pure and simple, that this man would be his true friend—and so time had proved.

And Oswald had, she knew—for Jack's blundering declaration had come as no surprise—really, Violet wondered, what *did* the boy think two married people spoke of when they were alone—the weather?—declared himself in favour of this unlikely, improbable wife for Jack. All of this passed through Violet's mind as she pursed her lips and delicately sipped her tea. She finally met the younger woman's eyes.

The long silence had frayed Miss Garnett's nerves. She had not even taken up, after her first sip, the cup of tea Violet had poured for her. Proserpine was perceptive enough to observe Violet's taking stock of her deficiencies—her age, her class, her lack of beauty—and knew herself to be under judgment. She blinked back tears, willing herself not to shed them and disgrace herself before Jack's mother.

Violet Effingham, as she had once been, had a warm heart, and age had not dimmed her compassion. Aware of the young woman's agony, she divined its cause, and immediately knew that here was no gold-digger, no title-hunter; rather, here was a strong, loving heart that had joined itself to her son's, and that feared to shame him before his mother.

She was everything Elizabeth Eustace was not.

Violet put down the cup of tea, and covered Proserpine's clasped, tense hands with her own.

"Oh, my dear," Violet heard herself say, in a husky voice that was not her normal tone, "we must be very dear to each other."

Proserpine's eyes reflected doubt for a moment, then hope, and then joy. Tears fell, but they were tears of happiness. "Oh, yes," she whispered, "I so want to love you; you are his mother, and I have none." They embraced, though whether it was the Countess who embraced Miss Garnett, or Miss Garnett who embraced the Countess, was never settled.

The skirmish was over; indeed, it had never been fought. Both garrisons had, simultaneously, surrendered.

THE TURN OF THE WHEEL

At the Beargarden, Dolly Longestaffe was brandishing a broadsheet, and declaiming while holding court—although, consistent with the new dispensation in his life, he kept his eye mindfully on the clock on the wall.

"Scuttle, McScuttle, like a roach/the villain flies at light's approach," he extemporised. "No, not quite right, is it, chaps?" he said. "Still it's good to see that plug-ugly won't be stalking Westminster any more, eh Vavasor?"

"Exposed by *The People's Banner*, too, Dolly, which is pretty funny when you think how he courted Quintus Slide," Vavasor replied.

"And what a down Slide used to have on your uncle-in-law, too, eh? They seem to have signed articles," said Dolly.

"I can't say I'm shocked to see that poor old Barrington Erle was done in by foul play. After all, whoever heard of a sitting PM being unseated in his own borough, absent senility or death. And sometimes not even then." Niven's comment drew a gentle chuckle.

"Where's Trubshawe these days, anyway?" Dolly asked. "Haven't seen him here for ages, I think."

"Courting, they say," Niven answered. "Apparently agog over some mystery lady—can't wait to find out who, hey?"

Vavasor repressed a groan with some effort, a symptom missed by most, but not by Dolly Longestaffe, who forbore to exacerbate the symptom. Live and let live, thought Dolly, and tactfully changed the subject.

"Speaking of those missing and believed matrimonially imperiled, I hear Jack Standish is to be married. To a—what was the lady's occupation—nursery governess?"

"No, Dolly," Savrola laughed, "she was a church secretary."

"Bit of a come-down for Lord Chiltern, heir-presumptive to the Earldom of Brentford, though, isn't she?"

"No, Dolly," Savrola answered quite seriously, "I don't think she is at all."

Dolly looked intrigued. "I thought you and Jack had made it up rather? I mean, you had the chap to your wedding, and all that."

"Indeed we have, Dolly. By the way, did we ever reply to his letter of resignation?"

"Don't think so," murmured young Charters from the back.

"Well, we can refuse it, as far as I'm concerned. Standish has turned over a new leaf, and that Miss Garnett of his is just what he needs. She may not be a noblewoman by blood, but she's made a nobleman out of him—or at least helped to do so."

From some corner of the room, where he was hidden, Sir Felix Carbury was heard to mutter, "American half-breeds instructing us about who's a b—y gentleman now? We'll be lettin' in nabobs next."

Before Savrola could react, Dolly again turned the conversation.

"So what do we know about the new Government? Who's to be what? Planty Pall seems to be keeping his cards close to his vest."

"I don't know anything," said Savrola Vavasor, and then, turning to his guest for the evening, "what about you, Powlett-Jones? Has Himself let slip any bits of intelligence you can share with us?"

"No, nothing," Ifor Powelett-Jones, in full fig, was enjoying his first excursion to a real club—he had smiled broadly on being invited to drape his cloak across the extended left paw of the Great Bear in the foyer. "Guest's privilege," Vavasor had assured him, adding that the right paw was reserved for the Senior Member's use, so Ifor must make note of that fact.

Sipping his whiskey and soda, Powlett-Jones thought about the matter more, and then, seeing that they were all waiting for an answer, he added: "It does seem peculiar to me, though, that Mr. Finn isn't more involved in the discussions. They've had him in once or twice, but it's mostly Mr. Laurel and Major Yeates meeting with the Duke."

Vavasor looked startled by this news; as indeed he was, having assumed that Phineas Finn's labours for his new party would have earned him a place near its head.

"But they'd be nowhere without him," he protested, "there'd be no coalition, and my side would be in power."

"Aye, but think how long Craig Laurel and the rest have been out there on the hustings for the working men and women," Powlett-Jones replied dourly. "I understand it, in a way, though unfair is how it seems to me."

"I suppose Greystock will be pleased, and so should I be," Vavasor muttered, taking a vicious pull on his cigar, which crackled threateningly. "After all, he's the only real Parliamentarian Labour has, and if he's shut out and it's just the old Liberal gang running things, well, that's better for our crowd."

"How so?" asked Ifor.

"Because the Coalition won't be stable enough; it'll lean too far to the center, Labour'll get fed up, and, hey, presto! General Election time again. No, if it weren't so dashed unfair to Finn, I'd be overjoyed."

"Phineas Finn shut out again," mused Dolly Longestaffe, "Poor chap used to be famous for his luck. I suppose it had to desert him someday."

At home in Park Lane, Phineas Finn sat in his study, in his smoking jacket, pipe in hand, reading Low's old favourite, Boethius's *Consolations of Philosophy*—or, rather, trying to do so, in the hope of persuading himself out of the feeling that he was being ill-used by those whom he had served, not only in his own opinion, quite well. Perhaps it had been that blasted Slide, he thought, overdoing the praise as he had once been wont to overdo the condemnation. Perhaps that had led Craig Laurel—a good man, but subject as are we all to the frailties of this fallen world—to feel imperiled by the newcomer to the Party.

Or, he reflected, it could be that the hard core of the Liberal Party wanted nothing to do with him—that they viewed him as a turncoat, and would rather deal with those who had never served alongside them.

Perhaps these, the finest months of his political life, were also the logical end of that life. He had thwarted an avaricious, bad man, who would have subverted a great party and corrupted the Government; he had avenged his fallen friend; and he had been instrumental in raising to the Premiership a man worthy of it, despite long odds. That just might have to be enough. The House would be in session in little over a week, and he had not been asked even to advise since those first few meetings.

He sighed, and turned the page, and read Boethius' description of Fortune spinning her wheel:

> *"Wealth, honour, and all such things are placed under my control. My handmaidens know their mistress; with me they come, and at my going they depart. I might boldly affirm that if those things the loss of which thou lamentest had been thine, thou couldst never have lost them. Am I alone to be forbidden to do what I will with my own? Unrebuked, the skies now reveal the brightness of day, now shroud the daylight in the darkness of night; the year may now en-garland the face of the earth with flowers and fruits, now disfigure it with storms and cold. The sea is permitted to invite with smooth and tranquil surface to-day, to-morrow to roughen with wave and storm. Shall man's insatiate greed bind me to a constancy foreign to my character? This is my art, this the game I never cease to play. I turn the wheel that spins. I delight to see the high come down and the low ascend. Mount up, if thou wilt, but only on condition that thou wilt not think it a hardship to come down when the rules of my game require it."*

Phineas sighed again. Low, for all of his admirable qualities, was clearly not the man from whose library to seek comfort. A knock at the door disturbed his reverie, and Marie entered.

"Knocking, my love?" Phineas asked. "Have I become that short-tempered lately?"

"Not at all, my dear Achilles," she answered, with the sly little smile he had always relished.

"Achilles? Sulking in my tent because my prize has been taken away from me? And what prize would that be?"

"You have seen the doors close upon you again, and assume that it is because you have been deemed unworthy. Could there be no other reason?" Her smile was openly teasing now; he was normally enchanted by this mood in her, but this evening, playfulness was not something he could rise to. He considered her question, though, with a professional's detachment, and after a few moments, answered.

"Possible, but unlikely," he opined. "With the House going into session so soon, most of the appointments would have been made by now. The Duke likes to fill the Cabinet and sub-Cabinet offices in that order, and to have the Department heads weigh in on who their juniors will be—so, if he was considering me for any position, I should have been summoned by, at the latest, this evening."

"A fine political analysis, my friend. Would you mind sharing it with another friend of mine?"

"Eh? A friend of yours, Marie?" His mood lightened if only a fraction. "What game are you playing at?"

"Perhaps an unkind one," she answered, and added, "Please come and see our visitor, Mr. Finn. You may find that you are not so undesired as you have come to believe."

Phineas rose from his seat, and walked out from behind his desk. Shaking his head a bit at his wife's odd humour, and his own lack of sympathy with it in this one occasion, he followed her into the parlor, where he beheld not one but two men, Craig Laurel and the Duke of Omnium.

Astonished that the Duke should have come to him, he suspected it was more out of motives of friendship than of State; still, he greeted his visitors, offered them refreshment, and, when both had refused and taken armchairs, asked point-blank:

"How may I be of service to you, gentlemen?"

The Duke of Omnium answered, with a small, tight smile, "I do hope, Phineas, that you mean that question as more than a conventional pleasantry."

Craig Laurel's solemn demeanour cracked utterly, and his smile was broad. "Aye, ye should be careful what ye offer, Finn; his Lordship is here tae ask heavy service of ye indeed."

Phineas's perplexity was written all over his face; taking pity, the Duke said, "You surely must have wondered why you have not been asked to our consultations these past few days."

Craig Laurel put in: "Thought we'd forgotten ye, Finn? Maybe just a bit?"

The Duke continued, "Our deliberations of late have been making peace among our more conservative members, even though they are members of the Liberal Party. What has been in my mind required the tact of Major Yeates, who in many ways is one of them–"

"Good hearted man that he is–" Craig Laurel interjected again.

"And immense patience on the part of Mr. Laurel. You see, Finn, there were those within the Party who thought you less than loyal. But when the evidence came forward of McScuttle's misdeeds against poor Barrington Erle, and with Mr. Laurel reminding the members how you and Erle walked arm-in-arm together into the House after he was counted out in the Naval Funding Bill, well–"

"The Duke was able to get his wish—and my wish too."

"And what is that wish?" Phineas asked.

"I sit in the Lords, Phineas, and when a Prime Minister does so, it means that many of his duties which involve the Commons necessarily devolve to the Leader of the House. In such a case, the Leader must effectively be a Deputy Prime Minister."

Phineas sat there waiting to see how this news affected him.

"And whom have you chosen?" he finally asked.

Craig Laurel roared with laughter, as Phineas had never before seen him do before.

"He really did think we forgot about him, my lord Duke," the Scotsman said.

"I never had but one man in mind for the position," the Duke replied to Phineas's question, "For this coalition to work, the Labour members must have a powerful voice in the Government, and we must bind ourselves as close as we can, so that we will not split asunder at the first difference, and lose our majority–"

"Which is, after all, slender enough," Craig Laurel interposed.

"So the Leader of the House must be a man whose integrity both parties can rely upon, and whom the Prime Minister can trust implicitly. Who else could it be but you, Phineas?"

Phineas was struck mute for a moment, and then muttered, "I had thought it should go to Laurel. He is our leader, after all–"

"Tosh!" The Scotsman would have none of it. "As a movement, aye, and as a party, perhaps. But in the House, right now, as part of a coalition? No, no; I know myself. Labour needs to show she can govern well, even if only in conjunction with the major parties. We need, as the Duke says, a man that Liberals as well as Labour can take the whip from. And that's you, my son, and not me."

"Well, Phineas," the Duke asked, smiling, standing and stretching out his hand, "you called me out of retirement—made me give up my wedding tour, too. Will you not take harness along with me, and see if we can do the Nation's business together?"

Phineas rose, and took the Duke's hand.

"With all my heart," he answered.

A bare moment later, Marie Finn entered, followed by Meier carrying a tray with four glasses and a magnum.

"Marie? Were you list–"

"My dear one, if you wish to have secrets, and hold meetings in the parlor, you must close the door. Besides, the Duke told me, so that I might be ready."

Meier opened the magnum, charged the glasses, filling Laurel's with soda water, and handed them around.

"Mr. Laurel?" the Duke invited.

"No, Your Grace, the privilege belongs tae you."

The Duke raised his glass, and said, simply, "The Leader of the House."

Laurel and Marie answered vigorously, "The Leader of the House!"

Had Phineas Finn finished the paragraph from Boethius when he turned from the volume in disgust, he would have read:

"What if not even now have I departed wholly from thee? What if this very mutability of mine is a just ground for hoping better things?"

The wheel had turned, and better things had arrived.

On a brisk morning in early September, Phineas Finn and his colleagues of all three parties were gathered in the House. The galleries were empty, for this was the day of the opening of the new Parliament, and the House of Commons would soon be deserted. Prayers were read, and, and an uneasy silence fell for a few moments.

"Taking their time in the Other Place, I suppose?" A young Tory was heard to mutter, leading Mr. Speaker to gavel for order. The Leader of the House, and Deputy Prime Minister, Mr. Phineas Finn, rose.

"Gentlemen," he began, "in a few moments, we shall be summoned to hear the Speech from the Throne. You will all hear the proposed agenda for the Session, and while there will be much we will not agree upon" (a buzz of laughter and derisory comment from the Tory benches) "there will, I hope, be much we can agree to do for the benefit of the Nation." ("Some hope!" a young Tory called out. Phineas cocked an eyebrow at Savrola, who was just getting into the spirit of the thing, and the younger man blushed, until he noticed the wry smile on Phineas's face.) "Today, there will be much ceremony, and little business; we hope to make up for that in the days to come."

Phineas took his seat, and Frank Greystock rose. He said, "I rise only to congratulate the Honourable Member for Tankerville and his fellow Members of the Labour Party, even if they did choose the wrong side with which to form a coalition." (Laughter both sides.) "We look forward to working with the Government where we can, and to frustrating its efforts where we must, for the good of all." (More laughter.)

And Frank Greystock took his seat. "Ah, well," he thought, "next time mayn't be that far off. Let's see if Finn gets any better change out of Planty Pall than he did out of Barrington Erle." He was still a young man, as politicians are deemed young, and his time would surely come. Things looked grim in South Africa, and he was unsure the Coalition would stand up to the Boers. And if they did not, why, some members might just defect. Patience, Frank, he told himself, patience.

The doors of the House were suddenly slammed shut, reverberating through the chamber. As soon as the last echo died away, three loud raps were heard, and the great oaken door swung open with a cry of "Black Rod!"

And indeed, it was the Gentleman Usher of the Black Rod, a portly gentleman who nonetheless became his spare black uniform admirably. He bowed to the Speaker, and processed with dignified, severe mien to the dispatch box at the bar, where he intoned "Mr. Speaker, The Queen commands this honourable House," he paused in his incantation to bow to each side of the House, "to attend Her Majesty immediately in the House of Peers."

The Serjeant-at-Arms plucked up his mace, and, with Mr. Speaker between them, he and Black Rod began the procession to the "Other Place," where the Sovereign and the Lords awaited them. In the first rank, Phineas and Frank Greystock discussed the possibility of hunting with Brentford at Harrington Hall, while the weather held good; the noisy, jocular tribe behind them, in paired Government and Opposition files, laughed and bustled, as tradition required, to show that they had no fear of the Lords.

As the unruly, somewhat undignified procession slowly made its way to the Lords, Phineas reflected on what was to come. So many friends and adversaries, all gathered in one room, with the Great Widow of Windsor herself there to address them, in words that he, Phineas Finn, had had a role in crafting! Brentford would be there, and poor old Fawn—Jack Standish, too. The Duke of Omnium—a friend for many years, but now a colleague with whom he would have to walk a tight-rope, balancing a delicate majority at a time of rising strife around the globe and at home. Difficult, but the British art of the compromise, joined with the Duke's own conscience and those of men like Craig Laurel, might just be enough to allow them to do the trick long enough to improve the lives of the long-neglected poor, like those miners in Wales.

And in the Ladies' Gallery would be the women who had shaped his life in so many ways. Violet, Countess of Brentford, who had had the wisdom to refuse him; Laura, the new Duchess of Omnium, who had helped launch him in politics, and from whom he had learned the dangers of disregarding the heart's felt necessities. Clarissa, who had brought to him late in life the joys of fatherhood that he thought he had missed forever, and next to her that vivacious mother-in-law of hers, who had thrown her influence behind his effort to free Powlett-Jones. Most of all, there would be Marie, whom he had loved now for many years, and who had brought sweetness back into his life when he thought it gone for all time. Marie, who had believed in him enough to bring him to this day.

"Think they'll let us in, old, chap?" Greystock asked.

"We could always storm the door," Phineas replied.

As the procession reached the door of the Lords, he heard Craig Laurel's voice: "What now, eh, Finn?"

"Now?" Phineas repeated. "Now, we begin."

THE END

FOR THOSE WHO ENJOY PEERING BEHIND THE CURTAIN: AUTHOR'S NOTE, ACKNOWLEDGMENTS, AND AFTERWORD

At the end of what is a fairly long novel—although *Phineas at Bay* is in fact considerably shorter than either of its direct predecessors *Phineas Finn* (1869) and *Phineas Redux* (1874)—some explanation as to why the enterprise seemed worthwhile to me is probably a bit late. The reader has, after all, read the novel, and has either enjoyed the experience, or has not, and any words of mine could all too easily shatter the spell, if it has been successfully cast. Still, the spate of Jane Austen sequels, and of other derivative works based on Victorian novels and themes suggests that the Victorian Age has a particular resonance for us in our own new Gilded Age—an age where income inequality, boom-and-bust economy and enormous swindles are everywhere about us. Bernie Madoff, though himself a little *passé* now, is a modern American version of Trollope's Augustus Melmotte in *The Way We Live Now* (1875), and has been often called out as such.

But my impulse to write more about Phineas, Marie, and their friends and associates comes from a much more basic place: I was unsatisfied with where Trollope left them and wanted to know the rest of the story.

The Palliser novels, also known as the "Parliamentary Novels," span six volumes. One (*The Eustace Diamonds*, 1873) is devoted to Lizzie Eustace, with Plantagenet and Glencora, tending to the ailing Duke of Omnium, and accompanied by Madame Max Goesler, present, but relegated to the margins as a kind of Greek chorus, commenting on Lizzie's exploits. Two are devoted to Phineas Finn. The first book in the series, *Can You Forgive Her?* (1864-5) takes its title from Alice Vavasor, whose story is given slightly more prominence than that of the rocky start, near failure, and ultimate survival of the marriage of Glencora and Plantagenet Palliser. In other words, Phineas Finn is, by any measure, the second most important male character in the Palliser novels—a fine contrast to the dutiful, sometimes dull, but honest and high-principled aristocrat who, ultimately, is the central figure in the series. Phineas Finn is lively; in youth, a little lazy, and easily imposed upon, and yet principled enough to dash his political hopes against the rocks on a point of principle. His marriage to Marie marks his full acceptance at the highest level of society—a fact that illustrates just how paradoxical a writer Trollope was.

Often written off as an author of comforting and conventional novels, Trollope in fact knew how to get away with murder in terms of flouting the conventions of his age, as he did in the two Phineas novels. An Irish Roman Catholic and a Viennese Jewish widow are the hero and heroine in these two novels, written in an era when anti-Irish, anti-Catholic and anti-Semitic sentiments were rife. He takes these two quintessential outsiders, the Irish Catholic and the foreign-born Jewish adventuress, and makes the reader root for them in an era when they would normally be suspect at best. It is an extraordinary achievement, all the more so for how quietly and with how little fanfare Trollope pulls it off.

And yet—Trollope concludes *Phineas Redux* with the words: "Of Phineas every one says that of all living men he has been the most fortunate. The present writer will not think so unless he shall soon turn his hand to some useful task. Those who know him best say that he will of course go into office before long." (Chapter LXXX.) We glimpse Phineas in office in *The Prime Minister* (1876), and see a little of him in *The Duke's Children* (1880), but the fire and radical sentiments that animate him in his two starring appearances seem lacking. He is, while happily married (though seemingly without children), drifting; acted upon far more than acting.

Was he disillusioned? I found myself asking. Or had he become cynical? Or had he become as conventional as Barrington Erle, and just stopped giving a damn? I was rehearsing these frustrations with Trollope's having left the story incomplete to my wife some years ago (it was in 2006, as I recall), and she simply said: "Write a sequel. Figure it out."

And so I wrote the first draft of chapters 1 through 3 of Volume 1, and, after having introduced Clarissa Riley, promptly dried up. Then the computer on which the manuscript was stored crashed, and the printed copy disappeared, and I put the matter out of mind.

Until, in April of 2013, I gave myself an inadvertent birthday present: I stumbled upon the print-out of chapters 1 through 3, lightly edited by my wife. Afraid I would lose them forever if I lost this copy, I entered them into my current computer, making revisions as I typed. When I had finished chapter 3, I knew exactly what would occur in chapter 4, and when I reached the end of that chapter, the events of the next chapter came to me—and I was off and running.

I've written quite a few scholarly articles, and one prior book, on freedom of speech and the First Amendment, but those were labourious, heavily researched, and even more heavily footnoted works. This? Writing *Phineas at Bay* was bliss—the characters ran the show, and I scribbled away frantically, trying to keep up. Not unlike the great novelist who inspired me, I found myself often laughing with them, and, occasionally, shedding tears with them. (Lady Laura Kennedy and Oswald, Lord Brentford, especially got under my guard.) I never needed to write an outline, as the characters were quite sure they knew what was to happen next, and only as I neared the end of Volume One did that change, as I needed my cliffhanger to fall at the right point in the overall tale.

In writing the novel, I took some liberties with time and place—good luck to anyone trying to figure out what years the novel spans; the days of the week on either side of the New Year come from the same year, events from the beginning and end of the decade are referred to as happening at the time spanned by the narrative, and the political scenario is reminiscent of events at one end of the decade, while a careful analysis of dates and days of the week would have you conclude the action was set near the other end. In other words, the action is truly set in 189_, a period spanning two years but not susceptible to being pinned down more closely than that.

This is, of course, consistent with the practice of many Victorian novelists. Arthur Conan Doyle was infamous for it, and there are learned articles trying to date the chronology of the adventures of Sherlock Holmes and Dr. Watson, a trend that reached its apogee in William S.

Baring-Gould's *The Annotated Sherlock Holmes* (1967) and *Sherlock Holmes of Baker Street* (1962).

Trollope himself kept the dates of his novels vague, and one criticism I received was that of tying the events of *Phineas Redux* to a specific year; at least one other reader faulted me for *not* tying my own tale to a specific year. I plead guilty to both charges; I felt that some level of temporal anchoring was necessary for any readers who are not Trollope fans but relish a Victorian setting, but that any more specificity would underscore the deviations from actual British history to the point that they would become a distraction.

A substantial level of deviation from Victorian political history was hardwired into my own story as a result of Trollope's own such deviations in his Parliamentary Novels. To give but one example, the closest analog to the first Omnium Government in *The Prime Minister* (1876) takes place decades before that novel, a union between the Whigs (later the Liberals) and the Peelites (more liberal Tories) in 1852-1855, under Lord Aberdeen. And yet *The Prime Minister* does not read like a tale of twenty years or more before its time of publication. In sum, Trollope warped British political history for his own purposes, and so must I do. The last thing I needed, though, was to highlight this, and really frustrate those readers who know their late Nineteenth Century history. So—189_, and welcome to it.

Many of the older characters will be old favourites for Trollope readers (Miss Allen's briefing of Quintus Slide in the Prologue covers some of the main ones, for those new to the series), and a handful of others (the Grantlys, the Duke's children, Slide himself, to name a few) are, I hope, welcome at the feast.

But a few comments on some old, some new and some borrowed characters.

Dolly Longestaffe (or Longstaffe, depending on which Trollope novel one is referencing) appeared both in *The Way We Live Now* and *The Duke's Children.* His history is pretty much as I have given it, although I must confess that Simon Raven's re-envisioning of Dolly, as portrayed by the late Donald Pickering, for the BBC adaptation *The Pallisers* struck a chord with me, and I have used him, as did Raven, for expository purposes, and occasionally to comment on the action.

Mrs. Winifred Vavasor, *née* Hurtle, also appears in *The Way We Live Now*, and is last seen in that novel heading back to America after being rather shabbily used by the hobbledehoy hero of that book, Paul Montague. Bad luck, as the present volume informs us, haunted her in America, where she met and married the appalling George Vavasor, last seen heading to America in Trollope's *Can You Forgive Her?* Her surname alone gave rise to an infinite amount of hair-pulling on the author's part, as some printings (especially early ones) style the family as *Vavasour* and others as *Vavasor*. (The Oxford edition of the Palliser novels settled the matter for me.) Her son, **Savrola Vavasor**, is my own creation, although he has a historical analog, himself the son of a dissolute, sickly Englishman and a beautiful American who charmed the Prince of Wales. His first name comes from the first, and to my knowledge the only, chronicle of the history of Laurania.

James Craig Laurel is not Keir Hardie in Trollopian guise, but he has a similar background, and, of course, the pun is awful. He fills a similar place historically, just as Winifred Vavasor fills the historical place of Jennie Jerome without being modeled on her in personality and biography.

Miss Proserpine Garnett found her way to this chronicle from the pages of G. Bernard Shaw's *Candida* (1894, published 1898). Trollope had no compunction borrowing characters from Dickens (albeit thinly veiled), and in naming at least one of his characters as a relative to one depicted in Sterne's *Tristram Shandy* (1759). When I found Jack Standish (himself based on several socialist peers and/or aristocratic Fabians) in need of a soul-mate, Miss Garnett put herself forward, and Jack agreed.

Finally, **Major Sinclair Yeates** (like his wife Philippa and his friend-and-foil Flurry Knox) is the brainchild of E. Œ. Somerville & Martin Ross (Edith Oenone Somerville and Violet Martin). Major Yeates is the narrator of, most notably, *Some Experiences of an Irish R.M.* (1899), which occurs well after or right around the time, of *Phineas at Bay*, and therefore further confuses the timeline. Major Yeates has the advantage of being authentically of the right era, and a decent sort whom Phineas could trust. He also has the advantage of being pretty decidedly apolitical, and, while more likely Tory at heart than anything else, prepared to go a long way to do his duty.

I should note that a handful of non-Trollopian cameos dot the book, filling out the late Victorian scene. Some are fictional, but not from the Trollope corpus (such as Eugene Marchbanks, or Rev. James Morrell, also from *Candida*, the Duke of Dorset and the lovely Miss Dobson, from the writings of Max Beerbohm). There are others, but I thought it might be fun for the Vic-lit buffs to hunt them out for themselves. Some cameos are by historical figures (Sir Arthur Sullivan, the lady friends of the Prince of Wales). Some appear in both historical and fictional guises—Bunthorne and Oscar Wilde in the same work, presented as equally real? Corno diBassetto and Bernard Shaw as separate men? What was I thinking?

One real historical figure whose appearance goes beyond a cameo is the **Right Reverend Charles Gore** (1853-1932). Gore's background and thought are presented based upon his own published works, and G.L. Prestige's rather hagiographic biography, *The Life of Charles Gore-A Great Englishman* (1935). The quotation attributed to B.F. Westcott, and its effect on Gore, is authentic; it comes from an 1868 sermon Westcott preached at Harrow, and is cited as having profoundly influenced Gore by Prestige at page 10 of his biography. Gore was, among other things, one of the founders of a politically liberal Anglo-Catholicism—that is, a belief in sacramental religion within the structures of Anglicanism. The prior generation of Anglo-Catholics, led by John Henry Newman, were politically affiliated with the Conservative Party, and can be fairly described as reactionary in their politics. For my own conspectus of Gore's place in Anglo-Catholicism and his teachings on social justice, see John F. Wirenius, "Not Charity But Justice: Charles Gore, Workers, and the Way," *Journal of Catholic Legal Studies*, vol. 50, p. 279 (2011).

In seeking to understand the feelings of a late-Victorian young lady before her wedding, in the hope of doing Clarissa justice, I went to a roughly contemporary source, and pillaged Eleanor Roosevelt's description of her own wedding, in her *Autobiography* (1961), at page 41. I did not exactly lift Mrs. Roosevelt's recollection verbatim—she was a very different young lady than is Clarissa Riley—but I used her formulation to structure her scene with Phineas before the wedding. Elizabeth Barrett Browning's poem, discussed between Clarissa and Phineas, was one which Mrs. Roosevelt reflects on in terms of marriage, too. Phineas's answer is my own.

The wise Frenchman whom Phineas quotes at Ifor's trial is Victor Hugo, and the work is *Les Miserables* (1862) (trans. Charles Wilbour, 1863); the quoted language comes from Volume Five, Bk. 4, ch. 1. The quotation from *The Consolation of Philosphy* comes from the translation by H.R. James (1897), and may be found at Bk. II, ch. 2.

Two descriptive passages in this book are not entirely original. My description of Matching Priory is based on Trollope's own in *Can You Forgive Her?* It is not taken word-for word from that book; I have tried to indicate the meaning the Priory had taken on in Palliser's life in his years since Glencora's death, and view it, if you will, through the lens of their lives.

Likewise, my delineation of Barchester Cathedral, where I had a very different problem: Trollope, despite all his visits there, never really gave a satisfactory description of the place. I know it's based on Salisbury Cathedral, but did not really wish to compose a methodical, historically accurate depiction of Salisbury Cathedral as it stood in the 1890s, and label it "Barchester Cathedral." Any reasonable man might have done that, but I preferred to adopt and adapt the depiction of M.R. James in the short story "The Stalls of Barchester Cathedral," from his collection *More Ghost Stories* (1911). The Rt. Rev. Mr. Emilius's good fortune in drawing back from the figurine of the cat will be clear to any so fortunate as to have read James's account.

My respect for tradition ended there, I am afraid. I was perfectly happy to determine for myself the Cathedral's patron saint, and elaborate on the décor using James as a starting point. Nor have I adopted the genealogies or histories suggested by Msgr. Ronald Knox in his *Barchester Pilgrimage* (1935; Trollope Society edition, 1990). This is most clear in comparing his unsympathetic portrayal of the younger Bishop Samuel Grantly—whom, I assure you, I had promoted to his grandfather's see before knowing that Msgr. Knox had done the same thing—with my own. I was very glad to read Msgr. Knox's work, but his project is not mine, and his Barchester exists in a world slightly askew from that you are able to visit in *Phineas at Bay*. I am reliably informed that passage to and from these worlds is easily arranged, and that one may enjoy the benefits of each without disparaging the other. I would say precisely the same, of course, of the Barsetshire novels of Angela Thirkell, the existence of which I have only recently discovered, and the canonicity of whose continuity and cast I neither confirm nor deny.

Which, I suppose, brings me to the more formal acknowledgements section. Of course this book, though different in many ways than what Trollope would have written, and set after his death, has been inspired by the love I have of the man and his works, and especially of his perception into human nature, and his ability to transcend the prejudices of his own day. I stand on his shoulders. Still, writing at over a century's remove, I had to consult other works to try to approach the period with some level of credibility.

For the overall political scene, I relied upon R.C.K. Ensor's *England, 1870-1914* (1936). David Cannadine's *The Decline and Fall of the British Aristocracy* (1990) gave me a more holistic view of the period. For the Fabians and their allies, I turned to A.M. McBriar, *Fabian Socialism & English Politics 1884-1918* (1966), supplemented by Michael Holroyd's first two volumes of his magisterial biography of *Bernard Shaw, Volume 1, 1856-1898: The Search for Love* (1988) and *Volume 2, 1898-1918: The Pursuit of Power* (1989). I also found helpful Philip Magnus's *King Edward the Seventh* (1964) and Ralph G. Martin's *Jennie: The Life of Lady Randolph Churchill—The Romantic Years* (1969) and *Jennie: The Life of Lady Randolph Churchill—The Dramatic Years* (1971). William Manchester's *The Last Lion: Visions of Glory* (1983) and *The Private Lives of Winston Churchill* by John Pearson (1991) both provided much food for thought, as did the magisterial multi-volume official biography by Randolph Churchill and Sir Martin Gilbert, as well as Roy Jenkins's *Churchill: A Biography* (2001) (especially helpful on parliamentary customs and terms).

For Phineas's two courtroom appearances, I consulted several works. For the procedure applicable to the trial of Ifor Powlett-Jones, I relied heavily on David Bentley's excellent and accessible *English Criminal Justice in the Nineteenth Century* (1998). I first encountered the story of Lady Eldon and her attempted felony when I was in high school, and read Alan M. Dershowitz's *The Best Defense* (1982), in which he describes his work on a case before New York State's highest court, *People v. Dlugash*, 41 N.Y.2d 725 (1977), which describes the origin of the famous hypothetical of Lady Eldon and her problematic attempt to smuggle French lace. *The Best Defense* was one of the books that hooked me on the law, that dangerous drug, for life, so let me thank Professor Dershowitz for that somewhat more questionable gift while I'm at it. The niceties of differentiating between handmade French and English lace are outlined in *History of Lace*, written by—I'm not making this up—a certain Mrs. Bury Palliser (Dover, 1984; reprint of the original 1911 Charles Scribner edition).

For the breach of promise action brought by Lady Eustace against Jack Standish, I consulted several sources: Charles J. MacColla's *Breach of Promise, Its History and Social Considerations* (1879) and Saskia Lettmaier, *Broken Engagements: The Action for Breach of Promise of Marriage and the Feminine Ideal, 1800-1940 (Oxford Studies in Modern Legal History)* (2010), were both extraordinarily helpful. I also found the contemporary Nineteenth Century forms in W.H. Michael & William Mack, *Encyclopedia of Forms for Pleading and Practice at Common Law, in Equity, and Under the Various Codes and Practice Acts*, vol. 16, at 1045-1063 (1897), to be helpful in capturing the authentic period flavor while clearly setting out the claims and defenses. (The last cited work is American, but captures the flavor of the Anglo-American pleading system well, and at a time when American courts borrowed British precedents and forms far more than now would be the case.)

Queen Victoria's pardon of Ifor is an elaboration of a similar document, catalogued as a "**Royal pardon, signed by Queen Victoria (1819–1901) and issued by M E Grimshaw [?] to Henry Justice, High Sheriff of Shropshire, 18 March 1842,**" displayed in Case 7 of the Exhibit "Our Will and Pleasure: Royal Autographs, Letters and Memorabilia of the British Monarchy," at the Reed Gallery of the Dunedin Public Libraries, archived at: http://www.dunedinlibraries.govt.nz/heritage/reed-gallery/our-will-and-pleasure/7

The Fall 2013 Trollope Society lecture, "The Qualities of a Swan: *Phineas Finn* and the *Bildungsroman*," by Nicholas Birns, inspired me to re-evaluate the parallels between Phineas and Emilius, and led me to bring them together at Phineas's chambers at night. Professor Birns also very kindly shared the lecture text, which I hope and trust will be published, as I think it offers fresh insights into what he calls the "Phineas Diptych," which I have, rather presumptuously, now made into a triptych. His comments about the unlikely friendship between Phineas and Oswald, Lord Standish (as he is in Trollope's novels) made me think more deeply about them, and his insight that the open ending of the Diptych invited continuation, leaving the reader wanting more, validated my own response: But what happened *next*? Beyond his lecture, he very generously read the first draft, and gave me much constructive feedback and encouragement.

On the Pallisers, that enormous cast of characters, the character index in the Oxford University Press 1973 edition under the general title "The Palliser Novels" was a helpful ready resource. More generally, Stephen Wall's *Trollope and Character* (1988), Ellen Moody's *Trollope on the Net* (1999) and her blog, "Ellen and Jim Have a Blog, Two," http://ellenandjim.wordpress.com, have been very useful in bringing to light facets of Trollope's work that helped me to reassess some old, beloved characters.

Trollope has been fortunate, as well, in his biographers: Victoria Glendinning, N. John Hall, Richard Mullen, and James Pope-Hennessy, have each (in very different ways) admirably explored the relationship between the man and his works. Michael Sadleir's classic *Trollope: A Commentary* (New and Revised Edition, 1945; originally published 1927) is still very worth reading, although I found Ellen Moody's critique of Sadleir's downplaying of the Irish novels especially salient in dealing with Trollope's most fully developed and important Irish character. I should add my thanks to the late Walter Kendrick, professor of English Literature at Fordham University, who encouraged me to delve into the Trollopean corpus.

None of these authors, of course, are responsible for any errors or omissions on my part, not to mention any artistic license I have taken. I should add that, since the action is set in Victoria's Great Britain, I have presumed to adopt primarily British spelling; I apologize for the errors I am sure that my American reflexes have missed.

Descriptions of women's clothing were a formidable obstacle. My own feeble efforts were materially aided by Karen Clark, my editor, whose knowledge of the period, love of fabric, costume, and precise detail stood me in good stead. While every chapter has benefitted from Karen's suggestions, sympathetic and insightful review (as well as her keen eye, and sense for the rhythm of prose), the ladies would have been drab indeed if dependent upon me for their style. But her contribution goes well beyond *couture*. She has truly been, to quote an accolade long ago accorded a considerably less deserving character, the Partner of my Labours.

Several early readers gave me invaluable feedback on earlier drafts: Nicholas Birns, as mentioned above, but also Ken Barry, Christiana Cobean, Anthony Vitrano, and my father, John David Wirenius. My father, in particular, helped me brainstorm a solution to the problem of how to on-board the reader unfamiliar with these characters, and orient them quickly without what has come to be known as an "info-dump." Novelist and good friend Susan Wright, herself a Trollope *aficionado*, did a careful, line-by-line review of the first draft, and offered me the benefit of her profound knowledge of the Trollope *oeuvre*, and her intuitive grasp of the characters, continuity, and relationships, sparing me from several significant blunders.

My wife Catherine was a steadfast support, listening to problematic passages at all hours, willing to talk through plot and character points, but wanting to hold off reading the whole until it was done. Some of my best ideas are in fact hers. My mother, Claire Wirenius has long urged me: Write a novel. Here, at long last, it is.

Jason Aylesworth, Esq., entertainment lawyer extraordinaire and old friend, gave me the professional's view of self-publishing's pros and cons, and led me through what needed to be done to protect my authorship rights, and make an informed business and artistic decision to publish through this new imprint, Monocle Press—a venture, I am profoundly glad to say, that my editor and friend Karen Clark has resolved to join me in. Matthew Arkin, Susan Wright, and Anthony Clark shared their experiences and viewpoints with me, and helped me know what we were getting into, and how to do it. I am deeply grateful to them all. Further confirmation came from Philip Sandifer's excellent *Tardis Eruditorum* series of books, as aesthetically pleasing as his content is enjoyable and illuminating, and his blogging about the fine work done by CreateSpace.

Judy Cummins's revamping of the great *Vanity Fair* caricature of William Beauclerk, the Duke of St. Albans, by Baron Melchiorre De Filippis Delfico (known as Delfico in the trade) and her cover design grounded the work in its political and literary *milieu*, fusing a Twenty-first Century to a Nineteenth Century aesthetic. Her cover brought to pass a thought I had on buying that caricature (and five others) from a street vendor on a wintry, Upper West Side morning a quarter of a century ago. "I'll be damned," I remember thinking to myself, "that one looks just like Phineas Finn."

And now he is, thanks to Judy.